HOPE OF ISRAEL

by

Patricia O'Sullivan

To Eamon,

Patty O'Sullivan

Llumina
Press

Requests for permission to make copies of any part of this work should be mailed to Permissions Department, Llumina Press, 7101 W. Commercial BLVD., Ste. 4E, Tamarac, Fl 33319

ISBN: 978-1-60594-578-1 (PB)

Printed in the United States of America by Llumina Press

Library of Congress Control Number: 2010910076

For my parents

Acknowledgements

I would like to thank Dr. Joseph Ward for advising me to cut the narrative digressions from my master's thesis. It was because I could not let go of these stories that I wrote *Hope of Israel*. Also, thanks to Karen Forgette, Susan Kelly, Monica Blondin, Kathleen Lucey, Gail Lucey, Joan Lucey, Dawn Hurley, Suzanne Wilkin, and Renee Hallam for reading the manuscript and making important suggestions to it, to Marta Chevalier for helping me with the Portuguese expressions, and to Deborah Greenspan and everyone at Llumina Press for making this book possible. Most of all, thank you to my husband, Dan O'Sullivan, and our children, Marion and Colm, for their constant encouragement and support.

There is no hope without fear,
and no fear without hope

≈ Baruch
Spinoza

I. *BEKHOR*, THE FIRST ONE

Lisbon, Portugal, April 1642

It had begun. Domingo moved quickly through the crowd, his small body easily weaving through tight groups of spectators. He would have nightmares the rest of his life for coming today, but he knew he could never forgive himself if he stayed away.

"Today Portugal atones for a grave sin of omission. In failing her duty to suppress the Jews, Portugal has advanced the reign of Satan and shamed the holy church!" The preacher's shrill voice could be heard halfway across Rossio Square, which, though full of people, was eerily quiet as if a foul curse had silenced even the beggars and their winged brethren, the pigeons.

A shiver ran through Domingo despite the heat of the day. The nightmares would be bad. But horror was preferable to shame when one was able to choose. More often than not, however, horror and shame were like demonic twins attached in such a way that a body did not know where one left off and the other began. But it was neither fear of shame nor courage in the face of horror that had brought him here. His brother still lived and Domingo held on to hope.

In coming to the square, Domingo had defied his parents, who had charged him with staying inside the house this day. But he'd considered the danger and thus had transformed himself into an urchin, knowing almost instinctively that the poor never drew notice, especially the children. Before he'd left the house, Domingo had removed his shoes and stockings; then he'd untucked and ripped his shirt. Stepping outside, he'd reached down and scooped up a handful of the dry, red dirt of Lisbon into his hands and had smeared it in his hair, on his face, and over his clothes. Domingo was pleased with his disguise and thought himself clever to have conceived of it.

He was closer now to the front of the crowd and he could see the preacher, the grand inquisitor of Portugal, Frade Francisco da Costa, a short, thin-faced Dominican in his middling years. Domingo cringed at the sight of the most powerful man in the land, the one who had sealed his brother's fate. Frade Costa was far gone into his preaching, and when he reached the climax of his sermon, he raised his fist to heaven. Sweat poured from every pore on his body under the heavy, rich robes of his office, but the inquisitor seemed to feel nothing except the swell of righteous anger bursting within him.

"Jews seek to destroy the true faith. They marry with Old Christian families and breed their heresy throughout Portugal! Jewish blood has infected families of all ranks. Only this holy tribunal can stand against them, routing them out and purifying our Christian nation!"

The inquisitor paused here and surveyed the crowd with his small dark eyes, as if he could tell just by looking at a man whether his blood had been infected with Judaism. Domingo dashed behind a matron's skirts, his chest constricted in fear. Looking about him, he saw that he was not the only one afraid of Frade Costa. Men cowered under the inquisitor's gaze, having learned from their priests that this was a holy man entrusted by God with the purity of the church. His was not a pastoral role. He was a defender of the faith, a seventeenth-century San Miguel, whose sword was meant to run with the blood of God's enemies.

The sermon continued for another twenty minutes. Domingo began to feel dizzy from standing still so long in the press of the crowd. The air around him, thick and hot, smelled of urine, wine, and sweat. Black flies alighted on every still thing, grooming their many eyes and rubbing the dust off their legs. They reminded Domingo of priests, droning on in their self-important, lazy manner, always watching for an opportunity or a threat.

Domingo felt himself sway on his unsteady legs. Every breath felt stale, as if he was breathing in what he'd just breathed out. When he felt he could no longer last, Domingo gratefully saw the inquisitor sit down. Then Domingo sank to his knees. The crowd's attention turned to a large group of men and women dressed in yellow and black *sanbenitos*, knee-length tunics decorated according to the fate of the wearer: yellow ones with large red X-shaped crosses on both

2

the back and front panels for those who would serve sentences of prison or slavery; black ones decorated with red hellfire for those who would burn.

Domingo knew from his catechism that these men and women were Judaizers, more popularly known as *conversos,* those who professed the true faith but secretly practiced the Jewish heresy and passed it on to their children. The friars taught that conversos were the Inquisition's worst enemies with their mixed blood, mixed religion, and, worst of all, mixed message about the saving grace of baptism. They were the termites of Christianity, living in secret, constantly breeding, and destroying from within. If not for the Inquisition, Jews posing as Christians would bring down the entire structure of the church.

Armed guards prodded the conversos to the lower part of the dais where they were instructed to kneel in front of the altar. In a lengthy speech, one of the Jesuit attendants read out the crimes of each converso: Juan Dias, convicted of honoring the Jewish Passover by bathing and not opening his jewelry shop for a week; Carlos Mendes, convicted of speaking Hebrew and possessing a Jewish prayer book; Louisa Cortes, convicted of secretly naming her daughter Gila before having her baptized with the name Isabelle; and Padre Filipe de Lacerda, convicted of falsely accusing a fellow priest of fornicating with a Jewess. There were dozens more crimes, similar in nature, read out loud as a warning to the listening crowd.

The church's official part in the affair ended when men and women sentenced to slavery and prison were shuffled aside, and six unlucky men, the condemned, were handed over to the secular authorities. The soldiers and confessors escorted each condemned man to Campo da Lã, the place of execution. The crowd in Rossio Square followed behind the condemned's entourage in a jovial manner, happily anticipating the spectacle a half mile away. Domingo trailed behind them, choking on the dust of their carnival, but determined to watch the civil conclusion to the Inquisition's act of faith.

When they arrived at Campo da Lã, the crowd spread out around two sets of wooden pikes: high ones accessible by scaffolding for burning the unrepentant and street level ones for garroting those who confessed to their crimes. Although the crowd preferred live burnings, Jesuits assigned to reconciling each of the condemned worked until the last moment to bring their charges back to the church. After an hour, only two of the six men remained on the upper pikes. The crowd was disappointed by this and began to clamor for the spectacle to proceed. Soldiers chained the four reconciled men to the pikes on the lower level. Domingo once again made his way furtively toward the front of the crowd, but by the time he arrived, one of the four reconciled had already been garroted.

Sancta Maria, please let him still be alive! Domingo thought. Heart pounding, he scanned the faces of the three men still living and saw his brother among them. Filipe! he screamed silently. Domingo tried to catch Filipe's attention with a discreet wave.

His brother's stringy brown hair clung to the sweat on his face and urine dripped from the hem of his tunic, though he tried to keep his composure by quietly chanting. "*Sancta Maria mater Dei . . . ora pro nobis peccatoribus, nunc et . . . in hora mortis . . . nostrae,*" Filipe stammered out the final line, a plea for Mary's prayers at his death as his executioner tightened the iron band around his neck.

"Filipe!" Domingo shouted, beyond caring if he was recognized. His brother turned his eyes toward Domingo's voice.

Domingo.

Filipe's lips formed the name but he didn't call out in response. Domingo saw, though, and took heart for a moment before he realized that no amount of love or courage would compel God to perform a miracle to save his brother. Filipe was already dead.

As Filipe's body slumped, Domingo's stomach wrenched and he began to heave. Remnants of last night's meal burst violently from his mouth, splattering the feet of those standing nearby.

"Christ's blood, you damned pig of a boy! You're like a God-damned woman, getting sick at the sight of death!" The speaker, a large, sweaty man standing behind Domingo, pushed him forward.

Onlookers laughed as Domingo stumbled and backed away, slipping in his own vomit. He regained his footing on the wooden ramp leading to the execution pikes, and then he dove back into the crowd, desperate to get away from his mockers. He felt disoriented. Filipe's execution was sickening, even as it seemed unreal.

Domingo's legs moved without his being conscious of running, and after some minutes, he cleared the crowd. Here in the middle of the dusty road he fell to his knees and coughed up swallowed tears. He tried to understand what had just happened. His parents had not told him why Filipe had been taken and condemned. Now he knew, but this added little to his understanding. Why would Filipe accuse a brother priest of fornicating with a Jew? Why had the Inquisition executed him for it? And worst of all, why did he have to die alongside conversos?

No answer came to him, but Domingo's attention was caught by one of the conversos condemned to burn alive on an upper pike. The man was screaming, not for mercy though. Standing, Domingo strained to hear. But the renewed chanting of the friars and the heckling of the crowd as soldiers lit the execution pyre made it impossible for him to hear what the man was saying. Domingo caught snatches of phrases and realized that the man was yelling in Hebrew rather than Portuguese.

Shema Yisroel, Ado-nay Elo-heinu, Ado-nay Echad. Baruch shaym kavod mal-chuso li-olam va-ed. It was the Shema, the holiest Hebrew prayer. Yet the condemned man shouted it like an accusation, "Hear O Israel! The Lord is our God, the Lord is One! Blessed be the name of His glorious Kingdom forever and ever!" Fearfully, Domingo crossed himself and ran home.

Though just eight, this was not Domingo's first lesson in death. Last year, his sixteen-year-old sister, Marial, had drowned in the river Tagus. Domingo had not really understood what had happened, but for many months he had thought that her death was his fault. He had lied to a priest, and it was common knowledge that this was one of the greatest sins. His father, a physician, had told Domingo not to reveal to anyone outside the family that he knew how to read. So twice a week Domingo had to hide this ability during catechism lessons. He hated pretending ignorance when he was as literate as the priests, and he was sure that his lie had cast a bad omen on his sister, leading to her death. But when he and his brother Jorge took the fever this past winter, Domingo realized that death took at random. Jorge, older than Domingo by three years, had succumbed to the fever while Domingo had lived.

Breathless, Domingo stumbled across the foyer into the house. Out of habit, he touched his fingers to the right side of the doorframe and then brought them to his lips. This ritual had to be done in secret for fear of the evil eye. His father had taught it to him; he'd said it was a way to thank God for the blessings of their home and family. But lately Domingo wondered if God no longer blessed his family. Perhaps they were cursed. There seemed to be no other explanation for their troubles from which not even their home was an escape.

The Lacerdas lived in a three-story attached house in a quiet neighborhood in the Alfama atop one of Lisbon's seven hills and upwind of the stench of the poorer parts of the city. The white stucco exterior, decorated with blue and white tiles, reflected the sun, keeping the inside cool. Domingo's dirt-encrusted feet thudded on the tile floor of the entryway, but otherwise the house was quiet. Even Louisa and Carla, sisters who'd served the Lacerda family since before Domingo was born, were not there to greet him with their motherly embraces and offerings of sweetbread baked just for his pleasure. He crept into the kitchen and, finding it vacant, took the opportunity to swipe some bread, despite the fasting required during an auto-da-fé. It was approaching sundown and this would be Domingo's first meal. Greedily he consumed two slices of *broa*, dense bread made with barley, and washed it down with watered red wine. This seemed to settle his stomach somewhat, even as it unsettled his conscience. There would be much to confess to Padre João at the cathedral this week.

He was brushing the crumbs from his shirt and breeches when he heard his mother's moans. She never left the house lately, except to attend Mass. He knew she would be in her chamber. He trudged up the stairs and approached the doorway. Looking in, he saw her kneeling on the four-poster bed, her voice muffled by a garment she held against her face. It was Filipe's christening robe, the one they had all worn as infants and that now served as his mother's fetish. Her long black hair, streaked with gray, rippled in waves down her back. She was forty-three but still a striking woman with her small frame, angular face, and large dark brown eyes.

"Aiey, my God! Why do you take my children from me? Santa Maria, help me in my despair!"

6

Domingo hesitated. As her last surviving child, he felt it was his duty to comfort his mother. On the other hand, he was repulsed at the thought of inheriting so much grief.

"Aiahhh! *Oh Mater pietatis et misericordiae, beatissima Virgo Maria . . .*"

Duty won out. He filled a silver bowl from the basin of water on her vanity and walked over to the bed.

Pushing aside the thin gauze sheers hanging from the bedposts, he held out the bowl to her. "Mãe, please drink."

She raised her head and her glassy, red-rimmed eyes searched for his. "Domingo? My son." She sat up and her head lolled for a moment, even with his, and then fell toward her knees.

"Mãe!" he cried. It was not unusual for her to have such episodes, but today she was beyond reason. He lifted her chin and placed the bowl to her lips. "Mãe, please." To his dismay, most of the water dribbled down her silk gown, staining the bodice. But his ministrations seemed to calm her, and she lay quietly on the bed now.

He heard heavy footsteps downstairs. It would be His father. Should he go to him or stay with his mother? Neither choice was appealing. During these last months, Domingo had been the one comforting his parents. The burden weighed on him like a slave's yoke. His tears were like poison drops that weakened his mother and father, so he was careful to weep only when he was sure to be alone. Thus he experienced a mixture of fear and relief when his father joined them, brandishing an open letter and pronouncing in a raspy voice, "We are leaving Lisbon."

His mother looked up, suddenly sensible. "You would leave them all here?" she accused.

His father understood her meaning. "We have Domingo, Teresa Maria. The others are lost to us. If we do not leave now, we risk losing him as well."

This revelation startled Domingo. He suddenly felt cold and unprotected, even though he was standing in the same room as his parents.

His father continued, "My nephew Cosme from Amsterdam has written to tell me that many are making the journey to Brazil. Hundreds have already gone. There is much opportunity there."

"Brazil! Mother of Jesus, save us! Are there not priests in that wilderness?" his wife argued.

"There is more freedom in the New World, Teresa Maria. Our nation is not scorned there as it is here."

Domingo did not understand, but he'd learned in the last year not to ask the questions he had, just the ones his parents would answer. "Papa, is it a long way?"

"Yes, Domingo," his father answered, looking at him more closely now. "We will travel on a ship for many weeks. But you must not tell anyone of our plans, not even Louisa and Carla. No one can know we are leaving. Do you understand, Domingo?"

"Yes, Papa."

"Good. Why are you so dirty? What happened to your shirt?"

"I . . . ah, there was a fight. Nothing important," Domingo answered lamely. It was one thing to disobey his father, but to directly lie to him made Domingo feel as unclean on the inside as he was on the outside.

He expected a disapproving glare but was surprised when his father looked concerned. Domingo waited for further questions; instead, he was given instructions. "Clean yourself up and go to bed, *filho*. I must talk with your mother alone." As Domingo passed him on the way to his chamber on the third floor, his father brushed his hand affectionately over his curly mop.

Once alone, Domingo allowed himself to grieve for Filipe. He wept for hours and still slept poorly afterward. Even after three months, he was unused to sleeping alone in the bed he'd shared with Jorge, and worse, images of the day's spectacle kept imposing on his dreams: the inquisitor's eyes boring into him, Filipe's body hanging from his pinched neck, the burning Jew yelling in Hebrew.

He was running from an angry crowd, and every time he seemed to be getting ahead of them, he would fall, slipping on a puddle of vomit. It was a pair of Dominicans who finally caught and chained him with iron rosary beads to several other prisoners. He struggled to break free, but stopped when he remembered that to destroy a rosary was a grave sin. Soldiers lit the pyres at his feet and soon the burning crept up his body and began to consume him.

Domingo forced himself to wake from the nightmare. Throwing off his quilt, he hurried to his balcony where a light breeze carrying the scent of lemons and hibiscus caressed his skin through his thin nightshirt. Though sweating, he shivered thinking of his dream. Had a demon taken him because of his disobedience? His boldness yesterday seemed such folly to him now. He may have avoided mortal detection but surely Satan's agents would not be fooled by his childish disguise.

His grandmother had once told him that demons were most powerful when a person slept; they could even separate a soul from its body. If your soul left, there was a chance it might never return. It would become a slave to the devil, and your body a living corpse. Once, his father had a patient who slept without waking for three weeks. Clearly the man was one of those possessed by the demons his grandmother spoke of. Domingo had tried to warn his father about the man, but his father had chided him for speaking of demons and had told him that the man had a head sickness that caused him not to wake. When the man died, it was hard to believe his father's explanation: the man had starved to death. Domingo had found the idea of the demons more believable. Sleep was a dangerous state, especially for the guilty.

He sat on the edge of his bed and tried to calm himself by reciting the rosary, but it was hard to keep track of the prayers in his exhausted and distracted state. Just before dawn, when thin bands of pink and orange began to cut through the gray darkness of the sky, he went downstairs, feeling defeated by his memories and his dreams.

In the kitchen he was surprised to find his father sitting at the table reading a letter. He looked up when he heard Domingo's footsteps approaching. "Domingo, how is it you are up so early?"

"My dreams won't let me sleep, Papa. May I sit with you?"

"Sí, come here." His father patted the space next to him on the bench. Domingo sidled up to him and leaned into his chest. His father, Joseph, was a tall, thin man with fine, straight brown hair that he wore just below his ears. As a younger man, he'd been more muscular, but now as a physician, his strength was in his mind and his hands. Domingo had been the child of his old age, being born when Joseph was forty-seven. Now in his mid-fifties, Joseph seemed weary of life. Nevertheless, Domingo took comfort in being near his father, his earlier feeling of being unprotected forgotten.

His father showed him the letter. "It is from my nephew Cosme Delgado in Amsterdam. We will join him there and travel to Brazil together. It will be a new start for us, Domingo." His father's optimism bothered him, so Domingo hung his head rather than reply. *Zakor*, he'd always been taught. It meant "remember." So why was his father so determined to forget? His father squeezed Domingo's shoulder affectionately. "Tell me what is troubling you, *filho*. Is it your mother?"

"No." Domingo hung his head in anticipation of his father's displeasure. "I went to the square yesterday, Papa."

Stunned, his father pulled his hand away and slammed it on the table. "Domingo! We forbade you from going there!"

"I had to see Filipe!" Domingo shouted, surprised at his own passionate defense of his disobedience. He could not claim to be a compliant child, but until recently he had always acknowledged his willfulness as a sin against his parents and the priests. But not today. Going to the auto-da-fé was impulsive, even dangerous, but he remained convinced that he was right in going.

Without warning, his father began to sob. Streams of tears ran down his face and soaked the letter, making the ink run off the paper and onto his father's fingers. Domingo willed him to stop. Why was his father so weak? The feeling of being unprotected washed over him again and he resented his father for it. But as his father wept for several more minutes, his body heaving with the violence of his emotions, Domingo began to feel compassion for this broken man next to him. His father had not forgotten. Domingo put his little hands over his father's larger ones.

"Papa, he saw me. He wasn't alone when he died."

This did not seem to have the comforting effect Domingo expected, though his father did more decently put his head on the table and muffle his weeping with his arms. Domingo laid his head next to his father's and soon fell asleep.

London, England, April 1642

Her labor was not going well. They never did. This was the second one in Lucy's memory, but Nettie said that there had been two others when Lucy was too young to remember. Four pregnancies in seven years. Three dead babies. All girls. Lucy shuddered at the thought. That she had survived seemed almost incomprehensible. She tried to shut out her mother's screams by pressing her hands against her ears and then pulling her shawl over the back of her head. But it was no use. The screaming penetrated the walls and floorboards like a poltergeist. Lucy yearned for the comfort of another human soul, but Father had locked himself in his study and Nettie was assisting the doctor upstairs. Father had paid dear for the doctor, who generally tended only to royals and courtiers. But in the anti-royal climate of Cromwell's England, a London doctor did well to expand his practice to the minor gentry. Her father had been grateful for the doctor's attendance, but from the way her mother was yelling, the doctor presented a far bigger problem than the child stuck in her womb.

"Mother of God, get this damned Jew out of here! I won't have him touch me!"

Lucy could hear Nettie trying to soothe her mother. "Shh, there's a girl, Missus D. You jest let 'im do his job. Well qualified, 'ee is, Missus. Well qualified."

Two hours later the baby finally came, a scrawny weak thing. But now her mother's yelling took on a new urgency. "Where is my husband? Where is John? The child needs to be baptized straightaway!"

Nettie lumbered downstairs and into the kitchen where Lucy sat by the hearth. "It's a boy, but 'ee won't live. Get yer father," she said panting, her large breasts rising and falling like drowning men struggling for air.

Lucy jumped up and ran to the door connecting the kitchen to the countinghouse. Father's study, the accounts room, was an interior chamber that could be locked from within.

"Father!" Lucy shouted, pounding on the heavy oak door with her fists. "Mother's had a boy. Come quickly."

She heard shuffling from within and then the sound of the lock slowly turning. When he swung the door open, Lucy saw that her father looked disheveled and disoriented.

"Lucy?"

She grabbed his hand. "Mother needs you. The baby is come. It's a boy."

They made their way back into the house and had just started upstairs when her mother started screaming again. "What have you done to him? Get out of my house! John!"

The doctor gathered his instruments and hurried downstairs, almost knocking into Lucy and her father in the narrow, winding passage. "Senhor Dunnington," he said, bowing nervously.

The doctor's presence made her father sensible again. He put up a hand to stop the doctor's speech and turned to her. "Lucy, take Dr. Añes downstairs and give him some rum. I'll be along shortly."

After settling the doctor in the parlor with his spirit, Lucy lit several candles against the dark and then looked to the empty fireplace.

"There is no need to light a fire. The cool air is refreshing after the birthing chamber. And it is a mild night, no?"

His voice startled her, but she liked his accent. It had a kind of sing-song quality to it that reminded her of the priests in the Queen's Chapel. He looked a bit like them as well, short and swarthy-skinned with cropped dark hair under the wig he'd just put back on.

"Is my brother dead?" she asked him.

He set down his mug and brought his hands together under his nose. Then he rocked back and forth. "Yes, menina Dunnington, he is with God. But have no fear about your mother. She will live."

"He was the first, you know."

The doctor shook his head, not understanding.

"The first son. My mother had four girls before him."

"Four daughters," he mused.

Lucy nodded, unsure of what to say next. "Are you French like the queen?" she asked finally.

"No, no," he replied with a nervous wave of his hand. "I am a Portuguese from Lisboa, the most Catholic city in the world."

This information gave her some comfort. Her family was Catholic, even if her father went to services once a month at the state church, the Anglican Church of England. Her mother didn't like it when he did though. On those days it was best to stay out of her way for her rage. She'd call Father all manner of names and tell him that it was his fault, his sin that caused their babies to die in her womb. When Lucy was born seven years ago they'd lived in Yorkshire and her father had not attended Protestant services. According to her mother, this was why God had allowed Lucy to live.

Lucy and the doctor sat in companionable silence until her father came downstairs. Dr. Añes stood. "Senhor Dunnington, please forgive me. I wanted to help. She was distraught and his life slipped away so fast."

Her father nodded. "I know. There is no cause for you to be concerned. Nettie administered the infusion you prepared and Mrs. Dunnington is resting comfortably."

"And your son, *bekhor*, the first one. I am sorry, Senhor. But he was so weak. If he had not died tonight, he would have died tomorrow. I can assure you of that. He came too soon and could not breathe." Lucy's father said nothing and the doctor continued in a nervous rush, "I will have Masses said for him. It was, you know, a legitimate baptism. Your servant can testify to this."

"I never questioned that," replied her father, noticing for the first time that Lucy was in the room. "Come Dr. Añes, you must be tired. I will see you to your carriage."

When he returned, Lucy had extinguished the candles in the parlor and Nettie was banking the fire in the kitchen. Without his asking, Lucy poured her father a cup of mulled wine and they sat down at the kitchen table together.

"Will ye be needin' anything else, sir, 'fore I retire?" Nettie asked, clearly not in the mood to serve any more that night.

"No, Nettie. You've been a great help this evening. Take your rest now," Lucy's father answered.

"I'll jest check on the missus then." She took a candle and trudged up the stairs.

Her father turned to Lucy and said, "Well, pet, it seems you are destined to be an only child."

But Lucy was troubled over a different matter. "Father, what did Dr. Añes do to make Mother so angry?"

13

He sighed deeply. "The good doctor baptized your brother, John Francis Dunnington." He took a deep swig from his cup and held it out for her to refill.

"But why did that anger her? Isn't that what she wanted?" Lucy asked, lifting the jug and pouring more of the warm beverage into his cup.

Her father shook his head. Then he said, "I don't know what she wants anymore, Lucy. I just don't know."

"Father, what is a Jew?"

He looked up startled, but then quickly composed his features. "Nothing, pet. Just something your mother made up. You know how she gets sometimes."

Lucy nodded, not from true understanding, but because that was what her father expected. But this much she knew: Jews were real and her mother feared them.

II. *EXODUS*

He was only allowed to bring what he could wear. So even though it was a warm April day when they left Lisbon, Domingo dressed in three layers of clothing. He stuffed his pockets with his childhood treasures: a smooth gray rock streaked with pink that he and Jorge had fought over during one of their excursions to the shore, a long blue ribbon that had belonged to Marial, and a little figurine of the Virgin carved out of wood that Filipe had given him. And in the lining of his coat, his mother had sewn her jewels. They bore into his back when he sat down, but she was insistent that he keep the jacket on. Domingo knew that his father carried several books and a purse of crusados in his sack. What was hidden in the skirts of his mother's walking dress remained a mystery to Domingo, but he was sure that it was as richly lined as his coat. They had not closed up the house, leaving it as if they had stepped out for a normal morning outing. But they would never return to this place. They walked quickly and silently toward the wharf.

Fleeing was no simple matter. Now that Portugal had finally won its independence from Spain, New Christians who tried to leave the country were suspect and often detained by Inquisition spies, who charged that these emigrants were both heretics and traitors to the king, João IV. Added to this was the fact that many of the New Christians created a viable middle class and could be counted on for bribes and fines to supplement the coffers of the king and the inquisitor general. This much Domingo understood from the discussions and arguments his father and Filipe had had in the months leading up to his brother's arrest. What he had not understood, and had been afraid to ask lest they had recalled his presence and sent him from the room, was what they had meant by "New Christian." They had used this strange term with baffling familiarity, these two common words placed together to create a powerful secret.

So he'd learned that theirs was a blameless New Christian family until Filipe had been arrested. Now everything was different. Secrets surrounded them like a fog, their fear infecting every ordinary act and conversation. He heard it in his parents' whispers, saw it in the way they walked about the city. But his father was still respected by many in Lisbon. In the last weeks before their departure, his father had made a few careful bribes and had earned a favor from a ship's agent by performing an illegal procedure on the agent's son. The child had been born with a clubbed foot, a sure sign of God's judgment for the family's sinfulness. The agent had approached Domingo's father, begging the doctor to fix his child's foot. The only other person who had seen the deformity was the midwife, and she could be paid to keep quiet. Domingo's father had refused at first, but when Filipe was arrested his father had said it was only a matter of time.

So his father broke the child's foot and reset it, carefully cutting the tendons that had been pulling the limb out of place. The child would never walk easily, but the deformity was now masked and, with proper healing, the child would not be lame.

Thus a child's misfortune became the Lacerdas' means to escape Portugal. The grateful agent agreed to book them on a Dutch ship bound for Amsterdam and to keep their passage a secret. However, it would be up to them to get safely to the wharf. The only way was to go before dawn, before the gossips were awake. God, so long absent from this family, was with them as they made their way to the ship and embarked without incident. After losing so much, Domingo's father said that they deserved this relatively easy escape. And as his father wiped his brow and sat down on one of the two narrow wooden bunks in their small, windowless cabin, Domingo realized how tired his father looked even though it was still morning. Feeling woozy himself, Domingo stripped down to just one set of clothes. This did not please his mother, whose scolding spewed forth like a shattered dam after her silence these last weeks.

"We're not even out of the harbor and you act like we are already in Amsterdam. Look at your clothes scattered all over the place."

"Mãe, it's so hot," he whined, but he began to gather up and fold the discarded shirts and breeches into a neat pile anyway.

"He's hot! You think we are on a pleasure cruise, then? Look at how you've dirtied them already," she said, pointing to a smudge of dirt on one of the linen shirts. "Give them to me."

After he handed over the clothes, his mother set to refolding them and Domingo slipped out of the cabin and up to the main deck.

When the *Drie Koning* pulled out of Lisbon's harbor, Domingo was fascinated and a little sad. He had never been on a ship before and the adventure of it thrilled him. Although, in some deep part of his consciousness, he suspected that the journey to the New World would be difficult. Terrible things were happening here, but Lisbon was the only home he'd ever known.

He'd grown up in a neighborhood full of cousins, aunts, and uncles, who were as much a part of his life as his own siblings. Over the years, though, they had all moved away to Amsterdam or Spain. Then Marial and Jorge had died and the house echoed with emptiness. And when Filipe was arrested three months ago, the children in the neighborhood shunned Domingo. And he had become consumed with loneliness and shame.

The worst part was not knowing why all of this was happening. Each day he conjured up a different scenario of his family's secret sins, trying desperately to make sense of their fate. Was it his fault? Domingo had examined his conscience a hundred times a day trying to figure out what he might have done to have caused his family's suffering. Guiltily, he even cast a suspicious eye to his parents, even as he knew how unlikely it was that either of them harbored a secret sin. His mother was devoted to the Blessed Virgin Mary and went to Mass almost every day. His father was a respected physician and scholar in Lisbon. Why was God so displeased with them?

Recalling all that had happened during the last year caused a ball of pain to form deep in Domingo's chest. He knew this feeling well and had even managed to suppress it several times in the last few weeks. All he needed was a space to be alone. He went down to his family's cabin, laid down on one of the hard bunks, pulled his knees to his chest, and faced the wall. His throat throbbed from the ball of pain trying to make its way out. He took several deep breaths, trying to beat it back.

But his mother would not suffer him being ill like his father. "Domingo! What is wrong with you? Why are you lying down? Joseph, you are pale. Sit down. Domingo, go find some ale for your father."

Domingo reluctantly rose and left their cabin. He made his way to an upper deck where large barrels of fresh water, rum, and ale were kept. One of the crew, a dirty, stocky man with several black teeth, stood guard over the barrels. Domingo knew that he could get his flask filled if he passed the man a coin. He held his empty flask out and said, "Ale please, sir."

"You'll get drink at mealtimes." The sailor didn't even look at Domingo.

Domingo was ready for this response. His father had told him once that some men liked to obstruct others purely for sport, but persistence was the key to success. "Sir, that's three hours from now. My father is not well." He showed the man his coin. "Please?"

The man roughly snatched the coin from Domingo's hand and grabbed the flask. He dipped it in the barrel of ale for a moment, filling it perhaps only halfway, and then he shoved it back toward him. "It'll cost you more each time, Jew boy." Domingo opened his mouth to protest this insult, but then he realized that if he angered the man, he might never be able to get ale again. Defeated, he jammed the cork into the flask and walked away.

Just outside the cabin, Domingo's shoe caught on a nail and he tripped, causing him to drop the flask and slam to the floor on his knees. Pain shot up his legs, into his hips, and his eyes filled with tears as the ball of pain forced its way up, closer to making its escape. Abruptly, a hand reached down, grabbed him by an armpit, and pulled him to his feet. Domingo looked up to see who the hand belonged to. He could tell by the finely woven black robe that it belonged to a Jesuit priest. They were inquisitorial confessors, as opposed to their white-robed Dominican brothers who oversaw Inquisition trials and autos-da-fé. It was a strange cooperation between the orders. The Dominicans routed out and broke accused Judaizers, while the Jesuits were charged with saving their souls. Domingo looked up. The Jesuit had short blond hair and twinkling blue eyes that seemed kind.

"Are you hurt?" He spoke in a language Domingo did not understand, so Domingo stood mute, hoping his silence did not offend the priest. But the Jesuit recognized his difficulty and switched to Latin. "Quem appeletur?"

This language he understood. "Domingo Maria Rodrigues de Lacerda, Senhor Padre," Domingo answered, bowing respectfully.

The Jesuit smiled; then he raised his right hand over Domingo's head and pronounced the Trinitarian blessing, "*Benedicat te in nomine Patris, et Filii, et Spiritus Sancti. Amen.*"

"*Agradeço-lhe*, Senhor Padre," replied Domingo dutifully. He reached down to retrieve the flask and limped into his parents' cabin.

"Who were you talking to out there?" his mother asked him after he closed the door behind him.

"There was a priest, Mãe. He wanted to know my name and then he blessed me." He handed the flask to his father, and when he turned back to his mother, she slapped him hard across the face. "Mãe!" he cried, cradling his stinging cheek as he tried to keep from falling backward onto his father, who was lying on the bunk behind him.

"Stay away from the priests, Domingo!"

"Teresa Maria, there is no need to strike the boy. He doesn't understand," his father said sighing. He sat up and reached for Domingo. But Domingo moved away and sank down into a corner of the cabin where he pulled his scraped and bruised knees to his chest, trying to make himself as small as possible. When had his father lost the power to protect him? No longer able to fight it, the pain in his throat finally got out and he began to sob quietly.

"Domingo," pleaded his mother. "I'm sorry. I was frightened." She knelt down and embraced him. And as much as he wanted to punish her by pushing her away, his need for his mother was overwhelming. He fell into her arms and gave full vent to his hurt and frustration. His mother pulled him onto her lap, touched her forehead to his, and gently rubbed his back. "Amiel, my little one," she murmured, "there is so much sadness in you."

♦♦♦

When she was well enough, Lucy's mother insisted on going home to Yorkshire for the summer as was her custom. But not to stay with her parents. They were long dead, and for reasons Lucy did not understand, her mother no longer spoke to the uncle and aunt who had raised her. They would stay instead at the Dunnington family home in Thorganby Parish, Thicket Hall. The manor was a modest, two-century-old structure belonging to Lucy's uncle Richard, and Lucy had spent every summer there for as long as she could remember. It was a two and a half-story stone building with semi-hexagonal windows, three high chimneys on an arched roof, eight hearths, and a wonderful hexagon-shaped tower that rose an entire story above the rest of the house. Originally, the house had been part of Thicket Priory, which was acquired by a Dunnington ancestor during the dissolution of the monasteries under Henry VIII. But during the last century, the vast acreage of the priory had been carved up and sold off to minor gentry who were eager for land to secure their status in England's new order. Thicket Hall was the prize of the priory, at one time being the primary domain of the abbot with several rooms for guests of high birth.

Lucy loved to climb to the top of Thicket Hall's tower and pretend that she was a kidnapped princess. She'd stare out the window searching for the knight who would come to her rescue, but generally the only men on horseback who passed outside the tower were Uncle Richard, her father, and their cousin Charles Dunnington coming back from a hunt. Although disappointed, Lucy knew her hopes of rescue were foolish. The most interesting captives, Queen Maude, Queen Eleanor, and Queen Mary of the Scots, all immortalized in the stirring ballads of the minstrels, always managed to arrange their own escapes.

Richard Dunnington had generously set aside one of the better kept residences on the property, Chapel House, for his only living sibling, his younger brother, John, Lucy's father. Chapel House was a typical Tudor-style cottage with a large upper floor that hung slightly over the lower floor. With only six rooms, it was a cozy house compared to the elegance of Thicket Hall. Lucy loved its informal manner and, as much as she enjoyed running through Thicket Hall's corridors, she preferred living at Chapel House.

Her father joined Lucy and her mother in July, but it was not a good visit. The whole time her parents argued.

"John, Father Lacy is staying with my cousin James. I've done my duty. Now you must do yours," her mother said before her father had even settled in.

He sighed and rubbed his hand over his forehead. Lucy noticed that he did that a lot lately. "Mary, I am not going to confess what I don't believe. As for your condition, there is something inside you that prevents the womb from expanding. Dr. Añes said he could feel it during your labor."

"How dare you cite that heretic to me! It's his fault our son is dead, not mine. I heard what he said. It was a curse, not a baptism."

"I'd like you to see another doctor. One who can treat the hardness in your womb."

"*Again* you say it's my fault. I am not the sinner, John. You are! It is your hardness, not mine, that destroys our children. It is *you* who's betrayed your faith. And for what? Money. Just like all the other apostates in this family. My brother is the only one who stayed faithful."

"Yes, Mary. And now he has to live abroad because of it. Is that what you want? For me to lose my property and livelihood and have us have to flee to France? What would we live on, prayers? Or would you have us be like your parents and die in prison, leaving our child an orphan? Is that what God asks of us? If so, then I will have no further commerce with him."

"You speak blasphemy! This is why God punishes us. It is not God who wants this; it is the king and his councilors who preach the Protestant heresy. In its glory, England was Catholic and it shall be again soon. I know this to be true. Please, John, go to Father Lacy."

"If I speak heresy, then you speak treason. I'll take my chances with God, as the king is more reliable with his punishments."

"Then go stay with your brother," she said, pushing him toward the door. "I won't have a blasphemer in the house, and I certainly won't have one in my bed."

He left, but he returned a few days later. He seemed drunk, but penitent. It was nice for several days, her parents together with her at Chapel House. But then the fighting began again. This time her father did not leave, and as much as she loved him, Lucy wished he would. The house was silent with tension. Her mother, generally kind and attentive to Lucy, became sharp and spent long spells of time away visiting her cousin and his priest. When her mother came home, her parents argued; this time about Lucy.

"I want Lucy to take lessons with James's children, Sebastian and Claire. James tells me Father Lacy is an excellent tutor," her mother said one day at the dinner table.

"Absolutely not. You may pass on your beliefs to her, but you will not endanger her or this family by letting her be tutored by a Jesuit. I've already arranged for Lucy to be tutored by a fellow in London, a Mr. Bithcuts."

"I suppose he is a Protestant?" her mother huffed.

"He is certainly not a Jesuit."

"Why do you do this to me, John?" Her mother began to break down in tears. "Can't you see what a misery my life has become? What are you doing to me? To our daughter?"

Her father threw his shoulders back and sat up straight in his chair. "I am trying to give her a chance at a decent life. Let her be a Papist at home. But in society, Lucy will be a good Anglican."

"But *why*? I don't understand, John."

"Because in truth, I don't know if it matters what religion she professes, wife. No, hear me out," he said when she opened her mouth to speak. "Think of what is happening around us. England has not gone back to Catholicism. It's been nigh over eighty years since we've had a Catholic monarch. Catholicism is outlawed, Mary. We've been to war with Ireland over Catholicism and we've been to war with Scotland over Presbyterianism; now we will most likely have a civil war because the Puritans hate the Catholic queen. It is ridiculous. Of course, a child must be raised to some kind of faith, and it is my duty to prepare Lucy for her place in English society. Anglicanism is the safest choice even though the bishops deify the very nation. I'll not have Lucy be a Separatist like those damned Baptists and Quakers. Indeed, I suspect all religions to be hopelessly against logic and peace, but the reality is that one must at least seem to be aligned with one, rather than be accused an atheist. So, Lucy will conform, at least publicly, and that is my final word on the matter."

With that, he threw down his napkin, rose from the table, and ordered the servants to begin packing for the journey back to London.

♦♦♦

After the first couple of days at sea, Domingo spent most of his time on deck away from his parents. He loved the feel of the cold, wet ocean spray on his face; and the rocking of the boat did not sicken him as it did Papa. The air, salty and fresh, made him want to throw his arms wide and breathe it in like a glutton until his lungs burst. Gazing for hours at the vast expanse of ocean made him feel free to dream about what his life might be like in the New World. Brazil seemed to be a land of adventure and promise compared to Lisbon, now in Domingo's mind a city of fear and death. Below in their cabin, Papa remained on his bunk and Mãe busied herself by tending to him and worrying about the long journey ahead. He could not identify why, but Domingo felt that when he was with his parents he was bound to unspoken, but very real, expectations about his future. If only he could trust his parents, he might have taken comfort in knowing that they had already mapped out the course of his life. But, guiltily, he realized that he did not trust them. Not now that his siblings were dead, and especially not after his parents' erratic behavior during the last few weeks. Glumly, he concluded that he had only himself to rely on now.

Occasionally he saw the blond Jesuit on deck. The priest always had a large smile for Domingo, and as much as he felt drawn to the man's paternal demeanor, he did not want to risk another scene with his mother. Though she'd been tender toward him these last few days, Domingo had seen her weeping as she prayed her rosary. He knew that beneath her gentle manner she was still grieving. To agitate her further, just to alleviate his boredom, seemed selfish and cruel.

Their ship pulled into Amsterdam's harbor on a chilly morning in early May. Cosme had arranged passage for them on the *St. Peter*, which was due to leave for Brazil in two days time. Their destination was Recife, a Dutch-ruled region in northeast Brazil. Domingo's father spoke of Recife as a land of milk and honey. The terrain was mountainous, the land rich and fertile, and the people there lived free from fear of the Inquisition. It became mythical in Domingo's imagination, a paradise in the New World. He longed for this promised land of goodness and warmth.

It became frustratingly clear, though, on arriving in Amsterdam that his father was now too ill to travel any farther. It took all his father's energy to disembark and find lodgings for them near where the *St. Peter* was docked. Climbing the steep, narrow staircase to their chamber, a single room on the third floor of a boarding house on the Damrak, his father nearly collapsed from exhaustion. Domingo carried his father's heavy sack and seethed with disappointment. Why did his father have to get sick now? Why, when Domingo had finally allowed himself to hope that Recife would be better than Lisbon, was his father ruining everything with his weakness?

The next morning his father sent a message, via the landlady's son, to Cosme, who called on them later that day.

"Good day, young sir," his cousin greeted Domingo when he opened the door to him. "And which one are you?" He was a broad-chested man, but still young, and perhaps only in his early thirties. Domingo noted his cousin's suit of blue-and-gold striped silk trimmed with black velvet, his draping wig of dark curls, and his wide hat trimmed with two green feathers. Cosme looked like a peacock stuffed for display.

"I am Domingo, sir."

"Excellent," Cosme replied, as if Domingo had given him the correct answer to a difficult question. "Take me to your father then."

His father had told him that Cosme was a widower with no children. As he led Cosme inside, Domingo wondered what his cousin would make of his sickly, soberly-dressed father.

Indeed, it was a brief interview in which Cosme concluded that his uncle was unfit for the long journey to Brazil. "My brother, Manuel, lives just a mile from here. He is a good man. He will give you shelter until the next ships are scheduled to make the voyage. I can take the boy."

"We will not be separated," his mother interrupted, placing a protective hand on Domingo's shoulder.

"Yes," his father said panting. "There has been too much loss already. We must stay together now. None of my family will go to Brazil tomorrow." Turning to Domingo he said in a raspy, but commanding voice, "You must fetch your cousin Manuel. Cosme will tell you where to go."

Domingo caught Cosme scowling at this arrangement, but his cousin did not argue with his uncle. Cosme turned to Domingo and said, "Follow this street west until you come to a garden square. From there you will go south to Nieuwe Houtmarket. There is a school at one end of the street. My brother's house is two blocks east of the school. His name is Manuel Delgado. He is well-known. So if you get lost, you need only ask anyone in the neighborhood to show you to the house of Manuel Delgado. Do you understand?"

"Yes, sir." Domingo silently repeated the directions to himself.

His mother walked him to the door and handed him a small sack of coins. Then she whispered to him, "Give these to your cousin so he can hire a cart." She cast a glance at his father and Domingo understood her meaning. Then she grasped his head in her hands and kissed each of his cheeks. "You are a good boy, Domingo. Please hurry." And with that, he ran off.

After getting lost twice, Domingo finally found his cousin's house, a narrow wooden structure that was raised several feet off the ground and that was only accessible by a wide set of wooden steps. Out of breath from his haste, he trudged up the stairs and rapped soundly on the door. The servant who opened it, a young girl with dull looks and a fierce scowl, did not speak Portuguese. But she did gesture for Domingo to wait outside. He scowled back at her. After she closed the door, he stood alone on the stoop, nervous and humiliated. What if the servant had been telling him to go away rather than to wait? Even worse, what if his cousin was not at home? However, after ten minutes of worrying, Domingo was rewarded with an invitation from Manuel himself to enter. Trying to walk in a dignified manner to make up for his earlier shame, Domingo entered the foyer where his cousin stood. Manuel was almost thirty years younger than Domingo's father, but he was unmistakably related to him. They were both tall, thin men with pale brown eyes and straight light-brown hair.

"Sir," Domingo addressed his cousin, giving him a low bow. "I am the son of your uncle Joseph de Lacerda. We arrived from Lisbon yesterday. Your brother, Cosme, waits with him. He asked me to bid you come at once. My father is not well and cannot travel to Brazil." Domingo held out the sack of coins. "For a cart," he said.

Manuel seemed taken aback. "What is your name?"

"Domingo Maria Rodrigues de Lacerda, sir."

"And what is your age?"

"Eight, sir."

"You came here alone from the docks?"

"Yes, sir." Domingo was afraid that he had suddenly done something wrong. He tried to explain, "I got lost, but I hurried as fast as I could when I realized I went wrongly."

Manuel's expression became warm and he shook his head incredulously. He then turned around toward the inside door and, pushing it open, called out something in Dutch. Presently, a pretty woman, with yellow curls bursting from underneath her white cap, came bustling into the foyer. Domingo could hear a baby whining from a back room.

The woman stood close to Manuel and seemed about to speak, but then she noticed Domingo and moved back a step from his cousin. She said something in Dutch to Manuel.

Manuel sported an amused grin and replied, nodding at Domingo.

Certain that this was an introduction, Domingo bowed to the woman and said, "Senhorita."

"Mevrouw," she immediately corrected.

Speaking in Portuguese, Manuel explained, "Domingo, Ana is my wife. She does not speak Portuguese." Domingo nodded, embarrassed at his error but linguistically unable to make amends for it.

After taking his leave of Ana, Manuel put his arm around his young cousin and led him out the door. As he tucked Domingo's money sack into his cloak, he outlined their plan. "Three blocks from here we will find the butcher, Isaac, who will lend us his horse and cart for a few of these coins. Then we will go collect your father."

"And my mother."

Manuel raised an eyebrow at this new information, but then he nodded. "And your mother. Anyone else?"

"No, we are just three now," Domingo replied in a dampened tone. Fortunately Manuel asked no further questions, but somehow Domingo knew that his cousin would not let the matter rest. Conversations about why they'd left Lisbon would be unavoidable.

They arrived at the boarding house an hour later. Cosme was visibly relieved and he embraced Manuel warmly.

"Brother, I had thought not to see you again for years, but here I stand with you just a day after saying good-bye," exclaimed Manuel.

"A happy meeting for us," Cosme replied, "but our uncle and his family are not so fortunate. I was set to take them with me to Brazil, but now I must ask you to give them shelter until Joseph can travel."

"Of course, brother," responded Manuel, who seemed eager to accommodate his older brother.

After making introductions, Cosme drew Manuel back into the landing where they spoke in hurried whispers for several minutes. Seated by the door, Domingo could not hear what they were saying, but he saw Cosme try to give his brother a sack of coins that Manuel pushed back at him. Then Cosme sighed and forgot to whisper his response, "I did not mean to burden you with this, brother. Thank you for taking them in."

"What are we if we do not help each other?" answered Manuel. "The Lacerdas are strangers in a strange land. It is my duty to shelter them."

Cosme smiled and placed his hand on his brother's shoulder. "You are truly Papa's son, brother. I am glad one of us is. God will certainly bless you for your generosity."

When the brothers returned to the inner room, Cosme made his good-byes and assured Domingo's parents that he would expect their arrival in Recife in the fall. Then he was gone.

Domingo helped Manuel settle his parents and their few belongings into the butcher's cart. As he and his cousin walked beside it, Manuel, leading the horse through crowded streets and over a complicated series of bridges, kept up a steady stream of chatter.

"My mother, Isabelle Delgado, was born Isabelle de Lacerda. She was your father's youngest sister. She married my father, Gaspar Delgado of Lisbon, when she was sixteen. Shortly after Cosme was born, they moved to Amsterdam where I was born. When I was five, my mother died in childbirth, and my father, heartbroken, never remarried."

"Was your father a merchant, sir?" Domingo asked, feeling an obligation to encourage his cousin's story.

"No, he worked as an accountant, but he was better known in our neighborhood as 'the job finder.' When Portuguese refugees came to Amsterdam, my father arranged for their employment with the merchants, agents, and artisans. And when Cosme and I came of age, he did the same for us. Cosme apprenticed with a tobacco merchant and my father trained me himself. I hope to train my own sons when they are of age, but that won't be for some time as neither are in breeches yet. Ah, here we are, back where you began just a couple of hours ago, yes?"

Domingo looked up and saw that, indeed, they were back on Nieuwe Houtmarket, standing just yards from Manuel's house. Back from where he had begun two hours ago, but a lifetime away from Lisbon.

III. *AMSTERDAM,* 1642

The Delgados easily made room for Domingo's family. His parents were given the anteroom bed, which was built into a large wardrobe on the wall opposite the fireplace. Manuel's sons, three-year-old Marcos and one-year-old Gaspar, were moved into their parents' chamber, which also served as the parlor. And Ana made a pallet using a canvas sack stuffed with straw and mule hair for Domingo, who preferred to sleep in the kitchen. Being alone at night gave him time to think about all the changes of the past year. After swallowing his disappointment about not continuing on to Recife and being taken in by the Delgados, he thought he would like living with cousins again. But he found himself too unhappy to enjoy their company. So much was different here that it was a constant effort to adjust. He concluded at the end of the first week that he didn't like Amsterdam. The weather was generally wet and windy and the fog cast a pall over his already gloomy mood. He missed the warmth and the brilliant blue sky of Lisbon.

In addition to the foul weather, his family did not go to Mass anymore. And instead of fasting on Fridays as the church required, the Delgados served an elaborate meal. Domingo could not understand why his parents, so observant of Catholic traditions in Lisbon, were meekly accepting these changes. The numerous rules about washing and prayers irritated him as did his prickly pallet on the hard floor of the kitchen. In Lisbon he'd had a wooden bed with a down mattress and cotton sheets. Now he huddled under a coarse woolen blanket and slept near the hearth for its warmth. His pallet was certainly more comfortable than his bunk on the *Drie Koning,* so he knew that he shouldn't complain, it was just that this arrangement did not seem as temporary as the ship bunk had been. Autumn was still a long way off, and even then, the journey to Brazil would take many weeks. The comfort of a real bed would not be a possibility until at least the end of the year. Annoyed, he pulled the blanket tighter around his body and closed his eyes, trying to imagine himself already in Brazil where he could once again feel the warm sun on his face.

More days passed, and even though he was living in a house full of people, Domingo continued to feel lonely. His parents were preoccupied. And even if his little cousins had been old enough to play with, he could not properly speak to them because he did not understand the Dutch they spoke. Papa's illness had ruined everything. All was now gray, chill, and hopeless. Domingo grew sullen and often found himself in trouble with his mother, who had little patience for his mood.

"Mãe, it's always so cold here and it smells like fish," he whined.

Her response was a swift cuff to his head with the back of her hand. After that, he kept his misery to himself.

Everything changed a week later when Manuel arranged for Domingo to attend the neighborhood school. On the day he was to begin his lessons, Manuel took Domingo and his father to meet the master teacher, a round-faced man of middle height with a long mustache, goatee, and wavy brown hair that he wore cut above the collar in the Dutch style. He looked to be the same age as Manuel, perhaps a few years older, but still young for a master teacher. Despite his youthful appearance, the master teacher's large, almond-shaped brown eyes seemed kind and wise. Manuel made introductions in Dutch.

His father and Manuel bowed to the master teacher. From his dress, a sober black woolen suit with a simple white collar, Domingo concluded that the man was not a priest. Why had Papa bowed to one such as him? If this was a Dutch custom, he did not like it. Did the master teacher know who his father was? Had Manuel not told him?

Manuel spoke again. Domingo did not understand what his cousin was saying to the master teacher, but after hearing Manuel speak the name "Amiel" a second time, Domingo grew agitated. Why was his cousin speaking that name? Amiel was his mother's pet name for him. Why would Manuel embarrass him by telling it to the master teacher?

The master teacher then turned to Domingo and addressed him in Portuguese, "I am Menasseh ben Israel. You may address me as

Haham." The master teacher's lips formed a strangely eager smile. "Amiel, you are most welcome here," he said. Then he gestured to a youth standing behind him whom Domingo had not noticed until that moment. The boy appeared to be slightly older than Domingo, and his large oval eyes, wavy brown hair, and round face surely indicated that he was related to the master teacher. "This is my son Semuel Soeiro," the master teacher said. And responding to Domingo's look of confusion, the master teacher added, "Semuel is known by our Portuguese surname. He will acquaint you with the ways of the yeshiva. Now your father and I will speak." With that, the master teacher dismissed Domingo, who then followed the older boy out of the master's chambers.

Semuel led him down a narrow passage that led to a spacious room filled with a large table and a dozen chairs. Light streamed in from several high, east-facing windows. Neatly piled on the table were several scrolls and books of all sizes. Amazed, Domingo's gaze lingered on the books. At the cathedral school in Lisbon, the students were never allowed to read, or even *touch*, the few books available. Most of what they learned had been read to them by the priests, and the boys had been expected to memorize the lessons word for word and then repeat them back. This was thought to demonstrate a mastery of the material. Here in this new school, Domingo eagerly looked forward to the kind of instruction he'd received at home, studying a text with his father and then discussing its meaning. These lessons were harder to prepare for as there was a lot of reading he had to do on his own; but in the end, they were more satisfying than summary and memorization.

Semuel, who also spoke Portuguese, explained that the boys studied each day from eight to eleven in the morning and from two to five in the afternoon. Domingo reveled in the thought of so many pleasurable hours spent away from his cousin's house and in the presence of boys his own age.

"Where did you study in Lisbon?" Semuel asked, making polite conversation.

"I had lessons at the Cathedral of Santa Maria, but my father and brothers taught me to read Latin and Hebrew at home," Domingo answered with pride.

Semuel laughed heartily, as if his answer were some kind of joke. Domingo was pained, both at Semuel's reaction and his own failure to understand the source of it. "Amiel, my friend, I trust you know your Catholic catechism well, but what of your Jewish learning?"

Domingo was dumbstruck. Why would he know anything about the enemies of the Inquisition?

His silence seemed to be answer enough for Semuel. "*Meu Deus*, Amiel! You have been turned Christian after all!"

Confused and irritated, Domingo retorted crossly, "I am Domingo. Amiel is what my mother called me when I was young. And we are Catholic." He made the sign of the cross, hurriedly touching the fingers of his right hand to his forehead, his breastplate, and each side of his chest.

Semuel sighed knowingly, which irritated Domingo all the more. "Amiel is your real name, your Jewish name, which you have because you are a Jew," Semuel said. "It means 'God of my people.' Think about it. Why do you read Hebrew? Why was your family hunted and driven out of Lisbon? You have been brought here to study with my father, who is called 'Hakham,' scholar of highest rank. He is the greatest haham in Amsterdam. He will make a Jew of you yet!"

Domingo had no answer to Semuel's charges. He had been taught by the friars that the Jews were a people accursed by God, and Semuel was convinced that Domingo was a part of this forsaken race and that his childhood name was a secret Jewish phrase. Semuel seemed proud that his father was a Jew and that he would turn Domingo into one.

"Mother of Christ! Are you a Jew, Semuel?" Domingo imitated his mother's strongest language, when he was finally able to answer that is.

Semuel suppressed a laugh at Domingo's awkward Catholic curse. "Yes, Amiel. We are all of the Hebrew nation in this neighborhood: your parents, your cousins, and everyone in the yeshiva. How can you not have known this?"

Domingo backed away from the older boy in shock, searching his young mind for an answer to Semuel's question. He couldn't have known his family was Jewish because they were not! It was some kind of cruel trick Semuel was playing on him. Jews were despised in Lisbon. His family went to Mass regularly. Domingo had been confirmed and partook of the sacraments. His mother kept a rosary and recited its litany every day. Many of their family prayers had been spoken in Hebrew, but did not Jesus himself speak this language? And yet, they had fled Lisbon under the cover of darkness, leaving almost everything behind like fugitives rather than a respectable family. And then there was the matter of Filipe's execution alongside heretic Jews.

Domingo suddenly felt lightheaded. Wishing to further distance himself from Semuel, he turned around and ran back the way they had come in. He had to get outside into the fresh air, but he could not find the door. The hallway seemed to be closing in on him. Where was his father? He heard Semuel's voice as if from a distance. Yet he could see Semuel standing next to him, reaching out his arms. "Amiel? Amiel! Sit down."

Everything began spinning, and there was a great white noise in his head. It was like being in a giant whirlpool of sound and air. Oddly it was not frightening. It seemed to beckon him to enter, and he knew he'd be safe there. Domingo gave himself over to the spinning and soon there was nothing.

He awoke to his father's voice, ". . . wanted to protect them . . . we taught them without telling them why . . . has been through a great deal these past months." In and out his father's voice went until Domingo regained full consciousness. He was lying on the floor of the yeshiva, although he could've sworn that he had never left his pallet that morning. Looking up, he could see his father leaning over him.

The old man, made suddenly well again by his purpose, placed a cool hand on Domingo's forehead. "*Filho?* Nod if you understand me." Domingo obeyed, wanting to reassure his father, even though he felt muddled and the back of his head ached. The men began whispering among themselves and Domingo shut his eyes against their anxious stares. He felt wet and cold. Discreetly patting his breeches, he realized that he'd wet himself when he'd passed out. His face grew hot with shame. This was too much to bear. He opened his eyes and tried to sit up, but he was gently held down by

Semuel, who was carefully arranging a blanket around him. Their eyes met. Domingo was sure that Semuel would disdain him for his weakness, but to his surprise, the older boy's expression was full of compassion.

"I'm sorry, Amiel," Semuel whispered. "I didn't know."

Someone was lifting him. It was Manuel. The sudden movement brought back the whirlpool and Domingo lost consciousness again.

When he woke, Domingo stretched and, hitting the hard oak of the inside of the wardrobe with the tips of his fingers, realized that he was in his parents' bed. He sat up and his stomach rumbled. Gathering up the long hem of his nightshirt, he hopped down from the bed and carefully made his way in the dark to the kitchen where the low hearth fire gave a dim light to the room. His mother was sleeping in a rocker and his father lay on Domingo's pallet in front of the hearth. "Mãe. Papa," he whispered. His mother stirred. "Mãe," he said again, pulling at her sleeve. At last she awoke.

"Domingo!" She grabbed him and pulled him into her arms. "*Gratia*, Santa Maria. My Domingo." She began to cry, burying her face in his thick hair. He wanted to wriggle away, but her grasp was tight and he did not want to struggle against her.

"Mãe, I'm hungry." Domingo knew that his need would distract her from her weeping. "Oh, my Amiel. Of course you are." She released him, rose from her chair, and, within a few moments, placed a thick slice of bread and a generous serving of cheese in front of him at the table.

Domingo eagerly consumed it under his mother's watchful eye. "Mãe, why are you and Papa sleeping here?"

"Domingo, you've been ill. Do you remember this morning at the yeshiva?"

The details were slowly returning to his conscious memory. The darkness hid his burning cheeks. It was a relief that the rest of the household was sleeping now so he did not have to face them. Hopefully by morning they would've forgotten all about his childish reaction to what Semuel had told him. Yet he had to know the truth. As she set down a mug of watered wine before him, Domingo met his mother's eyes. As much as he desired answers, something in his mother's face told him to let the matter be for now.

"I'm recovered, Mãe," he said in a voice that he hoped sounded older, as if the boy who'd fainted and shamed himself at the yeshiva was another child, unrelated to him. "I will sleep on the pallet."

"No, Domingo," his mother answered firmly. "Tomorrow perhaps. Your papa and I will remain here tonight. You must go back to sleep now." He was frustrated but not surprised by her response. He would always be the youngest, the smallest of her children, the one who most looked like her, and now the only one left on whom to direct her maternal energies. She led him back to the anteroom bed where, despite himself, he fell asleep within minutes.

The next morning he tried to speak to his father alone, but Papa had taken to the sick bed and his mother would not have Domingo pester him. It was Manuel who took Domingo for a walk along the harbor and explained to him the strangeness of Semuel's revelations.

"Once, the Lacerdas were a noble family related to the king of Spain himself," Manuel began, "but the massacres of 1391 changed everything. Over ten thousand Jews, even those who were professed New Christians, were murdered or burned alive in that year alone. The church and the king were not able, or were not willing, to stop the killing. When the Old Christians finally tired of shedding Jewish blood, thousands of survivors chose conversion. A hundred years later, in 1492, the Spanish monarchs, King Ferdinand and Queen Isabella, banished all the Jews. Again, New Christians were often targeted as Jews. After thousands of Jews and New Christians fled Spain for Portugal, King João II of Portugal ordered the children of those with Jewish blood to be taken from their parents and raised by Old Christians. Even when this king died, his son continued the practice. Jewish children were taught to hate their parents and to believe that their blood was tainted. Some parents resisted separation and their children were slaughtered before their eyes. So, you see, conversion to Christianity allowed families to stay alive and to stay together. And because of their choice, we are alive today to reclaim our faith. Had they all died martyrs, there would be no Jews left in Spain or Portugal."

Domingo considered this lesson a moment. "So I am no longer Christian?"

"Domingo, you were never a Christian."

Domingo frowned at this. "I was baptized and confirmed. Doesn't that make me a Christian?"

"According to the church, yes it does," admitted Manuel. "But Domingo, our family is Jewish. Judaism is your heritage and your blood. Christianity was a guise to ensure your survival. In Amsterdam, Jews live freely. There is no longer a need for you to practice the Christian deception."

"But I don't know anything about being Jewish. I don't know if I want to be Jewish. They are ill loved."

He thought his cousin would be angry with his words, yet he nodded knowingly. "Domingo, you cannot choose to be or not be Jewish. It is who you are. Whether you like it or not, you are a member of the nation of Israel."

Domingo was silent. The North Sea wind pummeled him, pushing through layers of clothing, skin, and muscle to chill his very bones. Pulling his woolen cloak tighter around his shoulders, Domingo wondered if he'd ever feel the warmth of a sunny day again. Looking up at his cousin's expectant face, he felt simultaneously trapped and exposed. He was not who he'd thought he was and everyone seemed to know this, even strangers like the sailor guarding the ale on the ship from Lisbon. "Why did Papa not tell us this?"

"I cannot answer that, Domingo," Manuel said uncomfortably. "My guess is that he was trying to protect you from the Inquisition. You cannot accidentally reveal what you do not know."

"But you cannot know to hide it either!"

Manuel bowed his head in understanding. "You speak of what happened to your brother," he said. "This is why you left Lisbon. There will be no peace for your parents because of what happened. It is better to not speak of it to them."

◆◆◆

So he learned to be a Jew. It was undemanding, for learning had always come easily to Domingo. It was the unlearning of his Catholic habits he had trouble mastering. In Portugal, he'd been taught to call on God's blessing by making the sign of the cross throughout the day on hearing a curse, seeing a cripple, before eating, on waking, when the weather threatened, and for countless other reasons. He was instructed by Manuel and his parents to not make the sign of the cross anymore, yet he ached with the loss of this blessing's protection. At first, his parents were indulgent of his lapses. He was a child. But then his little cousins began to imitate him. Now when Domingo was caught unconsciously invoking the Christian god, his mother would slap his hand down and his father would give him a stern look. He didn't understand. Even his mother occasionally crossed herself when she thought that no one was looking.

Because there were so few questions his parents would answer, he figured out how to glean information by observing them. What he discovered was that they seemed to be learning how to be Jewish just like him. Nonetheless, Domingo felt vulnerable against his parents' admonitions. He turned to the Virgin Mary that Filipe had given to him. The small carving had been in his cloak pocket since leaving Lisbon. When he held it in his fist, he felt safe, protected. The Blessed Virgin Mary would never forsake him, even if, in the eyes of the church, he was a heretic. Surely her love must supersede the teachings of the church? Was she not a Jew like him? He was sure Mary understood his confusion and his fear. Just touching her image gave Domingo the same feeling of protective power that crossing himself had. At night, he held Mary close to his chest, under his blanket, and she helped him sleep. But he was careless with her. Ana found the carving one morning while she was tidying up his bed things and Mary had to be surrendered to Manuel. Domingo pleaded with his mother to be allowed to keep the carving of Mary. In her eyes, he could see her struggle. She had not given up Mary either.

His father explained, "Domingo, Jews do not trust in the Virgin. They trust in God and his law." But Domingo felt he did not know God. The friars tortured and killed Filipe in God's name. God was the scripture, the law, a dead man on a crucifix. But Mary was a loving mother. Men did not slay one another in Mary's name. Domingo trusted Mary.

Manuel called Filipe's carving an idol and playfully told his cousin to stay away from Catholic women. Mary was not welcome here, not even by the Christians. Domingo was learning that in Amsterdam, where most Christians belonged to the Reformed Church, Catholics were hated almost as much as Jews were hated in Lisbon.

37

Learning Jewish traditions was easier than unlearning the Catholic ones. The Sabbath began on Friday at sunset. This was the holiest time, the time set aside by God for rest. Any work that imitated what God had done during Creation was forbidden on this day. Even servants and animals were given rest on the Sabbath. The Jewish ritual seemed oddly familiar, even as it took place at home rather than in a church. Domingo liked when Ana lit the Sabbath candles on the dining table and chanted the prayer welcoming the Sabbath in her airy, lilting voice. Ana was like a priestess presiding over their family altar. Domingo loved the blessing of the children best. Manuel would lay his hands on the boys' heads and recite, "*Ye'simcha Elohim ke-Ephraim ve'chi-Menash, Ye'varech'echa Adonoy ve'yish'merecha.* May God make you like Ephraim and Menasseh. May God bless you and watch over you."

Next, Manuel and Domingo's father would bless the wine. "Blessed are you, Lord, our God, king of the universe who creates the fruit of the vine." Then everyone at the table would respond, "Amen" and drink his or her portion of the Sabbath wine. Ana would then circle the table with a basin and a pitcher of water that each member of the family would ritually wash his or her hands in, reciting, "Praised are you O Lord, our God, king of the universe, who has sanctified us by giving us the command to wash our hands." And finally, there was the blessing of the bread; two loaves were used to symbolize the double portion of manna God gave on the Sabbath when the Israelites were in the desert. As the loaves were passed around the table, everyone would rip off a piece. Together they would eat and then joyfully shout, "Shabbat shalom!" It was a ritual that Domingo came to love for the feeling of immediate inclusion in this extended family. Sabbath gave him hope that God would forgive his obstinacy and confusion and that someday his family would be restored.

They went to the synagogue now instead of church. Manuel and Domingo's father sat downstairs, while Domingo and his young cousins sat with their mothers in the balcony in the back of the synagogue. It was hard to see and hear up there. This part he did not like, being penned in with the women and children. And when

Domingo complained, his father said, "When you are a man, when you are thirteen, you may come up front."

One night, Domingo heard his father arguing with Manuel. "I will not allow this. Not Domingo. I was not circumcised and neither shall he be."

"But Joseph, he is young and you are all safe here. There is no need to deny him his part in the covenant," argued Manuel in a conciliatory tone.

"No. It is too much of a risk. Our safety is never guaranteed." Domingo strained to hear more of their conversation, but they had shut the door to the parlor. Thus, the mystery of circumcision remained hidden to him. He would have to try to discover what it meant. Perhaps Semuel would be able to tell him.

Three days after his first, embarrassing, visit, he returned to the yeshiva and was warmly welcomed by Semuel and his father. No mention was made of his passing out, and for this he was grateful. There were ten students who studied with the haham, including Domingo and Semuel. The cleverest student by far was a boy about his own age named Baruch, who was prone to question everything. It was almost as if he were trying to test the haham's patience as well as his knowledge. To Domingo's relief, Haham ben Israel rarely lost his temper. Domingo was a little intimidated by Baruch's superior intellect, but he enjoyed his daring. Everyone assumed Baruch would be a famous hakham one day, but Baruch himself said little about his own desires.

Another student who intrigued Domingo was Josef, Semuel's older brother. In appearance they were clearly brothers, although Josef was taller and thinner than Semuel. But in personality they couldn't have been more different. In contrast to Semuel, Josef had a quiet and studious manner and did not feel the need to express his every thought. Their father often charged Josef with instructing the newer students like Domingo. Neither of the ben Israel boys was being trained to be a haham like their father. Menasseh desired that his sons make their livings as teachers and scholars. Josef was also expected to take over the family's printing business.

Semuel was not as accomplished as Josef, but what Semuel lacked in intellectual talent he made up for in other ways. There was a joyful quality to his personality that made the other boys listen to Semuel and secretly want to be just like him. Semuel was given to jokes and could imitate the voices and facial expressions of anyone he chose. He often had the other boys in stitches laughing at his antics.

Their studies included the Torah in Hebrew and the Talmud in Spanish and Aramaic. The Talmud Torah School did not teach Latin. Domingo's father insisted that he study Latin at home as it was the language of physicians, philosophers, and poets. His father scorned the Portuguese and Spanish immigrants who were trying to prove their new Jewishness by rejecting Latin as the language of Christians. He impressed on Domingo that God did not wish his people to wallow in ignorance. "Dullness of the mind," he told him, "does not prove a man's love for God, Domingo. Remember this."

Domingo enjoyed the hours he spent studying Latin texts with his father each evening, but he found that Talmud studies were, by far, his favorite subject. He found it strange at first to read so many different interpretations of Biblical passages. The hahamim whose commentaries filled the Talmud, actually debated with one another and with God, the author of the scriptures. It was unsettling to know that holy men often disagreed on points of law, but Domingo soon grew to enjoy these debates. There was still a great deal of memorization and rote as he'd been used to at the cathedral school, but in the yeshiva, students were expected to read and were trained to attain the same level of learning as their teachers. Domingo thrived in the Talmud Torah School and soon his cathedral education was a hazy memory.

Domingo's command of Hebrew was quite good, so Haham ben Israel assigned Josef to help Domingo with his Spanish. He could read it well enough, but despite its similarity to Portuguese, Domingo found it difficult to speak Spanish. Josef believed it was because Domingo kept mixing Spanish with Portuguese and translating everything in his head rather than thinking in Spanish. And because most of the students in his class spoke Portuguese, Domingo did not have the opportunity to hear or practice speaking Spanish. He happily discovered, however, that Josef Soeiro was a patient tutor. Josef wanted Domingo to learn Dutch before trying to master Spanish. But Domingo would have to learn Dutch outside the yeshiva. In this, he would have help from his young cousins, who spoke their mother's Dutch. At first, Domingo rebelled against learning the common language of Amsterdam. If they were going to Brazil in a few months, why should he learn Dutch? But he soon realized that Brazil was a story that his mother and cousin used to keep up his ailing father's spirit rather than a real destination for his family.

His father's condition worsened through the summer. Late at night, Domingo could hear him coughing through the wall that divided the kitchen from the anteroom. By August his father could not leave his bed; by September he was dead. Domingo watched Manuel pray with the men from the synagogue who came to the house. Other than their chanting, the house was quiet. Domingo, restless from sitting Siete, guiltily felt unmoved by his father's death. Numbly, he toyed with the frayed edges of his shirt, ritually torn in grief. Such a waste, he thought, to tear and then discard a perfectly good shirt. Within a few days, however, anxiety set in. What would become of him and his mother?

Three days following the end of Siete, Domingo summoned enough courage to ask Manuel if he'd made a decision about where he and his mother would go next. Manuel seemed shocked by the question and quickly assured Domingo that they would stay under his care. Nonetheless, Manuel insisted that, in addition to his studies, Domingo begin training in some practical skill so that he could apprentice when he turned thirteen. Because Domingo showed promise with languages and ciphering, it was decided that he would follow Manuel in the accounting profession. Thus, beginning in October, Domingo began accompanying Manuel on his rounds of agent countinghouses to justify accounts for his merchant clients.

In a typical week they would meet with a ship's captain to obtain the bill of lading, visit the warehouses and inventory the goods after they were unloaded from the ships, and then call on the agents who sold the goods to match the sales records with the warehouse inventory. Generally they did not have to deal with coin, as most of this trade operated on credit. The actual selling of the merchandise, mainly wine, fine textiles like silk and India cloth, gemstones, spices, and tobacco, was carried out by agents at the Bourse, a covered courtyard of sellers and buyers that operated from two o'clock until five o'clock each weekday. Accounting was tedious, but not difficult work, and Domingo grew to enjoy the rounds in Amsterdam's busy port. He also looked forward to his time with Manuel, who was older than a brother but too young to be Domingo's father. Manuel served both roles for Domingo without the burden of his dead siblings between them.

His cousin's serious, formal manner did not bother Domingo overmuch, as he enjoyed Semuel's mirthfulness several hours each day. He and Semuel had become fast friends: Semuel finding an eager audience in Domingo, and Domingo realizing that he was still able to laugh despite the losses of the last year that weighed so heavily on his heart. Sometimes, doubled over with laughter at something Semuel did or said, he would guiltily remember how sad and unhappy his mother still was. He wished he could help her, but she did not seem amused at his stories about Semuel. At home he learned to adopt a quieter demeanor so as not to agitate his mother, or worse, Ana.

Because Domingo and his mother could not communicate in Dutch, the language barrier with Ana created tensions in the house. However, Ana seemed pleased that by the end of his first year in Amsterdam Domingo was able to speak with ease in Dutch, and he was even reading and writing well enough to be useful to Manuel. Eventually the warehouse clerks began asking him to translate and copy documents from Portuguese and Latin into Dutch, and for this service they paid him a small fee.

For his mother, acclimation did not come easily. After his father died, she had little to do during the long hours she was confined to the house. Occasionally other Sephardic women from the neighborhood came to visit, but without an escort, his mother could not return these social calls. And without encouragement from their Dutch hostess, the neighborhood women began to come less frequently. Wounded by her isolation outside of the household, his mother tried to become useful within it, but she found that pleasing Ana was beyond her understanding. Whenever his mother tried to ease Ana's burden with the household tasks or with the children, Ana resisted, and then she complained to Manuel about having two more people to care for. Thus, his mother did her best to stay out of Ana's way, busying herself with the care of Domingo. But he no longer needed her constant attention. As a result, his mother grew cross and kept to the parlor where she furiously mended the children's clothing and anything else she could get her hands on. And when she was finished mending, she would cry.

Ana seemed to feel sorry for his mother at first, for she had suffered so much, but by December, she had had enough. "I will not see our house become a stage for Teresa Maria's scenes of self-pity. You must do something, Manuel," she yelled for all to hear, forgetting, perhaps, that Domingo could now understand Dutch. It pained him to see his mother so sorrowful, but deep down he agreed with Ana. He, too, was tired of his mother's need.

During his first winter in Amsterdam, Domingo worked with Manuel in the evenings to make the unused top floor of the house habitable. This large new room would be his mother's to decorate and clean as she liked. But even when it was completed, Domingo continued to sleep in the kitchen, and his mother's sorrow fermented into anger.

"You would still sleep in the kitchen like a servant? Am I that odious to you, then? Your brothers and sister cried out for me to the last, but you reject me as you live."

"Mãe, please," he pleaded, ignoring his mother's inventive reconstruction of the last moments of his siblings' lives. Indeed, Jorge had cried out to her before he died, but his mother had not even been with her other children at their deaths, and it was Domingo's name that Filipe had spoken last, not his mother's.

"No! I don't want you upstairs anyway. You speak Dutch and behave like a stranger to me. What would I want with such a son?"

But when Domingo began giving his mother his earnings from his translation work, her spirits lifted and she began to praise him in front of an uncomprehending Ana.

In the spring of Domingo's second year in Amsterdam, the haham had to go to Poland for business and he took Josef with him. Menasseh and Josef were going to deliver dozens of prayer books and copies of the Talmud to the Jewish communities in Poland; they would be gone for at least a month. Domingo was invited to stay with Semuel and his mother, Rachel, while his father and brother were gone. He eagerly accepted the invitation and, even though he realized early on that his presence was intended to keep Semuel out of trouble and to prevent the boy from driving his mother mad, he reveled in living in a household free from the tensions in his own. Even better, he got to sleep in Josef's chamber in a real bed with a wooden frame and a down-filled mattress. For four weeks Domingo pretended that this contented woman, Rachel Soeiro ben Israel, was his mother and that mirthful Semuel was his brother. It was then that he decided that someday, when he had a family, they would love each other like the ben Israels did.

IV. *TO LONDON*, 1645

Manuel's reputation as an honest and competent accountant grew, and he took on more clients during the next three years. "Four years from now, I will send you out on your own to do rounds as my apprentice," he told Domingo, explaining that this arrangement would cut the time it took them to see all their clients by half; thus they would be able to take on more of them. This plan changed, however, when Manuel was offered an exclusive contract. One of his most important clients was Senhor Antonio Rodrigues Robles, who dealt mainly in the West Indian trade of sugar, tobacco, and coffee. Senhor Robles lived in London, and he had requested that Manuel relocate to take over his accounts there. It was an important move for Manuel, and he spoke of it to Ana that evening after their sons were in bed.

"Marcos and Gaspar are young and can easily adapt to a new country."

"And what of me?"

"I would not ask this of you if it were not so beneficial to all of us, Ana. Think of the salary Senhor Robles has offered me. Think of the opportunity for our sons. This move will be the making of me, I promise you."

"And your cousin and aunt? Will they come as well?"

"I will speak with Teresa Maria," Manuel replied, pensively stroking his short beard. "They've settled here well enough and I would not like to displace them again so soon, but I'd hate to lose Domingo. He's a good worker and it is my duty to care for my uncle's family." Manuel looked over to where Domingo sat at the dining table, converted this evening to a desk so he could study. "What say you, cousin? Would you like to move to London?"

Domingo hesitated in answering. He did not want to leave his studies or Semuel, yet he was also sure that he did not want to live alone with his mother in Amsterdam. The Delgados had served as a buffer between them for so long now, and besides, he'd grown used to the rhythm of life with his cousins and enjoyed his work with Manuel. Who would support him and his mother if Manuel moved to London without them?

"I've been very happy with your family, cousin. I would not wish to live apart from you," Domingo answered, earning him an affectionate smile from Ana.

"Then let us go talk to your mother then, yes?" Manuel said, rising from his seat and heading for the stairs to Teresa Maria's rooms. Domingo dutifully followed, hoping the news of the move would not send his mother into one of her fits of melancholy.

Surprisingly, it went better than Domingo had expected.

"Aunt, there are matters we need to discuss," Manuel began after he and Domingo had taken seats in Teresa Maria's parlor. "A business opportunity requires that I move to London. As soon as I am able to rent a house, I will send for Ana and our sons. There is opportunity for Domingo in London, and I should like him to come as well."

"And what of me, nephew?" Teresa Maria asked, oddly echoing Ana's question to Manuel earlier that evening.

"Of course you will come if that is what you desire," he answered. "When Haham ben Israel is satisfied with Domingo's studies, you and the boy will come to London. My new position will allow me to formally apprentice Domingo. By twenty-one, he could be a master accountant and would be able to afford a home of his own."

Teresa Maria seemed pleased with this account of Domingo's prospects and Manuel hesitated before telling her the rest, things he had not even told Domingo about London. "There is one more thing you must know. In London, Jews do not live openly as in Amsterdam. The families we will join in London pray together in secret, and they register as Spanish Catholics under the protection of the Spanish ambassador. Posing as Catholics is the only way for us to lease property and conduct business. This means that we will have to attend Mass."

Domingo was sure that his mother would balk at these conditions. He hadn't forgotten how she'd slapped him for speaking to a Jesuit on the ship that had brought them to Amsterdam three years ago. And yet, he knew that she'd kept her rosary, and last year, on his tenth birthday, he'd woken to find his confiscated figure of the Virgin resting on his pillow. He'd never mentioned it to anyone, but he knew it had been his mother's doing when she'd cryptically instructed him to be more careful with his belongings.

"When the haham agrees, we will go to London," she answered Manuel.

◆◆◆

Lucy watched the two butterflies circle around each other in their funny little dance. Both were a brilliant yellow, providing a warm contrast to the gray day. They alighted on a cluster of bluebells and Lucy stayed still so as not to startle them away. Engaged among the flowers, the butterflies were blissfully unaware that Lucy's mother lay dead underneath them and that Lucy had resolved that she would never be happy again.

It had been five days since Mary Dunnington had died, not even enough time for Lucy's father to receive word and make the week-long trip from London. Lucy stretched out her long legs on the soft ground. Both of her feet had fallen asleep from her prolonged kneeling, so she wiggled her toes to speed up their recovery. Loose dirt clung to her stockings and skirt, but it mattered little now that her mother could no longer admonish Lucy for this violation of propriety. From a distance she could hear her name being called. The voice was coming from the manor house. Soon they would come for her. Lucy sighed, not wanting to be thrust back into that world just yet. She ran a hand across the dirt of the fresh grave, startling the butterflies away. "Mother, why did you leave me?"

Lucy's first thought on learning her mother was dead was disbelief. She'd survived so many births before. But the midwife had explained that there was no child in her womb, just a hardness that had bled until her mother's soul had floated away in the flow of blood that had soaked the sheets and mattress where she'd lain. Uncle Richard had ordered the entire bed burned and had taken Lucy with him to Thicket Hall after he'd dismissed the servants at Chapel House and closed it up. With sheets covering the furniture and the shutters bound tight, it seemed as if Chapel House had died as well.

When the shock wore off, Lucy had been inconsolable, weeping constantly and unable to eat. Her uncle, unused to female carryings-on, had decided to summon someone better suited than he to console his niece.

"Lucy!" The girl ran the last few yards to where Lucy was sitting in the dirt. "I've been calling, didn't you hear me? Oh, Lucy, I've missed you so."

Frances Dunnington, the daughter of Uncle Richard and her father's cousin Charles, was a year older than Lucy. Although plump and blonde, in contrast to Lucy's thin frame and dark brown hair, Frances shared her cousin's love of mischief as well as a loyalty to the secret Catholicism of their mothers. They had been friends since childhood, but they had become closer during the last three years when Lucy and her mother had spent their summers in Yorkshire. Like her cousin, Frances had survived many siblings who'd died in infancy. Two brothers had preceded Frances and there was a sister, born when Frances was three, who had been taken by fever when she was just a year old. Frances remained an only child, another unfortunate similarity between her and Lucy. They were both survivors, but to their families' disappointments, they were girls.

"Frances!" Lucy tearfully greeted her cousin. As she poured out her grief, her cousin enfolded her in her arms and tried to absorb it. The afternoon sun gave way to evening shadows and the air grew cold.

Then Lucy began to come out of herself. "Frances, I am such dull company for you."

"Shall we go eat, then?" Frances suggested. "Everyone is here waiting to see you."

Lucy sighed. Then she said, "Perhaps I can face them now."

Thicket Hall was full of neighbors and cousins. In the main hall, the women fussed over Lucy, clucking over her appearance and plying her with food and advice on how to manage her father's loss, while the men retreated into the library with tumblers of strong spirits.

A tall, plain, stately-looking woman approached Lucy and took her hands in her own. "Lucy, darling," began her Aunt Anne. "Your cousins would very much like to see you." She led Lucy to a back corner of the hall where the three Bretton children sat. Sebastian was the oldest at thirteen, his sister Claire was a bubbly eight-year-old, and Catherine, the baby, was just five. It had been some time since she'd seen her cousins, over a year anyway. Again, her mother's stubbornness had led to a family rift, this time with her Uncle James and Aunt Anne. But all seemed forgiven now that her mother was dead.

The girls embraced Lucy while Sebastian stood looking awkward. "Lucy, I'm not sure what to say. It is good to see you again, but I wish our reunion had a different genesis." Lucy noted that Sebastian had grown taller and that he had become more formal since she had last seen him. He was losing his soft boyish looks and beginning to look more like the man he so eagerly wanted to appear.

Lucy did not share Sebastian's sense of decorum and she threw her arms around him. "Oh, Sebastian! I am so glad you are here." After a moment, during which he coolly returned her embrace, Lucy stepped back and drew Frances forward. "You remember my cousin on Father's side, Frances Dunnington?"

Frances greeted the Brettons with a curtsey.

Sebastian bowed to her. "Yes, I have not forgotten Frances Dunnington," he said.

Frances blushed and suggested that they all get something to eat.

"Lucy, what news of your father?" Sebastian asked as they made their way to the side tables loaded with food.

Her response was curt. "He is expected by carriage within the week. If he takes a horse, it will take less time. I cannot say what he will do." She looked away from her cousins. Sebastian and Frances exchanged a concerned look, but they said no more about her father.

When her father finally arrived from London, Lucy was beginning to feel the dull ache of acceptance. It would have been natural for her to take comfort in her father's presence, but she found that she was too angry with him. Not until her father openly wept did Lucy soften toward him. She had never doubted his love for her mother, but she had hated his inability to fully reconcile with her. Somehow his sorrow, while it did not make her father more attentive, made him seem more accessible to her. Even if he would not tell her so, she knew that he understood her sadness.

They did not stay long in Yorkshire after her father's arrival. He explained to her that the country's general instability and the demands of his business meant that the sooner they got back to London, the better.

For Lucy, the return to London was almost harder than her mother's death. The emptiness of the house was unbearable. Her father spent most of his time either in the countinghouse or in coffeehouses, where he met with buyers and transacted business. Lucy's loneliness grew acute with only aged Nettie to keep her company. Her father considered sending her back to Yorkshire, but with civil war raging in the countryside, he said that it was not safe to leave London.

He explained it to her as if she was a son or an apprentice, "The army is increasingly powerful and Parliament is losing control of it. Mark my words, there will be trouble over this. I don't disdain the loyalty of your Bretton cousins to the king, but I trust far more in the social aspirations of our merchants. Of course, many of them are fools as well. They speak of leveling the social order, but I tell you, only those with an eye to business will survive the new order."

By June, the king surrendered to the army in Oxford. The violence seemed to be over, though Lucy's father continued to remain alert. Parliament was now controlled by Presbyterians and Puritans who quickly set to work instituting their vision of England. The English Church was stripped of its bishops, and Catholics were more hated than ever, especially in London.

When Lucy begged her father to let her visit Frances that autumn, his response was firm. "Absolutely not! Yorkshire is overrun with Papist loyalists. It's not safe. And for God's sake, Lucy, please mind what you say, even around Nettie. There will be no more talk of Catholicism. Are we clear?"

"Yes, sir," she replied meekly.

"Come, then, Mr. Robles is expecting me within the hour. Go make yourself ready," he said.

Lucy trudged up the stairs to her chamber, wishing her mother was there, wishing she was back at Chapel House where everything had been pleasanter. Wishing her father would stop chastising her for holding on to her mother's religion. It was all she had left of her mother and she thought it was unfair of him to demand it.

When Lucy reappeared, her father scowled at her appearance. "Did you brush your hair? Where is Nettie? That damnable woman is never around when she is most needed."

"I did brush it," she stated, stomping her foot in frustration.

"All right, never mind," he said, his tone softened to soothe her ire. "Put on your cap and cloak and let's be off."

Lucy hated attending business meetings with him. They were so tedious. Even Uncle Richard had protested when he'd learned of his brother's strange practice during his visit in October.

"It's just not done, John. What will people think?"

"Lucy will not be rendered dull by a few hours in the company of merchants, and surely they cannot object to her presence. She is well-behaved and as smart as any boy."

"But surely you could leave her with the servant?" Richard had pressed.

"Bah!" her father had scoffed. "Leaving her with Nettie is like leaving her alone. Lucy's only ten, too young to stay by herself."

Richard shook his head. "Why don't you dismiss that woman? Get someone who can look after you and Lucy better."

"Ah, there's the rub. Lucy loves Nettie, don't you, pet?"

"You are far too indulgent with our girl," Uncle Richard had scolded, even as he winked at Lucy.

Lucy thought about that conversation and the irony of her uncle thinking she was indulged as she and her father walked east through the city. Indulged! Her father hadn't even hired a carriage. To be sure, the cool November winds drove away most of the stink of the streets, which were strewn with animal dung and garbage, but the walk to the parish of St. Catherine Cree took them an hour. But when they arrived, Lucy was delighted at what she saw. The homes in this part of the city were freestanding, unlike their attached house on Fleet Street. Entranced by the golden deciduous crowns peeking above the walled gardens, Lucy began to fall behind her father.

"Lucy! Keep up," he snapped uncharacteristically.

She picked up her skirts and ran to catch up with him, as he did not slacken his pace to accommodate her.

When they arrived at the home of Mr. Robles, a servant led them to a parlor to wait. The room was richly decorated with tapestries, vases, and other curious foreign-looking items. Her father caught the eager look on her face as she looked about the room. "Now Lucy, you are not to say or touch anything. Can I depend on your obedience in this?"

"Yes, Father. I'll be like a portrait. I'll just sit and watch you," she demurred.

"That's a good girl, Lucy." Her father leaned down and kissed the top of her head.

The servant returned and escorted them to another, larger, room that was perhaps intended as a ballroom, but it seemed to serve as an office and warehouse. Against two walls, crates were piled up to the ceiling. There was a wonderful mix of smells in the room: coffee beans that she recognized from the coffeehouses on Fleet Street, there was a sweet smell that she was not familiar with, and there was an earthy, dirt smell that she guessed was tobacco.

Two men had risen from a large table in the center of the room when Lucy and her father had entered. The more finely dressed one, Mr. Robles, was older than her father, perhaps in his mid-fifties. With his large moustache, long goatee, and green brocade doublet, complete with a wig of brown curls, he had the look of one used to having his commands obeyed without question. The other man was younger, perhaps only thirty. He stood at least a half a foot taller than her father and sported a simple black wool suit and short beard like the Puritans, although he wore his straight brown hair long and bound at the nape of his neck like the king's cavaliers.

Mr. Robles spoke first. "Senhor Dunnington, thank you for coming. I was most grieved to hear of the death of your wife. I have arranged for Masses to be said for her at the Spanish ambassador's chapel for the next year."

Lucy liked him immediately. He reminded her of the Portuguese doctor who'd attended her mother all those years ago. She wondered if he, too, was a Portuguese, but then she remembered that her father had told her his employer was a Spaniard.

Her father was speaking, "Mr. Robles, that is most kind of you. My wife would have wished no better remembrance."

Mr. Robles nodded his acknowledgement of her father's thanks. "And who is this lovely child?" he asked, nodding to Lucy.

Her father placed his hand on Lucy's head. "Mr. Robles, this is my daughter, Lucy. She has been my constant companion of late. I beg you not mind her presence. Lucy knows how to comport herself when I am engaged with business."

"Not at all, Senhor Dunnington. Your daughter may sit with us or, if she would be more comfortable, take a seat by the windows."

Lucy, knowing what was expected of her, curtsied to her father's employer and then to the other man, because it seemed that he was being ignored by the other two. He nodded courteously, but did not return her smile, turning instead to be introduced to her father. She then removed herself from their circle and found a chair on the far side of the room to wait.

Mr. Robles began the meeting. "Senhor Dunnington, I'd like you to meet Manuel Delgado from Amsterdam. He is to be my new bookkeeper."

"It's a pleasure, sir," Lucy's father said to the younger man, bowing respectfully.

Mr. Robles continued, "Senhor Delgado has been in London these three months learning how things are done here. Senhor Mendes has been training him, but he is headed for Barbados to oversee our business interests there. As you know, planters in the islands are increasingly moving from tobacco to sugar production. I would like to try this spice on the English markets."

Her father nodded but did not interrupt, so Mr. Robles continued, "You and Senhor Delgado will be working closely together, so I felt we should all meet with one another." He then addressed Manuel. "My two ships, the *Tobias* and the *Three Brothers*, are registered in Senhor Dunnington's name. Through him, we sell our cargo to the London distributors. You will need to justify the accounts at his office."

Mr. Delgado finally spoke in heavily accented English, "Senhor Dunnington, I look forward to working with you."

Lucy was not sure what to make of Mr. Delgado. He seemed reserved, serious. He was clearly a foreigner like Mr. Robles. She wondered if he was a Spaniard like Mr. Robles or a Portuguese like Dr. Añes.

The three men sat down and a servant brought in coffee for them to drink. Lucy had been sitting still for a quarter hour and she was feeling restless. The windows closest to where she sat looked out over a lovely garden. She pressed her face to the glass to see outside more clearly. She could see a bench, some small fruit trees, and lovely flowers throughout the small enclosed space. Lucy was amazed that there was not a vegetable garden. Most Londoners kept a small garden for family consumption, but Mr. Robles did not.

She turned back to studying the inside of the house. There was a small arched door to her left. It seemed like a door fit for a child's room. Intrigued by its shape and size, Lucy slid off her seat to investigate. The dark oak door contrasted with the door handle, which was made of a light-colored metal that was cool to her touch. Lucy looked behind her and saw that her father and Mr. Delgado were engaged in conversation. Satisfied, she pushed the handle, opened the door, and slipped in, being careful not to fully shut the door behind her. A high window provided light in the small room, allowing her to see a beautiful walnut table embossed on the sides and legs with carvings of birds. At the center of the table sat a pile of books and a curious woolen garment. Tentatively, she reached for it and held it up. The garment appeared to be a rough shawl that was poorly made or unfinished because of the many strings that were hanging from its bottom hem. But on closer inspection, she realized that the strings were evenly spaced and intentional. There were knots in the strings, also evenly spaced. Lucy swung the shawl around her shoulders and hugged it across her chest. Despite its rough weave, she liked the weight of it and the warmth it provided.

"Do you like the tallith, Senhorita Dunnington?" a voice behind her asked quietly.

Lucy whipped around, embarrassed to have been caught snooping. It was Senhor Robles. "I apologize," she said quickly, placing the shawl down on the table, trying to position it as she'd found it. "I was curious. It is not a fine shawl, but I am sure I am ignorant of its value."

To Lucy's relief, Senhor Robles seemed amused rather than angry. "Sometimes the value of a thing lies not in its beauty but its function."

"It is good for keeping warm," Lucy noted.

He smiled. "Yes, it may serve that purpose. But what of the strings and knots? What is their function?"

"Function, sir?" Lucy asked. She paused to think for a moment; she had not considered that the unfinished parts might serve a purpose beyond preparing for a finished product. The knots were evenly spaced, like those on the counting strings her mother had used to teach her to cipher years ago. "Perhaps the knots are for counting?"

"Yes, very good, Senhorita Dunnington, you are a clever one. What do you suppose they count?"

"I am sure I don't know, sir." She fingered one of the strings, her nervousness giving way to curiosity. "Pray, tell me."

"They are for counting prayers."

"Oh! Like a rosary but more practical," she answered, knowing it was safe to say this to him because he was Catholic.

"Why more practical than a rosary, Senhorita Dunnington?"

"A rosary cannot keep you warm in church on a winter's day."

Her response made him chuckle. "Yes, yes. One should be warm when praying. Come, let us return to your father. He and Senhor Delgado have concluded their first meeting and I believe they are going to be good friends."

V. *The New Apprentice*, 1647

In late March, Domingo and his mother arrived in London. The city was awash in religious dissent and fear over the growing hostility between England's Parliament and the army. But the little neighborhood on Cree Church Lane, where they joined the Delgados, seemed to be insulated from the drama. About twenty crypto-Jewish families had settled in London's northeast corner, most of them merchants and jewelers, or involved in finance like Manuel. They were a close community, meeting Saturdays for prayers and working together during the week. Only half a dozen families had young children, but as Domingo would be apprenticing with Manuel for Senhor Robles, he would not join them for study sessions. Manuel had promised Haham ben Israel that Domingo would continue his studies in the evenings, though. In addition, as soon as the Lacerdas settled into their new home, Domingo would begin tutoring Marcos and Gaspar in exchange for a small weekly allowance that Manuel agreed to provide Teresa Maria.

The Lacerdas' rooms sat atop the Delgados' house but had a separate entrance, which pleased both Teresa Maria and Ana, although Domingo noted with amusement that the two women became close after their reunion in London. Ana and his mother clung together in their cultural isolation and their fear of being discovered as Jews. Manuel was constantly reassuring them that the English did not burn Jews, but he was pleased nonetheless that the two women had ceased their feud.

Two weeks after his arrival, Manuel took Domingo on rounds. The work was not unlike what they'd done in Amsterdam, and Domingo was happy to note that the weather seemed milder in London, although its port was larger so rounds took longer. Today, Domingo and Manuel would spend the morning inspecting the cargo of the *Three Brothers*, and then, in the afternoon, they would justify accounts with Mr. Robles's English agent, John Dunnington.

"I am eager to speak to Senhor Dunnington today, Domingo. Remember how I told you that Parliament has placed new restrictions on Catholic merchants?" Domingo nodded and Manuel continued, "He will be able to explain the particulars of those restrictions to us. I would also get his advice on an English tutor for you. It is important for you to learn this language without an accent. The English are not like the Dutch in this. Here in England, a foreign accent is a great liability. You will see soon enough that my accent makes some Englishmen mistrust me. I will not make this mistake with you."

Again, Domingo said little in reply. He found that Manuel was happiest being able to speak without interruptions, playing the role of teacher almost in the same manner as the priests in Lisbon.

It was past noon when they finished the cargo inspection, so they went directly to Dunnington's on Fleet Street, rather than going home for a midday meal.

"Senhor Dunnington! 'Allo and good day to you," Manuel said in his stilted English as he and Domingo entered the countinghouse. With Senhor Dunnington sat a young girl, about Domingo's age, and another man, apparently unfamiliar to Manuel as his cousin did not greet him.

"Good day to you as well, Mr. Delgado," Senhor Dunnington returned the greeting. "I don't believe you've met Mr. Knevett," he said, indicating the man seated next to him. "He is a notary at Doctors' Commons. Invaluable at translating Spanish cargo manifests for me."

Knevett stood and bowed to Manuel, then said, "It is always my pleasure to meet the business associates of Mr. Dunnington." He was a short man, about five and twenty years, with nondescript features who dressed like one trying to blend in, his clothes being neither too drab nor too fine to raise any notice.

Manuel nodded and said, "Likewise, Mr. Knevett."

"Who is your young companion?" Senhor Dunnington gestured toward Domingo.

"Ah, Senhor Dunnington," began Manuel, "this is my cousin, Domingo de Lacerda. He is newly arrived from Amsterdam to apprentice with me. Like Mr. Knevett, Domingo has a talent with languages."

This comment drew a scowl from Mr. Knevett but piqued Senhor Dunnington's interest. The older man turned to Domingo. "What languages do you command, Master Lacerda?"

Domingo looked at Manuel inquiringly. He'd only been able to follow bits of their conversation and had gotten lost toward the end. Manuel translated in Dutch for Domingo, who then searched his head desperately for the right words in English. "Senhor Doo . . . ning," he began in a halting manner, "I am speak . . . ing Portuguese and Dutch. . . . Little English. Latin and Hebrew . . . I read . . ."

Manuel shot Domingo a look of annoyance and interrupted him. "His English, you see, needs improving, Senhor."

Knevett frowned and mused aloud, "Hebrew, why on earth would he know that? But he must speak Spanish?" He turned to Manuel and asked, "Why did he not list Spanish among the languages at his command? Is he not a Spaniard?"

"Ah! Senhor, it is his mother tongue." Manuel laughed and put his arm around Domingo's shoulders with uncharacteristic affection. "So easy to forget to point out when it is not something studied but learned as a child!"

"Yes, I see how easy it would be to make that error," conceded Knevett disingenuously.

Manuel blanched but then recovered quickly, asking, "Senhor Dunnington, when you have completed your work, I may meet with you in private?"

Senhor Dunnington nodded. "Mr. Knevett and I are just about done here."

"Sir," interjected Knevett, "I can finish this on my own and leave it with the girl."

"Thank you, Mr. Knevett." Mr. Dunnington then spoke to the girl in a low voice and Domingo was unable to follow what he said.

But then Manuel turned to Domingo and said in Dutch, "I'll just be a few moments. You may speak with the girl. She is Senhor Dunnington's daughter. I don't trust the other one." Domingo nodded and watched with dismay as Manuel disappeared with Mr. Dunnington behind the counting room door.

◆◆◆

He felt the gazes of the girl and the translator, Knevett, on him, and he suddenly saw himself through their eyes, a foreigner and a heretic. Unlike fair-skinned Manuel, Domingo would never be able to pass as an Englishman. Heavy brows framed his large dark eyes,

58

the irises indistinguishable from the pupils. His hair, as black as his eyes in the dull candlelight of the countinghouse, hung in thick ringlets just above his shoulders, a look fashionable wigmakers imitated but that he was naturally blessed with, which would never be accepted by the generally thin-haired English. He felt exposed to their curiosity and their prejudice.

Suddenly, the girl spoke some command and then began to walk toward a door that was to the right of the counting room.

Domingo hesitated, not sure what she said. He saw that Knevett watched them, amused at their inability to communicate. "Ella quisiera que tu la siguieras," he said to Domingo. Knevett's accent was not right and it took Domingo a few moments to understand that the Englishman was telling him to follow the girl. Knevett narrowed his brows at Domingo's hesitation. "Tu entiendes?" he challenged.

"Sí," replied Domingo, giving Knevett a dark look.

This was the wrong response. It increased Knevett's hostility. "No creo que el español sea tu lengua materna," Knevett said with a sneer. He sat back in his chair and folded his arms across his chest.

Domingo realized his error immediately. The man did not believe he was Spanish. He was afraid but he held Knevett's gaze. How would he get out of this? His mouth went dry and he felt muddled. He dare not respond in Portuguese, but the proper Spanish response eluded him in his nervousness. Quickly, he grasped at the little English he had picked up in the last two weeks.

"Five years I am living in Amsterdam."

Knevett scoffed at this response, then he hissed, "You're a damnable liar, foreign scum."

Domingo wanted to flee back to Amsterdam—no—to Lisbon where his appearance and his speech did not mark him as a stranger. But then he remembered that even in Lisbon there was no place for one such as him.

The girl stepped forward so that she was standing between Domingo and his adversary. "Mr. Knevett, thank you for your help," she said, grabbing Domingo's arm and pulling him away.

Domingo wanted to trust the girl, but he did not know where she was taking him. He was furious with himself for letting Knevett suspect that he was not Spanish. Manuel would surely be disappointed in him. Two weeks in this city and he had already given himself away. Feeling defeated, he gave himself over to the girl and let her lead.

"He's not what he says he is, Miss," Knevett called after them. "He doesn't even understand Spanish. I wouldn't trust him."

The girl's response was swift and conclusive. She turned to Knevett and spoke with surprising authority, "Mr. Knevett, this apprentice is the cousin of one of my father's most important associates. I don't think Father would be pleased to know that you'd insulted him."

Knevett worked hard to arrange his features into a pleasant demeanor. Domingo wondered if the girl understood how much Knevett despised her. "Not at all, Miss. My mistake."

She led Domingo through the door to a short passageway that led to a kitchen. He held back under the door frame, not wanting to fully cross the threshold. The girl went to the hearth to ladle out some stew.

"Nettie, as usual, is not about," she said. "She's in charge of the cleaning and cooking but I fear that she's not very good at either. I'm much attached to her though. She was my mother's maid when she first married my father. Anyway, I shan't call her now. I want you to myself. Do you understand? I don't think you do, else I'd never speak to you like this. You have secrets, new apprentice, and I want to know them all."

He followed the better part of her speech but felt it better to pretend that he did not. How was he to respond to such boldness? She was speaking again. "He was horribly rude to you, my father's translator. I've never liked that man. Always railing against the queen as if she and her advisors are foreign spies. Father just ignores him, but Nettie told me that she knows men who've had their ears clipped for slandering Her Majesty."

The girl brought two steaming bowls of stew and a loaf of oat bread to the table and then poured two generous cups of small ale and set them by the food. "Pray come sit," she said, motioning to the table. Hesitantly, he took a seat opposite from her. His ill ease seemed to bristle against her sense of hospitality and she made an even stronger effort. Pointing to herself, she said, "My name is Lucy."

"Loo-sea," Domingo repeated quietly.

Lucy grimaced then smiled warmly. "That will do. Now, my turn. What is your name?"

"Domingo."

"Do-ming-go," Lucy imitated him poorly and he rewarded her with a weak grin. "Dominick in English I think. Right, now we are friends. Shall we eat?"

Domingo would normally be uncomfortable being alone with a girl, even if he knew her language. In Amsterdam, he had not interacted with girls at all. His cousins were boys and Semuel and Joseph's sister, Hester, was already married when he came to know the ben Israels. Baruch had once shocked him with their hakham's writings regarding a husband's conjugal responsibilities; he'd laughed at Domingo's naiveté about women and sex. All he really knew about girls was that they did not attend yeshiva and that someday he would have to marry one. Biblical women did not act in the same manner as his mother and Ana, and this girl displayed yet another variation of female behavior.

Although she seemed to be about his age, and she was fair of face and figure, this girl did not affect the demure mask of a maiden like the Sephardic girls in Amsterdam. On the contrary, she had a disarming confidence that made Domingo feel at ease. It was surely a violation of Jewish law to be breaking bread with her and eating a stew made by Christian hands, but Domingo was hungry and would rather be in here with this Loo-sea, than in the countinghouse with Knevett.

As they ate, Lucy tried to teach him the names of the items about the kitchen: bread, bowl, table, and chair. He sensed that his awkward pronunciations amused her, though she did not mock him. "All right now, try this: 'I am eating stew.'"

"I em eet-eeng stoo," he tried to mimic.

"Very good! Let's see, how about this one?" But before she could complete her thought, the door opened and her father and Manuel walked in.

"Lucy, Mr. Delgado is ready for his cousin now," John informed his daughter.

"Domingo?" inquired Manuel, giving Domingo an expectant look.

Domingo carefully laid down his spoon and looked up at his cousin, replying, "Yes. Please, I em eet-eeng stoo." Lucy erupted in giggles at this.

"What is going on, Lucy?" asked her father in a tone that seemed pleased rather than shocked as Domingo had expected.

"The new apprentice is learning English, Father," Lucy answered, still giggling.

Domingo rose to leave, noting Manuel's troubled look. He knew that if his mother found out that Manuel had left him alone with a girl, a Gentile girl at that, she would have his head.

"Senhor Dunnington, we will take our leave," Manuel said.

"Of course, Mr. Delgado."

Domingo flashed a dimpled smile at Lucy and nodded to her father as he turned to follow Manuel.

The next morning Manuel received a letter from Senhor Dunnington and translated it for Domingo. "He suggests his own daughter as an English tutor for you. He writes that conversation with her would allow for a more natural acquisition of the language than a formal tutor, and he would not charge us for the time you spend with her. Moreover, he wishes that once you are able to converse in English, you begin tutoring his daughter in Latin. For this, he will pay you a monthly salary." Manuel looked up from the letter and addressed Domingo directly, "His terms are generous, cousin, but I fear you will not progress as you might with an experienced tutor. I shall decline his offer and put the question to others among our brethren here in London."

"Wait, Manuel," urged Domingo, surprised at his own eagerness toward the proposal. "Shouldn't we perhaps consider Senhor Dunnington's offer? If he feels he is doing us a service and we reject it out of hand, would that not sour our relationship with him?" Manuel opened his mouth to respond, so Domingo continued quickly, "What I mean to say is that I am willing to try this arrangement for the sake of pleasing Senhor Dunnington."

Manuel regarded him curiously. "She's a girl, Domingo. How could you learn English from her?"

"I learned Dutch from my infant cousins. They were the best of teachers for they knew naught else. This child, Senhorita

Dunnington, can be no worse. And think of how it would please my mother for me to earn another income from teaching."

Manuel scoffed. "Think of how it would vex your mother to know who your student is."

"It is a job, cousin. Nothing more. We work alongside Gentiles each day. My mother understands that. It is the nature of our trade, no?"

"Yes, Domingo, but you must be careful. Dunnington does not treat his daughter as a man should. She is an unnatural child."

"I understand my duty, cousin," Domingo said. "But let me do this. It will please Senhor Dunnington and my earnings will please my mother."

So Manuel took Domingo back to Senhor Dunnington's countinghouse a few days later. The two adults agreed that Domingo would practice English with Senhor Dunnington's daughter as long as the servant was present.

John Dunnington found this arrangement irksome, complaining to his daughter, "Why should I pay Nettie to just sit with two children for several hours each week? Surely she could be mending or cooking if she has to be in the kitchen with you?"

"Come Father," Lucy chided. "Nettie is not young. Indeed, she is a decade your senior. I know her housekeeping is poor, but I love her so. Please don't be so hard on her."

John sighed. "I cannot give Nettie more leave to sit at ease just because of Mr. Delgado's overly cautious sense of propriety, Lucy. If it ever got out . . . why, I'd never get an honest day's work from anyone I hired."

"Well, Father, you've hired Dominick, and I promise he won't short you. I will see to that personally."

"It's 'Domingo,' Lucy. His name is Domingo, not Dominick."

"But he's in England now, Father, and he needs an English name."

He gave a loud *humph* by way of response and left her for the peace of his counting room.

While his cousin did his rounds about London on Senhor Robles's business, Domingo sat for lessons with Lucy Dunnington. She often fed him to teach him new phrases for foodstuffs and cutlery. It was, as John Dunnington had promised, a natural way of learning English and Domingo found himself learning this language far more quickly than he'd learned Dutch. However, after two months he still had not reached the competency that was required for his work with Manuel, and this frustrated him keenly. He did not blame the Dunnington girl. Indeed, she worked tirelessly to create new lessons for him. It was, he realized, the fact that no one in his immediate family spoke English. Home life was conducted in Dutch or Portuguese. English did not come easily to him because it was not a language he was forced to learn through constant exposure. With no way to change these circumstances, he redoubled his efforts with the Dunningtons, speaking with Senhor Dunnington at every opportunity. And over the next few weeks, he improved enough to make himself understood to most Englishmen he encountered on his rounds with Manuel.

Early in August, the civil war made itself felt to even the most disinterested Londoner. Disputes between the army and Parliament over pay and legal reforms led to a standoff that came to a head when the army decided to take action. Londoners, divided between those who supported the army, those who supported Parliament, and royalists who wanted King Charles I returned to power, waited in trepidation for the outcome of this confrontation.

Lucy and Domingo sat at the kitchen table discussing an English translation of the life of St. Mary Magdalene. Lucy had been using a collection of saints' lives to help him learn to read English. She was amazed at how quickly he was learning the language, but he dismissed her awe by telling her that English was similar to Dutch. He had little trouble following the narrative of the vita and was more interested in discussing the meaning of the story.

"This I do not understand, Lucita. Why the Jews send the Magdalene in a boat with no rudder?"

Lucy smiled inwardly. She loved hearing him speak her name in his tongue. Often, on days that he did not come for lessons, she would speak the name aloud, savoring it like a secret, "Lucita."

"The Jews despised St. Mary Magdalene's faith in our Lord. By putting her in a boat that was unmanageable, they hoped to drown her. But the Lord saved her, and thus she landed on the shores of

France. Their ill will was foiled by God's intervention, much like when he saved Moses and the Hebrew slaves from Pharaoh's army."

Domingo raised his brows at this comparison. "But with Moses, God saved Jews. How are they saved in one tale and enemy in another?"

"Because the Jews rejected Christ, Dominick. When they did this, they became forsaken by God."

His eyes blazed at this comment. "To forsake his people is not of God." He struggled with a clearer way to tell her what he meant. "It is dishonor to forsake. God does not do this."

"But they betrayed him. He had to cut them off," she explained.

"You forsake your family if they make you angry?" he asked in a challenging tone.

"I . . . I don't know," she faltered, thinking of her mother's constant fights with family members, "I guess it would depend on why."

"Do you forsake your children?"

"No, Dominick! But that is not the point. The Jews killed his son, Jesus."

"But, Lucita, the Jews, too, are his children."

"I—" She was cut off by her father's shout.

"Lucy!" John burst into the kitchen from the countinghouse. One look at his stricken face told them that something terrible had happened. "The army is marching through London and headed this way. Upstairs now, both of you."

"Mãe!" exclaimed Domingo, springing up. "I must go—"

"No!" thundered John, and then he more gently pleaded, "Domingo, please, it is not safe for you to be out on the street. You must stay here with us. Your cousin left an hour ago and is most likely safe at home. He knows you are here under my care. He'd never forgive me if I let you leave and something happened to you."

"Father, what is happening?" Lucy asked fearfully, her voice cracking into a sob.

John shook his head. "I'm not sure, pet. I doubt they will attack London, but it is best for us to stay out of sight, especially Domingo."

Even though he no longer resisted, Domingo was not happy about being ordered to stay put. John pulled him aside, whispering furtively, "I don't mean to scare Lucy unnecessarily, but I must impress on you how dangerous it is for a Spaniard to be roaming the streets right now. Your dark looks mark you as a foreigner, and possibly a royalist."

He then turned to his daughter. Lucy's eyes had filled with tears. Her father gave her a quick hug and then turned her toward Domingo. "Go upstairs, darling. I have to close up below. I'll be up as soon as I can."

Domingo was torn. He should go to his mother, who was most likely frantic with worry. On the other hand, Mr. Dunnington had entrusted him with his daughter, who was clearly upset. Offering up a silent prayer that his mother would forgive him, he led Lucy to the upstairs parlor where she took a seat on a settee that was away from the windows that faced the street. Domingo could hear the marching drums and hoof beats of the cavalry and hurried to close the shutters and draw the drapes. The army seemed to be marching west, toward Whitehall Palace. This route would take them right past the Dunningtons' house on Fleet Street. Standing behind a drape, Domingo peeked through a crack in the shutters to the street below, waiting. The army was in sight now. Domingo counted dozens of mounted officers trotting through the empty street, followed by hundreds of marching soldiers, their bayonets pointed upward and glinting in the summer sun. He felt a hand on his back and he jumped. Turning around quickly, he saw Lucy's tear-streaked face. Without speaking, she leaned her head against his chest. He could feel her shaking and, taking pity on her, placed an arm around her shoulders while slightly pulling back the drape with his other to keep an eye on what was happening outside. The army's march was a spectacle of power, but thus far, not one of violence, although Domingo had to admit that he was probably as afraid as Lucy. What had he and his mother gotten themselves into by moving to this place?

◆◆◆

By September, Domingo's proficiency in English enabled him to spend most of his time on rounds with Manuel. Soon, he only went to see Lucy two afternoons a week for their lessons. By then, it was Lucy's turn to be the student as Domingo began tutoring her in Latin for part of the time they spent together. Other days she would see him in the countinghouse when she brought in her father's midday meal, but he did not often acknowledge her, except to follow her with his eyes when he felt that she was unaware. But Lucy was aware, and she quickly learned to avoid meeting his eyes for fear of pushing him away. She so wanted to learn his secrets, but she knew that to press him was folly. She knew that she must sit quietly and patiently and, like her beloved butterflies, eventually he would come to rest.

Oddly, Mr. Knevett was just as eager to learn more about Dominick. By listening at the kitchen door, Lucy overheard him arguing with her father about him one day.

"I must insist, Mr. Dunnington. There is something not right about your new associates, the boy in particular. He's as much a Spaniard as I am. You know I have the best contacts in Doctors' Commons and even more exalted offices in the government. It would be nothing for me to learn more."

"And I say no, Mr. Knevett. Mr. Robles has my complete trust, as do the men he hires to oversee his business."

"It is unwise to not learn what you can, especially as the boy spends so much time with your daughter. What if he is a spy or a fugitive? You've got to be careful with Papists. I make it my business to know everything there is about the men with whom I associate. Naturally I know about your wife."

"Mr. Knevett, you go too far."

Lucy could tell from his deliberate speech that her father was on the verge of losing his temper. Mr. Knevett realized this too late.

"I meant no harm, Mr. Dunnington. I just want to impress on you that these Spaniards may not be what they proclaim. There is something about them, especially the boy. I can tell he is hiding something. Something important."

"Leave the boy alone. And leave my wife out of this."

"My apologies, sir. May I offer you my resignation as testament of my error?"

There was a moment's silence before her father answered, "That would be best, I think."

Lucy smiled as Mr. Knevett's mask of breeding slipped in his shock at his insincere offer being accepted. "You would let me go? And who will do your translations now? The little foreign bastard?"

Amazingly, her father attempted to console the man. "Mr. Knevett, please. You and I both know how little time you have for such small jobs as I can give you since you've begun working for Mr. Prynne."

"But how did you know that? I mean—not that I kept it a secret," Knevett sputtered.

Suddenly her father seemed to regain his usual good humor. "Yes, well, I make it my business to know a thing or two about the men with whom I associate, Mr. Knevett. I had meant to congratulate you on your good fortune. I don't agree with his politics, but Mr. Prynne is a prolific writer and I know that your talents will distinguish you in his service. Pray you avoid the displeasure of the king, though. I'm sure you don't fancy having your ears clipped like your new employer."

"Mr. Prynne bears the marks of his honest reporting. Truly, he is an inspiration to all Englishmen committed to freedom and true religion. I serve him with honor as I have served you, sir, and I thank you for releasing me from your service so that I may commit myself more fully to his noble work."

Lucy couldn't believe what she was hearing. After every vile thing Knevett had said about Dominick, her father was allowing the man to walk away a friend. How had he allowed his anger to dissipate so quickly, and for so unworthy a man? One who presented himself as something he was not, even as he accused others of the same. She felt unmoored, like a small craft suddenly cut away from a tall ship, drifting in sight of it, but no longer tethered.

VI. *"LOVE'S SOLE EFFECT,"* 1648–1649

Lately during their lessons, Domingo found Lucy to be distracted and unprepared. This day in May, she was alone in the kitchen drawing pictures in the dust on the window. He sat down with his books and waited for her to join him at the table.

"Your mother is a widow?" she asked, suddenly.

"Yes," he answered with hesitation, knowing how easy it would be to give away his identity in an unplanned answer.

But Lucy was persistent. "When did your father die?"

"Six years ago. After we arrived in Amsterdam."

"Why did your mother not remarry?"

"I don't know," he answered, still not happy about Lucy's interrogation but giving himself over to it. "I never really thought about it. I was the youngest of four, so my mother was no longer young when my father died."

"You have older brothers and sisters? Tell me about them," she commanded, finally seating herself at the table across from him.

Domingo looked down, not daring to meet her eyes, and said nothing at first. Finally he simply stated, "They are dead."

Lucy blanched. "I didn't know. You must think me terribly rude."

"It's all right," he said, willing himself to look up from the table. Without meaning to, Lucy always challenged his defenses. It was not her prying, however, but this strong desire he had to share everything with her that was dangerous. Being with Lucy meant constantly being on guard, and yet he could not imagine not being with her. Their few hours each week were his refuge from the expectations of his family, the *kehilla*, and the church. Lucy had no high expectations of him. Everything he said or did seemed to please this girl who was starved for affection. "It seems like such a long time ago now, almost like a different lifetime."

"I understand," she smiled sympathetically. "I was the first child. There were four others, but none survived more than a few days. It was hard on my mother."

69

Patricia O'Sullivan

"What happened to her?" he asked, hoping his question would not lead Lucy to expect more answers about his own family.

"She had a cancer in her womb. She thought it was a child it was so large. It was two years ago this week that she died. Now Father wants to marry again."

He detected resentment in her voice. "Does this upset you, Lucita?"

"I don't know. I've only just gotten used to our being alone and now Elizabeth is more and more with us. She's not unkind, but she's only twelve years my senior. When they marry, she'll want to change things in the house. Father has already had me put away Mother's devotionals."

"Devotionals? But those are Catholic worship items, yes?"

"My mother was a recusant," Lucy said proudly.

"What is 'recusant'?" Domingo asked.

"She did not attend the English Church. Father had to pay a fine each year for her absence. She hated the English Church for destroying the Catholic religion in England and she refused to be part of it. All her family is Catholic, and many of them have suffered greatly for it. My grandparents lost their land and died in poverty. My mother and her brother were orphaned and raised by their mother's brother. Father told me after she died that my mother wanted to become a nun, but her uncle refused to allow it. She married my father when she was eighteen. He was Catholic then. But he converted to the English Church when they moved to London. My mother's brother, my uncle Hugh, insisted on becoming a priest, against his uncle's counsel. My mother gave Hugh money from her dowry to help him flee to Flanders; her uncle was furious. He accused her of marrying my father as a means to get the money Hugh needed. But her uncle was wrong. My mother loved my father, just hated his conformity to the state church. Once, she took me to Mass at the Queen's Chapel. I'll never forget how beautiful it was, especially this one statue of the Virgin holding the infant Jesus. There was such comfort and strength in her face. I cannot explain it properly, but her image is the strongest memory I have of my mother."

So Lucy was Catholic. For some reason this pleased Domingo. "My mother also finds great solace in the Virgin. Every morning she recites the rosary," he said.

70

Lucy continued, encouraged by his revelations about his mother, "My mother used to kneel at my bedside and whisper it as I fell asleep. When she died, I begged Father to do this. But he wanted us to put aside the Papist traditions. I tried to recite the rosary myself, but I could not remember the order of the prayers. I often fell asleep angry with myself and, I confess, at my mother for dying and my father for trying to forget her . . ." She trailed off, taking several deep breaths to suppress a display of weeping. "I'm sorry. I've said too much now and have made you uncomfortable. Surely you'll begin to think like Elizabeth that these lessons are wasted on me."

Her confession had almost the opposite effect on him. "Not at all, Lucita. My father was a physician. He often treated the poor without charge, and when my mother complained that he labored in vain, he would say, 'It's not a loss, but an investment in my soul.' You see, Lucita? He taught us that knowledge is the key, but the heart, that is the treasure chest."

"I miss my mother," she replied with her usual finality.

Domingo considered the anger he had toward his mother for dwelling on the deaths in their family. It was strange to think that Lucy yearned for her dead mother while he yearned to be free of the constant memory of his father and siblings. And it was in this moment that Domingo realized that their deaths made him ashamed. But it was not the secrecy of their deaths that plagued him. It was much more than that. It was that he was forbidden to discuss them, while at the same time, he was forbidden to forget them. Thinking about the dead made him feel weak, vulnerable, and deceptive.

"Dominick." He was deep in his thoughts and had forgotten where he was. Lucy stared at him with concern. Then she slid her hand across the table and enfolded one of his. "Dominick, are you all right?"

"Yes, I . . ." He looked down at her hand covering his. Another challenge.

"What is it?" she pleaded, but he quickly pulled his hand free.

"Nothing."

◆◆◆

John Dunnington married Elizabeth Barker just after Candlemas at St. Bride's Church on Fleet Street. Days later, the Dunningtons traveled to Yorkshire. Lucy stayed with her uncle Richard at Thicket Hall, while the newlyweds took up residence at Chapel House. In the fourth week of her absence from London, Lucy wrote to Dominick.

March 10, 1649
Dearest Dominick,

I have sorely missed your company these last weeks. Uncle Richard is kind, but he is consumed with the trial and execution of the king and has little mind for any other topic. Father and Elizabeth came for dinner last evening. It was wonderful to visit with them, but Father and Uncle Richard spent hour upon hour going over every detail of the past two years' political intrigue. General Cromwell was one moment a butcher and the next a hero in their debates. It made my head swim!

Uncle Richard held a fine ball at Thicket Hall on Friday last. I fear I was all feet and disappointed the young men who asked me for my hand to dance. At least Father and my uncles suffered my ill grace with charm. My cousin Frances, who is my dearest friend, tried desperately to teach me in the week leading up to the ball, but my clumsiness and lack of experience were too much of a challenge for her instruction. Everyone in Yorkshire believes London to be so sophisticated, but in this they are mistaken. They forget that dance and theatre are banned by Parliament as sinful. So how am I ever to learn these arts? Frances has just about given me up to be a preacher's wife; she claims I am more attached to books than a gentlewoman's arts. Marriage to a preacher should be a fine trick as I will only marry one of the true faith.

I suspect that Frances is eager to marry me off to someone because she fancies my cousin Sebastian. He makes our days brighter with his stories about the foibles of his tutor, Father Lacy, who is a Jesuit but has the misfortune of being an Irishman. Sebastian puts us in stitches mimicking Father Lacy's accent and Irish mannerisms, both of which my cousin finds crude. Frances no longer has a tutor, her parents believing her too old at fourteen to continue her education. I hope that

Father does not make a similar decision about my education. I want to learn everything you know, even if I am still under your instruction at twenty!

Father and Elizabeth are very happy together. They rise late in the morning and take long walks together in the afternoon. My new mother is kind and has been sitting with me after dinner when Father and Uncle Richard retire to the study to speak of politics. Because Elizabeth speaks quite a great deal, I do not have to worry so much about making conversation with her. I did try to discuss my favorite books with her, but she feels that books make a woman dull and has warned me that suitors will find my education a distasteful quality in me. What think you of this, Dominick? Do gentlemen prefer ignorant wives? My cousin Sebastian does not seem to mind my studies. We've even had many lively debates about what I've learned from you. But, in an effort to please my new mother, I am turning to poetry.

I pray you are well and that you are planning wonderful lessons to make up for my weeks of intellectual fasting.

Your dear friend,

Lucy

Lucy sat with Sebastian on the divan in Thicket Hall's music room listening to Frances sing "The Ballad of Flodden Field" while Father Lacy accompanied her on the harp. Frances's voice was strong, rarely sharp or flat, and Lucy loved listening to it.

> King Jamie hath made a vow,
> Keepe it well if he may:
> That he will be at lovely London towne
> Upon Saint James's day.

> Upon Saint James his day at noone,
> At faire London will I be,
> And all the lords in merry Scotland,
> They shall dine there with me.

> March out, march out, my merry men,
> Of hie or low degree;
> I'le weare the crowne in London towne,
> And that you soon shall be.

Sebastian was restless during Frances's performance, more interested in learning what Lucy had overheard her father and Uncle Richard discussing regarding the late king and his successor.

"Tell me again, Lucy," he whispered, leaning in so close to her that their shoulders touched and she could feel his breath on her cheek. "Did they say that Parliament had voted to abolish the monarchy?"

"No. It was definitely being considered, as well as the abolition of the House of Lords, but there is no formal measure yet," she answered, hoping her voice did not betray her discomfort at being so physically close to him.

"It's treachery!" Sebastian whispered fiercely. "First the king, now the House of Lords! Who will be left to rule England except the ministers and the army?"

> Now heaven we laude that never more
> Such biding shall come to hand;
> Our King, by othe, is King of both
> England and faire Scotland . . .

"Shh! Listen to Frances," Lucy scolded.

"I'm just so angry," Sebastian replied, his tone rising. "How can they let Cromwell get away with this?"

Frances stopped mid-verse. "You two are so tiresome!" she shouted. "Can we speak of nothing but politics?"

Lucy laughed. "Frances, your ballad is political. It celebrates our new king's ancestor, James IV of Scotland." Frances sighed. In an attempt to appease her cousin, Lucy continued, "Your singing, as usual, was delightful. I'm sorry we ruined it."

The compliment and apology seemed to soothe Frances, even as Father Lacy slipped out of the room, a look of annoyance on his face. "Why must we spoil our time together speaking of the evils of Parliament?" Frances asked. "Is there nothing happier on which we might dwell?"

"What do you suggest, Frances?" Sebastian asked in a manner that, while polite, bordered on sarcastic. "Pray, tell us a topic we might speak of that does not completely ignore our nation's peril."

Frances smiled coyly. "I would like to speak of Prince Rupert. I've heard he has given his support to Prince Charles."

"The prince is now King Charles II, Frances," Sebastian corrected her. "If not for that knave, Sir Warwick, Prince Rupert and our new king would have rallied the navy to reclaim his throne! When I am eighteen, I shall join the king's army and help stamp out the Puritan treason."

"He is a romantic figure to be sure," simpered Frances.

"Of whom do you speak, cousin? Prince Rupert, the Lord Warwick, or Sebastian?" Lucy asked giggling.

Sebastian groaned at the turn in the conversation, but Lucy could tell that Frances was relieved by her attempts to move the topic to one in which Frances could participate. Lucy was well-versed in current issues and could have easily shut Frances out, but she did not, feeling sorry for her cousin and thankful that her father had allowed her a son's education.

March 15, 1649
Dearest Dominick,

We leave for London next week, but Father says that the poor condition of the roads will make our journey longer than usual. I pray we will be home by April. On a happier note, I've been invited to visit tomorrow with the Dunnington and Bretton cousins for a luncheon arranged by my Aunt Lettie to celebrate Frances's fifteenth birthday.

I am enjoying Uncle Richard's library. I wish you were here to see it because I know you would love it so. He has the most wonderful edition of Master Shakespeare's sonnets. My favorite so far is thirty-six, but I confess that I have only read up to forty-four. I've copied it for you:

Let me confess that we two must be twain,
Although our undivided loves are one:
So shall those blots that do with me remain,
Without thy help, by me be borne alone.
In our two loves there is but one respect,
Though in our lives a separable spite,
Which though it alter not love's sole effect,
Yet doth it steal sweet hours from love's delight.

I may not evermore acknowledge thee,
Lest my bewailed guilt should do thee shame,
Nor thou with public kindness honour me,
Unless thou take that honour from thy name:
But do not so, I love thee in such sort,
As thou being mine, mine is thy good report.

I have found myself drawn to this sonnet. It is so beautiful and sad. I have not read Master Shakespeare's plays, but Sebastian tells me that there is one very much like this sonnet called *Romeo and Juliet* in which two lovers cannot be married for the hatred between their kin. Elizabeth has advised me not to let Father know that I am reading the works of Master Shakespeare. In truth, I don't believe he would disapprove in the way that Elizabeth fears. Father is actually much more open-minded than he lets on, even to his wife. I did not tell her that I wrote to you about this. I hope it causes no offense. Apparently his works are not approved fare for godly English. But, as you are neither English nor godly in the Puritan sense, you might enjoy this sonnet.

In loving friendship,

Lucy

Domingo did not know what to make of Lucy's letters. Her sonnet made his heart race. But who was this Sebastian? Domingo instantly hated the boy's foppish name and strongly disapproved of his discussing *Romeo and Juliet* with Lucy. He was not familiar with the play, but he had heard that this Shakespeare was no friend of the Jews. What if Lucy learned through this poet to hate his people? He felt helpless, except to pray she would return soon. It caused him no end of anxiety to think that some cad was trifling with Lucy's affections, but he was slightly reassured from her letters to know that she did not seem to be completely taken in with this cousin of hers.

Domingo wasn't sure when he began to love her, but he knew that it was shortly after he met her. That first day when she had claimed him as her friend was forever burned into his memory. It wasn't just that he found her fair, although her deep brown locks and her eyes the color of the Lisbon sky were enough to earn her many suitors when she came of age. Perhaps she was taller than most girls and not talented in the female arts of music and needlework, but Lucy's other qualities more than made up for these deficiencies. Domingo loved her curiosity and her confidence. He loved her desire to learn even when she knew that learning made a girl less attractive to a man. Lucy had a sharp mind and was not afraid to use it. Marial had been the same. Against their mother's protests, their father had allowed Filipe to teach Marial Hebrew and Latin. Marial had soaked up knowledge like a sea sponge. He remembered, when she died, that Filipe and his father had had violent arguments about Marial. Filipe had wanted revenge for whatever had caused her death, but his father had insisted on their doing nothing. It was shortly after her death that Filipe became a priest.

Domingo felt conflicted, associating Lucy with his dead sister. Marial had died eight years ago, yet her spirit, as well as those of Jorge and Filipe, seemed to pervade Domingo's life. He found himself thinking about them at odd times like this when he was thinking about Lucy. What was it about Lucy? She shared the loss of a parent and siblings. She understood what it was like to keep the faith in a hated religion. But she did not know he was Jewish. Manuel had recently confided in him that he and Mr. Robles had told Mr. Dunnington their true identity as a precaution, as the climate in London was becoming intolerable for Catholics now that the king was dead and the queen had fled back to France. To his credit, Lucy's father had not seemed bothered by his employer's or his associate's Jewish religion. But Domingo was sure that Lucy did not know his secret. It would be unlike her to not say anything if she did know.

He could not decide if the sonnet was a warning or a declaration of love. On the other hand, it might not have a deeper meaning for Lucy, other than being a beautifully tragic poem. He carefully folded her letter and slid it into his pocket. Lucy mailed her letters to him to the countinghouse so neither Manuel nor his mother knew of their correspondence. It was hopeless, he knew, for him to allow himself these feelings for a Gentile, but he reveled in having something that was just his, unknown to them. Someday he would have to marry one of his own, and he accepted that. But what he would not accept was becoming so obedient that he ceased to exist.

◆◆◆

Frances was sitting on Lucy's bed watching her pack. "Will you be back this summer?"

"I don't know," Lucy answered. "If so, Father will most likely not come. He hates to be away from the countinghouse for long. I'll be fourteen next month so perhaps he'd let me take the coach alone."

Frances scowled at this remark. "Lucy, it would not be proper for you to travel alone, even if you were ten years older and married. Perhaps Elizabeth will accompany you . . ." She trailed off when she noticed Lucy desperately pushing on the lid of her trunk, hoping to close it despite it clearly being over packed.

"Lucy, what's in there?"

Lucy smiled slyly. "I borrowed some books from the library for Dominick. I can return them the next time I visit. I don't think Uncle Richard will even notice they're gone."

Again, Frances minded her cousin's boldness. "Lucy, I thought you said he was an apprentice. And he's not even English. You're lending your uncle's books to a foreign apprentice? What if he pawns them?"

"He's not just an apprentice, Frances. He's my tutor *and* I consider him a friend. Also, he is very well educated. He speaks four languages and can read and write in two more. I trust him completely with these books."

Frances shook her head. "Lucy, will you be borrowing books for the servants next? Perhaps Nettie would like to learn Greek."

"Frances! It's not like that. Dominick is training to become an accountant. He will surely be a gentleman, like Sebastian, someday."

"But he cannot be, Lucy. He's not English," Frances argued. "And anyway, Sebastian's family is very old and respected in Yorkshire. I bet your apprentice has no such bloodline."

"Frances, you *are* impossible! Just because Dominick lacks a prestigious ancestry doesn't mean that he shouldn't be able to read fine books."

"Of course not, Lucy, it just doesn't seem proper, you lending him books. What if he thinks you fancy him?" She suddenly looked at Lucy intently. "Oh, dear! You don't fancy him, do you, Lucy?"

Lucy was growing angry. Frances could be so disdainful sometimes. "No, Frances. I don't fancy him. It just doesn't make sense to me that Uncle Richard, who never seems to read anything except pamphlets and broadsheets, has an entire library, while Dominick, who cannot afford books, loves them. Besides, I would have thought you'd be happy if I fancied someone other than Sebastian." This comment had the desired effect as Frances indignantly stood to leave.

"That was undeserved, Lucy."

Lucy realized she had gone too far. "Oh Frances, I am sorry. I don't fancy Sebastian or Dominick, but please don't abuse Dominick to me. It's not . . . it's not been easy these last few years and . . ." She faltered here, unsure of what she meant to say, but then she suddenly concluded, "It makes me feel useful to be able to do this for him."

The anger left Frances's face and Lucy knew that her cousin was pleased with her admission that she did not have romantic feelings for Sebastian. "I won't try to understand why you are friends with this Spaniard, but I promise not to abuse him any further." Frances pecked Lucy's cheek. "Please write, Lucy. I'll miss you."

When Frances left, Lucy felt guilty for her lie. She tried to tell herself that she didn't have feelings for Sebastian but she felt drawn to him in a way she couldn't explain. He was Catholic and educated and did not disdain to speak with her about politics and literature. Both Frances and Elizabeth scorned these topics as unbecoming for a gentlewoman, but it was not their opinions that held weight with Lucy. Her father had continued to allow her education, and she and Sebastian had spent many happy hours talking about all manner of topics, even Dominick had pushed her to learn more. But more than this, Sebastian had become the handsomest boy Lucy knew. At sixteen, he stood at least a half foot taller than her. His flaxen hair fell full and straight, and his blue-green eyes gave him the look of a Greek hero. If tales of the French Sun King were to be believed, Sebastian could probably rival him in beauty.

Lucy was eager to speak with Dominick about Sebastian. She had already written quite a bit about her cousin in her letters to him.

She wondered if he understood that her love for sonnet thirty-six grew out of her frustration over not being able to openly admit her admiration for Sebastian while it was clear that Frances fancied him. She had gathered that Dominick did not have much knowledge of the fairer sex, but Lucy was sure that he would be able to help her discover how to please Sebastian without openly competing with Frances. She knew that she had to rely on her wit, as Frances outshone her in looks and grace. She gave the lid of her trunk a furious push and quickly latched it. Dominick would be so pleased with the books and it would be a great relief to get back to their studies. Despite her attraction to Sebastian, Lucy had grown bored with Yorkshire these last weeks.

VII. JEWS IN AMERICA, 1650

Thomas was born a year after Lucy's father married Elizabeth. Lucy instantly loved her brother and eagerly helped Elizabeth with his care. Elizabeth, pleased with her stepdaughter's devotion to Thomas, often went without care to the market or to visit friends and acquaintances, leaving Lucy and Nettie with the baby. On these days, Domingo would come in through the countinghouse to visit with Lucy so they could discuss the readings he had assigned to her. One afternoon, toward the end of summer, Lucy was in the kitchen rocking Thomas, who was asleep on her shoulder. With one hand she held her brother in place and with the other she held a thick book. Domingo watched them for a few moments from the doorway. He imagined that she was his wife holding their son. It was so commonplace a hope and yet so fantastical given their backgrounds and Lucy's infatuation with her gentleman cousin. It drove him mad to think of it. When she spoke of Sebastian, he tried to be helpful. But inside, he felt his heart tearing. Their close association had worked against him as it seemed that Lucy considered him nothing more than her tutor. It seemed hopeless, yet he felt he would never stop loving her.

He decided to break the silence. "What are you reading so intently?"

"Hello," she said, looking up and blushing at being caught reading a book that he had not assigned and one translated into English at that. "I borrowed this from Father. It's called *Hope of Israel* and it's the most fascinating tract about the lost tribes of Israel and the restoration of the Jews. Have you heard of it? The author is a rabbi from Amsterdam, Menasseh ben Israel." Domingo tried to hide his surprise. He took the book she held out to him and examined it.

"Yes, I've heard of it," he answered. "I've heard there are Jews in the New World, but I don't think they are descendents of ancient tribes. It is more likely they are descendents of those driven out by the Inquisition."

"Are there many Jews in the Americas?" Lucy asked.

"When I lived in Amsterdam there were several ships that transported Jews to Brazil. Other than that I cannot say," he answered, not meeting her eyes.

"The Americas seem like such a barbaric place. Why would anyone want to live there?" Lucy asked with distaste.

"The Jews live there because the barbarians in the New World let them live in peace, while the civilized nations of Europe do not," Domingo answered.

She made a motion to stand up but hesitated for fear of waking Thomas. Domingo reached down and gently lifted the infant off her shoulder and instinctively cradled him next to his chest. Thomas started but then relaxed in Domingo's arms. Within seconds he was asleep again. Domingo looked up and found Lucy smiling at him. "He feels safe with you, Dominick."

He tried to keep his expression neutral at her praise. "Where does he sleep?"

"Follow me."

Lucy led the way upstairs to the bedchambers. Thomas slept in his parents' room. When they stood before the cradle, Lucy held out her arms to take the infant, but Domingo laid him down as gently as any mother and the child never stirred in the transition. He flashed Lucy a look of triumph. She smiled widely, grabbed his hand, and quickly pulled him out of the room. They laughed heartily, yet quietly, in the hallway. It was a release to laugh so. Dominick carried the weight of a thousand cares and it was not often that he felt free to forget them.

"Let's go downstairs," Lucy said. "I want to hear more about the Jews in America."

He nodded his assent but then impulsively raised their clasped hands and softly brushed her fingers against his lips. Lucy held his gaze for a moment, her brilliant blue eyes wide with surprise. Then Dominick released her hand and she pulled it to her breast, turned, and ran down the stairs. He stood alone for a moment on the stairs reproaching himself for his stupidity. To even touch her hand was a violation of the laws of his people and most certainly a violation of English manners. What if she thought him too bold and asked her father to dismiss him? Determined to exercise more discretion and self-control, he descended the stairs.

Lucy was bustling about preparing a midday meal. As soon as he emerged from the stairwell, her words came out in a rush, "Reverend Wall translated the book into English. He writes in his introduction that the Jews should be allowed back into England. What think you of this, Dominick?"

Good, she was still willing to speak to him. "Are there Jews who wish to live in England?"

"I don't know," she answered. "One might think that Rabbi Menasseh ben Israel desires this. He wrote that God will take vengeance on those nations that mistreated the Jews. I could not fathom whether he meant that England was now suffering for her sins against the Jews or if England would prosper for not mistreating Jews as sorely as Spain."

"That is well argued, Lucita. Perhaps the good haham cherishes a desire that is inopportune to speak of directly just yet."

"Haham?"

"It is the term the Sephardim use for 'rabbi.'"

"Who are the Sephardim, and why do they not just call a rabbi a rabbi?"

God's blood! Her curiosity was going to get him into trouble. "Sephardim are Jews from Spain and Portugal. They don't say 'rabbi' because of living so long among the Moors. In the Moorish language, *al-rab* is one of the names of God. You can hear how close it is to the Hebrew term 'rabbi,' no? It is blasphemous to call a man by God's name so the Sephardim use 'haham,' which means 'learned man.'"

Lucy remained silent a minute, thinking hard. Finally she spoke, "I don't understand, Dominick. Are you saying this rabbi, this haham, desires the Jews to live in England but will not speak of it openly?"

Domingo chose his words carefully. "The haham seems to have planted the seeds and now must wait to see if they grow. England must come to a decision about the Jews on her own and not because the Jews insist on it. The haham courts England on behalf of the Jews, but it would be better if England courted the haham on behalf of the Jews."

Lucy laughed. "You speak in riddles, Dominick. To talk of planting and courting as if they are the same thing either debases courting or ennobles planting."

"How are they different?"

"One can plant any number of things, and with the grace of God, they will grow. I should think that in courting, one's heart is set on one other heart with no thought for what else lies in the garden."

This allegory caused Domingo to roar with laughter. "Now who is mixing planting with courting?"

Lucy blushed and set the meal on the table. "'Tis your fault, Dominick, for planting that silly image in my head." She looked at him slyly and they both set to laughing again.

"In all seriousness, Lucy, what do you think of Mr. Wall's proposition that the Jews be readmitted to England?"

"It would seem an act of Christian charity, although I wonder why the Jews would want to come here at all."

"Why do you say that?"

"Reverend Wall writes that, in England, God will finally convert them to Christianity. If this is God's will, then who can argue? But I wonder if it is more the will of the Protestants than of God. They've given up on converting Papists like us, so now they prey on Jews. It stinks of a plan to shame Rome with a victory over the Jews more than a desire to provide safe haven for them. If I were Jewish, I would not want any part of the battle between Protestants and Catholics in England."

Domingo was impressed with her assessment. As a crypto-Catholic, Lucy was not taken in with the English Protestant millennial schemes to bring about the second coming of Christ by converting the Jews. Still, she had not given him the answer he sought. "That is very wise thinking, Lucita. But tell me, if they remained unconverted, would you object to Jews living in England?"

"I think I should if the tales about them are true. It is said that Jews kidnap Christian children and murder them in their Sabbath rituals. But after hearing the lies that are told about Papists in this country, I wonder if these stories of the Jews are true. My uncle has just returned from Flanders to tend to the few Catholic families left in Yorkshire. Every day we live in fear of his being discovered a priest. Just last year one of his brethren was hung, and before his body was cold, it was disemboweled. Then his head was posted on the city gates and his corpse left to rot." She shuddered and then continued earnestly, "Many of my family are Catholic and they are not treasonous. They simply want to practice their religion in peace. I suspect that Jews and Catholics share a similar defamation." Her passionate diatribe completed, Lucy fell silent.

While he was heartened by her speech, Domingo found that he was troubled over her portrayal of Catholics as victims of Protestant fanaticism. He knew too much about Catholic bigotry and Inquisitional violence to feel the sympathy that Lucy felt. Yet he realized Lucy's experience as a Catholic in England was not so different from his own as a Jew in Portugal. She had never known the horrors of the Inquisition but a similar system of forced religious conformity had broken her family as well.

"Lucita, you have given me much to think on. But now I must return to your father's accounts. Thank you for the meal." He stood and gave her a low bow and then disappeared through the door that connected the kitchen to the offices. It was a long time before Lucy got up from the table. She too had much to think on.

◆◆◆

When Domingo arrived home, his mother was waiting for him at the door. "Son, we must go downstairs."

"What's wrong, Mãe?"

She patted his arm affectionately. "It is for your cousin to tell."

The family gathered in the Delgados' parlor. The mood was somber. Manuel put his hand on his cousin's shoulder. "Domingo, sit down. A letter has arrived from Semuel." Domingo obeyed and Manuel continued, "Josef Soeiro is dead."

"Josef? No! But—how?" Domingo was in shock.

"They don't know. All they've been told is that he was struck with a sudden illness. Menasseh is not well and he won't let Semuel go to Poland for the body. Thank God the Ma'amad agreed to delay the burial so that Josef could be interred in his family plot. One of the hahamim in Poland is making arrangements to send Josef back to Amsterdam."

"Oh! It is a terrible day when a parent has to bury a child," Teresa Maria said moaning. Ana sat quietly, a stunned expression on her face.

"Shall I go to them?" Domingo asked.

Manuel considered this. "No, they have not requested it. I would like you to return to Amsterdam, but not now."

Domingo nodded. He was only three years into his apprenticeship and, until he was twenty-one, Manuel was the master of his comings and goings.

"Teresa Maria, please stay for dinner," Ana urged. "We should all be together tonight." Teresa Maria embraced the younger woman and they began to weep together. The younger boys shifted uncomfortably in their seats.

"I don't remember Josef," confessed Gaspar.

"No, you were just four when we left Amsterdam," mused Manuel. Turning to his older son he asked, "Marcos, do you remember the haham and his sons?" Marcos strained to remember even a fragment of a memory, finally admitting that he was also too young to recall the ben Israel family.

Gaspar collected his books from an alcove, brought them to the table, and then pulled out a stool next to Domingo, who had said nothing for several minutes. Manuel turned to the boy. "Son, you will not have your lessons tonight. Your cousin needs some time with his own thoughts." Domingo was grateful for Manuel's sensitivity to his mood. Generally he enjoyed tutoring his cousins, but tonight his sorrow threatened to consume him. He wanted to be alone with his grief. They all knew the ben Israels, but none of them knew Josef as he had. Josef had been like an older brother to him, so gentle and patient. Semuel made him laugh and Baruch made him think, but Josef had been a steady presence of calm intellect. It was unbelievable that he lay dead so far from his family. He had only been twenty years old. Domingo also grieved for Semuel, who couldn't even take comfort in bringing his brother's body home. He knew what that was like.

"Come, Domingo, let us retire to my study." Manuel's voice broke through his private thoughts. "A shipment of Madeira wine came in today and Senhor Robles gave me several bottles. We will share one in honor of Josef."

After a glass of wine, Manuel shared more of Semuel's letter with Domingo. "Josef was engaged. They were to be married when he returned from Poland."

"And what of the press?" Domingo wondered aloud. "Josef has been running the press for the last four years."

"Semuel will take over Josef's responsibilities."

"Will he have to give up his teaching post?"

"I don't think he can afford to right now. Apparently when Josef died he was delivering a large order to their Polish clients. None of the merchandise or payments he had already received were recovered. Semuel wrote that almost half of the worth of the business was lost in Poland." Manuel shook his head in disbelief. "It is so much loss at once. That can break a man. I wish I knew how Menasseh was holding up. You know, Domingo, the haham's loss reminds me of your father. I'm sure your siblings' deaths and the loss of his practice broke your father all those years ago."

"He spent a fortune getting us out of Portugal," Domingo admitted.

Manuel leaned forward toward his young cousin. "He would be proud of you, Domingo, if he were still alive. You are a credit to his good name."

Domingo did not trust himself to speak. Josef's death seemed to bring back his father's death all those years ago in Amsterdam. It was as if through the tragedy of Josef's death he finally understood the tragedy of his father's. He closed his eyes against the tears that threatened to flow. Manuel said nothing and Domingo appreciated his cousin's understanding. It meant a lot to him that Manuel thought well of him. Manuel did not grant praise lightly and his expectations of Domingo were demanding, even as they were fair. In the past year Domingo had sensed a change in their relationship. Manuel increasingly treated Domingo as a colleague, enlisting his advice on business matters. With Marcos approaching the age of an apprentice, it seemed to Domingo that Manuel was transferring his instruction to his son. Domingo was glad that Manuel saw that he was no longer a child to be commanded but a man with his own ideas.

Later, after he and his mother had returned to their own apartment, Domingo wrote a letter to Semuel. Though he fought to control his emotions, he couldn't stop his throat from constricting. He heard his mother quietly walk up behind him and felt her place her hands on his shoulders.

"Such a sorrowful life for you, child. Yet you are not really a child anymore, are you? Soon we will arrange a marriage for you."

"Mãe!"

"No, I've already spoken to Manuel about this. He has said that he will send you back to Amsterdam soon. I will write to Haham ben Israel about a match for you, yes? I trust the haham to find you a nice Sephardic girl. One who will come to London. That would be nice, Domingo, you see? A wife for you, a daughter for me. We'll just have to make sure she knows how to be a Catholic, eh?"

"A Jewish girl who loves the Virgin, Mãe?" he said sarcastically.

Predictably, his mother bristled at his speaking aloud her deepest beliefs. "The Blessed Virgin was no priest. She lost a son to them just as I did. She protects you, Domingo. Never forget that!" And with that, she stormed off to her own chamber, slamming the door for emphasis.

◆◆◆

Lucy's cousin Frances had come from Yorkshire to London with her mother, Lucy's aunt Lettie. They were purchasing a winter wardrobe for Frances in preparation for her coming out. Consequently, Lucy spent most of her time during those weeks with Frances and her aunt, shopping and calling on London acquaintances. Domingo felt the loss of their time together keenly and was surprised at how easily Lucy had turned from their lessons to accommodate her cousin and aunt. Now he spent a great deal more time alone with Mr. Dunnington and found he enjoyed the older man's company. There was an ease about John Dunnington that Domingo found refreshing after spending so much time with the exacting Manuel and his mother, who drained him to the point of emotional exhaustion. Of course, he knew that Mr. Dunnington's easy personality often led him to overlook Lucy's need for attention and affection. The poor girl was so often left alone by her father and his new wife that Domingo was surprised at her continued good humor regarding her family.

Today was the last Wednesday in September, the day before Michaelmas invoices were due, and Domingo planned to spend the

entire day helping Mr. Dunnington settle his quarterly accounts with
Senhor Robles.

Early in the afternoon, Lucy burst into the quiet diligence of the
countinghouse. "Father, Aunt Lettie has come. Elizabeth bids you
to attend."

John Dunnington sighed heavily. "Yes, Lucy. Let's go pay our
respects to my cousin's wife and her prize peacock."

"Father!" Lucy scolded. "What an awful way to refer to Frances."

"Ah, Frances is with her? This might be tolerable then."

Domingo looked up, amused at this family scene. Mr. Dunnington
was generally quite at ease with visitors; it was odd to see him so
put out by having to entertain his family from the country. "Sir, shall
I lock up when I finish here, or do you expect to return within the
hour?"

"An hour! God help me, Domingo." John thought a moment and
then snapped his fingers. "I have it! I want you to come to the parlor
and ask for me in about twenty minutes—no—make it fifteen."

"Sir? I do not think I can complete this in fifteen minutes. I'll
need another hour at least," replied Domingo, looking about at the
scattered papers and ledgers on the desk. It would take him fifteen
minutes just to organize them for storage, never mind checking their
figures against his account book.

"I don't care if it takes you the rest of the day! You will come get
me in fifteen minutes, young man."

Suddenly understanding, Domingo smiled and nodded. "Yes, sir."

"Father, you are horrible for involving Dominick in your
schemes," Lucy chided. Then she addressed Dominick, "You will
meet Frances when you come up. At least *then* there will be some
good to this deception."

John rolled his eyes to Domingo as he and Lucy exited to the
house.

◆◆◆

Exactly fifteen minutes later, Domingo followed them. As he
climbed the stairs to the parlor on the second floor, he heard a loud
female voice saying, "So Frances received ever so many invitations.
But of course one must be selective about these things." This must
be Aunt Lettie.

He entered the parlor seeking out Mr. Dunnington. But Domingo was suddenly uneasy about what Lucy's relations might think of him, especially Frances, whose opinion seemed to mean a lot to Lucy. He patted his head to make sure that all of his hair was secured at the nape of his neck by the simple black ribbon. As a boy he'd worn it loose, but in the last two years, he'd taken to tying it back like Manuel. He cleared his throat nervously. "Excuse me, Mr. Dunnington, sir."

John jumped up from the settee where he was sitting with Elizabeth. "Ah, yes, Mr. Lacerda. You need me back downstairs, then. Ladies, I must apologize. I look forward to dining with you this evening."

Elizabeth did not look pleased. "You're leaving us so soon, John?" But her husband was already halfway out the door.

"Wait. Please, Father," urged Lucy. She strode over to Domingo and took him by the arm to draw him into the room. "Frances, Aunt Lettie, I'd like you to meet Dominick Lacerda. He has apprenticed these last three years with his cousin who works with Father."

Lettie Dunnington nodded stiffly to Domingo, but her daughter stood and offered him her hand.

"Mr. Lacerda, I have heard much of your learning from my cousin. It is a pleasure to finally meet you."

He took Frances's hand and obligingly planted a quick kiss on it before releasing it.

"Oh! How cavalier," Frances simpered, ignoring the guttural sounds coming from her mother. "You have a foreign look about you, Mr. Lacerda. I hear that our late king's son also has dark eyes and swarthy skin. But, of course, his mother is a Frenchwoman. Are you French?"

"I have lived many places, Miss Dunnington. Alas, never in France."

His effusion seemed to only spur Frances on. "Oh, Lucy! He is gentlemanly and mysterious. And here I've thought you to be captive to a dull scholar all these years."

Her mother was glaring at him. She was a large woman, not half as attractive as her daughter, especially because of the scowl on her face. If she were a Portuguese, Domingo was sure that she would've cast him the evil eye. He had long ago learned not to make the sign of the cross but he was sorely tempted at this moment.

Mr. Dunnington saved him. "Come, Mr. Lacerda," he commanded. "We've a busy afternoon ahead of us."

Domingo bowed to the ladies and quickly followed Mr. Dunnington out of the room.

◆◆◆

Later in the day, when her mother's attention was engaged with a dressmaker, Frances pulled Lucy aside. "Cousin, you enraged Mother this morning by introducing your apprentice to us."

Lucy faltered in her response, "Frances, I . . . I am sorry. I just wanted you to meet him as you're both my friends." Then she noticed that Frances was smiling. "You are wicked, Frances. You are pleased with your mother's discomfort."

"It was wonderful, Lucy. She was speechless for once." Lucy opened her mouth to reply but Frances continued, "He has a very foreign look about him."

"Of course he does, Frances. He is Spanish," Lucy responded, exasperated with her cousin's silliness.

Frances smiled slyly. "He is a handsome figure. A girl could drown in those eyes! His accent is ever so slight but still charming. I love how he kissed my hand, Lucy. I've heard this is how all the gentlemen of the French court greet the ladies. It is so cultured. When might we see him again?"

Lucy stared at her cousin incredulously. "Frances, stop, please. Your mother is already upset with me over him. I will not risk her anger just to satisfy your need to trouble her." Frances just laughed in response. For the remainder of the day, Lucy found herself irritated with her cousin. Lucy had sacrificed her feelings for Sebastian for Frances's sake months ago, and now her cousin was interested in Dominick. As much as she loved Frances, Lucy burned at her cousin's games. Dominick was her friend, not some foreign cavalier on whom Frances could practice her country charm.

VIII. *Good Christians*, 1651–1652

Millennial fever was raging through London, and Lucy had become fascinated with the popular search for signs of it. Thus during their lessons, Domingo found himself drawn into discussions about the end of the world with her.

"See, this passage, Lucy." He pointed to the Hebrew transcription that he'd copied for her to compare to the Latin one she'd been studying. "The prophet Isaiah speaks of the scattering of his people to the ends of the earth. Haham ben Israel believes that England, *Angle-Terre* in Latin, is the prophetic edge of the earth. When the Jews are allowed to live in England, this will fulfill the prophecy for the redemption of the nation of Israel. Your English preachers believe that the redemption means Jewish conversion to Christianity, but naturally this is not what the hahamim teach about redemption. In the Amidah, Jews pray for the coming of the *Moshiach*, or Messiah. He will gather the exiles back to Jerusalem, restore the law, end the persecution of the Jews, and rebuild the temple."

Lucy said nothing for a moment. "How do you know this?" she finally asked, staring deep into his eyes, as if hoping to see beyond them to his unspoken thoughts.

Realizing that he'd slipped again, the natural teacher in him overpowering his Catholic disguise, he made as if such knowledge was not so unusual. "I've had a varied education, Lucita," he replied with a shrug. "Schools in Amsterdam teach very different things from schools in England."

"Such schools defy even my father's liberal nature," she said. "It is well that he is fond of you, else he'd wonder how you come to know so much about the Jews."

After that, he made an excuse to leave early, frustrated with himself, his masquerade, his very existence.

◆◆◆

At home, he walked into the middle of a row between Manuel and Marcos. For some months now, Domingo's young cousin had been hinting to his father that he did not want to apprentice as an accountant. Because at twelve, Marcos was restless. So he argued with his father about his future, and at one point said, "I want more than the drudgery of small offices in the homes of wealthy men."

Manuel riled at his son's uncharitable description of his profession. "And what is it, exactly, that you wish to do then, Marcos?"

"I don't know, anything but accounting. I want to travel. Perhaps I could go to Brazil and find Uncle Cosme, or even the Canary Islands where Senhor Carvajal's son lives," Marcos answered, his voice pitching in excitement.

Manuel sighed deeply. "I see. Yet traveling is not a profession. How would you live? Who would train you?"

"I'd find work, Papa. Domingo gets paid for translating and tutoring. I could do this too!" Marcos looked at Domingo for help, and Domingo felt torn. This was not his fight, yet he could sympathize with Marcos. The boy was not meant for desk work and Manuel refused to see that, wanting to mold each of his sons in his image.

Domingo was saved by his mother calling for him from the kitchen. With a sympathetic glance at Marcos, he heeded his mother's call. In the kitchen, Teresa Maria and Ana were preparing a seven-tiered cake for tomorrow's Shavuot meal. Each creamy layer of the *sete céus* symbolized one of the seven celestial spheres that God descended to meet Moses on Mount Sinai to give Israel the gift of Torah.

"Domingo, I need you to go to the market for eggs," his mother commanded. "Be sure to buy them from the widow in Leadenhall, the one with the big black dog; she sells the freshest ones."

"Yes, Mãe," he dutifully answered, despite his fatigue. He'd just walked from Fleet Street to Stoney Lane, more than halfway across the city, and his feet ached.

All work in the kitchen paused, as Manuel's voice could be heard from the parlor yelling at Marcos, "Is this why I brought you to London? To live like a half-wit parasite without a trade!"

"Domingo." Ana stepped toward him, reached into her apron, and then pressed some coins into his hand. "Please take Gaspar with you."

◆◆◆

When they were out on the street, Gaspar walked beside his older cousin. Domingo could tell that the boy was agitated, but he waited for him to speak rather than press him. After a moment, Gaspar said glumly, "I've not seen Papa so angry before. I wish Marcos would just do as he bids and let us all live in peace."

"Even if your brother is unhappy apprenticing as an accountant?"

"You like it well enough. Why cannot Marcos?" Gaspar answered with a child's simplicity.

Domingo shrugged. "We are different, Marcos and I. I like books and figures. He does not."

"Well, he should learn to like them," insisted Gaspar.

"And what of you, cousin? Is there anything that you would have to learn to like to make your father happy?" Domingo asked, intrigued with the child's reasoning.

"No, I don't think so," replied Gaspar. "I like what Papa likes. I don't like the fighting. It happens more than you know, although I've never seen it this bad. At least you and Aunt Tettie get to live upstairs, away from them."

This revelation startled Domingo. He'd always imagined the Delgados to be a loving family. It seemed strange that Gaspar would envy Domingo's living with his mother. Did the child not notice how she had a more bristling personality than his father's? At least Gaspar had the buffer of a brother and a mother.

"I remember my brother fighting with my father," Domingo finally said. "The last words they ever spoke to each other were in anger. Pray that this does not happen with your father and Marcos." Gaspar said nothing, just stared at the ground as he walked. They were approaching the market now. Domingo mussed Gaspar's hair. "Come, cousin, let's get some apples and go sit by the river awhile."

◆◆◆

Lucy found her father alone in his counting room that evening. "Father, may I join you?"

"Of course, Lucy. I'm just finishing up."

"Father, I have a question about Dominick and Mr. Delgado. I've been thinking about it for some time."

"What is it, Lucy?"

"They are not like us, are they?"

"What do you mean, darling?" he asked, his tone suddenly guarded.

"Mr. Knevett was right all those years ago, wasn't he? They are hiding something. Why does Dominick read Hebrew? Why are so many in his family dead? Why did they leave Spain and then Amsterdam?" She knew the answers to these questions, but it was important to hear them from her father's lips.

Her father sighed deeply. "Lucy, these are things that are private to Mr. Delgado and his cousin. It is best to not ask too many questions."

"Father, are they Jews?" He said nothing so she tried again. "Father, I won't betray them. I know how hard it was for Mother."

He took her hands in his and sighed heavily. "Lucy, this is important. Do you remember visiting Mr. Robles with me about five years ago?"

"Yes, Father. That is when we both first met Mr. Delgado."

Her father nodded. "Yes. I thought then that Mr. Robles and Mr. Delgado were Catholics and Spaniards. I am not only an agent, Lucy. On paper, I am the owner of Mr. Robles's ships. That way we can sell his merchandise to the London markets."

"He cannot sell directly because he is Jewish?" she asked.

"No, Lucy. Because he is Portuguese. Foreign merchants may not operate out of London. Jews are not even allowed to live in England. Up until three years ago, I believed them to be Catholics. Only foreigners are allowed to be Catholic. Even then, they must register under the authority of one of the king's ambassadors. That is why Mr. Robles, Mr. Delgado, and Domingo are registered as Spaniards. The Spanish ambassador allows Jews to register under his protection as long as they are discreet in their worship and outwardly appear to be Catholic. Naturally there must be heavy bribes involved, but neither Mr. Robles nor his associates have ever shared such information with me.

"Mr. Delgado told me their secret shortly after the army brought the king to London for his trial. Mr. Robles gave me the opportunity to leave his service, and I chose not to, Lucy. I respected his integrity. I have never had cause to complain about his treatment of me, and I feel, in some small way, I am helping those who dearly need our goodwill. They are honorable people who've spent years running and hiding. Many of them, like Domingo, have lost family members because of their religion. We need to just let it be, Lucy. Please say nothing of this to anyone. I thought at one time that Nettie suspected, but she's not turned me in after all these years. But whether that's out of loyalty or ignorance I've not been able to ascertain. Of course, this is why I never hired any other servants despite Elizabeth's constant requests for one. She does not know Mr. Robles's secret, and I don't want to burden her with it. Can I trust you?"

"Of course, Father. But may I speak to Dominick about it?"

He drummed his fingers on his desk as he considered her request. "I'll leave you to your own judgment in this. Please don't vex the boy unnecessarily. I like him well and would not wish to lose his company because you've upset him."

"I understand, Father. Thank you for trusting me." She then kissed him on his cheek and left him to his accounts.

So much of Dominick's reticence made sense now, but Lucy felt saddened at the wall of deception between them. He was her closest friend besides Frances. In fact, she was sure her feelings for him went beyond friendship. Lately, she'd found herself distracted just looking at him, his mysterious eyes, his angular Iberian face, and his thick black curls forever resisting his attempts to tie them back. Lucy realized that she had lost something important today. Being Catholic was something she'd thought they'd had in common. But it was a deception they shared, not a faith.

A fortnight later, Domingo was alone in the counting room, pouring over the large record books, when Lucy brought in his midday meal. She set down a cloth filled with brown bread, cold chicken, and cheese, along with a mug of small ale, onto the table. Domingo looked up. He looked worn but smiled a welcome to her. "Thank you, Lucita. There is so much food here. Will you join me?"

"Yes, of course." She sat down next to him and began to absently pull apart a slice of bread. "Dominick, what was it like as a child in Amsterdam?"

He looked at her quizzically. "Why do you ask?"

"Well, I was thinking about how you learned English so quickly and was curious about your education in Amsterdam."

He felt he needed to be on his guard, but there was nothing untoward about her question. "Amsterdam wasn't easy. I hated the cold winds and the constant grayness. My father was ill, my mother was fretful, and I did not speak Dutch at first. When my father died, I worried about what would become of us. But Manuel cared for us as if we were his own. He started training me when I was just eight."

"What of your formal education?" she asked.

"I attended a neighborhood school. My friend Semuel was a gift to me in those days." Domingo's story took on a brighter tone. "In the winter, lessons were wretched for the cold and the constant darkness. Semuel hated seeing us so miserable, so he would cause a distraction so that we were able to slip more coal into the fire without the master seeing. Semuel was forever in trouble to keep us warm. I think the master knew about the deception, but as long as we were willing to maintain it, he played along."

Lucy smiled warmly and leaned forward to search the food basket for more bread. Under the table, her foot brushed his leg. She'd taken her shoes off and the friction of her wool stockings against his gave him shivers. Stealing a look at her, he saw her face redden. And he understood that what she'd done had been accidental. He leaned back in his chair, his eyes twinkling. "Why do you tempt me, Lucy Dunnington?"

She was pensive, and then she grinned coyly. "I fear I am not a good Christian. Nor do I think that you are a good Christian either, Domingo Maria Rodrigues de Lacerda."

He caught his breath at her words. "What do you mean by this, Lucy?"

She held his gaze. "I know who you are, what you are."

"And what is that?"

She leaned toward him. "You are like me, Dominick. You play a role, and yet you are not sure what you truly are. Are you a Jew or a Papist?"

He rose with a sudden violence that overturned his chair. "I know who I am," he uttered through clenched teeth.

"I am sorry. I thought . . ." She faltered then. Taking a deep breath, she continued, "Dominick, why do there have to be secrets between us? I would never betray you."

He closed his eyes for a moment before responding. "I had an older brother, Filipe. When he was nineteen, he asked my father if he could take the vows to become a priest. My father forbade it, but he would not give Filipe a reason. We were Catholic and, even though we kept many of the Hebrew traditions, we did not know that this was not so for all Catholics. Filipe took vows without my father's permission. Within six months, he was brought before the Inquisition for being a Jew. He was tortured and maimed during his trial; I watched his execution during a public penance. The worst part is that he *was* a Catholic, a priest. He had Jewish habits, but he was not brought up in the knowledge of the Jewish faith. He died because my father wanted to protect him from being Jewish."

Domingo paused. Then he said, "You see, Lucy? I know who I am and what that means. Jews don't pay a fine for being Jewish. We pay with our blood and the blood of our children. You see now why my mother loves the Virgin so? Jewish women are used to watching their children being murdered. Your Jesus died in one day. Filipe was tortured for weeks and then strangled to death."

"I'm sorry," Lucy whispered, horrified. Domingo did not look at her; instead, he reached down for the overturned chair and righted it. The hurt silence made the moment seem unending. His hands were shaking when he began gathering his books. Lucy reached out and took them in her own, stepping close so there was little space between them. With each move, she was breaking down walls that he'd carefully built over a lifetime. He determined not to meet her eyes. Gently, Lucy pulled apart his hands, moved into the circle of his arms, and laid her cheek against his shoulder. "Please forgive me, Dominick."

She hadn't rejected him. On the contrary, she pressed against him, as if trying to absorb the bitterness of his past with her body. Her closeness unnerved him. He wanted to explain why he'd lied to her, but he wasn't ready to talk about it yet. He needed time to think, yet he had to say something to her. "Lucita, I've wanted to tell you. But I didn't want to lose your friendship."

"I would never forsake you because of your people, Dominick." She looked up at him, her sky-blue eyes wide and her face just inches from his. He knew this was the moment that could change everything between them. But it was all wrong.

During the past year, he'd imagined scenario after scenario in which he'd saved Lucy from ruffians in the street or the unwanted advances of a churl like Mr. Knevett. In each fantasy, he was able to demonstrate his strength to her against the villains and win her love. And they would always end with a passionate kiss, full of the promise of other physical delights. But now she stood before him, perhaps feeling pity rather than love, and awed by his deceit, not his manliness. And yet, her arms rested securely on his shoulders, her expression expectant. It was not how he'd imagined it would be, but clearly it was the moment. Fearfully, he pressed his mouth against hers. To his relief, her lips were moist and welcoming. He was nervous that he was doing it wrong. He was nervous that he was doing it at all, but Lucy did not pull away. As the minutes passed, it occurred to him that he did not know what he was supposed to do afterward. Would she expect him to say something charming? Worse, would she want him to reveal more about his secret Jewish life?

Lucy ended the kiss first. She leaned her head on his shoulder and, relieved, he understood that she did not expect him to say anything. It was almost as if she knew how much she'd pushed him out of his protective shell and was wise enough to allow him time to recover before questioning him further. But he had questions for her.

"How long have you known?"

"Two weeks ago I confronted Father with my suspicions. He told me not to speak of it, but I had to hear it from you. I'm sorry for insulting you."

"No, I shouldn't have thought you were attacking me. I'm just not used to talking about it. How did you know?"

"There were so many clues. I can't believe I didn't guess earlier. You sometimes said things. I think you wanted me to know."

"Yes," he said. "I suppose I did."

"Dominick, I have a question for you."

Instinctively, he pulled out of their embrace. He still wasn't ready to talk about his true identity. "What, Lucita?"

She blushed. "Will you kiss me again?"

With happy relief he accommodated her, this time feeling confident in his ability and her response.

♦♦♦

Over the next year their friendship deepened into an undefined, yet comfortable, state. In an unspoken agreement, they did not speak of their relationship. Neither of them attempted to temper their inner feelings or discourage the other's attentions, although they were both very careful to disguise the nature of their relationship around others. This was easily accomplished with John Dunnington's absences from the house, busy buying and selling Mr. Robles's cargo in London's coffeehouses, and Elizabeth's frequent outings to call on her friends, leaving Lucy at home caring for Thomas. Manuel kept a watchful eye on Domingo, but his monthly visits to Dunnington's countinghouse were expected.

Both skilled in the art of deception, their secret proved a simple matter to keep. What became important was that there were no more secrets between them. Domingo told Lucy of his life in Lisbon and Amsterdam, and she received his memories like precious gems belonging to a great treasure. With Lucy, Domingo felt a freedom to become who he was, rather than what was expected of him. She respected his past, but for her, it was a story of his origins, not a burden or a horoscope. She became his refuge from a difficult past and an unwelcome future that would be shaped by others. But most importantly, she loved him despite his being a Jew. He reveled in this for many months, but he knew that someday it would be important for Lucy to love him because he was a Jew.

They were in the upstairs parlor one morning in August. Lucy was sitting on the settee struggling to read a Hebrew text that Domingo had assigned her after she'd begged him to teach her the language. Domingo was sitting next to her, intending to work, but his hand kept straying to her hair. He wound one of her silky dark locks loosely around his fingers and smiled when he let it go, enjoying watching it swing. It was amazing, even a little irritating, how focused she was on her reading despite his attentions. Gently, he brushed her neck with the back of his fingers and earned the reaction he sought.

She let out a soft moan. "You are a terrible tutor, Dominick." She could tell by the way he touched her lately that he desired more than kisses, though he never pressured her. She flashed him a mischievous grin and, pulling him close, kissed him deeply. Grasping the hand caressing her neck, she inched it down her shoulder until it covered her breast. His hand shook, but he did not pull away. Slowly, his fingers curled into the top of her bodice and found their way beneath her shift. Lucy trembled. Dominick raised his head, gasping for air as if coming out of deep water.

"Lu-cy," he panted, "if . . . if your father walked in—"

"He'd make you marry me and I'd be a happy woman," she said matter-of-factly.

But Domingo's light mood dissipated. He moved back and settled himself on the far side of the settee. "Your father would not like for you to marry a Jew."

She frowned at him as she sat up and smoothed her skirts. "That is unfair, Dominick. You don't know that to be true. My father does not hold to any religion. Besides, he thinks well of you."

He shook his head. "Lucita, it's different with Jews. You know that. We are a despised people, even in countries that allow us to settle freely."

"So what are you saying, Dominick?" she asked darkly.

He stared at the floor. "I don't know. I've been unfair to you, Lucita. I try not to think about our future."

"Dominick, don't tell me you are without hope. I love you, and I won't give up that easily."

It was the first time he'd heard her say she loved him, though he'd suspected for many months. Her declaration made anything seem possible, even marriage with a Gentile. Yet he couldn't let this go any further without knowing if she could truly love him for what he was.

"Could you get away tomorrow for a few hours?"

"I could tell Elizabeth I have to go to the market for Nettie."

"Good. Meet me at the west gate of the Tower at noon. I have something I want to show you."

◆◆◆

Just after noon the following day, she came. "Lucy, draw your hood," he instructed her.

She obeyed, pulling it forward so that her face was obstructed, and they walked several blocks to Cree Church Lane in silence.

Domingo stopped at one of the largest homes on the street and turned to speak to her. "This is a special house, Lucy." He took her around the back. The back garden was walled in, an iron gate being the only point of entry. Domingo unlatched the lock and they entered. He strode over to a low back door and drew a large key from his cloak. After unlocking the door, he bade Lucy enter.

Lucy hesitated. "Dominick, is it permitted?"

He smiled. "Most definitely not, but I insist you see."

He took her hand in his and led her through a narrow door that appeared to be a servant's entrance. At the end of a short hallway, they emerged into what looked like a large parlor with four long benches pushed up against the side walls. Above the benches, built-in cupboards lined the walls. A large platform, about two feet high, dominated the west end of the room. An ornate table and matching chair sat atop it. In front of this platform sat a slightly lower table with four brass candlesticks adorning each corner. A long, narrow latticed window divided this room from another smaller one, which was empty except for two long benches. Domingo took Lucy to the front of the larger room and showed her a handsome cupboard flanked by candlesticks that were similar to those on the table. There were also two ornate crystal lamps hanging from the ceiling in front of the cupboard that lit the darkness of the space around it.

"What is it?" she whispered in awe. "What is this place?"

"This is our synagogue. And that is the tabernacle," he answered proudly, pointing to the cupboard.

"Tabernacle? Catholics have tabernacles in their churches. Jews have these as well?"

"Yes, but they do not hold bread and wine."

"What is in it?"

"The words of God himself."

"You mean that is where you keep your bible?"

"They are like a bible, but they are not books. They are scrolls of parchment that must be unrolled carefully and never touched directly."

"But how do you read them?"

"We don't. They are chanted," he replied, not really answering her question.

"Show me," she exclaimed.

Domingo felt self-conscious but began in a low tone, "*Vayehi ka'asher ra'ah Ya'akov et-Rachel bat-Lavan achi imo ve'et tson Lavan achi imo vayigash Ya'akov vayagel et-ha'even me'al pi habe'er vayashk et-tson Lavan achi imo.*"

"How beautiful," she whispered, sighing. "What does it mean?"

"It is the moment when Jacob met Rachel. He was so overcome with love that he kissed her."

Lucy raised her hand to his face and caressed his cheek. "I've never heard that story. It's wonderful." Her eyes sparkled in anticipation.

He did not disappoint her. "It is how I feel about you, Lucita." Domingo drew her closer. It was most definitely a violation of the law to kiss her here, but he didn't care. It was important for him to tell her he loved her in the synagogue.

When they left the house on Cree Church Lane, Lucy brimmed with curiosity. Scanning the houses in the neighborhood, she asked, "Dominick, which house do you live in?"

Domingo hesitated before answering. During the last few years, he'd done his best to hide his poverty from Lucy, but now he was determined to show her his circumstances. She should know up front that marriage to him would not bring her the comfortable lifestyle she was used to with her father's earnings and her uncle's property in Yorkshire. "My mother and I live with Manuel. There are rooms above his home that we occupy."

"So you all live together?"

"Well, yes and no. We often take meals with them, but there is a separate entrance for our apartments."

"Do you live on this street?"

"No, it is just over there." He pointed to a small lane just ahead. They walked one block north to Stoney Lane and stopped outside a house that was modest compared to the others in the neighborhood but was grander than the one Lucy shared with her father, Elizabeth, and Thomas. Domingo began to walk toward the house, but Lucy held back.

"This is your house?" she asked.

"It is Manuel's house. He's supported my mother and me since my father died."

"I don't know how to greet your family. What should I say?"

"They took the boys to Bristol a few days ago. Manuel is trying to expand trade relations with the colonies, and a good deal of the Atlantic trade operates out of Bristol. He also finally convinced my cousin Marcos to apprentice as an accountant and wanted to introduce him to the merchants there . . . ." He trailed off, embarrassed at his nervous rambling. "Anyway, I'm here alone this week."

A side entrance led them to a steep staircase. At the top, he unlocked a door and ushered her in. The apartment was simple, yet tastefully decorated. A large fireplace dominated the center room, and two other rooms served as bedrooms. A small pantry completed the living quarters. Lucy found it charming and told him so, but he was uneasy. They stood for a moment in awkward silence. Then Domingo drew a deep breath and spoke in a rush, "Lucy, now you know all there is to know. If you would have me, I offer you my pledge."

She closed her eyes and considered his sudden declaration. It was no light matter to accept. She knew her father liked Dominick, but he would not approve of their pledging themselves without his permission. Opening her eyes, she tried to regard him dispassionately. Despite his current poverty and his religion, he was a good match for her. Surely when his apprenticeship was completed, Dominick would earn a comfortable living and, more importantly, he did not try to dissuade her from her own religion or her learning. His offer was not rooted in her dowry or a false impression of her personality. Her parents had a mixed marriage of sorts, so her religious differences with Dominick did not seem an impossible obstacle. But, given his past, would he be able to marry a Catholic?

"It is I who bear the guilt of a thousand trespasses of my religion against your people, Dominick. If you can forgive this, then I accept your pledge and give you mine."

Domingo's anxious expression dissolved into joy. "Yes, Lucita, yes!" He kissed her for a long moment, but he soon began to feel overwhelmed by the battle between his body and his conscience. He could not dishonor her; this had to stop.

But when he tried to pull away, Lucy held him fast and murmured into his ear, "Dominick, I want to stay here with you awhile."

Lucy's way was to make simple what was, to him, a complicated matter. She wanted to stay. It was simple. Yet his mind rebelled against this resolution. Things were never as simple afterward as they often seemed beforehand. But the hope in her expression, her sweet feminine smell, and the swell of his desire for her won out.

"Lucita, are you sure?"

She smiled and nodded; this gesture seemed to clarify everything for him. They were pledged now, as good as married. It was simple. Eagerly, he led her to his chamber where they consummated their union in the awkward, but sincere, manner of inexperienced lovers.

Despite their clandestine relationship, Domingo had never felt so emotionally safe or so true to his feelings. He felt hopeful, and this emotion seemed to banish a past full of pain and fear. As a child, Domingo had watched butterflies break out of their protective cocoons, now he felt he understood this transformation. Lucy knew him completely, and she loved him. He was ready to fly.

It was inevitable that his mother noticed Domingo's altered mood. He was careful to never meet Lucy outside of her father's office or home, but these weekly meetings never satisfied his desire to be with her. When the weather turned fine, they arranged to meet in Hyde Park. Nettie always accompanied them, believing at first that Domingo had just happened on them. But after several similar coincidences, Lucy's elderly maid caught on.

"Master Cerda, I ain't a prudish woman but neither am I a fool. Eyes in my head I have," she said, tapping a gnarled finger to her temple.

Lucy threw Domingo a quick grin. Nettie left the particle off of Domingo's surname as a matter of course.

"Of course, Miss Greer. Anytime you wish me to leave I shall. Until then, I shall enjoy strolling the gardens with you. I'm sure no one in London has a finer eye for spotting the blue swallows than you."

"Hmph! Let's get on with it then."

"Oh, Nettie, you are a love," Lucy said, linking her arm with her maid's. "I've a mind to see the west gardens today. I hear the roses are in full bloom and the king's fountain is working again."

An hour later, as they relaxed at the fountain's edge, Nettie amused them with stories of Lucy's childhood.

"This one here," she pointed at Lucy for emphasis, "always in trouble with her ma over wearing out her stockings. Never one for wearin' shoes, even in the cold, mind you. A little imp she was."

"Oh, Nettie, come now. I was a perfect angel as a child."

Nettie snorted. "You's forgot then the time you decided to wash your hair in honey. Near took me two hours to get it off you."

"Weren't all the fine ladies washing their hair with honey then, Miss Greer?" Domingo asked.

"Sure they didn't dump a pail of it on their heads, Master Cerda."

Domingo's head shook so hard with his laughter that one of his side locks escaped his ribbon. Without thinking, Lucy reached up and tucked it behind his ear, brushing his cheek with her fingers.

"That's better," she said.

"Domingo?" Like a sudden squall, his mother strode up in her usual black satin and veil, threatening to drench them in her fury.

"Mãe!" He jumped up and kissed her hurriedly on each cheek.

"Where is Manuel? Is there no work today?"

With effort, he kept his tone pleasant, as if it was completely normal for her to be walking alone through Hyde Park. "I completed my work, Mãe. I was on my way home when I saw Miss Dunnington and Miss Greer."

Lucy stood and curtsied to his mother. "Mrs. Lacerda."

Teresa Maria's eyes bored into Lucy. She acknowledged her with ill grace by only nodding; then she turned back to her son. "Escort me home, Domingo."

"Yes, Mãe." He bowed to Lucy and Nettie while saying, "Miss Dunnington, Miss Greer." Then he took his mother's arm and they began to walk home.

She said nothing until they were in their apartment. "Domingo, what is this girl to you?"

"She is the daughter of Senhor Dunnington. She is no threat," he answered.

"She is a Gentile! What if others in the kehilla saw you? Would you bring shame on your family so easily? What does this girl know about you?"

"I didn't tell her anything. She figured it out herself, Mãe. She's known for a year. She's even seen the synagogue."

It was the wrong thing to say.

"Don't you realize the danger in this? How do you know she is no threat? How do you know that she won't tell this to others? Does your brother's sacrifice mean nothing to you?" She was screaming now.

He suddenly wanted to hurt her, to show her that he was no longer a little boy she could bend to her will. "His death was not a sacrifice, Mãe. It was your mistake."

She stood there stunned. Then the slap of her hand against his face, so powerful, so unexpected, knocked him to the floor.

"Don't you ever speak of this to me again!"

He dared not get up until she left the room. When he heard the door of her chamber slam, he quickly grabbed his cloak and left the house. For some reason, he found himself at the synagogue. He slumped to the floor and sat there for hours as the sunlight slipped away, leaving him in darkness. It was cold and uncomfortable, but Domingo did not want comfort. He didn't know what he wanted, really. He wanted Lucy. He wanted to stop pretending to be something he wasn't. He wanted a life he could probably never have. The last two months had been the happiest of his life. It was not just the bliss he felt in being loved by Lucy; it was that when they were together he was truly himself, not a Jew in hiding or a converso trying to conform to the expectations of the kehilla. With Lucy, he had autonomy over his identity and his conscience.

He heard the door open and saw light. It was Manuel. "Domingo, cousin, why do you stay here in the dark? Come home and eat."

"I cannot."

"Domingo, I am going to sit down and talk to you now." Domingo nodded his assent as Manuel joined him on the floor, setting his lamp between them. "You broke a confidence, cousin."

"I told Mãe that Lucy could be trusted!"

"Yes, I know. But can we trust you? You have shared our secret with a Gentile, and without our consent. You have also put a business relationship in jeopardy. She is young, Domingo."

"She's seventeen. Old enough to be married," Domingo countered.

"Nevertheless, she belongs to her father and you have no business trying to make her yours."

"I love her, Manuel. I gave her my pledge."

Manuel raised an eyebrow. "Have you lain with her?"

Domingo did not answer, but he knew that Manuel could guess from his stony stare.

"I see," Manuel said, sighing. "Domingo, if she were Jewish, you would be obligated to take her as your wife. Even the Catholics have this law. We are fortunate that this girl is Protestant."

Domingo fumed, but he would not reveal Lucy's secret to his cousin. If he had remained Catholic or if she was Jewish, they would already be considered married according to the laws of both their faiths. The agony of it exploded in him and he shouted, "I would love nothing more than to claim her as my wife! Don't you see? It is because she is not Jewish that I cannot!"

"Domingo, I am warning you. Do not get entangled in this relationship. What happened to your sister should be lesson enough for you."

This warning confused Domingo. "What happened to Marial? What do you know, Manuel?"

His cousin cursed, but then caught his temper. "It is not for me to tell you. Suffice it to say that your sister also trusted and was betrayed. I do not want that to happen to you."

"Lucy would not betray me. She would not betray us."

"Domingo, you have not completed your apprenticeship. Even if you wished a wife from among our people, you would have to wait three more years. You have put us all in danger, including the girl. If she is with child . . . do you realize what that means for us *and* for her? Her father works with us, but do not think this means he will accept what you have done to his daughter. He will not consent to your marriage. And how would it be if others discover that a Jew did this to a Christian girl? Do you think you would be safe from their wrath simply because she consented? No. This cannot be. For the next month, you will do your job—but do not meet with this girl alone. If she is with child, we will have to beg her father for mercy. I cannot say what will happen to you or the rest of us in that case, but I assure you that it may mean the end of our safety in London. If she is not with child, you will go to Amsterdam. I will write to Haham ben Israel tomorrow about this."

"No! I cannot break my promise to her."

"Domingo, do not argue with me. You had no right to make such a promise. You are part of this community and therefore you may not act alone. If you truly loved her, you would not have done this. Do you think you could ever be with her openly? What kind of marriage would that be? You would both be excommunicated, and you would grow to hate each other for it. Think also of your mother. She has no child but you. If you are cast out of the kehilla, she will have lost all her children. End it now, cousin." He stood to leave. "There will be a meal for you when you return home."

Domingo was devastated. The full consequence of what he had let happen for his own pleasure was like a series of waves that threatened to drown him. He had only thought of himself when he'd pursued Lucy. It had never occurred to him that their relationship might harm the kehilla or Lucy's future. What he'd thought was noble love had been base passion. His behavior with Lucy had put her in danger and shamed him in the eyes of his family. The loss of Manuel's trust was especially biting. He did not know if he would ever be able to earn it back.

◆◆◆

Arriving back home, he went to confront his mother in her chamber. She was sitting up in bed, her hair awry, her eyes red. "Tell me about Marial," he demanded.

She glared at him. "You would betray us to satisfy your lust. She died to protect us."

"Mãe, what does that mean?" he asked angrily. "How did she die?"

The story came out between her sobs. "He discovered . . . during her confession . . . that she knew the prayers of our people. She begged him. . . . She had to buy his silence with her body."

He felt sick. He remembered what happened now. "Mãe, Marial drowned herself because she . . . ."

Her eyes narrowed in anger. "She was pregnant with the priest's bastard. Even after what he did, he refused to bury her. He told us she was damned!"

This was why Filipe and his father had argued. This was why Filipe wanted revenge. But then, why had Filipe taken vows? "I don't understand, Mãe. How could Filipe become a priest after that?"

"Don't you see? He did it to be able to save her from damnation. He wanted to say Masses for her soul. Only a priest can."

"But why? Dear God! Even then you didn't tell him." Domingo's head spun. Stumbling to his own chamber, he tried to make sense of his childhood memories. He had always known that Filipe had died not knowing he was a Jew. But now Domingo realized how deeply his parents had conspired to keep this knowledge from Filipe, even when it could have saved him from seeking atonement for Marial. His parents had lost not one, but two children to the Inquisition. Children lost because of a religion they did not even know.

It was days before he could speak to his mother again; it was even longer before she would speak to him. Worse were Manuel's questioning looks every time they were together. He knew what he had to do, but their silent damnation of him made it worse.

After finishing up Mr. Dunnington's account books the next week, he found Lucy upstairs in her parents' chamber putting Thomas down for a nap. Her expectant smile drove him mad with desire.

"He's just about asleep." She took Domingo's hand and started for her chamber. He stopped her in the hallway.

"What's wrong, Dominick?"

His heart hammered with dread. "Lucy, I need to know if you are with child."

She sighed as if relieved. "No, Dominick. It's all right." She leaned in to kiss him but he turned away, determined to end this cleanly. "Dominick, please, have I done something to displease you?"

He felt his heart would break. "I am to go to Amsterdam. Manuel wishes for me to reacquaint myself with the agents there as part of my training. Senhor Robles is expanding his trade, and I must be ready to take on new responsibilities when my apprenticeship is done."

"And how long will you stay?"

"I am to complete my training there. Three years."

She caught her breath in shock. "What about us?"

He had to tell her, but the words refused to form on his lips. Her hand still clasped his. Gently, he pulled it away. "Lucita, I don't know. It is best if we end this."

Lucy felt as if she'd been struck. She began to swoon. Domingo grabbed her about her waist to hold her up. "Lucita, please," his voice wavered. "I love you, but we can't. My mother knows. She told Manuel."

"When will you leave?" she whispered.

"I sail in two weeks."

She sank into him and tried to beat back the pain in her heart. If she could just shut out everything except his touch and the rise and fall of his chest, she might make it through the moment without falling to pieces. They were sending him away.

"Why?"

"You know why, Lucy. I'm bound to him by law."

Suddenly she found her voice. "Manuel would never have you arrested."

"It's not just that. Where would we go? What would we live on? It's not going to work, Lucy."

She pushed away from his embrace, disgusted at his easy submission even as she knew he was right. "Did you try to convince them?"

"Lucy . . ."

She started pummeling his chest with her balled fists. "Did you fight or just give in?"

"You don't understand," he cried, grabbing her wrists and pulling her close again. "I love you. God, how I love you. But I'm a Jew, Lucy. Tell me how to love you without denying who I am."

It was then that Lucy realized that life refused to remain undefined. What was happily muddled in their childhood was taking shape as they grew into adults. It would soon have to be decided if they were friends or lovers, Catholics or Jews, conformists or violators of a sacred order that dictated that faithfulness to one religion required disdain for the other.

IX. *FALL FROM GRACE,* NOVEMBER 1652 – DECEMBER 1653

In Amsterdam, Semuel met Domingo at the dock and greeted him with a warm embrace. "Amiel, it's so good to welcome you back after so long."

"Semuel! But how did you recognize me after so many years?"

Semuel's expression became mischievous. "I scanned the passengers for a lovelorn Jew in Puritan black."

"Ah, so Manuel wrote of my banishment," Domingo said, embarrassed.

Semuel laughed. "Poor Amiel. So few Jewesses in your little neighborhood. There will be no need to court Christian maids in Amsterdam. If it is a wife you desire, I can make more than one excellent introduction. My own intended has two younger sisters." Domingo ignored this last comment and bent down to lift his trunk, grasping one of the side handles. Semuel reached for the other and together they carried it to a waiting carriage. After setting the trunk on the luggage rack on the back, they took their places inside. Domingo crammed himself into a corner and stared out the window as the carriage took them to the haham's home.

"My father has great plans and wishes to speak to you about them," Semuel said.

Domingo sighed. "Why me?"

"Because these plans concern England. He is eager to confirm information he's received from his correspondents about Jewish readmission to England."

"Readmission? So he plans to pursue this course?" Domingo turned to face Semuel.

"Yes. He is eager to meet with Mr. Cromwell about it."

"And what of those of us who live there as Catholics? What does your father expect from us?" Domingo asked, fearing the answer.

"Ah," exclaimed Semuel. "That will be the subject of your discussions, Amiel."

◆◆◆

The ben Israels' house was located in Nieuwe Houtmarket in the Jewish quarter of Amsterdam. The three-story structure housed a printing facility on the third floor and living quarters in the lower floors. Menasseh ben Israel had started the first Hebrew language press in Amsterdam thirty years earlier, printing thousands of copies of prayer books, Bibles, and theological tracts. Unfortunately for the haham, the press was only periodically successful and, of late, had operated at a loss. Semuel had been managing the printing business for the last two years; but, in their poverty, the family had sold much of their print type and the rights to a good deal of their material, including many of Menasseh's own writings. It bothered Domingo that such a learned man still had to worry about his income. His own profession would never make Domingo as wealthy as Senhor Robles, but he certainly could expect to support a family comfortably as long as he could win substantial clients and prove himself useful to them. The haham's worth could not be measured by his income. While wealthy merchants spoke of their love of scholarship and wanted their sons educated, they did not seem to be willing to pay scholars like Menasseh ben Israel a salary that would allow them the leisure to pursue knowledge and share it with the young.

◆◆◆

The haham and his wife, Rachel, greeted Domingo as he and Semuel entered the house. "Amiel Lacerda! Welcome back to Amsterdam." Domingo found himself wrapped in one of the haham's warm embraces.

"It is good to see you, Haham."

"Amiel, give me your cloak," instructed Rachel, giving him a welcoming smile. She still exuded a maternal feeling even though she'd lost her plumpness and now seemed thin and pale, her dark hair completely gray under her white cap. "Semuel, show him where he will sleep. I've got a hot meal for you after Amiel settles in."

Semuel led Domingo to Josef's old room on the second floor. "It's been empty for too long, my friend. I'm glad you are here to fill it."

The sadness in Semuel's voice betrayed how much he still mourned for his brother. Feeling ashamed of his own selfish unhappiness, Domingo placed a comforting hand on Semuel's shoulder. "I could never replace him, but I hope to prove myself worthy of Josef's memory. Forgive me. I've been so ill-tempered since I arrived. I have not been a very gracious guest thus far."

Semuel smiled. "Josef would tell you to stop berating yourself and go downstairs to enjoy my mother's cooking."

"And so I shall."

◆◆◆

After dinner, Menasseh began questioning Domingo. "What do you know of Antonio Carvajal?"

"He is one of London's most powerful merchants, Haham, with contacts in France, Amsterdam, and various parts of the New World. A few years ago he won an exclusive contract to ship corn to the army, and he imports all manner of fine goods from Brazil and the Indies. The house we use as a synagogue is leased in his name, and he is known in our community as a pious man. I've heard that shortly before my mother and I moved to London he was charged with recusancy by the English Church, but he was never tried."

Menasseh nodded. "Does he wish for you to worship freely in London?"

"We've never discussed it. Few people know we are Jews and that identity is tightly guarded."

"The English speak of religious tolerance and greatly desire the conversion of the Jews. I am convinced that they will welcome Jewish resettlement there. Many of my English friends have assured me of this," Menasseh said.

Domingo found this line of thinking disturbing. "Haham, even if Jews are welcomed under these conditions, how long will the welcome last if Jews do not convert?"

"Conversion is not forced in England, Amiel. Christians there will be patient and try to persuade us with their example. They expect that we are living in the end times. The civil war was just the beginning of England's trials. The English long for redemption for what they did to their king and to one another, and this redemption involves the Jews. Their prophecies and ours point to this coming to pass."

Domingo worried that Menasseh's friends had given him an incomplete picture of English attitudes toward religious tolerance, particularly toward the Jews. Continued persecution of Anabaptists, Quakers, and Catholics in England did not bode well for Jewish acceptance there. How could the haham's English friends think that Jews would be welcome? Perhaps they didn't, and they were just using him to justify their own strange beliefs. It angered Domingo that English millenarians might be manipulating this well-intentioned scholar for their own theological ends. Despite his resolution to put aside his own feelings, Domingo found himself growing angry.

"Amiel, imagine having the same freedoms in England that we enjoy in Amsterdam," Semuel interjected.

"Like being free to marry the woman I love?" Domingo shot back with more bitterness than he intended.

"Amiel, that is the law of God that no state can or cannot allow. A Jew may not pledge himself to a Gentile. On this, the law and the hahamim are clear," Menasseh replied firmly.

Domingo swallowed hard. He should not have brought this matter up at the haham's table. "I apologize, Haham. You were asking about Senhor Carvajal and the sentiment in England toward the Jews. I don't know that our community is ready for exposure. Our present situation is bearable, but with the upheaval from the civil war, there is much uncertainty about religion in England."

"Exactly!" Menasseh exclaimed. "This is the time to gain acceptance for our nation. If we gain permission now, even if things change, it will not be easy for them to expel Jews again. This is the time. Christians are divided against one another, so some are now willing to befriend our nation in opposition to the others. In England, the Protestants hate Catholics now more than the Jews. We do not threaten Protestant identity as Catholics do. In fact, the Protestants in England love our law and our prophets as their own. I have even read tracts in which they view the history of our people in ancient times as their own."

Domingo thought of what Lucy had said years ago about Jews getting involved in the battle between Catholics and Protestants in England. "Haham, are you sure that the Protestants would not just be using the Jews as a way to prove their authenticity as Christians to the Catholics? What if they like the idea of us more than our actual residence?"

Menasseh grinned as if he were about to reveal a great secret. "Because, Amiel, besides our history, they also want our money and our skill in trade. We can be useful to the English in more than one way. Senhor Carvajal was not harassed for his religion because of the wealth he brings to England. Your Oliver Cromwell knows what Senhor Carvajal is. He knows that we can help him build his New Jerusalem in England. Even if the Jews of London are not ready, Cromwell is. So we must push our case soon."

Domingo did not concur, but he was unwilling to openly disagree with the haham. He simply nodded and then made his excuses to be off to bed. He planned on getting an early start tomorrow visiting Senhor Robles's agents at the Bourse.

◆◆◆

As the winter days darkened so did his mood. Domingo found himself angering easily, especially in matters concerning religion. Menasseh was pressuring him to undergo circumcision. Because of his father's objections, he had not been circumcised as a boy. When he'd turned thirteen, the decision had been his alone. And there had been no haham in London to insist on it or mohel to perform it. The *parnassim* in Amsterdam frowned on uncircumcised men worshipping in the synagogue, although, with so many refugees from Portugal and Spain, it was a common enough situation. The parnassim's attitude irritated Domingo. It wasn't that he feared the procedure; well, he did not fear it entirely. He knew many who had undergone it as grown men. It was just that the expectation of absolute conformity, which had comforted him as a child, was a vexation to him now.

Semuel tried to comfort Domingo with humor. He even introduced him to the sisters of his betrothed, Miriam. They came with their older brother Aaron one Sabbath afternoon in late winter. Esther and Leah Mendes were dark-eyed and shy, and neither one of them was older than fifteen. They were so unlike Lucy that Domingo could not even feign interest, yet Semuel and his father urged him to try. They told him that either girl would make a fine match, and Menasseh even offered to write to Manuel about arranging an engagement. But Domingo's wound was too fresh, the memory of stolen moments with Lucy too strong. He told them he would not consider marriage until his apprenticeship was completed.

◆◆◆

During the spring festival of Purim, the haham brought home a guest for dinner. "Amiel, do you remember your schoolmate Baruch Spinoza?" Menasseh asked as he ushered a young man into the parlor. "He works in the importing trade with his brother."

"Baruch, how wonderful to see you." Domingo jumped up to greet his old school friend. "But I thought you were to be a scholar?"

"It was not to be, Amiel. My duty was to my family." Baruch cast a furtive glance at the haham. Menasseh nodded in understanding. Domingo noticed their unspoken exchange and guessed that there was more to Baruch's decision than family obligations.

"Come, gentlemen, dinner awaits." Menasseh led them to the table where he said the blessings before they set to eating. Rachel had laid a fabulous table of cod, challah bread, chickpeas and pine nuts drenched in olive oil, and *folares*, hard boiled eggs that were wrapped in pastry and decorated as characters from the Purim story. Domingo's egg was Esther, the dough over it forming a long veil that Rachel had dyed a deep green.

Baruch got Haman. For a moment, he considered the dough-encrusted egg, shaped like a man's head topped with a red tri-cornered hat, then shrugged, and popped the treat into his mouth. "Amiel, are you living in Amsterdam now?"

"It is a temporary stay. I've been sent to . . ." He hesitated here. What should he tell Baruch about his banishment? "I've been sent to learn lessons about work and faith."

"Three years is not so temporary, Amiel," Semuel said, carefully cutting up his Mordecai egg. "Perhaps we can convince you to stay." Domingo did not reply to this comment. Instead, he concentrated on eating his dinner.

"What is the nature of your work, Amiel?" Baruch asked with genuine interest.

"I am apprenticed to an accountant. I have also done tutoring and translation."

Baruch gestured impatiently. "I see. So tell me what you seek to know about faith?"

Semuel did not look pleased at Baruch's question. Domingo, however, was glad for a chance to vent some of his frustration before a man who did not seem likely to just quote the law to him. "I seek to know whether a Jew, who has pledged himself to a Gentile, is obligated to the law for the sake of the community, thereby losing his claim on his wife; or, is he obligated to his wife, regardless of the community?"

"You have a wife?" Baruch seemed pleased at Domingo's troubles.

Menasseh waited, fork poised above his plate, for Domingo's answer.

"That seems to be a matter of contention," Domingo answered.

"But marriage outside of the law is not valid, Amiel. This the hahamim have made plain," Semuel said.

"Then I question the validity of the law," Domingo said defiantly.

The haham put down his fork and folded his hands in front of him on the table. He leaned toward Domingo and spoke slowly and clearly, as if they were back in the yeshiva. "The law is God's way of protecting us from our own weaknesses, Amiel. We also build a fence around Torah to protect ourselves from overstepping the law. Without the law we are prone to selfishness. Without the law we are no better than the beasts."

"We've inherited this fence, but dare we look at it critically? What is the nature of this fence? Perhaps it is a fence of fear rather than a fence of protection," argued Baruch.

"There is no truth beyond the law!" yelled Semuel.

Menasseh held up his hand. "Peace, son. Baruch, there may be many realities that lay beyond the law, but are they all worth your attention? The good Lord chose us for the truth of the law. Will you drop dead from eating pork? No. In fact, many Christians enjoy it. This is allowed under their law. But pork, to us, is poison."

"Ridiculous," muttered Baruch.

"You see this from a digestive perspective, Baruch. What I mean is that it is a spiritual poison. Once you transgress the law, you make yourself and our people vulnerable to spiritual decay. This is why your reliance on reason is so threatening. You believe men can be gods and can see all consequences as God does."

"That is not what I teach, Haham! Reason is a tool God gave to humanity. It is a gift that we should not reject," protested Baruch.

"As is the law," said Menasseh ben Israel with a finality that ended the conversation.

In June, Domingo received a letter from Lucy. He broke the seal in a rush, but then decided to take a walk along the canals so he could be alone with her words.

Dearest Dominick,

I pray my letter finds you safe and happy. Thomas's baby sister, Emma, continues to thrive, and Elizabeth is quite recovered from her recent miscarriage. The doctor tells us that it was perhaps too soon for her to carry again after bearing Emma. Thomas asks after "Mingo" still. He is just three but remembers you well as the man who used to bring him honey cakes. Would that Elizabeth and I knew how your mother made them as Thomas has rejected each attempt we've made as "not Mingo's."

Father has been bringing home associates of late; I suspect that he and Elizabeth are conspiring to have me engaged to one of them. Naturally they are all Protestant, but only one of them, Edward Polestead, a former cavalry officer for Parliament, is aligned with the English Church. The others are Separatists and Baptists, insufferable Evangelists all of them. I would naturally be expected to conform to my husband's church, and the very thought of this fills me with grief. Father seems determined to stamp out Catholicism in this family even though I know he does not really care about religion.

Please, Dominick, you know my heart in this. Two years is not so long to wait as I know you must complete your apprenticeship. I have tried to speak to Elizabeth about my desire not to marry yet, but now that I am eighteen and there are two full-grown women and two small children in the house, we are all not so easy together as we once were. I have asked Father to allow me an extended visit with Uncle Richard. It would certainly cheer my uncle in his illness and I would be relieved of Father's parade of suitors. I have written to Frances and she also wishes me to come to Yorkshire. She hints at an engagement of her own, and I wonder if she has finally won Sebastian's heart. My mother's brother, Hugh, is staying with the Brettons and I desire to speak with him about Father's plans. Perhaps Uncle Hugh can speak to Father about the situation. I know he greatly desires to keep me within the Catholic fold.

The talk of London concerns General Cromwell. It is said by some that he will be crowned king. Father does not believe it will come to that because a crown would limit the Lord Protector's powers rather than expand them. I am not sure what to think anymore. I must confess that I have not been reading as I used to. So much of my time is now spent helping Elizabeth with the children, and without our reading and conversations, I have become as ignorant as any London maiden.

Perhaps in Yorkshire I might be able to revive both my mind and my spirit.

Yours,
Lucy

Back at the ben Israels' that evening, Domingo wrote over twenty different responses to Lucy, all of which ended up in the fire. He finally sent this one:

August 29, 1653
Dear Lucy,

Semuel and his father are increasingly at odds with the Ma'amad, which is the ruling council of Jews here in Amsterdam. It would seem that the Jewish community here is divided in more ways than one. Ashkenazi, the eastern European Jews, do not view the Sephardim as faithful to the law. The Ashkenazi are mostly farmers and laborers; they suffer in poverty here, while the learned Sephardim live comfortably. There is dispute on both sides over how much

Gentile scholarship should be taught in the yeshiva for it is feared that this learning will turn Jews away from the law. Jews here, as in London, live in fear of attracting the attention of those who would wish them harm. Because of this, the haham's efforts to secure a haven for the Jews displaced by the wars in Poland are met with little support among Amsterdam's congregations, particularly the Sephardim. I fear the haham will encounter similar problems in London when he travels there to petition the Lord Protector for their readmission.

Please tell Thomas that I have not forgotten him. At the Leadenhall market, there is an old widow with a large black dog who sells eggs; she makes the finest Madeira honey cakes in London. They are known as *bolo-de-mel*. I think your going to Yorkshire is a fine plan. Stay true to your faith, Lucita. I know how much it means to you.

Dominick

November 13, 1653
Dearest Dominick,
I returned from Yorkshire two days ago. Uncle Richard died in late September and there was much to arrange for his funeral and the transference of the manor to my father. I am happy to report that Uncle Richard left Chapel House and many of his library books to me. Someday I should like to live there permanently, but Father says it is unthinkable for me to live alone and that I must marry. In my daydreams you return to London and we make our home together in Yorkshire. Is this a false hope, Dominick? I had once thought you my intended husband, now I fear that I no longer know your heart. I wonder that I ever did; it seemed to turn so quickly against me. Frances counsels me to forget you and is convinced that I have been ill-used. Is this true? If I knew there was hope of your return to me, I might find peace. But as it stands, I am as a leaf fluttering in the wind.

Yours,
Lucy

Her second letter seemed to break something inside him. He knew that she must marry another, but he couldn't bear the thought of Lucy despising him, thinking that he'd used her for sport. After the Bourse closed, he found himself at the Spinoza house in Amsterdam's *Houtgragt* neighborhood. Baruch lived with his father, Michael, a pious man and a warden of the synagogue, who, of late, had been ill and was staying with his married daughter, Rebekah.

"I am going to return to London on the next ship. I've already booked passage on the *Cloe*. I sail in four days," Domingo announced to Baruch when he opened the door.

"Hello, Amiel. Come in." Amused, Baruch ushered Domingo to the second-floor parlor. "What event has inspired your desire for flight? Has the Ma'amad discovered that underneath your breeches you remain outside of the nation?" Baruch laughed at his own joke.

Domingo couldn't tell if Baruch was serious or not. "There is a family matter."

Baruch eyed him knowingly. "Amiel, you are a poor liar. Sounds more like a matter concerning a woman. Has your Gentile bride begged you to come home?"

"No. She is beginning to despise me. And now I despise who I am, what we are."

"Careful, Amiel. You sound like a heretic," Baruch cautioned.

Silencing his doubts, Domingo tried to direct the conversation away from them. "I am told the Ma'amad is considering your own excommunication, Baruch."

Baruch's mirthful expression instantly became sober. "Yes, they have actually been considering it for several years now. I think they hold off because of my father's status in the community, but as the political situation in this country becomes more tenuous, the council grows more fearful of dissent. I am a Jew but I find it no sin to interact with Gentiles. My greatest teacher is a former Jesuit, I correspond with Quakers, and I take coffee with the Reformed. Even Haham ben Israel has Gentile admirers, but he is concerned with the integrity of the community first. He does not agree that a Jew should pursue a course that could reflect poorly on the community. His is a position of fear, not of reason. Remove the threat of Christian persecution and you remove much of the justification for conformity."

"But he wishes to speak for the Jews without the support of the Ma'amad in Amsterdam or the community in London."

"He seeks the good of all Jews, even if he alienates himself from the Ma'amad. In his own way, the haham will also be cast out just as I am sure to be. Why do you think he has not yet traveled to England? If he leaves, they have threatened to replace him at the Talmud Torah School and remove him from the Ma'amad."

"I gathered as much from Semuel, but I hope it will not come to that."

"He is willing to make great sacrifices so that Jews may live unmolested."

"I suppose that makes me selfish. But I am tired of sacrificing and I am tired of hiding. I often wonder if happiness itself is a violation of the law."

"To be cut off is a terrible thing, Amiel. I risk it but I do not seek it," Baruch said sadly.

"So you advise me to conform, just as Semuel and the others do?" Domingo felt disappointed in his friend. He had been sure Baruch would support him.

Baruch shook his head. "Amiel, you must first know your own heart, your own inclination, before you can even begin to defy others. What kind of man are you, Amiel Lacerda? What is it you want, and what will you risk to get it? Can you claim your wife and then stand on your own? Because that is what you will have to do. If you cannot do that, then do not claim her."

"It is wrong that I should have to choose!" exclaimed Domingo, fearful that he could not stand on his own, even with Lucy. He had been taught for the last eleven years that being a Jew meant never standing alone. Every action, no matter how trivial, affected other Jews. God and his angels monitored the Jews. The Christians monitored the Jews. Even Jews monitored their brethren to ensure conformity to Jewish law and to Christian sensibilities.

Baruch's speech grew animated, like a haham reaching the climax of a sermon. "I agree with you that the law is wrong in basing our redemption on our exclusivity. Of course it is not just the Jews who do this. It is a universal failing. Why are we happier when we have what others do not? Why do we define holiness so narrowly?

Why is redemption cheaper when it is available to everyone? On the other hand, is it not true that if we allow for the beliefs of all people, we then stand for nothing?"

Lost in his own circumstances, Domingo said nothing in response to Baruch's philosophizing. He realized that all of them—Baruch, Haham ben Israel, and himself—were suffering from an excess of community. The security of religious conformity felt like a yoke when one had experienced acceptance outside of the kehilla. It was hard for those who had been persecuted to understand that not all Gentiles sought to harm the Jews and that not all Jews found comfort in submission to their religious authorities. He recalled the Talmudic debates among the hakhim regarding the law from his boyhood lessons with the haham. What had happened to that Talmudic spirit of debate and compromise? Was Baruch correct in concluding that fear had become the true ruler of them all?

Nonplussed by their sober discussion, Baruch regained his high spirits. "Come, let us stop being so dour and raise a glass to your imminent departure!" He poured out two glasses of wine and handed one to Domingo, who drank deeply. Baruch seemed to have an unending supply of cheap wine and tobacco. Domingo gave himself over to these vices and felt satisfaction in knowing that both his behavior and the company he kept would displease those who wished him to give up Lucy. After sundown, Baruch introduced two more young free thinkers to the gathering. It was not long before they were all drunkenly philosophizing.

Domingo was amazed at the power of inebriation to engender wit and sophistication in men. He'd never felt so liberated. If only Baruch would serve them something to eat, it would be a perfect gathering then. Domingo's stomach lurched with hunger, and he decided that he would clear his head and then go downstairs to Baruch's larder to search for food. Anticipating his companions' praise for his resourcefulness, he staggered over to a window to open. But he found that he could not open the shutter for the latch was jammed.

Not to be outdone by a simple locking mechanism, he grabbed a stool by the wall and stepped up onto it so that he could better assess the problem. To his surprise, the latch gave easily and Domingo pushed the shutter open, his head swimming. The rush of cold air did not clear his head, but it felt good in his chest for its freshness, compared to the smoke-filled room. He leaned forward, bracing himself on the window frame. Looking down at the canals, he became entranced with the moonlight dancing on the lapping water. Amsterdam seemed beautiful to him in this moment.

"Amiel. What are you doing up there?" Baruch called out to him. Domingo turned around to answer, but suddenly the stool was sliding out from under his feet. He gripped the window frame and tried to regain his footing on the sill, but it was too late. He was falling out of the window to the cobblestones below. Instinctively, he raised his arms to protect his head. Then, with a sickening crack, his shoulder hit the ground followed by his hip. At first all he felt was shock, but when he tried to move, pain shot through his body like a hundred knives stabbing him from the inside. The pain was overwhelming. He began to retch. Then he heard Baruch frantically calling his name, "Amiel! Amiel!"

Footsteps pounded toward him. Someone's hands grabbed his shoulders and turned him onto his back. This was worse than the impact of the fall. He heard himself screaming; then white noise and spinning took him away from all consciousness.

X. *A Case of Conscience,*
December 1653 – September 1654

When Domingo woke, he saw a strange face leaning over his. It was a man of about fifty with blond hair tending toward white, a bushy white mustache, and twinkling blue eyes. Domingo sensed a familiarity about the man. In his mind was a vague image of those eyes looking down at him once before in kindness. But he could not place the memory as being from a time long past or the recent present. How long had he been unconscious? He was so cold.

The stranger had cut off Domingo's bloodied clothes and was daubing the battered right side of his body with a rag soaked with warm water. Domingo felt sticky and the smell of his own blood and vomit made his stomach churn. He closed his eyes, hoping to shut out the smell and the pain. Then he drifted into unconsciousness again.

The slam of a door followed by a chilly draft woke him. How much time had passed? The stranger still tended to him, but the reek of his sickness was gone. Thankful for having been cleansed, but also too weak to care about modesty, Domingo only minded being unclothed because of the cold. The stranger suddenly spoke, but not to Domingo. "Excellent timing, Baruch. I've just finished cleaning him up. Did you find my medical bag all right?" A pause. "Good, now find some blankets and keep the fire high. Your friend is lucky to be alive, you know. Your rabbi will have your head for this."

"I know," Domingo heard Baruch say in a voice choked with guilt. "I'll send a message there shortly."

"Send it now," replied the stranger firmly. "He lives, but I cannot tell what damage he may have done to his insides. He seems to have protected his head with his arm but it still must have hit with some force." Domingo heard Baruch's footsteps leave the room. When the stranger turned back to him he saw that Domingo's eyes were open. "Ah, my friend, you are back among the living. You've learned now that men are not angels and cannot fly."

126

Domingo opened his mouth to reply but the stranger held a finger to his lips. "Sht! I will do the speaking for now. My name is Franz Van den Ende. I am a friend of Baruch's. I've been trained as a doctor so you can trust me. It would seem you've broken your shoulder. Also, your elbow is badly bruised. It is possible your hip is cracked. I won't be able to tell for sure until we can move your leg, but that can wait." He held a lit candle close to Domingo's eyes and then clapped his hands by each of his ears. Apparently satisfied with Domingo's responses, he set the candle back on the table by the bed. "Your pupils are not dilated, and your hearing is intact. Also, your breathing is not labored. Hopefully God has spared you for some unknown purpose. Mayhap it is one of his little jokes, eh?"

Franz turned his attention to Domingo's wounds. He worked with a silent intensity, and though his touch was gentle, Domingo nearly passed out again when Franz began to bind his shoulder and elbow in thin strips of a light linen cloth that was soaked in what smelled like gin. When he was done, Franz rose and walked over to a table near the hearth. Domingo remained cold and nauseous; every part of his body hurt. Franz returned with blankets and carefully spread them over him. Warm now, Domingo minded the pain less, but he had to remain perfectly still so as not to feel it ripping through his flesh.

Franz then brought over a wooden bowl that was half full of water. "I am going to spoon some of this water into your mouth. Don't move your head if you have trouble drinking it, just let it go." This exercise satisfied Domingo's thirst but left pools of water behind his ears. Like most beds in Amsterdam, the one in Baruch's anteroom was enclosed in a wardrobe. It was shorter than a full-grown man, which meant that Domingo was forced to sleep half sitting up. This arrangement enabled him to have a better view of the room, but it caused great pain in his hip. After clumsily drinking his fill, he drifted into an uncomfortable sleep.

It was the yelling that woke him next. "What have you done, Spinoza! Why couldn't you leave him alone! Must you try to turn everyone atheist!"

"Damn you, Semuel! Why did he come here if your counsel is so valuable? You barrage him with platitudes hoping to stem his questions and his anger!"

127

"Yes, I see your way is better, Baruch. Ply him with drink instead and let him throw himself out a window."

"He fell. I told you that," Baruch replied sullenly.

The door opened and Semuel rushed over to Domingo. "Oh, Amiel. What have you done to yourself?"

"I fell," Domingo rasped.

"Yes, Amiel. You've been falling for a long time now. I should have seen it sooner. I am so sorry, my friend." He turned to Franz, who was sitting in a cushioned chair pulled up close to the head of Domingo's bed. "You are a doctor?"

"I have been trained as one," Franz answered.

"Will he live?" Semuel's tone was matter-of-fact, yet his eyes betrayed his fear.

Franz eyed Semuel as if trying to assess his ability to take the full truth. "I expect he will develop a fever. I've found that soaking the bindings with a strong spirit helps sometimes." Semuel looked puzzled by this treatment but didn't say anything, so Franz continued, "It is possible there is something damaged inside. We shall know within the next day. If he is bleeding inside, the blood will fill his stomach or his lungs and he will die. He must remain here until we are sure."

Semuel nodded. "Then I too will stay." He posted himself by Domingo's bedside and began to chant the prayer for the sick. Domingo was grateful it was not the prayer for the dying; he fell asleep comforted by his friend's hopefulness.

◆◆◆

He woke later in the day and saw that Semuel was still by his side. Seeing that Domingo had survived thus far, Semuel recovered his humor. "How is your hangover, friend?"

Even if he could have laughed without pain, Domingo was not ready to be mocked. "I might never recover from it, Semuel. Too much wine and too little food. Lesson learned."

Semuel looked hurt. "I didn't mean to lecture you, Amiel. We both know that it was not the wine that caused your accident."

"What did then?"

"You are clearly meant to remain in Amsterdam," Semuel pronounced with confidence.

"What do you mean?"

"Amiel, have you not considered why you fell? I believe God wants to keep you here. I knew you were planning on leaving; I was going to beg you to stay. Now it seems I don't have to."

"I don't belong here, Semuel."

His friend smiled and nodded in agreement. "No, you don't belong here with Baruch Spinoza. That is for certain! As for Amsterdam, I think God has a purpose for you here." He gave Domingo a pleading look. "You are like a brother to me. Please let me help you find your way. I believe that with your fall God was foiling your obstinacy. It is obvious that more than your body needs healing. In fact, were your body whole it would not matter for your spirit is broken. Perhaps God has broken your body so your spirit has a chance at wholeness."

Domingo felt he would weep at his friend's perception. He did feel broken. Like a hammer had smashed his family back in Lisbon leaving them with only sharp edges that they'd been cutting each other with ever since. And yet "broken" was not the right word. Broken implied that at one time there had been wholeness. He'd never wholly been one thing; rather, he was a mixture of religions and cultures. Wholeness would mean choosing one part and forsaking the others. Wholeness would require a sacrifice even greater than giving up Lucy.

"Semuel, I don't know who I am," Domingo admitted.

"Then we will discover God's will for you together," Semuel reassured him. "Don't give up hope, Amiel."

When Franz returned that afternoon, he proudly offered Domingo a pair of Turkish pantaloons he'd purchased at the market. With a great deal of effort, so as not to jar his friend's hip, Semuel helped Domingo into them. They were amazingly comfortable despite their garish orange and blue stripes. The lightweight silk was a welcome change from woolen breeches and the loose-fitting style of the pantaloons was ideal for his convalescence. Despite this improvement, however, his pain worsened. He tried to sleep, hoping to find a reprieve, but in the early hours of the second day, sleep was beaten back by the pain. There was no escape from the throbbing of his right side, and his exhaustion only seemed to exaggerate it.

Nausea gripped him and the fear of his stomach heaving added to his misery. Any movement at all seemed to wrench his shoulder. As dawn approached, his moans and sharp breaths began to scare Semuel, who woke Baruch to fetch Franz. He returned less than an hour later with his friend. Franz carried a clay pipe that he lit and then offered to Domingo.

"Trust me, Amiel," he said in more of a command than a plea. "This will help."

Domingo no longer cared enough to doubt or fear Franz's strange remedies, but he was too weak to take the pipe. Understanding the younger man's difficulty, Franz inserted the pipe into Domingo's mouth and instructed him to breathe deeply of its embers. At first, it smelled of tobacco, but as he inhaled, he noted that it tasted sweet. Not used to the smoke, Domingo fought the urge to cough.

Franz gently urged him to puff on the pipe again. "Just a few more deep breaths, my friend, and you'll be able to sleep without pain."

Domingo inhaled deeply and soon felt the pipe's effects. Franz was right; the pipe did help ease the pain. Yet Domingo was suddenly afraid of the dullness that began to envelope his mind. What if he never woke? But then he realized the ridiculousness of that particular fear. If he never woke, there would be no more pain, no more confusion, no more hopeless dreams of the future.

He had nightmares about falling. In his dreams he had large, light wings like a butterfly, and each time he tried to fly, they were cruelly plucked off. Sometimes Manuel did the deed, sometimes the haham, and sometimes it was people he could not even identify. After losing his wings, he was then pushed by a hooded figure in a dark robe from various heights: his balcony in Lisbon, the upper level of the synagogue in Amsterdam, and even once from the crow's nest of a ship's mast. Occasionally he was able to wake himself before he fell in the dreams. But more than once he woke from the pain in his side and his own screaming after he'd jerked in his sleep from anticipating the impact of a fall. In one of his more disturbing dreams, he stood with Lucy in her chamber. As they kissed, she inched him toward the window and then, suddenly, with one great shove, she pushed him out. Even after he'd hit the ground and the pain was searing through his body, he couldn't wake up from the horror. He didn't want to leave her, even in a nightmare.

"Amiel!" Baruch gently slapped Domingo's face. "Wake up!" He opened his eyes to Baruch's worried face. They had not spoken in the week since Domingo's accident. Baruch pulled a chair over to Domingo's bed. "Tell me about your dream."

"It . . . it's . . . a de-mon, Bar-uch," Domingo said panting. "While I sleep . . . he plagues me . . . making me . . . making me fall . . . each night."

Baruch smiled sympathetically. "It is not a demon, Amiel. You've given yourself over to despair. Your mind is grasping for answers that elude you. Don't rely on superstition to guide you. That will only lead to more despair or false hope."

"Semuel sees the hand of God in my accident. It is chastisement for my obstinacy. Do you think God has turned from me, Baruch?"

"Your accident was caused by your lack of judgment about a stool, not because of your lack of judgment about a woman. If God punished every man who loved a woman, well, he could not have. There would be few men without broken bones. God did not cause your fall."

Domingo began to take some comfort in Baruch's reasoning. "So you are saying that my fall was just a random action unrelated to the state of my moral soul? That even a righteous man could fall from a window?"

"Of course, Amiel! Consider what you already know about tragedy and joy. Do not righteous men suffer all the time and evil men prosper? Where is the hand of God in that? Why must you assign God's hand to these occurrences? Doesn't that make God himself random in choosing whom he will punish and whom he will reward? Would you rather believe in the unpredictable nature of life or the unpredictable nature of God? For my part, I don't understand why men choose to believe that God would act in so capricious a manner. It is man who is irrational, not God. You are unaccustomed to drink and this impaired your judgment. It was your impairment that caused you to fall, not the unsystematic punishment of God. Do you understand, Amiel?"

He did, but his mind sought to reject the sense of it. Belief in God's justice, no matter how mysterious, was still more comforting than a world in which tragedy and joy were unpredictable. If life was so random, how could a man know his place in the world?

◆◆◆

After three weeks, his friends hired a litter to move Domingo back to the ben Israels' house. And with great effort, he was able to walk the short distance from the street to the parlor. Franz pronounced Domingo's hip set, even though it was not healed. His shoulder would take much longer to heal. Semuel and Baruch settled Domingo into a wardrobe bed in a back room on the ground floor. Then Baruch made a quick exit. Although he and Semuel had not quarreled since the night of Domingo's fall, their childhood friendship seemed beyond repair. This bothered Domingo even though he knew that their differences went much deeper than his accident. Baruch's studies with Franz, his challenges to the law, and his belief that God worked through nature rather than superseding it undermined the integrity of the kehilla and the authority of the Torah. What's more, Baruch's having been Menasseh ben Israel's student at the yeshiva also seemed to cast doubt on the haham's own teachings. Domingo wondered if Semuel felt the same way about his own digressions from the law. Did his unacceptable behavior also create problems for the haham? He was too ashamed to ask Semuel.

"You will sleep down here until you heal, Amiel. Father is eager to see you, but he is with the council presently," Semuel said in a drained voice.

"Baruch told me they were considering sanctions against your father."

Semuel sighed heavily. "Yes, he has petitioned the queen of Sweden for safe haven for the Polish Jews. The situation there is increasingly dire. There are massacres every day. Thousands are dead and many more flee east to the Turkish Empire where they are made slaves of the Muslim sultan. We used to sell the bulk of our books in Poland. Now we hardly do any business there. We still don't know exactly how Josef died. I think part of my father's mission in helping the Polish Jews is his way of coming to terms with whatever happened. He couldn't save Josef so he wants to save as many others as possible. But the Ma'amad in Amsterdam does not want to get drawn into the conflict between Poland and Sweden. They feel that any involvement in state matters draws attention to our numbers in Amsterdam and will only lead to sanctions, perhaps even expulsions."

"But how can they do nothing?"

"It is complicated, Amiel. Amsterdam's ruling council has allowed us freedom to work and worship, but this charter was based on our success as merchants. In the last few years, thousands of Ashkenazi Jews have settled here. How many poor Jews will Amsterdam allow before it changes the charter? This is also true in London. Your small community brings wealth into the city, so you are tolerated by those who know of your existence. But even if you won acceptance as Jews, would England accept poor Jews? Queen Christina is said to be a kind-hearted monarch and is considering her kingdom as a shelter for Poland's Jews. If she does not take in our nation, however, we must find another sovereign with similar sympathies. Your Cromwell is the most likely candidate."

It was dawning on Domingo how very complicated the situation was. Menasseh ben Israel was championing safety for all Jews, but in doing so, he endangered the Sephardic merchants and their families who were few, self-supporting, and practically invisible when they needed to be so. Jewish emancipation seemed dependent on their ability to support themselves and to create wealth to support their poor. Yet most Christians disdained the rich Jew as a violation of some kind of natural order in society. Christians hated rich Jews for their wealth, poor Jews for their need, pious Jews for their religion, irreverent Jews for their atheism, and even converted Jews for their very blood. It was a fixed game that the Jews could never win.

It took two months before Domingo was able to walk free from pain. Franz told him that he needed to walk every day else he would never heal properly. Semuel had to help Domingo get about during the first month of his recovery, but as he grew stronger, Domingo was able to move about with just a cane. Favoring his weak right hip gave him the appearance of having a limp. He hoped it would not be permanent, although he knew that he should be thankful that he could walk at all. An even longer time passed before he had any use of his

Patricia O'Sullivan

right arm. The elbow healed cleanly, but his shoulder continued to pain him whenever he tried to lift or pull with it. Franz told him to be patient and that the shoulder would heal with time. Domingo was able to write again by late spring, but he did not answer Lucy's letter from six months ago. It was part of a past he no longer wanted.

Determined to leave his life in London behind him, he began to study the Talmud again with Semuel. By summer, he was able to resume his duties for Senhor Robles, and a new peace began to grow in his heart. He was a Jew in a Jewish community and, despite his physical state, he felt whole for the first time in his life. He also finally agreed to be circumcised, because after the ordeal with his shoulder, it seemed to be a minor thing. Perhaps he would stay in Amsterdam, marry, and eventually join the Ma'amad.

This plan sustained Domingo until September, when Menasseh decided that he would send Semuel to London. Miriam's father was furious with the delay of their marriage. They had been engaged for almost two years. Had Semuel not been the son of Menasseh ben Israel, her father most certainly would have brought a case against him to the Ma'amad. Twenty-two and eager to marry, Semuel was also unhappy with the delay, but his father's wish for him to go to England had priority over all else. The mission to Queen Christina had failed and now it was imperative that they convince Oliver Cromwell, Lord Protector of England, to provide safe haven for the Jews.

Menasseh composed petitions for Cromwell and Parliament and entrusted them to his son. Sending Semuel would provide Menasseh a second chance if things in Amsterdam or London went badly. The Ma'amad in Amsterdam would have no cause to dismiss Menasseh from his post and a rejection in London would not preclude Menasseh himself from speaking before the great Puritan leader. Semuel's trip was, in a sense, a testing of the waters.

Semuel begged Domingo to accompany him to London. Although Semuel spoke passable English, his friend's superior linguistics and his London contacts would be a great help to the mission. Domingo had mixed feelings about returning to London. It would be good to see his family again, but he resented being used as a pawn in a mission that would surely be unsupported by the London kehilla.

In the end, he agreed to go out of love for the ben Israels. He did not agree with their mission, but he loved them as family. They had saved his life and restored his health, and for this, he could never forsake them.

XI. *A HUMBLE PETITION*, 1654

They arrived in London in early September. Manuel, Marcos, and Teresa Maria met them at the docks.

"Domingo!" His mother uncharacteristically rushed to him and threw her arms about him. Then, after brushing a tear from her eye, she composed herself and began her usual interrogation. "You are limping still? But how is your shoulder? Show me your arm."

He was embarrassed but pleased with her affection. Two years ago he'd left London in anger and defeat. Since then, he and his mother had exchanged few letters. However, after his circumcision, he had committed himself to being a better son to her.

"Hello, Mãe." He kissed her cheeks. "I'm fine."

"What of your arm? Is it healed?" she asked.

"I cannot lift it high, but otherwise it is healed," he assured her.

She squeezed his arm tenderly. "I am glad you are home, Domingo."

He touched his forehead to hers in reply. In the particular language of their family, her words and his gesture were exchanges of peace. No further words would be spoken on the manner of his leaving two years ago. All was forgiven.

He made introductions. "Manuel, you remember Semuel."

"Welcome to London," Manuel said coolly. "This is my son Marcos. He is my apprentice here in London." Domingo smiled warmly at Marcos, now fifteen, who winked in reply. His cousin had grown a great deal during Domingo's two-year absence and showed promise of the man he would become in his self-assurance. Despite his resolve to leave the past, Domingo could not help but wonder if Marcos worked on Dunnington's books and if he ever saw Lucy. Probably not. Manuel would've made sure to keep Marcos far away from Gentile girls.

"Senhor Soeiro, arrangements have been made for you to stay with the Lacerdas during your visit."

Domingo knew that Semuel would be grateful for this kindness for he did not have the funds to rent lodging. "That is most generous of you, Senhor Delgado. My father will be most appreciative of your kindness toward me."

Manuel gave a slight bow in reply and then led them all to a carriage, borrowed from Senhor Robles, which would deliver them home to Stoney Lane.

◆◆◆

As Lucy and her little sister made their way through the narrow, smelly streets of London, Emma persistently tugged at Lucy's cap so that she continually had to readjust it to keep her head covered as was befitting a woman in public. But, in the end, Lucy let the child have the cap rather than fuss over it. At two years old, Emma was a healthy size and too heavy for Lucy to easily carry for such a distance. When they finally reached Covent Garden, Lucy bought a sweet cake for Emma. She set her sister down on a closed crate and the child was soon occupied with her treat, allowing Lucy to recover her cap and to scan the stalls for Elizabeth and Thomas. Her stepmother had been of late engaged in purchasing material for the children's winter wardrobes. The more specialized pieces would require the help of a milliner, but Lucy and Elizabeth would be able to cut and sew the children's everyday wear, like their skirts, trousers, caps, and shirts. Looking about her, Lucy suspected that many a London wife had similar ambitions because the market was particularly crowded this October morning.

As she filtered the sights and sounds of Covent Garden, a familiar, yet unbelievable, voice registered in Lucy's ears. She turned toward it and spied Dominick with another young man standing at a clothier's stall. Dominick seemed to be negotiating with the tailor on behalf of his companion. Only two years had passed, but Dominick looked much older now. He sported a closely trimmed beard and was wearing his hair shorter in the Dutch manner, his wild waves tossing about in the breeze.

Lucy quickly picked up Emma and made her way over to them, her heart racing. How was it that he was in London and he had not called on her? She was about twenty paces away when he seemed to notice her. But instead of coming toward her, he oddly moved behind the stall out of her sight. Perhaps he hadn't seen her after all. Nonplussed, Lucy strode up with Emma in her arms. Dominick's companion was turning to leave. She looked behind the stall for Dominick, but he was gone. Looking past the row of stalls and carts, she scanned the crowd for him knowing that it would be difficult to follow him, even if she could see him, burdened as she was with Emma. But there was no sign of him in any direction. Did she simply imagine that she had seen him? She called out his name, but it was Dominick's companion who responded. He smiled at her and bowed. He was an attractive man, with warm oval eyes and an easy manner.

"Senhorita," he said, bowing politely.

"You are a friend of Domingo Lacerda?"

"Semuel Soeiro," he answered her in a thick accent. He sounded Dutch, even though he looked Portuguese. This must be the Semuel of whom Dominick always spoke.

"But where did he go?" Lucy asked, scanning the crowds again.

"Ah, Senhorita, he was called away. Is there a message for him?"

Lucy was hurt and confused. It had been so long since they'd spoken. How could he run off like that? "Sir, if you could tell him . . ." She did not know what to say to Dominick's friend. She wanted to tell Dominick that she still loved him. She wanted to hold him and feel the warmth of his skin against hers. "I am gladdened to see him home in London. My name is—"

"Lucy Dunnington," he finished for her. "I have heard of you."

This lifted Lucy's spirits. "Is he well?"

"Do not fear," he began dramatically. "Our friend is as gloomy and hard-working as ever."

She smiled. "He said you were funny."

"He said you were fair," he shot back. Lucy blushed and looked away. Emma had finished her treat and was now wiping her sticky hands on Lucy's bodice. Semuel laughed as if he had planned this performance to follow his compliment. "But who is this?" he asked, motioning to Emma. "Has Senhorita Dunnington become a Senhora?"

"Oh no," Lucy said quickly. "Emma is my sister. We came to the market to meet her mother and—"

"Maaaaama!" Emma cried suddenly. Lucy tried to quiet the child, but then she soon realized the source of Emma's excitement.

"Lucy! Emma darling!" Elizabeth lifted Emma away from Lucy and, although she was relieved of the child's weight, she realized with dismay that her bodice was ruined as it was covered with sweet cake and drool. Holding Emma had at least disguised most of the damage. But now there was nothing for it. Elizabeth was clutching her daughter lovingly. "Lucy, who is your gentleman friend?"

"Elizabeth, may I present Semuel Soeiro of Amsterdam. He is a friend of Dominick Lacerda's." She turned to Semuel. "Mister Soeiro, Elizabeth Dunnington, and this little one hiding behind her skirts is Thomas." Lucy made the introductions, but even after five years, she was still unsure of how to formally address her father's wife. She liked Elizabeth, but as Lucy matured it was clear that the two women could not live in harmony much longer. Elizabeth was firm about her place as lady of the house and Lucy's role as elder daughter. Now that Lucy was nineteen, this arrangement was becoming untenable.

"A pleasure, sir," Elizabeth said.

"The pleasure is mine, Senhora Dunnington." Semuel bowed to her. This seemed to please Elizabeth. He turned to Lucy. "Menina Dunnington, I am happy to have met you and I will give your regards to our friend." After a tip of his hat, Semuel disappeared into the crowd.

"What a charming gentleman, Lucy. You must tell me all about him. But first, I am bursting to show you the most delightful fabric I've found for Emma's new dresses." And so Lucy's attention was captive to cloths of various colors and textures for the next hour.

◆◆◆

Lucy was sure he would come during the next week, but she was disappointed in this hope. The weather turned chill and soon it was winter. Lucy knew she could simply ask her father about Dominick, but she did not want to arouse his ire about her noncommittal stance with Edward Polestead. In December, her father brought up the issue one evening after the children had been put to bed.

"Lucy, I saw Edward this afternoon and he asked after you." Lucy paused in her mending, and her father continued, "He is hopeful of a bride by Candlemas."

Lucy looked over at Elizabeth, who caught her eye before addressing her husband. "Darling, with winter upon us, I do so need Lucy here to help with the children. Could we agree on a spring wedding?"

Lucy did not know whether to be thankful or furious. Perhaps Elizabeth had just bought her three more months, yet to set a wedding date meant that the engagement would be final. Further delays after this would result in a loss of face for her father.

"What think you, Lucy?" her father asked her enthusiastically.

She hated herself but replied obediently, "Come springtime, Father, you may give me as a bride."

"Excellent!" He rose from his chair, arms open. "Come here, daughter, and let me kiss you!" Lucy went to him and offered her cheek. Then her father said, "I will speak to Edward tomorrow. You may expect him to call on you soon." Lucy nodded, feeling numb. In pleasing her father by agreeing to marry Edward Polestead she was simultaneously giving up on Dominick, her Catholic religion, and any hope of living in Yorkshire at Chapel House. Yet Dominick had not come and her father would not let her remain unwed.

That night and for several nights after, she cried herself to sleep. Elizabeth came to her chamber once to comfort her. "Lucy, I cannot bear to see you so unhappy. Please tell me what's troubling you. Are you so afraid of marriage?"

Lucy wiped her eyes and shook her head. "No, Elizabeth. I want nothing more than to marry soon, and Mr. Polestead is very kind. It's just that," she stopped, realizing that if she said out loud that Dominick did not love her it might actually be true.

"What, Lucy?" Elizabeth pressed.

"I saw him in October at the market. He was in London and did not come."

"Who, dear?"

"Dominick," she said, sobbing.

Elizabeth rubbed Lucy's back tenderly as if she were an infant. "That man from Amsterdam, he was a friend of his?" Lucy nodded and Elizabeth continued, "You saw Dominick? What did he say to you?"

"That's the point, Elizabeth," Lucy said between sobs. "He said nothing. He left before I could speak with him. I was so sure he'd come." She began weeping afresh. Elizabeth just held and rocked her stepdaughter gently in her arms.

"Lucy, darling, shall I speak to your father about Dominick? Perhaps—"

"No!" Lucy exclaimed. "Please, Elizabeth, say nothing. If Dominick does not come of his own will, then there is little hope."

"I always suspected you had an attachment. I do wish you had told me, Lucy. Tell me, what caused its rupture? Is it that Dominick is a Catholic?" Lucy did not respond, just wept all the harder. "Did you misunderstand his intentions, Lucy? I know you were friends, but when a man is choosing a bride, he seeks not a scholar but a helpmeet. Domingo is very young and surely does not know his own mind yet. Edward Polestead is a good match for you. He is older, established, and will provide handsomely for you. In many ways, he reminds me of your father when I married him."

Lucy did not respond to Elizabeth's words, but she allowed her stepmother to comfort her with promises of happy days ahead. It was not the comfort Lucy wanted, but Elizabeth meant well and eventually Lucy began to accept Elizabeth's vision of her future.

◆◆◆

Domingo and Semuel had been in London for six months and still Cromwell would not give Semuel an audience. Semuel's letters to his father remained optimistic, but Domingo could see that his friend was increasingly frustrated with his failure. Even the London kehilla hesitated to welcome the son of Menasseh ben Israel, and many in the Cree Church Lane neighborhood treated Semuel coolly. He was cordially received in the synagogue and in a few individual homes, but no outpouring of support followed his arrival.

Winter seemed endless to Domingo. It was bitterly cold and his shoulder ached constantly, even as his hip gave him less trouble of late. Senhor Robles had his physician attend to Domingo but, other than rest and steamed cloths pressed against his shoulder to ease the ache, there was little that could be done. Dr. Abrunel suggested opium to ease his discomfort, but Domingo feared the dullness that accompanied the relief that the pipe gave. Now that the pain was not so acute, it was better to suffer it than to spend half a day recovering from the opium. He realized that, even though well over a year had passed since his accident, this pain would never leave him and he would have to learn to live with it. He grimly placed it in the same category as his love for Lucy: that which could not be banished had to be managed somehow.

On Domingo's twenty-first birthday in March, his apprenticeship to Manuel was formally completed and he subsequently began to work directly with Senhor Robles at his home in Duke's Place as his personal bookkeeper. Domingo welcomed the change as it meant he was less likely to run into Lucy. Once or twice he'd spied her with Elizabeth and the children in the market. He wanted so much to speak with her, to write to her, even though he knew that any communication between them would only prolong the pain of their parting by creating a false hope.

◆◆◆

In early spring, Semuel learned from one of Cromwell's courtiers of his wish to meet with Menasseh ben Israel in person. Disappointed in Cromwell's decision, but relieved that there was finally some resolution to his efforts, Semuel planned to go back to Amsterdam to escort his father to London. Despite Semuel's cheerful response to the news that he would be able to return home, Domingo suspected that his friend felt like a failure for not being able to personally press his father's petition with the Lord Protector of England. When Semuel asked Domingo to accompany him to Amsterdam in May, Domingo knew for sure that his friend was hurting from his shame. He tried to speak with Semuel about the situation, but Semuel, usually so open, preferred to keep his own counsel regarding his father's petitions and the mission to Oliver Cromwell.

Five days before Semuel and Domingo were due to leave for Amsterdam, Manuel asked to see Domingo privately. They met in a coffeehouse on Fleet Street. Manuel wanted to speak of the haham's upcoming visit to London. "I don't sense support among our people for what the haham and Semuel seek. You must try to convince him not to do this," he instructed Domingo.

Domingo sighed heavily. "Manuel, I don't know that Haham ben Israel would be deterred. He's sacrificed so much already for this mission, and with the endorsement of the Lord Protector, he is closer than he's ever been before."

Manuel bristled at Domingo's response. "What if he fails? What happens to our families? We have so much to lose. Some are already talking of relocating to Jamaica and Barbados. Haham ben Israel seeks to save the Jews, but his mission could expose us and lead to our destruction. Your haham cannot protect us from those in London who wish us ill, Domingo."

Domingo hung his head. "I understand. I will do what I can. Senhor Carvajal will want the haham and Semuel to board elsewhere while they are in London?"

"Yes, cousin. They cannot board in our neighborhood. It would bring too much suspicion on us. It would also be best for you to limit your association with Semuel and his father. The haham has many Gentile friends; if these men see you with him, they will know you are a Jew." Domingo nodded sadly at his cousin's request. He understood Manuel's concerns, but they conflicted with his friendship with the ben Israels. He had lost one friend out of duty to the London kehilla; now Manuel was asking him to forsake another.

Manuel took a long sip of his coffee and set down the empty cup awkwardly. "There is another matter I would discuss with you, cousin." He took a deep breath before continuing, "Dunnington's daughter is to be married tomorrow. I thought you should know."

It was as if Manuel had just thrust a knife into his heart. It took several moments for the pain in his chest to subside enough for Domingo to breathe again. As he opened his lips to speak, his eyes began to water, and he screwed them shut against Manuel's knowing gaze.

"Where?"

"Domingo, please. Do not interfere in this," Manuel said gently.

He fought the urge to strike his cousin. "I won't. You know this. You told me to give her up, and I did. I've been in London for nine months and I haven't contacted her once. I just want to see it concluded."

"St. Bride's at eleven o'clock."

♦♦♦

The Church of St. Bride's was modest despite its steep tower that seemed to penetrate heaven itself. It was squeezed in among the tightly packed houses and printing shops on Fleet Street so it was easy for Domingo to blend in with the morning bustle. He watched the wedding procession from a coffeehouse nearby. As he caught sight of Lucy, he felt the tightening in his chest again. She looked beautiful and, to Domingo's relief, happy. Soon she would be the wife of another, and when Domingo left for Amsterdam in three days, he could do so with a clear conscience. Not speaking with her while he was in London had taken every bit of willpower he possessed. He was worn out from guilt and the fear of running into her in public.

After what seemed like just minutes, the doors to St. Bride's opened and the wedding party spilled out in joyful disarray. Domingo turned away from the scene. He did not want to see her face as another man's wife. It was enough to know that the deed was done. No matter how the hahimim interpreted the law, he believed that she'd been his wife first. But now he'd truly lost her. He felt sick and dizzy. As soon as he returned home, he took to his bed. Despite his mother's ministrations and Semuel's pleas for company, he did not leave his chamber until the morning he was due to leave for Amsterdam.

◆◆◆

Summer passed quickly for Lucy. Edward's home was located in the fashionable neighborhood between Aldwych Street and the Strand. One might think it a handsome place given the address, but Lucy found Edward's home to be adequately furnished but bland and cheerless. She threw herself into making his house her home, changing the drab window drapes for colorful ones and adding warmth and color to the rooms with rugs and wall hangings. In addition to these efforts, there were frequent visits with Elizabeth and the children back on Fleet Street. Because of Elizabeth's pregnancies, she had not made the long trip to Thicket Hall in Yorkshire for several years. But in July, Elizabeth and Lucy took the children north for two months, leaving their husbands to the noisy, dirty streets of London.

Summer in Yorkshire renewed Lucy's spirit. She luxuriated in the fineness of Thicket Hall, its quiet gardens, and Elizabeth's informal management. Now that she was married, Lucy sensed a pleasant shift in her relationship with Elizabeth. Each was mistress of her own home rather than a competitor for John Dunnington's attention; Lucy found she better appreciated Elizabeth's company and conversation on this equal footing, even as she still cherished the time she could steal away to be alone in Thicket Hall's gardens. She often spent hours doing nothing but staring at the birds, flowers, and bugs. It was a welcome relief to be an observer of their world rather than an actor in her own. Late in the summer, though, she found that her solace could have pleasant interruptions.

"Lucy, there you are," exclaimed Elizabeth, coming upon her in the garden late one morning. "Look at you sitting in the grass like one of the children. Whatever are you doing?"

Lucy greeted her stepmother with a warm smile. "I'm waiting for butterflies, Elizabeth. If you sit very still and have patience, they will come."

"Well, while you wait on your garden creatures, your cousin Frances has arrived. She's only just back from France but she insisted on seeing you straightaway. You'll find her in the music room visiting with the children."

Lucy jumped up. "Frances!" They walked back inside together and joined in the playful songs Frances was teaching Thomas and Emma.

After lunching with Elizabeth and the children, Lucy and Frances walked the wooded path from Thicket Hall to Chapel House together. Frances linked her arm through Lucy's. "So, cousin, how are you enjoying married life? I envy you so. Sebastian promises to make me a bride when his law studies are completed, but that is still two years away."

Lucy gave Frances's arm a little squeeze. "Patience, Frances. He will honor his promise. Sebastian loves you."

Frances glowed at Lucy's pronouncements. "Tell me about your husband, Lucy," she asked by way of response.

"Edward is kind. He works hard," Lucy replied, adding, "He is a good match."

Frances stared hard at her cousin. "You still think about the apprentice, don't you?"

"Please, Frances, don't." Lucy hung her head. "That is over. Edward is my husband and my affection belongs to him alone." Frances said nothing; they walked in silence for a while. When they came upon Chapel House, Lucy took a deep, satisfied breath. "Look, Frances. My house. Someday our children will play together on these grounds."

Frances laughed. "Yes, well, you must get pregnant and I must get married."

◆◆◆

Back in London later that month, Lucy reflected on the silences in her conversation with Frances. Edward was a good husband. She'd not lied to her cousin. He gave her a comfortable home and treated her with kindness even if he did not encourage her opinions while often instructing her in his own. She was particularly disturbed by his hatred for Jews and Catholics. In this he really wasn't so different from most other Englishmen she knew. All the same, she was determined to try to be a good wife to him.

But she found it difficult to forget Dominick. It had been three years since she'd spoken to him and a year since she'd spotted him at the Covent Garden market. She often felt that if she could just understand why he had severed their friendship she might think about him less. Whenever she thought about seeing him in the market, a surge of frustration and anger would rise in her breast. Despite her anger, however, she also burned to know if he was all right.

As the year ended, it became increasingly difficult for Lucy not to worry. Menasseh ben Israel had arrived with his son in London and had presented petitions to Cromwell and Parliament for Jewish readmission to England. These petitions had caused an uproar among the merchant community; Edward was particularly vexed about the latest developments concerning readmission.

"Blasted Cromwell," he spat one day. "Now there's to be a conference at Whitehall to discuss letting the Jewish filth back into the country. I swear His Highness believes himself to be Moses leading the Hebrews to the Promised Land. Well, England is not going to be their Canaan, I can tell you that. Good Englishmen are not going to suffer this without a fight. Next he'll be letting Papists and Turks into the country!"

"Edward," Lucy began, trying to produce a sweet and ignorant tone so as not to irritate him further. "What harm could the Jews do to us? Are we not strong in our faith?"

146

Edward switched to the pedantic tone he used when instructing her and said, "Lucy, I don't expect you to understand the finer points of this issue. Suffice it to say that these people are a poison to Christianity and to commerce. They are vile usurers and cheats. Their worship is lewd, they are diseased, and they smell of the rotten flesh that they are."

Lucy hated to hear these accusations issue from her husband's mouth even though she knew they were commonly held among Londoners. She recalled the sweet smell of Dominick's skin and hair. Contrary to what Edward claimed, Dominick was perhaps the cleanest man she had ever known, fully bathing before each Sabbath and frequently washing his hands and face during the day in accordance with the Jewish cleanliness laws for prayers. "I see you know much about the Jews, Edward. Have you had many dealings with them?" Lucy asked, trying to mask her defiance of his views in a light, girlish voice.

Edward frowned at this suggestion. "Of course not! Why would I have anything to do with the Jews?"

"Oh, I see. I just thought that since you know so much about their ways that you must have some experience with them . . ." Lucy trailed off when she noticed how agitated Edward was becoming.

"Lucy, the ways of the Jews are plain to anyone who bothers to read our sacred scriptures with the accounts of their deeds," he sputtered, his face reddening in anger.

She knew better but she could not stop herself from arguing with him further. "Scripture tells us that the Jews are God's chosen people and that he will redeem them. Our own Savior was of their nation."

Edward narrowed his eyes at her. "Wife, I do not like the direction of your words. You begin to sound like one of the Separatists. Why do you defend the Jews to me? Do not be blind, Lucy. You must know what they are—cursed, cast out, and rejected by our God. There is no hope for their conversion, and their settlement will only bring ruin to England. Tell me you see this!"

She shook her head defiantly. "I do not, Edward."

He was shocked. He stormed out of the room and made to leave the house, but then he suddenly came to her once again, clearly still angry, but controlling his temper. "You are a woman; therefore I will forgive your foolish compassion and inability to understand what is truly at stake. But I forbid you to speak of this again to me or to anyone else. I'll not have Jews living in England, and I will not have my wife oppose me in this." He turned and strode out, leaving Lucy feeling her heart harden a little against him.

◆◆◆

Oliver Cromwell had set up the ben Israels in a house on the Strand. Domingo was pleased at their fine accommodations. The Cree Church Lane community was unwilling to support Menasseh ben Israel's mission to Oliver Cromwell and Domingo had feared that the ben Israels would live in poverty while in London. He and his mother still lived above the Delgados, even though he'd completed his apprenticeship over eight months ago. He was saving as much as he could so that he could lease a home for the two of them, but it was too soon yet for them to move to Amsterdam. Besides this, Senhor Robles had been cool to Domingo's request to take on the Amsterdam business. Domingo supposed he should take it as a compliment, Manuel had not even attained such an intimate position in Senhor Robles's household, but he found, instead, that he was vexed with Senhor Robles for insisting that he remain in London to oversee his personal accounts.

◆◆◆

It was now October and the first Sabbath following Sukkot. Despite Manuel's warning six months earlier, Domingo was celebrating the Sabbath with the haham and Semuel. To his surprise, the haham had also invited two Gentile friends to the meal, John Sadler and Henry Jessey, Englishmen who supported the readmission petitions Menasseh had presented to Cromwell and Parliament.

When Domingo arrived, Semuel detained him in the foyer. "What we have feared has come to pass. My father received notice yesterday that he has been expelled from the council of hahimim in Amsterdam and has consequently been relieved of his post at the Torah Talmud School."

Domingo knew this was not a surprise, but it was sure to greatly dishearten the haham. "How is he?"

Semuel shrugged. "As well as can be expected. He busies himself with other matters and dismisses my concern for him. He's

148

had a constant stream of visitors since we arrived, including Mr. Sadler, who has been a strong advocate for Father's petition. I am glad you've come, Amiel. It is good for Mr. Sadler to see that Father has friends of our nation in London."

Domingo recalled Manuel's warning. "Semuel, I came here as your friend, not as a representative of the London kehilla. They don't know I am here and, to be honest, they wouldn't like it. There is a lot of fear."

Semuel's expression darkened. "I see. We'll tell our English guests that you are our friend from Amsterdam." He briskly turned away from Domingo and strode into the parlor where his father sat with his Gentile guests. Domingo held back for a moment, not sure if he should feel ashamed or relieved. It seemed he could not avoid disappointing the people he loved. Reluctantly, he followed Semuel into the parlor.

John Sadler was an elegant figure of a gentleman, about forty years old and sporting a head of thinning gray hair. His speech was animated, although it seemed as if each word was carefully weighed before he spoke. This was a man whose conversation was deceptively offhand. The second visitor, Henry Jessey, was older, perhaps by fifteen years or more, and appeared more careworn. He wore a black suit that made his balding head all the more apparent for its pinkness under the thin strands of his mousy-brown and white-flecked hair. Jessey possessed the slow, commanding speech of a practiced preacher.

The five men made polite conversation over dinner, but later, back in the parlor, their discussion centered on the redemption of the Jews and the millennial hopes of the Protestants in England. Mr. Sadler was advocating readmission as a means for the Jews to see Christianity in its true form as practiced in England.

He explained, "Naturally Jews living in Papist countries have not been convinced to convert for the corrupt version of Christianity practiced there. If it were not for the Papists, most peoples of the world would have likely already converted to Christianity. In England, the Jews will be able to see true Christianity lived out each day. Only in England will they come to know the Lord."

Domingo was curious to learn more about this scheme, but he also found it insulting. "Mr. Sadler, it would seem that the majority of Englishmen do not favor Jewish readmission as you do. Why do you think this is so?"

"It is fear, Mr. Lacerda. Fear of past blasphemies, fear of the anger of God, and fear of what they don't understand."

"What do you feel they do not understand about Jews, sir?" he asked, feeling himself being drawn into a trap but unable to resist arguing with this sincere, but arrogant, Christian.

Mr. Sadler leaned forward toward Domingo. "Christians do not understand why you reject Jesus when it is so obvious that he is the Messiah."

Domingo unwittingly took the bait. "Then they ignore our teachings about the Messiah. Jesus was a reformer of merit but he was not of David's line. According to the Gospels, that bloodline runs through his earthly father, Joseph, whom Christians claim was not the true father of their Lord. Neither did Jesus restore Israel or bring peace to his people as the prophets' state the Messiah must do. Within forty years of his resurrection, the temple was destroyed and the Jews were scattered over the face of the earth. Given this evidence, he cannot have been the anointed one."

"Amiel, please," begged Menasseh. "No good can come from dismissing Christian beliefs about the Messiah."

"We cannot expect you to understand," Mr. Jessey said in the confident, condescending manner of Christian clerics. This earned him a frown from Semuel. But Mr. Jessey did not see Semuel's disapproving look as he fixed his eyes on Domingo. It was as if he felt that with his sincere gaze alone he would convince Domingo of his error. "Christians see the prophecies already perfectly fulfilled. In a spiritual sense, Jesus was in the line of David, the anointed king of Israel. Jesus created the church, which is a restoration of his kingdom on earth, and the peace he brings is the peace of the soul, free from eternal damnation. God's salvation, beginning with Abraham, and then rejected by the Pharisees, is being fulfilled here in England in our age. This is Jerusalem, not that pile of dirt the Catholics and the Muslims squabble over."

Domingo scoffed at this. "With respect, sir, that is a creative interpretation of the prophecies. And how is it that England fits into the redemption? Are you saying that God would forsake the Jews for the English?"

"All our scriptures point to this," Mr. Jessey answered matter-of-factly, leaning back in his chair and taking a satisfied sip of his brandy.

"But they are *our* scriptures that Christians have taken and twisted to meet their own ends," argued Domingo, feeling his anger rise. "Is England's own history so poor that she needs to steal that of the Jews? We've lost our land and our freedom, and now you suggest that our history is no longer our own."

Menasseh looked uncomfortable, but he said nothing. It was Mr. Sadler who answered Domingo in his diplomatic manner. "In rejecting Christ, the Jews reject their own history. When the Jews convert to the true faith, they will be restored to God's graces and the history of salvation."

Before Domingo could respond, Menasseh interjected, "We can all agree that Mr. Sadler is correct in his assessment of Papist Christianity. The hand of God is not in the Inquisition." He gave Domingo a knowing look.

Domingo thought of what Baruch had said about seeing the hand of God in man's irrational acts. Of course the Inquisition was not God's work, but the Catholics believed that it was, just as these men believed that England was the new Promised Land and the English were the chosen people who graciously allowed the Jews to eat the crumbs from their spiritual feast. These thoughts angered him, yet he understood the haham's look of warning. He had to somehow make up for arguing with the haham's guests.

"Certainly this is true, Hakham. God surely does not administer the Inquisition. Let us hope he advocates the restoration of Israel in England."

He looked over at Semuel, who had been silent during the conversation. His friend looked tired but smiled at Domingo, at once thanking him for standing up to the Christians but also for not embarrassing his father. There was so much that they would never agree on, but they understood each other, and both trusted that their bond of friendship would sustain them through any difficulties.

XII. *WHITEHALL,*
DECEMBER 1655 – JANUARY 1656

Huddled with Semuel by the ungenerous fire in his apartment's small hearth, Domingo read aloud the broadsheets reporting on the Whitehall Conference, the gathering at which Oliver Cromwell was sounding out his plan to readmit the Jews to England. "There's no author to this set, but they were printed at the Seven Stars," he said, holding up the large sheets for Semuel to see.

"How does that signify?"

"The Seven Stars is a press near St. Paul's Cathedral. They've printed tracts by some of your father's supporters."

Semuel nodded. "Let's hear them then."

Domingo cleared his throat and began to read: "An account of the first meeting of the Whitehall Conference, December 4, 1655. After conferring a moment with his trusted advisor Henry Jessey, the Lord Protector, His Highness Oliver Cromwell, took his place at the center of the floor and spoke, 'Gentlemen, truly it is our business to speak here today! The dispensations of God that are upon us do require it; and that subject upon which we shall make our discourse is of very great interest and concernment, both for the glory of God and the people within these three nations of England, Scotland, and Ireland. In the matter before us, the readmission of the Jews to our domains, I put before you two questions: First, is it lawful to admit the Jews? Next, is it expedient to admit them?'

"'On this day I welcome your counsel on the first question, as we cannot hope to proceed in this matter without lawful admission. My lord chief barons, lord chief justices, and most holy ministers of God, you meet here to advise by reason, by law-learning, and by scripture-prophecy the proposal of admitting the Jews, with certain privileges as of alien citizens, to reside in England. They were banished near four hundred years ago and now, at the request of the most noble rabbi of Amsterdam, Menasseh ben Israel, we solemnly consider his petition for readmission to the realm.'"

"Is that all?" Semuel looked up at Domingo in surprise.

"No, I'm skimming a bit. Here, I'm going to read the lord chief justice's speech regarding the history of the Jews in England. 'It has been documented that Jews accompanied the French conqueror, William of Normandy, in his suppression of this island six hundred years ago. He drew them chiefly from Rouen, where they engaged in money-lending. Within a short time of their settlement on this island, they began to carry out diabolical rituals on Christian children. It was reported by Prior Thomas of Monmouth that in 1144 an apprentice to a tanner, a William of Norwich, was brutally murdered by means of crucifixion by the Jews of Norwich, who then collected his blood for use during their Passover feast. Those responsible for this crime were not called before the law, nor were they punished in any way.'

"'We are then told of the martyrdom of Hugh of Lincoln, a nine-year-old child abducted by the Jews, crucified, and cruelly thrown into a well. Over one hundred Jews admitted to the boy's murder and testified that it was the custom for them to crucify a Christian child each year before the Passover. Of this pack of murderous men, only eighteen hanged for their crime. Let it be known that over twenty such murders of Christian children were reported in the kingdom of England from the time the Jews were brought in by the Conqueror to their expulsion. Good King Edward I saw fit to remove the Jews from the kingdom of England in 1290.'

"'Our present question of the law, regarding Jewish readmission, seems to rest on the nature of that edict, which some believe was the independent action of the king and others believe was at the request of the holy church and the lord barons. I do, very respectfully, present to you the edict of July 1290, which reads thus: "King Edward having willed it, all Jews, with their goods, children, and wives, are thus banished at the feast of All Saints from the land of England and of Aquitaine."'

"The chief justice concluded with, 'I am satisfied in this matter that the edict of banishment was not an act of Parliament but a matter of the king alone. I would not give my consent to the petition of the representative of the nation of Israel, yet I cannot find in our law any hindrance to its passage. After careful examination of the case, I must conclude that the original edict of banishment was issued solely by His Royal Highness, King Edward I, and directed only to those Jews living in his dominions at that time. It was, in my mind, not a permanent edict, and it was certainly not a law approved by Parliament. I must then answer to Your Highness, our Lord Protector of the three kingdoms of Britain, that there is no law preventing the resettlement of the Jews herein.'"

"Outrageous!" Semuel exclaimed, sitting up straight in his chair.

"Which part?"

"The recounting of those ridiculous stories about child murders before proclaiming no legal barrier to Jewish readmission. The chief justice was trying to predispose the council against us."

Domingo flipped through the broadsheets. "Here's a report from the second day on December 7. Shall I read it?"

"Yes, yes, go on," Semuel said, sighing.

"This bit is from a speech by Dr. Newcomen, an independent minister from London. He said, 'I respectfully submit to you that it is a grave sin to allow the Jews public worship service in which Christ will be blasphemed. It is well-known that they direct their prayers against Christians, they make a mockery of the sacrifice of our Lord, and their rituals are of the most provocative sort. The curses that God justly punished them with will certainly be visited on England should we allow those whom God has forsaken to settle among us. I have read the accounts of Jewish converts to Christianity and am deeply shocked at what they report of their former errors. It is well established among the Jews the ancient practice of offering a child, the firstborn son, to the pagan god Moloch for the satisfaction of his anger and the protection of their tribe. Let us not minimize the possibility of these Jews trying to seduce Christians to their false religion. Imagine, gentlemen, the danger of an Englishman converting to Judaism and then sacrificing his son to this murderous deity! Imagine an Englishman offering up his son as a sacrifice for the sake of some superstitious belief! It is a blasphemy, and we must not allow such barbarity in our Christian nation!'"

Domingo paused for breath, then continued reading, "A counterview was offered by two Anglican divines, Dr. Barlow and Dr. Wilkinson, who presented this statement, read by Dr. Wilkinson: 'We have agreed that there are certain merits to Jewish readmission that must not be overlooked. Of especial interest would be the merit gained by our Christian nation for encouraging the conversion of the Jews to the true faith. As the Jews mainly reside now in Papist lands, there cannot be any hope of their conversion or their redemption. We feel it to be the duty, nay, England's unique calling, to carry out God's will in this matter. We cannot hope for Jews to turn from error to salvation when they languish in Papist lands. For this reason, we must endeavor to settle those whose hearts have not been hardened by their false faith in God's New Jerusalem in England. It is, however, important that they not be forcibly converted, for that is a Papist custom abhorred by true Christians, but there must be certain limits placed on their practice while they persist in error. The mistaken ways of the Jews must be tolerated as they work toward their salvation, but their sins must be contained. It is with this in mind that we submit the following restrictions to their worship. First, while they reside in England, Jews may not seek divorce or the dissolution of their lawful marriages as is allowed according to their customs. Second, the circumcision of any male shall be prohibited; the circumcision of a Christian will be punishable by death. Third, unconverted Jews shall not be allowed to marry Christians. Fourth, the practice of working on the Christian Sabbath shall be prohibited. And finally, Jews shall not be exempt from swearing oaths of allegiance to the nation of England.'"

"Moloch?" Semuel huffed. "Offering up one's son to die for a superstitious belief? On what do these Christians think their own religion is based?"

Domingo ignored his friend's comment, too engrossed in rereading the passage suggesting a law against marriage between a Christian and a Jew.

"Amiel!"

"What?"

"I asked you to read the next report. There is one more, no?"

155

"Right," Domingo said, distractedly shifting the papers in his hands again. "December 12, 1655, Whitehall Conference. The day opened with a speech given by former army chaplain Hugh Peters, who, at one time, supported readmission but has now come around to the majority opinion. He said, 'It has come to me of late that there are a few Jews living among us now practicing as Papists. Deception upon deception! What honor, gentlemen, is there in such an existence? To use the religion of the anti-Christ as a mask to cover up the stink of their Jewish decay is unconscionable and blasphemous. This is allowed by their own tradition, even their rabbis participate in the deception. In admitting the Jews to our Christian land, we would encourage a self-seeking people who make little conscience of their own principles. We cannot hope to convert such a hard-hearted people.'

"Then Moses Wall, translator of Menasseh ben Israel's *Hope of Israel* and independent chaplain to Lord Warwick, gave an impassioned speech supporting readmission on the grounds that it was the duty of Christians to be merciful to those first called. He called the Jews God's 'first wife' and insisted that the Jews would be redeemed by God. He closed his speech in this way: 'I do firmly believe, and fear not to profess it, that the Jews shall be called as a nation and have an earthly kingdom again!' He received some small applause for his heartfelt words, but in general, this speech was not favored by those in attendance."

Semuel looked up at Domingo. "Is that all of it, then?"

Domingo nodded. "Yes, but there is another meeting next week. I don't want to wait for the broadsheets this time. If we linger outside, we can perhaps waylay one of the runners to find out what took place."

"All right," Semuel said. "Come by at three. We can walk over there together."

◆◆◆

A brisk, wet wind whipped about them as Semuel and Domingo waited by the riverfront for some word of the proceedings at the fourth Whitehall session. It was only four o'clock, but the sky was already darkening. Semuel paced about the street, frequently cupping his hands and blowing warm breath into them. He'd been edgy these past weeks, at once trying to reassure his father that his petitions would succeed while at the same time falling into long periods of worried silence about their mission in England.

Nervous with anticipation, Domingo scanned Upper Thames Street for runners headed for the coffeehouses or print shops. It was the job of runners, usually boys of apprenticing age, to deliver messages from conference members to their contacts, who, more often than not, were newspaper men and pamphleteers. In the growing dark, it would be harder to spot them. At one point, he thought he saw Mr. Dunnington's former translator, the hateful Mr. Knevett, rushing from Whitehall toward Fleet Street, but in the dark he could not be sure if it was him or not.

Domingo lit the wick of his lantern with the assistance of an accommodating carriage driver waiting outside a private residence, then he walked down the road a few yards for a better view. And then, coming out of the shadows, he saw her walking down the street toward him. Her charcoal gray walking dress was elegant, and it made her seem different from the girl he had loved. There was a sense of sober propriety about her that was new. As she came closer, he could see her breath in the cold air and found that he longed to feel its warmth on his face. His heart began to hammer wildly in his chest, but then he noticed she was not alone. The older man must be her husband, Edward Polestead. The couple stopped outside of a small warehouse and the man entered. Lucy continued on alone.

Without really thinking about it, Domingo ran toward her. Semuel followed, calling after him, "Amiel! Where are you going? Have you spotted a runner?"

"Lucy!" Domingo cried, trying to get her attention in the midst of the dark and the crowded street.

Hearing his friend's cry, Semuel shouted, "Amiel, no!" But Domingo was now just a few lengths away from her.

She stumbled at the sight of him, but she caught herself without assistance. As he stood before her, she would not meet his eyes, choosing instead to look at Semuel, who had just come up alongside his friend. Domingo seemed not to notice her discomfort. "Lucy, how good it is to see you," he said, staring at her raptly. At this, her countenance changed from shock to anger. Domingo reached for her gloved hand but she wrenched it away. "Lucy," he started, surprised at her reaction.

"How dare you," she accused hotly, trying at the same time to keep her voice from being overheard by passersby. "You refused to see me or answer my letters, and now that I am safely married, you greet me like a friend!"

"Lucita," Domingo said in almost a whisper, unsure of how to respond. Finally, he decided to tackle the issue head on. "It was not my place to sway your decision."

She looked at him incredulously. "Just one word, Dominick. One word of encouragement and I would have waited for you."

He was taken aback by this admission. "But, Lucy, I had no words of encouragement to offer. You know this is true."

"I know no such thing."

The tears welling up in her eyes threw his every resolve of the last year into confusion. "Please, may I speak with you? Tomorrow perhaps?"

"No. What is done cannot be undone. Please do not contact me again." The hurt look on his face pained her, so she looked away. "I must get home," she said weakly, staring at the ground.

Semuel stepped forward. "May I escort Senhora home?" he asked, offering his arm. Lucy noticed at that moment how thin and pale Semuel had become. When she had met him last year, she'd been struck by his good looks. Now she was struck by how depreciated he seemed. But Semuel's personality did not seem affected by his ill health. His smile, contrasted with Domingo's injured expression, heartened her.

"Thank you, Senhor Soeiro. But I am quite capable of making my way alone." She brushed past them without another word.

Domingo stood there stunned. He was not sure what he had expected, but it was not this. He had been so sure that their many years apart and her marriage would have cooled her feelings. Why did she seem so happy on her wedding day if she would have refused to marry with one word from him? She seemed to detest him now. His head was spinning. He looked at Semuel. "I need to get away from here."

The merchants of London brought the full might of their power to bear on the Lord Protector, so he agreed to open the next session of the Whitehall Conference to the public. Thus, it was early in the morning on December 18, a full two hours before the session was set to begin, that the Council Hall was packed with merchants, agents, and tradesmen. Today Domingo waited for word of the proceedings by himself. Semuel had claimed sickness and had declined Domingo's invitation to spend the day outside Whitehall.

It seemed that everywhere Domingo had gone in the past week he'd heard men heatedly arguing about the readmission question. In the coffeehouses, from the pulpit, even on the docks, the Jews were maligned as moneylenders, coin clippers, blasphemers, and foreigners who would only bring ruin to the nation. Domingo was certain that this was the work of William Prynne, whose pamphlet *A Short Demurrer to the Jews* was published just four days past.

Even the usually unruffled Senhor Robles had spouted off about the writer that morning before he'd sent Domingo to Whitehall. "He is a scoundrel who would stop at nothing to have his name in the news, and I wonder if he feels as strongly against the nation of Israel as his abuse of them suggests. He had his ears clipped for writing against the late king, yet Prynne does not support Cromwell either. He seems to push against whatever wind currently blows. Unfortunately, he has given voice to the bigotry of the English merchants."

Well after darkness fell, Domingo saw men begin to file out of Whitehall's banqueting hall and into the streets. Trailing behind those who traveled on foot, Domingo hoped to fall into conversation with a talkative merchant on his way to a tavern. But chance offered him an even better opportunity. Just ahead of him, John Dunnington walked alone.

"Mr. Dunnington, sir!" Domingo caught up with him as he crossed the Strand on to Fleet Street.

John was taken aback for a moment, but then he warmly embraced him. "Domingo! Good God, boy, it's been what, three years since you left us?"

Domingo bit his lip, ashamed of the mention of his banishment to Amsterdam. "Yes, sir. But I've been back in London since October. I traveled with Menasseh ben Israel."

John raised his eyebrows in surprise. "The rabbi from Amsterdam? I didn't know you were acquainted with him."

"The rabbi was my teacher when I was a boy. I lived with his family while I was in Amsterdam, but now I am home."

"Then I'm sure you've followed the events of this last week very closely, son."

"Yes, I have. Sir, I see you attended the session today. I was hoping you'd be willing to tell me a bit about what took place." Domingo looked at John Dunnington hopefully. To his great relief, John smiled warmly and clapped Domingo on the shoulder, fortunately his uninjured one.

"I can think of no one else I'd wish to discuss the day's proceedings with, Domingo. I was just about to take dinner at the Bull's Ring. I'd be honored if you'd join me."

As much as he burned to know how the session went, Domingo was uncomfortable at the thought of eating in a public establishment. He had never personally been harassed by Londoners, but in just the last week Semuel had been heckled on three separate occasions, once having to suffer being spat on by a merchant-class boy and his thuggish minions. And last night, a Jewish beggar had been beaten to death in Cheapside. Domingo was often in public with Semuel, and he worried that he might be recognized and that this would cause problems for Mr. Dunnington.

John noted the younger man's hesitation and tried to reassure him. "Domingo, there is no need to fear. I don't frequent businesses that cater to Prynne's crowd. Will you come?"

"Thank you, Mr. Dunnington. I would be honored to share a meal with you."

It did not take them more than ten minutes to walk to the inn. After they were settled at a private table in a back corner and had been served fish pottage in small carved-out loaves of bread, John confided in Domingo, "I won't lie to you, son. It was an ugly scene today. William Prynne prepared the merchants well with that despicable tract of his. There was a great outcry over the threat Jews pose to English trade."

"That's ridiculous! We've been here for decades, and contrary to what they fear, Senhor Robles and Senhor Carvajal bring hundreds of thousands of lire into London each year."

"I fully understand, and I agree with you on this point, Domingo. But in this case, perception is much more powerful than truth. To be sure, none of them know that Jews live here already. They imagine a threat that is false because Jews have been trading with them for years. Your Spanish-Catholic identity has served your community too well I'm afraid."

"What else, Mr. Dunnington?" pressed Domingo. "I'm sure more was said about our religion."

John nodded as he took a gulp of wine to wash down the bread he had just popped into his mouth. "Yes, more was said. The usual fears were expressed. Jews would blaspheme Christ, they would carry out diabolical rituals, and they would seduce Christians." At this last charge, Domingo seemed to choke on his food. "All right, son?" John asked, concerned.

Domingo understood that the merchants feared Jews proselytizing Christians, but he couldn't help but be reminded of his last year with Lucy, especially the last two months when he'd bedded her regularly. He'd never tried to persuade Lucy to convert to Judaism, but in the broader sense of the term, he was definitely guilty of seducing her.

"I'm fine, sir. Just swallowed too quickly," he managed with the lame reply. God, how he wished John Dunnington was not Lucy's father. He forgot how much he enjoyed spending time with this man, with his mild temperament, keen mind, and tolerant heart. If John ever discovered how poorly Domingo had treated his daughter, he would surely never speak to Domingo again. He took a deep breath and tried to steer his mind back to the conversation at hand. "Sir, how did the matter rest at the close of the conference?"

John shook his head. "Unclear, son, unclear. Cromwell was sorely vexed at the merchants and preachers, some of whom he thought would support him with the readmission. Even Henry Jessey argued for a limited readmission at the end of the day. He suggested that Jews be allowed to only live in minor port cities and that all their income from trade should be taxed double. Basically, the consensus was that there was no way to prevent Jews from settling in England according to common law, but that if enough limitations were put in place, the Jews could be controlled to satisfy the ministers and the merchants. If Jessey's compromise had been accepted, Jews would not be allowed to live or trade in London."

"What do you mean 'if the compromise had been accepted'? Was it not voted on?" Domingo asked, suddenly feeling hopeful.

"Absolutely not! It was one of Cromwell's finest moments, and believe me, I'm no fan of the tyrant." John looked about them for eavesdroppers and then lowered his voice. "Our Lord Protector cleverly dismissed the conference before any action could be taken. He likened the council's debate to a 'babble of discourses' and said he was in need of their prayers. But between you and me, I don't think Cromwell will be inviting any of those men to pray with him anytime soon. Shocking really. Just goes to show you how he's not as all-powerful as he appears. Believe me, I would have wanted him to prevail over that hateful mob. But despite your rabbi's hopes, Domingo, this is not the time to press for readmission. Even if Cromwell could push this through on his own, I fear for what will happen to you on the streets when your true identity is discovered. Trust me, Prynne and his followers are not done with the Jews yet."

Domingo nodded in understanding. It seemed as if the end of the Whitehall Conference was just the beginning of trouble for the crypto-Jews in London.

True to John's word, the pamphleteers were quick to publish responses to the issues raised at Whitehall in December. Although many of the tracts were anonymous, it was often known on the streets and in the coffeehouses who the authors were. William Prynne claimed the Jews coveted English land and would push god-fearing Englishmen out of their livelihoods and homes. Other polemicists charged that Jews engaged in financial fraud and the murder of Christian children. While none of the charges were original, their appearing regularly in newspapers and pamphlets meant that all of London was reminded daily of Jewish perfidy. In addition, England was preparing for war with Spain. The Spanish identity of the crypto-Jews would ill serve them when open hostilities broke out. It was a time of great uncertainty and fear, but there was little for the Jews to do other than continue on as before and pray that neither the war with Spain nor Menasseh ben Israel's mission would publicly expose them.

XIII. *A Case of the Jews Altered,* March 1656

The conflict with Spain had begun the previous October when British ships attacked Hispaniola and Jamaica. Cromwell argued that Spain had brought war upon herself by not granting religious liberty to Protestants living in her colonies. Despite the all-to-easy anti-Catholic fervor Cromwell and his Puritan supporters generated among the masses, it was clear to Domingo that Cromwell's primary intent was destroying Spanish trade in the Atlantic rather than earning religious freedom for Protestants abroad. This was not a war for God, country, or king. This was a trade war.

Thus Domingo began to worry. There had been troubles with Spain in the past, but this war seemed different, originating in the colonies and threatening to spread to Europe. Today John Dunnington had warned Senhor Robles about a Privy Council petition to impound all Spanish citizens' possessions. His source for that information had told him to expect a decision in a week. That gave them ample time to conceal Senhor Robles's unsold merchandise.

But two days later, the commissioner of customs impounded Senhor Robles's ships. Then customs bailiffs, finding his warehouse empty, searched his home and confiscated all his goods and papers. From his desk in Senhor Robles's study, Domingo watched, stunned, as the bailiffs rifled through his employer's private correspondence. Had the Jews unwisely concluded from the unsettled end of the Whitehall Conference that Jews would not be arrested? But the bailiffs did not take Senhor Robles into custody. When he came to his senses, Domingo examined the search warrant and found that the confiscation was part of an investigation of merchant aid to Spain based on a Portuguese citizen's denunciation of Senhor Robles. There was no mention of Senhor Robles being Jewish. But Domingo was familiar with the accuser, Philip La Hoyo.

In the midst of the commotion at his house, Senhor Robles pulled Domingo aside and said, "Go find John Dunnington. He needs to be warned. Tell him to meet me here at three o'clock this afternoon. The bailiffs should be gone by then."

"Yes, sir," Domingo said with a nod. Then he grabbed his cloak and headed for the door.

"Domingo," Robles called after him, "tell your haham as well. He needs to know this will affect us all."

He hurried from Duke's Place and made his way southwest through the city to Dunnington's countinghouse on Fleet Street. When Domingo reached the familiar overhang he was relieved to find the door unlocked. He hurried in and found John sitting at his desk. The older man rose and strode toward him in a leisurely manner.

"Domingo! Come in, son. How does your mother?"

"She is well, sir. Thank you." Domingo lowered his voice, even though they seemed to be alone. "Mr. Dunnington, we must talk of a matter of some urgency."

John's countenance suddenly changed. "Certainly, son." He took a seat at the large center table and Domingo followed suit.

It came out in a rush. "Senhor Robles has been publicly denounced as an enemy of the Commonwealth. His ships have been impounded. As we speak, his home is being searched. Mr. Dunnington, you are in danger."

John sat in startled silence for a moment before speaking. "Mr. Robles told me he was planning to send a petition to the Lord Protector about the Privy Council petition later today. I can't believe they would move so quickly on this. I don't understand. The Privy Council is Cromwell's select group of advisors. Is he no longer able to shelter the merchant Jews?"

"Sir, I am not sure this has to do with Senhor Robles being a Hebrew."

"Who made the denunciation?"

"A man named Philip La Hoyo. He worked for Senhor Robles for a few months last year, but Senhor Robles had to let him go because the man was stealing merchandise and claiming it as a loss. We thought he had returned to Amsterdam. We assumed wrong."

John rose quickly from the table. "Domingo, I need to see someone straightaway."

"Wait, Mr. Dunnington. Before you go, I must tell you that Senhor Robles wishes to see you at his home at three o'clock. Shall I tell him you will be there?"

"Yes. Hopefully by then I'll have gotten to the bottom of this. Thank you, Domingo. Until three, then."

◆◆◆

Domingo and Manuel were whispering furtively together by the window when John Dunnington arrived at Senhor Robles's home that afternoon. Senhor Robles was sitting at his large oak desk dictating a letter to his clerk.

"Ah, Senhor Dunnington, come in and sit." Senhor Robles indicated a cushioned chair next to his.

"Miguel," he addressed his clerk, "that will be all for now. I will call for you shortly." The clerk bowed respectfully and, without a word, left the room. Senhor Robles then turned to John and said, "Senhor Dunnington, please tell the others what you told me on Friday."

To Domingo, his tone seemed amazingly calm for one who had just seen his business shut down and who was facing accusations of treason.

"I was in Doctors' Commons on personal business when I happened on a former associate, Francis Knevett. Do you remember him, Mr. Delgado? He used to translate my Spanish documents before Domingo took over that task." Manuel nodded silently and John continued, "He asked me to his office, saying he might have information I would be interested in. He has contacts in the Office of Discoveries who told him that the Privy Council would soon take action against Spanish citizens. We agreed to meet back in his office later that day when he would be able to give me more specific details. At six o'clock we met again, and he told me the Privy Council would act against Spanish ship owners this coming Friday. I immediately conveyed this information to Mr. Robles. What I don't understand is who Philip La Hoyo is and what his connection is to the situation we are in."

"I believe Domingo briefly told you about Philip La Hoyo." Senhor Robles gave a nod in Domingo's direction. "He is a

Portuguese of New Christian parents. His father was a respected jeweler in Lisbon before being arrested by the Inquisition. He did penance twice after being accused of Judaizing, and even though he was set free, his health was never strong after that. He escaped to Amsterdam where he married and where Philip was born. Simon La Hoyo died four years ago when Philip was fifteen. When I last visited Amsterdam, I took pity on the young man and offered him a position and a new life in London. Philip seemed eager for the opportunity, but within the first few weeks, he was frequenting taverns and speaking too freely with English agents and merchants. Philip was not only indiscreet, he was dishonest. It was Manuel who discovered the loss of merchandise, particularly the metals and gems I import specifically for jewelers. It was when I let Philip go that I also realized he no longer considered himself a member of our nation. He claimed I fabricated a crime against him to discredit him for turning Christian. His denunciation is clearly his way of exacting revenge."

"Senhor Dunnington, might we learn more from Francis Knevett?" Manuel asked. "My cousin does not think well of him, but it would seem to me that this man may be able to obtain more information that might be useful to us." Domingo scowled at his cousin's comment but held his tongue.

"I agree, Mr. Delgado. In fact, I have just come from his office." Senhor Robles leaned forward expectantly at John's words, but John shook his head sadly. "I am sorry to report that I was not able to meet with Mr. Knevett today, but I assure you that I will make it my primary task to discuss our situation with him."

"Good," said Senhor Robles. "As you must know, Senhor Dunnington, any investigation into my citizenship and position here in London presents a risk to my brethren. We are meeting later this evening to decide on a course of action suitable for all of us." He turned to Domingo. "Tomorrow morning I would like you to apprise Senhor Dunnington of any new developments before he sets out for Doctors' Commons."

"Yes, sir," Domingo said. "Would eight o'clock be convenient for you, Mr. Dunnington?"

"That would suit."

With this, Antonio Robles dismissed them to their individual tasks.

◆◆◆

That night, the men of the London kehilla, including Semuel and his father for the first time, came together as Jews, as merchants, and as Portuguese. What they gathered to discuss affected all aspects of their identity. They clustered in tight groups in the great hall used for the last decade as their house of prayer. Anxious whispering buzzed throughout the room until the unofficial leader of the community, the powerful merchant Antonio Carvajal, arrived.

"*Boa vinda*, my brothers. If God wills it, we will survive this storm. But we have much to discuss this evening. However, I must warn you. The time for discussion moves quickly past us and the time for making decisions will be upon us soon. I would like Senhor Robles to begin by telling us how the situation now stands, and then, afterward, the floor is open for discussion."

Thus Senhor Robles stood before the representatives of his nation living in London and told them of Philip La Hoyo's betrayal, Francis Knevett's helpful but ineffective tip off, and the contents of the Privy Council's warrants against him. When he finished his narrative, he sat and Senhor Carvajal indicated that the others were free to respond.

Isak Lopes Chillon spoke first. "It was the indiscretion of Robles's agent John Dunnington that led to this! This is what happens when we trust Christians."

Manuel coolly rose to his colleague's defense. "Isak, tell me, how can any of us conduct business in England without working with Christians? I have known John Dunnington ten years. He is not indiscreet. He was trying to gain information to help us; he had no reason not to trust his source. Do not forget, it was one of our own who brought the charge. Philip de la Hoya is a Portuguese."

"So what is to be done?" asked Abraham Brito. "We are all registered as Spaniards. Antonio's fate will be ours within the week."

"I have sent a petition to His Highness asking for denization to England as a citizen of Portugal," Robles revealed to the group.

"If you are granted this protection, what of the rest of us and our families?" asked Brito, raising his voice. "You would seek to protect yourself without accounting for the position that you've placed us in?"

Before Senhor Robles could reply to this accusation, Abraham Gonzales spoke up. "It is not our way to live alone in exile. We must band together! Our strength has ever been in our unity. Of late some of us support the Commonwealth while others would like to see our late king's son restored to the throne." There was angry murmuring at this. "Brothers, hear me out," Gonzales said. "This past year we have argued over Haham ben Israel's petition to Parliament. We have been a divided community and this will be our undoing. Antonio's fate is our fate; this crisis concerns us all. We must be unified in our response or they will come after us one by one."

"What Abraham says is true," Jahacob Caçeres said as Senhor Gonzales sat down. "We should act as one in this matter."

"We must throw ourselves on the mercy of the Lord Protector," pronounced Menasseh ben Israel from the back of the room where he'd been sitting quietly with Semuel. Now he rose and strode authoritatively to the front of the room. "Oliver Cromwell is the only one who can help us. He has protected Senhor Carvajal in the past and he personally intervened with the king of Portugal to restore the property of my cousin David Dormido. Senhor Cromwell will protect the rest of you. His Highness knows of the Jews' plight and he is sympathetic."

Manuel slammed his hand on the table in anger. "This is madness! Cromwell could not even convince his own supporters to allow readmission and now you want us to expose ourselves and our families as Jews? Have you not been reading the pamphlets published by the merchants and their mouthpiece Prynne? They've set their hearts to violence at the very thought of our readmission. What do you think they will do when they discover we have been here, living among them, these many years?"

Semuel stood. His voice was deep and restrained as he tried to maintain control over his anger. "Or perhaps you will find the opposite reaction, Senhor Delgado. If the English learn how many have been here for this decade past and how many have been loyal to the Commonwealth, they might realize their error."

"That is highly unlikely. Our brothers' wealth is the only thing that protects them. What about those of us who don't own ships?

The English, nay, even the tolerant fathers of Amsterdam, do not wish to be overrun with Jewish poor."

"You are hardly poor, Senhor Delgado," retorted Semuel hotly.

Carvajal raised his hand to stay Manuel's response. "There is wisdom in what has been said here. I agree with Senhor Gonzales and His Honor, Haham ben Israel. We need to band together. However, I do not agree that every family need be exposed." He gave a slight nod to Manuel here. "There are some of us here who operate a significant source of trade with the colonies. I believe that if we petition His Highness as Jews he will grant his protection. I will sign such a petition, and I invite Senhor Dormido, Senhor Caçeres, and Haham ben Israel, along with other men of trade, to sign with me. In this way, we present our case as a small, yet powerful, community and do not risk the exposure of our brethren."

So it was decided that seven would petition Cromwell for protection against the seizure of their properties as members of the nation of Israel, as Jews, not Spaniards or Portuguese.

March 24, 1656

To His Highness Oliver, Lord Protector of the Commonwealth of England, Scotland, and Ireland, and the dominions thereof.

The humble petition of the Hebrews at present residing in this city of London, whose names are underwritten, humbly acknowledge the manyfold favors and protections Your Highness has been pleased to grant us in order that we may, with security, meet privately in our particular houses to practice our own devotions; and being desirous to be favored more by Your Highness, we pray with all humbleness to you that such protection may be granted to us in writing as that we may thereof practice our said private devotions in our own particular houses without fear of molestation, either to our persons, families, or estates, our desires being only to live peaceably under Your Highness's government; and being we are all mortal, we also humbly pray Your Highness grant us license to bury those who die of our nation in a place outside the city, which we shall think convenient with the proprietor's lease on whose land this place shall be; and so we shall, as in our lives, as at our deaths, be highly favored by Your Highness, whose long life and prosperity we shall continually pray to the almighty God for.

Menasseh ben Israel

Abraham Israel de Brito

Isak Lopes Chillon

David Dormido Abrabanel

Antonio Israel Carvajal

Abraham Coen Gonzales

Jahacob de caceres

April passed wet and gloomy. As he slogged home through London's muddy streets, Domingo did not even notice how wet his feet had become. What he had feared when the Robles trial began was now threatening to destroy the little community on Cree Church Lane. Their exposure as Jews had been accomplished in March with petitions signed by the most powerful men in their community; so far, though, these petitions were not part of the public record. It was not commonly known yet that Jews lived in London. A few weeks ago he'd signed an affidavit for his employer confirming Senhor Robles's nationality, family history, and religion. Manuel had been furious with him, arguing that, while it was a noble gesture, it guaranteed that his family would be caught up in any unpleasant consequences of the trial.

"With every step we move closer to exposure, closer to the Christian sword that always threatens us, Domingo," he'd said.

When he returned home, Domingo set himself to repairing a chair with an uneven leg. Since Senhor Robles's denunciation, there had been little for Domingo to do, so he'd taken to fixing things around the house. Teresa Maria and Ana were thrilled with Domingo's new hobby as he had installed a new door on Ana's pantry, replaced broken tiles around her kitchen hearth, and repaired several cracked drapery rings on his mother's bed. But his lack of urgency irritated Manuel, who now spent most of his time meeting with merchants and making contacts in the colonies.

Engrossed in his project, Domingo did not hear Manuel come in.

"Domingo, I would speak with you please."

Domingo left the chair on its side and asked, "What is wrong, cousin?"

"Soon the trial will commence. Senhor Robles requires a man from his employ to witness for him, to confirm his statements about his background. I thought, since you have already signed the affidavit, you would do this for him." Manuel looked away and nervously began to wring his hands. "Domingo . . . Ana and the boys."

Domingo understood his cousin's meaning. "I'll go in your stead. I have been working for Senhor Robles almost as long as you have; I can testify for him. Naturally you would continue to care for Mãe should I be arrested. And I don't have a wife . . ." He trailed off at this awkward subject between them. "Anyway, if I am deported, I could survive much better than you. I was raised a Catholic. I know how to play that role."

His cousin had never lived in Portugal, but, like the rest of them, he was registered as a citizen of Spain and would be deported there rather than to Amsterdam. Domingo figured that Manuel wouldn't last one day before the Inquisition caught up with him.

Manuel said nothing for a long moment. "You are the last of your father's line, Domingo. If you do this, you will save my family, but you may destroy yours."

Domingo understood that Manuel was posturing. He knew Domingo couldn't back down. Yet he appreciated Manuel's acknowledgement of his potential sacrifice.

Teresa Maria was beside herself when Domingo told her later that day. She ran downstairs and threw herself at Manuel's feet, weeping. "How could you let him do this? He is my only son. Why are you offering him up for the sacrifice? Why must he be exposed at a public trial?"

Domingo lifted his mother to her feet as Manuel answered her, "It was his decision, Teresa Maria. Senhor Carvajal and Senhor Robles have pledged to help him if this goes badly. They will protect him."

Predictably, Domingo's mother was not soothed by Manuel's reassurance of the merchants' aid. "They make promises, but they will first try to save themselves. If this Cromwell requires a scapegoat, it will be my son and not those powerful merchants."

At this, Manuel exploded in rage. "Yes, Teresa Maria, it is a risk. But Domingo has less to lose than me. Besides, I can't keep protecting him from every danger he will face. I saved you from destitution when Joseph died. I saved Domingo from his stupidity over Dunnington's daughter. *Damn* you for making me out to have forsaken him!" Then he turned his anger on Domingo, "You are your own master now. It is time for you to stand on your own."

As Manuel stormed off, Domingo took his mother into his arms and led her back up to their apartments. "It will be all right, Mãe. You'll see."

The upcoming trial drove a wedge between more than one family in London. When Edward Polestead learned of his father-in-law's involvement with the crypto-Jews, a deep sense of betrayal consumed him. Dragging Lucy with him to her father's house, he confronted Dunnington without even removing his hat and cloak.

"Sir, had I known you to be an agent for those accursed Jews, I never would have consented to marry your daughter. I have been shamed before my colleagues, who now suspect me of working with you. I also see now how my wife has been infected with affection for these people. It is unconscionable how you trained her in your folly. You have saddled me with an obstinate Jew-lover."

Her father bristled at her husband's speech, but he remained calm. "Mr. Robles is an honorable man, and my daughter is intelligent enough to make her own decisions about where she places her affection. I will also remind you, Edward, that you are the one who pursued Lucy. I did not beg you to take her as your wife."

Edward then attacked from another angle. "This is going to ruin you, Dunnington."

"Perhaps," John said, nodding thoughtfully. "But there is no need to punish my daughter. She is your wife. Condemn me if you will, but leave Lucy out of our quarrel."

Turning to leave, Edward addressed Lucy, "Your father is no longer welcome in my home, and I forbid you to see him or mention his name in public. Your association with him is a detriment to my good name and business."

Later, in their home on the Strand, neither her anger nor her tearful pleas moved her husband to make peace with her father, and when Edward retired to a separate chamber, Lucy began to fear for her marriage. Because he had not expressly forbidden her from associating with Elizabeth and the children, Lucy called on them the following day, prepared to comfort her stepmother in her grief. But Elizabeth was also angry with Lucy's father for his deception.

"For goodness sake, Lucy, it was bad enough when I thought he was working for Papists, but Jews? Please tell me you didn't know about this."

Lucy shook her head. "I'm sorry, Elizabeth. I've known for quite some time."

"And Dominick? Did you know he is also a Jew?"

"Yes."

"Lucy! Did you know this when you hoped he'd come for you? Did you know he was a Jew then?"

"Yes," she whispered.

"How could you, Lucy?" Elizabeth's face grew red and she began to pace the parlor. "Your father kept this from me as per his prerogative. He is a man and his business interests were served by his silence. Your involvement with the Jews, however, is a different matter entirely. You deceived me, Lucy. And in that, you have put my reputation, and that of your brother's and sister's, at risk."

She'd been prepared to be humbled by her stepmother for knowing the Sephardim's secret, but Lucy found herself growing angry instead. "My friendship with Dominick began *well* before you married my father. He is an honorable man, as is Mr. Robles."

"They are Jews!"

Lucy saw, like with Edward, that she could never convince Elizabeth of the truth. But unlike with her husband, she felt a softness for her stepmother. At heart, Elizabeth was kind; she'd just been trained to not question the beliefs she'd been raised to accept. Lucy stood and walked over to her. Grasping the older woman's hands in hers, she said, "Let us speak no more of this, Mother. It has been years since I've had Dominick's friendship, so have no fear of my association with him."

Stunned at Lucy's deference, Elizabeth said no more.

XIV. *VINDICATION OF THE JEWS,*
MAY 1656

The Court of the Admiralty held its proceedings at Doctors' Commons. The trial room was small and restricted to the public, unlike the criminal courts of the Old Bailey. Witnesses and defendants sat on a set of two-tiered benches along the east wall. Colonel Philip Jones, a weathered, but still imposing, navy man and deputy to the lord high admiral, sat in the center of the room at a great oak table. He was flanked on either side by fellow naval officers Colonel James Thewitt, a man of about thirty with the look of a Norseman, and Colonel Jonas Brock, whose advanced age and dark looks provided a marked contrast to Colonel Thewitt's person.

"We call Antonio Rodrigues Robles, also known as Abraham Robles, to the bench," said Colonel Jones.

Senhor Robles rose from his seat and walked in a dignified manner, as if he were approaching the podium to read a portion of the Torah rather than to give a deposition.

"Mr. Robles, we have read and discussed your numerous petitions and depositions over these last weeks. The aim of our questioning today is to resolve inconsistencies in previous statements."

Senhor Robles nodded in answer.

"Where were you born?"

"Fundao, Portugal."

"How is it that you have been known these last fifteen years as a Spaniard?"

"I was born in 1606, when Portugal was claimed by the Spanish crown. My family escaped the Inquisition after my father's death by their hands. I was a boy of ten. My mother, my brother, my sisters, and I traveled to Spain where we lived for many years. During that time, I lived as a Catholic and worked in shipping for King Philip. From Spain, I went to Amsterdam and lived there for nineteen years.

When I was there, Portugal gained her independence from Spain and I reclaimed my heritage as a Portuguese. In Amsterdam, I married my wife, also a Portuguese. We have lived in London since 1641."

"What is your religion, sir?"

"I am a member of the Hebrew nation."

"You are a Jew?"

"Yes."

"Did you practice the Roman religion here in London?"

"Yes."

"Can you explain to the commission how you can be both Jewish and Papist?"

"My family lived as Catholics to survive the Inquisition and to live free of harassment. But we are of the Hebrew nation. My father died at the hands of Inquisition torturers, my mother was maimed, and my three uncles were burned alive during an auto-da-fé. I myself have not been circumcised out of fear of persecution."

"Mr. Robles, are your ships in service to the king of Spain?"

"Absolutely not! I am neither a citizen of Spain nor a supporter of that wicked nation. My trade and my ships have been these last fifteen years in the service of England, which is my home. Gentlemen, in many nations I have lived, and I tell you this, England is not the country of my birth, but it will ever be the country of my heart. My family suffered greatly before coming to England. But here, this land is God's deliverance. God wills that my people find sanctuary in England. I have heard this, yes? It is the New Jerusalem. A land of peace. My ships are at the service of England. I would see the defeat of the Papist devils in Spain and Portugal."

"Thank you, Mr. Robles. You may be seated now."

◆◆◆

After a brief recess of the court, Domingo was called to testify. "We call the witness for Antonio Rodrigues Robles." Domingo stood and approached the table where the three admiralty commissioners were seated.

"State your name," commanded Colonel Jones in a bored tone.

"Domingo Maria Rodrigues de Lacerda."

"Age?"

"Twenty-two."

"Habitation?"

"Stoney Lane, St. Catherine Cree Parish."

"Profession?"

"I am an accountant."

"Employer?"

"Senhor Antonio Robles."

"Place of birth?"

"Lisbon, Portugal."

"How long have you resided in England?"

"Nine years, sir."

"Religion?"

Domingo took a deep breath. He made eye contact for a moment with John Dunnington, seated among the other witnesses, and then pronounced, "I am a Jew."

Colonel Jones made note of his testimony and then continued his questioning. "Can you testify to the nationality and religion of your employer, Mr. Antonio Robles?"

"He is a Portuguese like me. We communicate in this tongue. I know him also to be a Jew. He made no secret of his religion to me during my apprenticeship and employment."

"How many years have you known the defendant?"

"Nine."

"And you have always known him to be a Portuguese and a Jew?"

"Yes, from the beginning of my apprenticeship, I knew this to be his true identity."

"Mr. Lacerda, why did you leave Lisbon?"

This question took Domingo by surprise. He knew that Senhor Robles had joined the others in the kehilla in arguing for protection as survivors of the Inquisition, but he had not been prepared to do the same. His role was simply as a witness to his employer's nationality. "Mr. Lacerda?" Colonel Jones pressed, now curious.

"Yes, sorry. My family had been discovered by the Inquisition to be conversos. I lost a sister and a brother before we were able to get out of Lisbon."

"What do you mean by 'lost,' Mr. Lacerda?"

"Th-They," Domingo stammered on his reply. "My brother was garroted then incinerated, and my sister, she was driv—she was killed. They were accused of being Christians who knew Hebrew prayers."

"Thank you. That will be all. You may be seated."

As he walked back to the bench, Domingo realized he was shaking. Only now did he fully realize the danger he had put himself in. If he were sent to Spain, he was sure to be handed over to the Inquisition. Had his family been caught during their flight from Lisbon, Domingo would have been sent to an orphanage or been taken in by a Christian family and raised to hate the Jews. Now he was older than Filipe had been when he was tortured and killed. Yet Filipe had died a Christian. His strangulation had been a merciful death for a penitent. Domingo had just publicly confessed to being a Jew in a formal court. If he was convicted by the Inquisition, he would surely be burned on an upper pike for all to see. He sat down and took a deep breath to calm himself, but then a firm hand on his shoulder made him jump. It was John Dunnington. "All right, son?"

Domingo nodded, grateful for a friendly face. "Yes, sir. Thank you."

John was called up next. "Name?" asked Colonel Thewitt.

"John Benedict Dunnington."

"Age?"

"Fifty-one."

"Residence?"

"Fleet Street, St. Bride's Parish."

"Place of birth?"

"Thorganby Parish, Yorkshire."

"Religion?"

John raised his chin defiantly. "I hold to none, sir."

"Profession, sir?"

"I have been these sixteen years a merchant's agent in London."

"Employer?"

"Mr. Antonio Robles of Duke's Place."

"Can you testify to the nationality and religion of the defendant?"

"I know him to have escaped the Inquisition of the Portuguese nation. He is a Jew with no loyalty to Spain or Portugal. During my twelve years in his employ, he has proven his worth and loyalty to our nation of England."

"And could you now please tell this commission about your dealings with Mr. Francis Knevett?"

"He and I were acquainted some time back, about ten years ago. I paid for his services as a Spanish translator for documents related to my business. Until March of this year, I had not seen or spoken with Mr. Knevett for seven years."

"Why did you speak with Mr. Knevett in March of this year?"

"I was engaged in personal business at Doctors' Commons and I happened on him there. We spoke in his chambers, and then he invited me back several hours later to receive information he said might concern my employer."

"What was this information?"

"He told me about the Privy Council's petition to confiscate the property of all Spaniards. He then suggested to me that Mr. Robles take precautions."

"Did you understand that he knew the nationality of your employer?"

"Mr. Knevett made the assumption that Mr. Robles was a Spaniard. I did not confirm or deny this. And at no time during our discussion did Mr. Knevett suggest that Mr. Robles was a Portuguese or a Jew."

"You expressed to the investigating body that you had a third meeting with Mr. Knevett in April. What transpired then?"

"Mr. Knevett suggested to me that I would be denounced among the merchants for my association with Spaniards and Jews. He forswore any role in Mr. Robles's troubles, laying the blame for that with a Philip La Hoyo. Mr. Knevett then advised me to deny the nature of our meetings in March, as they did not bear on Mr. Robles's case and would only serve to darken our good names. He offered to use his influence in the Office of Discoveries to help me restore my reputation should I agree to this scheme."

"What was your response to Mr. Knevett's proposal?"

"I called him a knave and a coward! And after taking leave of him, I immediately went to Colonel Jones to tell him of Knevett's treachery. My own role in this affair may be judged with disfavor by the commission, but I will not be a party to perjury."

"Thank you, Mr. Dunnington. That will be all."

As John took his seat, Colonel Jones conferred with Colonel Thewitt and Colonel Brock. Witnesses and other trial participants shifted uncomfortably in the silence that was only broken by an occasional cough. Finally Colonel Jones spoke, "This court will adjourn until May the tenth."

As they filed out of the courtroom, John caught up with Domingo. "That was a courageous thing for you to do, coming forward like that."

"It was my duty, sir," Domingo replied. "Senhor Robles has been a great support to my family. I am happy to repay him in this. I hope it helps, or we are all doomed."

"What will you do if the verdict is not favorable?"

"I have arranged to move my mother to Amsterdam. I've already transferred all my property into her name in case I am detained in London or deported to Spain. If allowed my freedom, I will consider the colonies. Manuel plans to leave within the year for Barbados. The Lord Protector means to move many of our brethren to the colonies taken from Spain. He has decreed that Jews may worship openly in Barbados and Jamaica. We will not be allowed to own land or slaves, but we can live freely, worship freely, and trade freely. It is a much better situation than what we have in London at present." Domingo ran his hand through his hair in a tired gesture. "My father used to speak of Brazil as a new start for us. Instead, we remained in Amsterdam for five years, and we've been in London for another nine. I am tired of running, Mr. Dunnington."

"Domingo, you have always been welcome in my house," John said. "This matter has left me bitter against those I trusted, and I am quitting London as soon as I can settle my affairs. I would be honored if you would call on me before you make a decision about leaving."

"Thank you, Mr. Dunnington. I would like that very much. If all goes well, I am hoping to return to Amsterdam soon with Haham ben Israel and his son Semuel. We have not always agreed on the issue of readmission, but I owe them a great deal. Semuel has been a good friend to me since I was a boy of eight, and his father, as you know, was my teacher. Semuel is to be married on his return, and he's asked me to stand with him at the ceremony. Can you believe, Mr. Dunnington, that I have never witnessed the wedding of one of my own?"

John sighed. "I wish I could say I am surprised, but I am not. I married Lucy's mother secretly as a Catholic and then publicly in the state church. I understand this deception, son. By the way, did you know that Lucy married last year?"

Domingo's throat suddenly constricted. "Yes, sir. My cousin told me. Is she well?"

"Yes, I think so. She and Edward had their differences over the Whitehall affair. She was furious with him for supporting Prynne and the Lord Mayor of London. And I must admit, he was none too pleased to discover his father-in-law's involvement in this affair." There was an awkward pause, then John continued, "You know, she guessed early on that you and your cousin were Jewish."

"Yes, we spoke of it," Domingo replied in a guarded tone.

"You and Lucy were such friends, Domingo. I'll bet she'd be happy to see you again."

"It would seem that her husband would not approve of her friendship with a Jew. Out of respect for Lucy, it is best that I keep my distance."

"Well, I'll tell her that I saw you and that you look well. Although, I am curious about your limp."

Domingo hesitated to speak to Mr. Dunnington about it, especially as it seemed he would be reporting to Lucy. Carefully, he answered the question enough to satisfy Mr. Dunnington's curiosity without divulging the circumstances of his injury. "Two years ago I had an accident in Amsterdam. I broke several bones on my right side, including my hip. Occasionally it still bothers me."

"Good God! What happened?"

Domingo felt awkward. He knew Mr. Dunnington meant well, but he was tired of being questioned. "I fell from a second-story window. It took me the better part of a year to recover."

Mr. Dunnington shook his head sympathetically. "We can talk about it some other time perhaps. Until next week, then."

"Thank you, sir. Until next week."

◆◆◆

The final witnesses would be heard at the next session. Colonel Jones began the interrogation by saying, "We call before the bench, Philip La Hoyo."

A wiry youth sporting a head of cropped black hair and wearing a threadbare black wool suit approached the bench. "Please state your full name, Mr. La Hoyo," instructed Colonel Jones.

"I am Philip Tomás Alvares de La Hoyo, Excellency," he said, pronouncing each word carefully. Despite his attempts to appear Dutch, his accent immediately marked him as Portuguese.

Colonel Jones narrowed his eyes at the form of address. "You may address me as 'sir,' Mr. La Hoyo."

"Yes, sir," La Hoyo answered, giving a slight bow.

Colonel Jones began with the usual questions. "Age?"

"Nineteen."

"Place of residence?"

"Newton Street, London."

"Place of birth?"

"Amsterdam."

"Religion?"

"I am a Christian of the Reformed rite, sir."

"Profession?"

La Hoyo faltered here. "I am—I mean . . . I was an agent in the gem trade. Formerly, I worked for Mr. Antonio Robles, who, for personal reasons, terminated my employment. I am currently involved in translation work."

"Employer?"

"I have none, sir. I am a free agent getting work where I am able."

"I see." Colonel Jones made a few notes on the papers in front of him before continuing. "Mr. La Hoyo, could you please tell the commission how you came to believe that Mr. Robles was a Spaniard and an agent for that nation? We are particularly interested in the curious time-lapse between the termination of your employment and your denunciation of him this past March."

"I came to work for Antonio Robles a year ago in April. He had known my father, a jeweler from Lisbon, and, learning of his death, he wished to offer me a position. I had been trained in my father's trade and, although I did not possess his skill, I knew quite a lot about metals and gems. In this, Mr. Robles found use of me, and I assisted him in the importation of these products from India. After just two months of employment, Mr. Robles called me into his office to accuse me of theft. His senior accountant, a Mr. Manuel Delgado, had discovered irregularities in the Indian accounts and had concluded that I was pilfering gems from Mr. Robles. Naturally I denied the charge. I am not a thief! Nonetheless, I was relieved of my post and found myself seeking work elsewhere. This past winter, I contracted to do translation work. In the course of that work, I developed a friendship with one of my contractors and I shared with him the circumstances of my current situation. He seemed familiar with Mr. Robles and offered to help me improve my situation if I would act as a scribe to a private meeting he would be conducting. All I had to do was record the meeting, then sign an affidavit citing that Mr. Robles was a Spaniard who owned ships that were in the service of Spain."

"And did you know this to be true of Mr. Robles?"

"Yes, sir. He sometimes wrote correspondence to his agents in the Spanish language, and I remember my father referring to him as a 'Spanish merchant.'"

"What of his agency for Spain?"

"That I guessed because of his extreme secrecy regarding his accounts and his person. I later confirmed my suspicions with my contractor, who told me that he had, for several years, suspected Mr. Robles's apprentice, a Mr. Lacerda, to be duplicitous in nature. All my suspicions were confirmed when I heard Mr. Dunnington refer to his employer as 'registered as a Spaniard' and formerly under the protection of the Spanish ambassador during the reign of the late king."

John, visibly upset by this admission, stood and exclaimed to the bench, "I've never met this man before in my life!"

Colonel Jones rapped his gavel and boomed, "Take your seat, Mr. Dunnington." Then he turned back to the interrogation and addressed La Hoyo. "Mr. La Hoyo, it is curious. How is it that you heard Mr. Dunnington speak of his employer's nationality when he says that he has never met you?"

"He did not know I was in the room, sir. I was standing behind a screen in the office of my contractor."

It was all becoming sickeningly clear to John, and as Colonel Jones asked the next question, John did not need to hear the answer. "Who is your contractor, Mr. La Hoyo?"

"Francis Knevett."

John sank back into his seat humiliated. He had been set up and played for a fool. Even when Knevett tried to bribe him, he still did not suspect that he was the one who was behind the plot against Antonio Robles. John looked over at Domingo, who hung his head in defeat and frustration.

Knevett! Domingo thought. So long had that man plagued him. Why? Was it simply because he had done such a poor job of playing the Spaniard when he'd first arrived in London, or had Knevett always suspected he was a Jew?

He was jolted out of his thoughts by Colonel Jones's continued questioning of Philip La Hoyo.

"Mr. La Hoyo, did you know, either at the time of your employment or at a later date, that Mr. Robles was a Jew?"

La Hoyo blustered at this question. "It was not my intent to accuse Mr. Robles on this ground. I only wanted to clear my own name and show that he and his accountants were hiding their Spanish identities behind an English agent and were possibly a danger to England."

"Answer the question, Mr. La Hoyo. Did you know that Mr. Robles was a Jew?"

"Yes, I did," he said weakly. "But it was not my intent to—"

"That will be all, Mr. La Hoyo," Colonel Jones interrupted him. "You may step down now."

After a brief recess, the court gathered for the final witness. "We call Mr. Francis Knevett forward," intoned Colonel Jonas Brock.

And there he was, walking to the bench and taking his place with self-righteous calm.

"Name?"

"Francis Knevett."

"Habitation?"

"Doctors' Commons." Colonel Brock's quizzical look made Knevett falter a bit. "I . . . I live in my quarters there. It is plenty spacious."

"Place of birth?"

"London."

"Profession?"

"I am a notary, translator, and writer."

"Employer?"

"These past several years I have been in the employ of Mr. William Prynne, formerly of Parliament and a most celebrated pamphleteer."

"Please tell the commission how you came to suspect Mr. Robles, a merchant of London, of having ties to the Spanish cause."

"Gladly, Your Honor," Knevett said, smirking. "My father, William Knevett of Yarmouth, captained the cargo ship *Regina* for five years, until his death at sea. The owner of this ship was Mr. Antonio Robles, who I knew from my youth to be a Spaniard and a Papist. My father bade me learn Mr. Robles's heathen language because he feared, rightly so, that he was being cheated on his share of the profits from each voyage.

"After the *Regina* went down in '42, my mother and I waited patiently for the death right Mr. Robles had promised to the families of his captains. But when I called on him six months later, Mr. Robles claimed that my father was alive and living in Hispaniola on the profits from the cargo and ship he claimed my father stole from him."

"Did he offer any proof of this claim?"

Knevett shrugged. "Calling it proof is saying too much. Mr. Robles showed me a letter he'd received from one of his brethren, another Spaniard living in Hispaniola, explaining my father's supposed treachery. Naturally I did not believe it for a moment."

"And then what happened?" asked Colonel Brock, thoroughly engaged with Knevett's tale.

"Nothing, Colonel. Mr. Robles refused my mother the death benefit, and, were it not for me, she would have died in poverty. As it was, she died with a broken heart knowing that her husband was true and good, but that this Jew had made him out to be a knave to get out of paying her, her due. I have spent these last ten years looking for my chance to expose to the law what this man is, a foreigner and a cheat."

Colonel Brock conferred with his colleagues a moment, while those in audience murmured amongst themselves. From what Domingo could tell, many were with Knevett, having been moved by his story of family loss and the supposed deception of the foreigner against an Englishman. Yet there was something not quite right about Knevett's story. How was it that he had never independently confirmed his father's whereabouts? Why did Knevett wait until now, fourteen years later, to charge Senhor Robles with cheating him and his mother?

"Attention to the commission!" Colonel Jones called the court to order. "Mr. Knevett, you shall remain in witness."

Everyone, most of all Francis Knevett, seemed surprised at this order, but they soon settled in for the close of the session.

"Is it true, Mr. Knevett, that your parents were not legally wed and that you were born in Newgate Prison, registered a bastard to a Sarah Eli?"

There was a collective intake of breath in the court. Knevett grew visibly flustered. "My mother was, in common law, wed to my father."

"Was your mother a Jewess, sir?"

"She was no such thing!" Knevett thundered.

"Where were you born, Mr. Knevett?" asked Colonel Brock.

"I don't see how the circumstances of my birth bear on the matter of Mr. Robles's treason. I am an English citizen; he is not."

"Please answer the question, Mr. Knevett."

"I was born in London, 1615."

"Where exactly in London were you born, sir?"

Knevett hesitated, looking about the audience for any familiar face, any supportive countenance, but he found none. "I was born in Newgate, Your Honor. My father had been away several months at sea. She had not the funds to support herself."

"Was there no one to help her then? No family? No community support?" Domingo understood now. Colonel Brock was referring to the kehilla's upkeep of widows and other impoverished Jews in London.

"There was no one!" Knevett said vehemently. "Don't you understand? My mother had no one. Everything they offered came with conditions."

"What kind of conditions?"

"She had to conform, to once again become like one of them. She thought she'd escaped that life when she'd met my father."

"For the record, Mr. Knevett, who pressured her to conform?"

"Those bloody Jewish bastards!"

The outbreak among the audience was uncontainable. Colonel Jones shouted several times for order, but Knevett's revelations about his Jewish mother were scandalous.

Only when Knevett began speaking again did the court come to attention. "When he returned, my father took me in hand and raised me up a good Christian and loyal Englishman. Be damned the Jews and their conditions. We lived well and happy until this Jewish dog," he pointed at Senhor Robles, "plotted to cheat us. And that is when I knew I had to bring him, and all those connected to him, down. It is as Mr. Prynne says, Your Honor. The Jews are a cancer on our righteous nation; they must be cut out."

Stunned by Knevett's revelations, Colonel Brock only managed to dismiss the court before retiring with his equally astounded colleagues.

◆◆◆

At noon on May 14 they gathered for the verdict. Senhor Robles had assured Domingo earlier that morning that he would do whatever was necessary to secure Domingo's safety should the court rule against him. Domingo took some comfort in this, but then he realized that if Robles and the other Jewish merchants were arrested, there was little any of them could do.

Colonel Jones rose from his seat and a hush fell over the room. He read from the single document in his hands, "After careful investigation, the admiralty commission has concluded that neither the nationality nor religion of Mr. Antonio Rodrigues Robles can be ascertained with any certainty. As a consequence of our findings, we will suggest to the Privy Council and His Highness, the Lord Protector, that the property of Mr. Robles be released to his person and all charges against him dropped."

Relief washed over Domingo. Senhor Robles was free! And it was a victory for all the merchant Jews of London too, who could now shed their disguises and live openly as Portuguese and Jews. His mother and Manuel would be eager for the news, yet the first person he wanted to tell was Semuel.

He found his friend at the apartment in the Strand. "The charges against Senhor Robles have been dropped! We are free, Semuel!" Domingo went to embrace his friend but Semuel turned away.

"This is your victory, friend, not one for the nation of Israel. The Privy Council allows the Sephardim to remain in England because of your trade, not because they wish to aid the Jews. They are hypocrites, all of them! The English condemn the Jew for his interest in trade, but they allow rich Jewish merchants safe harbor in London because they are survivors of the Inquisition. Your brethren have benefited from English hatred for the Papists and English love of gold, yet you act as if they've pronounced an edict of tolerance for all Jews. Don't be deceived in this, Amiel. Your employer has been bought, not freed. My father will not give up until there is freedom for all Jews to settle in England."

"But, Semuel, why must you push this beyond what the English are willing to bear? The English are willing to tolerate our nation as merchants. Eventually the community will be able to support its poor, but let us build a strong foundation first. Asking England to take on all of Poland's persecuted Jews is unrealistic now."

"How many Jews must die in the meantime? Don't you understand, Amiel? This is not about the comfort of the English, or of the Sephardim of London. Who knows how many die each day because they have no safe haven."

"You and your father have achieved so much, Semuel. But you cannot save everyone at once. In time, people will come to understand the wisdom of the haham's petition."

"How can you say that? We've achieved nothing!" In frustration, Semuel stormed out, leaving Domingo alone in the ben Israels' apartment. Not wanting to face the haham after Semuel's tirade, Domingo went home to share the news with his mother.

◆◆◆

Menasseh ben Israel had been busy writing all through the spring. The day following the close of Senhor Robles's trial, he published *Vindiciae Judaeorum*, On The Vindication of the Jews. It was a writing masterpiece and would become the haham's legacy for future generations. Two weeks later, the Privy Council accepted the petition of the seven Hebrews; thus an era of an open Jewish presence in London began, even while there were no formal legal protections for them.

Lucy, openly defying Edward's orders after months in vain of trying to change his mind with deference, sat in her father's countinghouse reading a copy of *Vindiciae Judaeorum*. She found herself weeping when she came to the final passage:

> *Now, O most high God, to thee I make my prayer, thou who by so many stupendous miracles didst bring thy people out of Egypt, the land of bondage, and didst lead them into the Holy Land; graciously thy holy influence descended into the mind of Oliver Cromwell, who for no private interest, but only out of commiseration to our suffering, hath inclined himself to protect, and shelter us, for which neither I myself, nor my nation, can ever expect to be able to render him sufficient thanks.*

Dominick's people had been acquitted by Cromwell's Privy Council, but would they ever be acquitted in the minds of the Christians? "Father, what does this mean for them? Is England their promised land? Are the Jews free to live here now?" she asked when she finally trusted herself to speak.

John shook his head sadly. "I'm not sure, Lucy. The merchants are still against them, as are many of the clergy. And I'm afraid there is still little popular support for the Jews. So much seems to depend on Cromwell's ability to protect them, but I don't know how long he can stand between the Jews and his own people. If I were him, I'd do my best to find a distraction for Londoners so that they'd simply forget the Jews are here. The only problem, my dear, is that the best way to get Londoners to forget how much they hate the Jews is to remind them of how much they hate the Catholics. I urge you to be careful in these next few months, darling, and by all means, please act the pious Protestant."

Lucy grimaced. "Have no fear, Father. You taught me well. I promise to worship Cromwell himself if that's what it takes. Would that someday we can overcome this bitterness; I am so tired of hatred being a mark of piety. But tell me, Father, what became of Francis Knevett?"

John sighed deeply. "Naturally Prynne has disassociated himself from Mr. Knevett, and I've heard that he no longer keeps offices at Doctors' Commons. I can't say I approve of what he did, and I surely felt the fool for being set up by him, but still, I don't wish the man ill. It's a hard life he's lived."

Lucy shook her head. "Father, you have ever been too soft when it comes to that man. When I think of how hateful he was toward Dominick that first day we met him, well, I cannot summon any sympathy for Mr. Knevett."

"Ah, Lucy, Domingo is none the worse for Mr. Knevett's scheming, yet it was because of him that I released Mr. Knevett from my service."

"Because Dominick took over Mr. Knevett's translations?"

"In part, but it was mainly because Mr. Knevett seemed to have a personal grudge against the boy. His hatred of foreigners has twisted his mind, and now he conceives all manner of conspiracies at their hands. Colonel Jones told me after the trial that Mr. Knevett took a position with me all those years ago in order to have an ear to Mr. Robles's doings."

"So Dominick's presence in the countinghouse not only lost Mr. Knevett his job but also delayed his plan to ruin Mr. Robles," Lucy concluded.

"By God, girl! I had not even considered that. Yes, well, lucky for us that Domingo came to London, eh?"

"Yes, Father, lucky for us indeed," Lucy replied without conviction.

◆◆◆

Over the next year, Domingo saw the ben Israels infrequently. Following the Robles trial, Menasseh ben Israel and Semuel distanced themselves from the Cree Church Lane community. In October, the Delgados left for Barbados. With Manuel gone, Domingo's workload doubled, and it was clear to him that he would have to consider taking on an apprentice when he had worked at least three years as a master and could afford to board and clothe a boy of about twelve years. In the meantime, his days were spent managing Senhor Robles's private accounts and the accounts of his agents, and although busy, Domingo was overcome with a loneliness he had not felt since he'd been a young boy leaving Lisbon.

That summer, Domingo traveled north during the August heat to Thicket Hall at John Dunnington's invitation. It was an awkward visit. Elizabeth was cool toward him, and when she saw her children, especially Thomas, develop an affinity for him, she grew even cooler. Domingo was thankful that Lucy was not in attendance, until John told him that she no longer came to Yorkshire because her husband had forbidden it. It was not so much her husband's command that bothered Domingo but Lucy's acceptance of it. Such meekness was unlike her, and he wondered if marriage had wrought great changes in her personality. When he rode back to London in early September, just before the High Holy Days, it was with a heavy heart.

Arriving home, his mother met him at the door. Wordlessly, she handed him a small note. It was from the haham.

> It is with great sadness that I write to you that your dear friend, my son, Semuel Soeiro, is very ill and begs your company. Pray do not delay, as I cannot say if he will remain in this life much longer.

The shock of the message tore at his very soul. It had been two months since he'd last seen Semuel. How could his friend have failed so quickly? Domingo would have believed such news of the haham, whose health had always seemed precarious, but not Semuel. He immediately ran to the apartment in the Strand and was tearfully welcomed by Rachel ben Israel.

"Amiel, Semuel will be so pleased to see you. You are like a brother—" She stopped, overcome with weeping, and buried her face in a handkerchief. After a moment, she raised her tear-soaked face to him. "Go to him, Amiel."

He hurried up the stairs and found Semuel in his chamber. He was lying in bed, propped up by a mound of pillows. Semuel's face had a grayish color to it, and he had grown so thin that Domingo could immediately see that his friend had little hope of recovery. "Semuel," he choked, taking a seat by his friend's bed.

Even opening his eyes seemed to strain Semuel's strength. His breathing was labored, and Domingo could hear a distinctive rattle in it. "Amiel, my brother," Semuel rasped, reaching for Domingo's hand. "I'm sorry—"

"Shh, Semuel," Domingo cut him off. "Do not speak of our differences. It is I who should apologize to you for my distance these last months. It was poor repayment for the one who sat by my bedside after my fall and nursed me back to health. Please forgive me, Semuel. I never wanted to lose your friendship, and now it seems I shall lose you entirely."

"*Tikvah*, Amiel. Never lose hope." Semuel wheezed as he spoke and weakly squeezed Domingo's hand before a fit of coughing consumed him. Domingo watched helplessly as each spasm extracted the very life breath from his friend. Mercifully, Semuel's cough subsided after a few moments and he drifted into sleep. He still held Domingo's hand in his own, and after a time, Domingo's wrist and fingers began to tingle. But he would not remove his hand from Semuel's grasp. How could he let go of the hand that had stayed with him since he was a boy of eight? Semuel was only two years older but he was everything Domingo wished he could be: pious, dutiful, loyal, and humorous. It was so wrong. Semuel had a bride waiting in Amsterdam. His father needed him in their efforts on behalf of Poland's Jews. Semuel was a better Jew, a better son, and a better man than Domingo. Why was God taking him?

As he had learned to do as a child, Domingo wept silently; though this time he felt a surge of anger rise within him. When would God stop taking? Was his role in God's drama always to be the one left behind? The survivor without a purpose? What grand lesson was he supposed to learn from losing Semuel? What point was there to all this suffering? At sunset, Menasseh ben Israel came in to pray over his son. Wordlessly, Domingo embraced his former teacher and took his leave knowing, despite Semuel's encouragement to never lose hope, that he would never see his friend again.

XV. *Broken*, September 1657–1660

Lucy was in the parlor when Edward came down to breakfast the September day that would change the course of their lives. A basket full of stockings she'd been mending sat at her feet, even though she was presently staring out the window, lost in thought. She missed her family, but she would not give Edward the satisfaction of repeating his lecture against her going to Yorkshire. Everything she did, everything she said, and every expression on her face was in effort to avoid another confrontation with him. It was not that she feared him, because no matter how impassioned his words could be at times, Edward was not a violent man. But she understood her position quite clearly. He was her husband, her master, and she was tired of fighting all the time. Peace of mind now depended on the absence of harsh words and looks. How she longed for the buffer of children between them!

He sat down next to her and waited for her to turn from the window. It was only when she'd given him her full attention that he spoke. "I must travel to Bristol for a few days. Will you come with me?"

She shut her eyes against his gaze, hoping to hide her revulsion at the thought of being alone with him in a carriage for days; yet, at the same time, there was the temptation of getting out of London to break the monotony of her days. After a moment's consideration, she decided that the present dullness of London was worth a few days of solitude. "Thank you, Edward. But I have not felt well these last few days. I think I need to rest."

He smiled and patted her abdomen. "Do you have news for me, then?"

She did not, but she hated to tell him so. Lately she felt like one of his investments that had failed to draw profit. If she were barren, it would be yet another reason for him to be disappointed in her. "Perhaps, Edward. I will know surely by the time you return."

He kissed her forehead gently. "Then stay and rest, darling."

She packed his trunk while he visited his usual coffeehouse. His coach was due to leave at noon and she had to be sure his effects were in order before his departure. By late morning, he returned in a cheerful mood. "I've heard the most excellent news, Lucy. We are finally to be rid of that confounded rabbi, ben Israel."

"Oh, what news of him then?" She tried to seem disinterested.

"He's headed back to Amsterdam tomorrow. Apparently his son died and he wants to bury him there. Good riddance, I say. But blast it, too, Cromwell's given him the funds to go. It is criminal that Parliament supports that Jew in his affront to Christianity. If he could take the rest of those Christ-killers with him, it would be a happy day for England!" Edward seemed pleased with his invective and disappointed that she gave no response.

"I feel faint, Edward."

In a sudden change of attitude, Edward put his arm around her waist. "Wife, you must lie down. I want no harm to come to you or the child." He led her to their bed, where he helped her undress and slip under the quilts. "Just rest awhile and I'll send Nettie up to tend to you. I should only be gone a few days, a week at most. I'll bring you back some of those embroidered caps you like . . ." He trailed off as she turned her face into the pillow. Sighing heavily, he left without another word.

Lucy waited until she heard the carriage pull away and then hurried out of bed. Semuel was dead! She had to see Dominick. No matter what had transpired between them these last years, she had to know that he was all right. She slipped one of her everyday dresses over her shift and ran downstairs for her cloak and boots. From the kitchen she could hear snoring; Nettie was dozing again. Lucy gently shook the servant awake. "Nettie, I need to run out for a while. I'll return before dark."

"Mr. Polestead said you were ill . . . ?" Nettie began.

"I am most grieved over something, yes. I must see to a situation immediately," Lucy replied vaguely. "I can't say when I'll return so don't bother with dinner." Then she pecked her old nursemaid on the cheek, knowing she'd be asleep again within moments.

Pulling the hood of her cloak over her head, she started for Stoney Lane, not daring to hire a sedan chair for this visit. She estimated the walk to be about four miles from Aldwych Street to the Strand, then eastward down the length of Fleet Street, past St. Paul's, and then north on Leadenhall. It had been five years since she'd walked this route, but she would never forget the way to the secret synagogue or Dominick's house.

After an hour, Lucy found herself walking down Cree Church lane. It was still early afternoon, but the street seemed deserted. Nervously, she knocked on the door to Dominick's house and began to have doubts about coming. What if Dominick didn't want to see her? But there was no answer and she could see no movement through the windows. She knocked again in desperation and was surprised when Dominick himself finally opened the door. She caught her breath at the sight of him. He looked haggard, unshaven and barefooted, and his shirt was hanging loose and sporting a huge tear. The rings under his eyes bespoke of sleeplessness.

"Lucy, what are you doing here?" Nervously, he looked up and down the street to see if there was anyone who might have seen her. "Come inside," he ordered, grasping her arm and pulling her through the doorway, then quickly shutting the door.

She was still trying to catch her breath from the long walk and her cheeks were flushed. "Dominick, I heard about Semuel. What happened?" she asked after awhile.

He was speechless for a moment, trying to comprehend Lucy's presence after the way she'd so angrily walked away from him two years ago. He watched as she pulled back her hood, her unbound hair spilling down her shoulders and back like a waterfall of the richest brown cocoa. She exuded life while all he felt was death. She stood silent, waiting for his explanation. So he gathered his wits enough to speak.

"It was his lungs. Semuel wasn't well for a long time. He felt he'd failed his father when Cromwell wouldn't meet with him. When Whitehall faltered, Semuel took it as a personal defeat. He'd worked so hard to protect his father from the ugliness of the debate. But the vile things that Prynne published about the haham and then Senhor Robles's trial, it was all too much. He collapsed a month ago and never recovered. His parents were both with him . . ." Domingo trailed off, too overcome to continue. His oldest and dearest friend was dead, and Lucy, who was dead to him, had come back to comfort him. Did God allow no pure happiness?

"And you, Dominick? How are you?" Lucy asked, jarring him out of his thoughts of God's injustice.

"I don't know," he answered honestly. To the rest of the community, he said he was fine, but Lucy knew him too well to believe him if he told her his standard answer, even if they had been parted for five years. She was also not part of the politics between the London Sephardim and Menasseh ben Israel's supporters, so this gave him more freedom to answer her. "Semuel and his father were unsuccessful before Whitehall and forgotten afterward. Yet Senhor Robles was granted denization as a Jew and the rest of us bask in his success. I should be happy for our freedom, but I feel empty. The haham has sacrificed everything to save his people, including his only son. It is a twisted version of Christianity, no? But Semuel is dead and the Jews of Poland still have no safe haven from the Poles or the Crimeans. God only knows how many of them are molested and killed each day while we live free. Yet I cannot bring myself to carry on Semuel's fight. I'm tired. I don't want to do this anymore."

With this last statement, he couldn't meet her gaze. Lucy shivered at the nakedness of his pain. Misunderstanding her reaction, Dominick gestured for her to follow him. "Come, I have a fire in my chamber. You could use some brandy to warm you, too." She removed her mud-encrusted boots and followed him.

"Where is the rest of your family, Dominick?" she asked as they made their way upstairs.

"Manuel and his family left for Barbados last year. I moved downstairs after they left. My mother insists on remaining in the third-floor apartments. She thinks it makes a more attractive arrangement for a bride."

"You are to be married then?"

"If Mãe has her way," he answered curtly, refusing to elaborate. What was it to Lucy, married herself, if he wed?

In his chamber, a large room with three floor-to-ceiling windows along one wall, there was a healthy fire blazing. Domingo poured an overgenerous glass of brandy and handed it to Lucy. She accepted it gratefully and moved closer to the fire, slipping off her cloak and handing it to him. He carelessly threw it across the bed before slumping into an armchair by the hearth.

"What happened to your shirt? I can mend it for you, Dominick," Lucy offered.

"It cannot be mended, Lucy. When a loved one dies, we rend our clothes as a sign of mourning. The shirt will remain as it is until I burn it."

He stared at the fire as if watching his shirt burn now, his silence like an accusation against Lucy's intrusive presence.

"Have you eaten, Dominick? When did you last? You are so thin."

He didn't answer her; so she gulped down the brandy, set the glass aside, and ventured downstairs to the pantry. When she returned, she set some stale bread, cheese, and an unopened bottle of Madeira on a small table by his bed.

"Come eat," she ordered, grasping his hands and pulling him up out of his chair and guiding him to the bed. He sat down and she pushed the table within his reach.

"I'm fasting," he protested, eyeing the food on the table.

Lucy's voice was firm. "No. You must eat now. No more fasting. It serves no one but the devil if you sicken as well." Over the next quarter hour he ate little, but it satisfied her need to care for him. The wine remained untouched.

"Dominick, what will you do now?"

He shrugged as if it didn't matter. "I will stay in London. I cannot live in Amsterdam. Not now. Maybe someday I'll follow Manuel to Barbados. He writes that the weather there is similar to that of Portugal. Funny, though, he's never been to Portugal. He's always lived in the north." He was drifting in his speech.

Lucy eased him back into his bed where he fell asleep almost immediately. As she pulled the quilt over him, it occurred to her how changed he seemed. The pall of fear and sadness she'd seen in him as a boy ten years ago had returned to his eyes. Instinctively, she knew that his unhappiness went much deeper than Semuel's death.

As he slept, she was not sure what to do. She did not want to leave him yet, but there was little to do after tidying up his chamber. Finally, out of boredom, she curled up in his armchair and, after draining a second glass of brandy, dozed off in front of the fire.

◆◆◆

A man was being strangled by two English merchants, yet he did not struggle. It was Semuel. When his dead body slumped to the ground, they turned to Domingo. He began running. The cobblestone street became a narrow hallway. He looked back and saw that the merchants had been joined by a rabble of ragged, hobbling Jews. Looking ahead again, he realized there was no exit to this strange place. Then he turned a corner and saw a door. His pursuers were close now, trying to grab his cloak. Domingo struggled out of it and ran through the door, but it was suddenly a window and he was falling.

Domingo's sharp cry woke Lucy with a start. As she hurried to him, he sat up, clutching his shoulder. "Dominick? What's wrong?" His breathing was fast and heavy, but his face was pale as chalk.

"I dreamed of Semuel. They strangled him. They were coming for me." His voice cracked and the next words came out with a sob, "I'm still falling." Pulling his knees to his chest, he buried his face in them.

She didn't understand his ranting, so she said nothing as she sat down on the edge of the bed, pulled him into her arms, and stroked his back. The force of his sobs startled her, and Lucy tried as best she could to soothe him, even as she felt incapable of beating back his demons. After a time, he quieted, though she continued to hold him, guiltily welcoming his need for her. To be necessary to another human being, especially Dominick, made her feel more alive than she had in years.

Hours ago the fire had died and it had grown cold. Lucy looked around for her cloak. When she spied it on the edge of the bed, she leaned forward to retrieve it. "Are you leaving?" Domingo asked, looking up at her.

"It's cold, Dominick. I need—"

"Please don't go," he pleaded.

"I'm not going anywhere, Dominick," she reassured him, pulling her cloak around her shoulders and huddling into its folds for warmth.

He took a deep breath in relief and stared at her for a long moment, his dark eyes drawing her dangerously toward him. "Lucita, you are all I have left."

"Dominick," but before she could complete her reply, he'd pressed his lips against hers, gently at first, but then with increasing urgency. A flood of emotions swirled through her brain. This was wrong, yet she felt herself responding to his kiss.

"Tell me you don't despise me," he begged, his hands pushing her cloak off and pulling her close. He felt her body relax against his and deftly pulled her onto his bed. She was shivering, whether from cold or passion he did not know, but it mattered not. He needed her and she had come to him.

In the morning Lucy woke first. She dressed and slipped out without waking Dominick. There was no point in saying good-bye. They could not meet again. He loved her still, and this comforted her, but it was not enough. Edward could be irritating and unfair, especially regarding her father, but he was still her husband. Dominick had had his chance all those years ago and now the moment had passed.

◆◆◆

Several hours later Domingo stood at the wharf listening for the signal.

"Heave!"

He and the other pallbearers, Senhors Carvajal, Robles, Dormido, and their sons, lifted Semuel's coffin and began walking up the gangplank to the *Carabella*. Behind them, leaning on the arm of his friend John Sadler, walked Semuel's father. Rachel followed at the rear of the entourage dressed in the black silk that she would wear the rest of her life.

Menasseh ben Israel was a broken man. This was the second son he would bury, and he was returning to Amsterdam with nothing. The mission to Cromwell was a failure and all his resources were spent. The Lord Protector had granted him a small pension, but he'd spent it in advance to transfer and bury Semuel. In the end, the people of England, including London's Jews, did not want readmission. After the Robles trial, it was clear that the London Sephardim's merchant status kept them safe from expulsion so readmission was no longer a compelling issue for the Christians who had initially supported it. Menasseh's campaign no longer had any champions in England.

Domingo hated to see the ben Israels go, but Semuel had insisted on being buried in Amsterdam. If only he had reconciled himself to London. Last year, Senhor Carvajal had been granted permission to purchase a plot of land to be used for Jewish burial; it was now known as the Mile End Cemetery. It would have been so much easier to bury Semuel there. But Menasseh was a loving father to the end. He was honoring Semuel's wish to return to Amsterdam, and even though poor and in disfavor with the Ma'amad, he would transfer his son's body back.

When Domingo arrived back at Stoney Lane, his mother was furiously tidying his chamber. She did not greet him or explain her presence. "Mãe, please stop," he said with a weary sigh. "Let the servants take care of this."

She turned on him viciously and said, "You had her here! What have you done, Domingo? She is married now. Do you realize you could be hanged for adultery? Why do you persist with this girl?"

He knew her accusations were just, though he was addled by her spying. But he would not be drawn into an argument, not today. "She came when she learned of Semuel's death. It was my fault. I won't see her again."

"It is time for you to marry, Domingo."

"No, Mãe. I can't talk about this now. Please, I just came from the wharf. The haham has gone with Semuel, with his body." He breathed deeply in an effort to hold back the despair that was cresting like a wave. "Mãe, please," he pleaded. "I need to be alone."

She shot him a disgusted look, but her tone softened when she said, "That is your problem, Domingo. You are too much alone." She turned and left the room, and Domingo threw himself down on his bed, falling asleep recalling every detail from Lucy's visit.

◆◆◆

By November, Lucy knew she was pregnant. Edward was thrilled and immediately began making plans for his son's education. His confidence that she carried a boy amused her, but his confidence that she carried his child racked her with guilt. She had not seen Dominick since that night in September, but she knew that he was still in London. Now that Lucy was married and an expectant mother, it was easier to glean such information from her father, who regularly corresponded with Dominick. Her father's continued friendship with him pleased her, even as it meant that Dominick remained on the periphery of her life, neither in it nor out, like a distant relative one hears of every so often without ever actually seeing. Of course, now Lucy had a new love to occupy her heart.

She caressed her belly with satisfaction. After two and a half years of marriage to Edward, she had not conceived and had feared never having a child. She also knew that he was disappointed that she hadn't borne him a child yet. Oddly, his desire for a child was not matched by his desire for her. Edward carried out his conjugal duty, but often it seemed just that to him—a duty. Ever since her night with Dominick, Lucy had not felt the same toward her husband's attentions. She smiled, remembering something Dominick had told her years ago about the marital duties of a Jewish husband. He'd said that the husband was required to please his wife in bed. If she was not satisfied, he had not fulfilled his duty to her. Dominick had also told her that Jewish doctors believed that a woman was more likely to conceive if she took pleasure in the sex act. This idea was shocking to Lucy, who had been taught by her Catholic aunts and the Protestant ministers that a woman's enjoyment of sex was sinful. Yet it was hard for her not to envy Jewish women, especially the one who would someday become Dominick's wife. She sighed and tried to put these thoughts out of her mind. He was not her husband. If, however, this was Dominick's issue, Lucy felt it was his special gift to her and she would cherish the child all the more for it.

Abigail was born on the Feast of St. John the Baptist in 1658. It was not a difficult birth. Her daughter was small, yet robust, and Lucy recovered quickly. She was thankful she had not inherited her mother's difficulties with pregnancy and childbirth. The child had dark hair, but it was still too soon to tell who her father might be. Edward and Dominick couldn't be more different in appearance: Edward was tall, broad, blond, and blue-eyed, while Dominick stood no taller than her and was slender with dark features. Perhaps as Abigail grew, the mystery of her paternity would reveal itself. During her pregnancy, Lucy had burned to know, but now that Abigail was born, it did not seem to matter as much. Abigail was her child, not the property of her unknown father.

♦♦♦

One day near Michaelmas, and shortly after the sudden death of the Lord Protector, Oliver Cromwell, a visitor came. "Madam Lacerda," announced Nettie. Lucy nearly dropped the baby in surprise. Why would she come here? After settling Abigail in her cradle, Lucy went downstairs to greet Dominick's mother. She curtsied to her visitor, remembering their unfortunate meeting six years earlier, and invited her guest to take a seat in the parlor. As Teresa Maria lifted the black lace veil covering her face, Lucy's heart skipped a beat. Then she remembered that his mother was a widow and always wore black.

"I wish to see the child," Teresa Maria said. Her accent was heavy and her voice commanding. Lucy liked to think she obeyed Senhora Lacerda to maintain decorum, but she knew deep down that she heeded the request because she feared her.

After Nettie left to retrieve the baby, they sat in an awkward silence, waiting for her to return. As soon as Nettie appeared at the door, Teresa Maria rose and possessively took the child from her. Lucy was taken aback by the older woman's boldness and began to worry about where this was going.

"Will there be anything else, Madam?" Nettie asked in a rare effort at formality, which told Lucy that she was just as worried as her mistress.

Lucy wanted to keep Nettie close, but she couldn't think of any reason to keep a servant in the room with her. "Please bring some wine for Madam Lacerda," she commanded, hoping her old servant would not linger overlong in the pantry. Lucy then turned to Dominick's mother, who was examining Abigail intently.

Teresa Maria looked up sharply. "This is a healthy child."

Lucy did not know how to respond.

"What is her name?" Teresa Maria demanded.

"A-Abigail . . . after my husband's mother, who has been deceased these four years," Lucy stammered.

Teresa Maria seemed pleased with this information. She held Abigail close to her chest and breathed deeply into the folds of her blankets. Lucy saw that there was no question in the woman's mind that Abigail was Dominick's.

"For this child, I have a gift. It will be delivered tomorrow."

"Thank you, Madam. That is kind of you—"

"There is more," the older woman interrupted sharply. "I will visit this child each month. She will know me as her mother's friend."

Lucy grew increasingly agitated but remained silent. She would not be rude to Dominick's mother. In that moment, however, she did develop a deep appreciation for Dominick's gentle manner. How he ever kept his temper around this woman was a mystery to her. Finally, she nodded her consent and Teresa Maria's tone softened. "Good, it is agreed." She kissed the baby and handed her over to Lucy.

Before leaving, she instructed Lucy about her next visit. "I will send a message to you with the day and time of my call. You must respond immediately to confirm the visit or to provide an alternate time. Do you understand that this is necessary?"

"Yes," replied Lucy, realizing how clever Teresa Maria had become living in the shadows of Christian London. She could not be visiting when Edward was home. Teresa Maria's discretion protected both of them, and Lucy was thankful for it.

◆◆◆

During the winter months, Teresa Maria came regularly to visit Lucy and Abigail. Lucy often invited other female acquaintances at different times so that Teresa Maria's visits did not seem unusual to anyone taking notice. When it grew warm, they met for walks outside. During each visit, Teresa Maria brought a gift for Abigail, usually a piece of clothing or jewelry, so that by her first birthday, Abigail had a trousseau worthy of a lord's daughter. Despite her earlier misgivings, Lucy grew to enjoy her visits with Dominick's mother. They never spoke of him, but his presence seemed to dominate their time together. Did he know that his mother came to call on her regularly? Did he know that his mother was certain he was a father? Lucy wished to ask Teresa Maria these questions, yet she knew that the older woman would never answer them and that she would only think less of her for asking.

Teresa Maria only spoke Portuguese to Abigail, which at first irritated Lucy. After some months, however, she grew to enjoy its lyrical rhythms and felt his mother was providing an unintended window into Dominick's world. Perhaps this was how his mother had spoken to him as a child. Lucy wondered what it was like to have grown up hearing this beautiful language. It had never occurred to her before Teresa Maria's visits how much Dominick had lost, having to flee his homeland at such a young age. Ever since she'd learned he was a Jew, she had only thought of him as one. Only now did she realize that he was as much a Portuguese as he was a Jew.

Teresa Maria also proved to be quite helpful, offering Lucy the counsel she lacked with Elizabeth in Yorkshire. When Abigail began teething, it was Teresa Maria who told her how to give the child a rag soaked in sweet wine to suck as a comfort. When Abigail finally walked at thirteen months, Teresa Maria eased Lucy's fears of her baby falling and hurting herself. Teresa Maria knew what was truly effective and what was superstition concerning the child's health. She frequently referred to her husband's experience when trying to illustrate a medical point to Lucy. Oddly, even though Lucy knew from Dominick that his mother had birthed four children, Teresa Maria never mentioned them. Lucy was careful to respect Teresa Maria's silence in this matter. Now that she was a mother herself, Lucy could not imagine the pain of losing a child. To have lost three after seeing them safely through infancy, as Dominick's mother had, was beyond Lucy's ability to comprehend. How could anyone survive so much loss? Yet here she was, helping to raise her only surviving child's illegitimate daughter.

As Abigail grew so did her affection for the older woman, whom she called "Avo," "grandmother" in Portuguese. Whatever their true kinship may have been, Teresa Maria became a grandmother to Abigail through her doting and constant presence in Abigail's life. It was an odd arrangement, seeing Dominick's mother regularly but never speaking of him, but Lucy saw how much Abigail and Avo needed each other and encouraged their bond.

And so, two years passed. Lucy thought of Dominick every day but tried to be a wife worthy of Edward. He did not press Lucy for her adoration. Edward was satisfied with a tidy home, an orderly life, and a compliant wife. In this, Lucy accommodated her husband and increasingly found joy in her daughter and her friendship with Dominick's mother.

XVI. *RESTORATION*, MAY 1660–1663

Bells pealed throughout England the sunny day in May when Charles II landed at Dover to claim his throne. After eleven years without a king, England welcomed back the exiled royal, son of the late king who had been beheaded by the army. But for all the rejoicing, many feared what the restoration of the monarchy would mean. Jews had lived openly in London for four years but without any formal protection from Parliament. If the new king determined to restore the kingdom to its pre–civil war status, he would certainly oppose Oliver Cromwell's project for Jewish readmission.

Charles II's manifesto *The Declaration of Breda* offered amnesty to those who supported Parliament against the Crown and even endorsed religious tolerance in the realm. *Breda* inspired hope in Domingo of tolerance for the Jews, but he still made preparations to move his mother to Amsterdam should the Jews be expelled from England. He worried what such a move might do to her. She was sixty-one now, and even though she remained in fair health for one her age, he hated to uproot her. Many in the Jewish community were active royalists and would weather this change in government easily, but Domingo was not one of them. He had tried not to become too involved in civil war politics in England. Cromwell had been kind to the Jews, but he had failed to effect any formal tolerance of them. As much as Domingo hoped for better days under the restored monarchy, he had learned from experience to plan for the worst.

◆◆◆

Edward Polestead became increasingly ill-tempered and secretive as spring turned into summer, worried about his status in the new order. Indeed, King Charles II was true to his word and did not move against those who had supported Parliament against the monarchy during the civil war, but those who had directly participated in his father's death he had arrested as regicides. Edward's position was uncertain. He had not been among those who had signed the king's death warrant, but he had been present at his trial and beheading. Those among the five dozen men still living who'd signed the death warrant were imprisoned, and there was an expectation that many would be hanged. As for the regicides who had since died, Charles II ordered their corpses, including that of Oliver Cromwell, disinterred, decapitated, and hung in public places.

The king's method of avenging his father's murder seemed excessive to many Londoners, but it soon became clear that as Charles II was willing to create a new kingdom from the ruins of the Protectorate, he would not compromise the honor of his family to do so.

It was July when royal magistrates came for Edward. His lawyer, Jeremiah Hosgood, waited for hours outside his client's home to give Lucy the news. Hosgood said that Edward had not been too roughly handled but that he was to be held at the king's pleasure at the Tower. What Lucy found odd about Mr. Hosgood's telling of Edward's arrest, even though she had been too distressed to mark it at first, was that Edward had not been taken at his countinghouse or at home. He'd been down at the docks on a Dutch merchant ship when the king's soldiers had come for him.

Within a week, Edward's property, including his home in London and all the merchandise in his warehouse, was impounded. He had left a good deal of money with a goldsmith banker, but when Lucy tried to withdraw it, she found the money was not available. The goldsmith curtly informed her that Edward had transferred the money to Amsterdam in anticipation of his removal to that city. She didn't understand what he'd done until after meeting with Jeremiah Hosgood a second time in his office at Lincoln's Inn.

"Your husband made arrangements to move to Amsterdam. I'm afraid his assets are tied up there, Mrs. Polestead," he informed her.

"But Mr. Hosgood, that's not possible. He knew I couldn't travel in my condition." She ran her hands over her swollen belly. She'd finally conceived Edward's child this past Christmas season.

Hosgood tried to appear sympathetic, but his tone remained firm. "I believe, Madam, that he planned to travel alone."

Her first reaction was disbelief. Surely Edward would not have left her alone with the children? Then she realized that he would have if it meant saving his life. Did he plan on sending for them later? Why had he kept his plans from her? She took a deep breath and tried to think logically about her situation.

"Mr. Hosgood, could we simply have the money transferred back?"

"It's not that simple, Madam. Only your husband may transfer the money, but if he does this, he risks it being confiscated like his other assets."

"Mr. Hosgood, this situation is untenable. How am I to live without money?"

"That, Madam, is a question for your husband. I would be happy to deliver a message to him for you." He slid some parchment and a quill across the desk to her. As surprised as she was at his informal gesture, she quickly penned a note to Edward and slid it back to the lawyer. There was no point in sealing it as the Tower magistrate would inspect it before passing it on to Edward.

Lucy had some small savings that she'd managed to keep from Edward, money her father had collected from renting out Chapel House. Thus she was able to take rooms for herself and Abigail in Cheapside. Her landlady, a beefy widow named Charity Butts, took pity on Lucy's condition and made the tenant on the second floor move to the fourth so that Lucy would not have to climb so many stairs. Her living situation settled, Lucy tried to adjust to her change in circumstance, but her resources would not last much beyond the birth of her second child.

As Nettie's last service to the family she had served for almost thirty years, she and her nephew Peter, who drove a hackney coach, moved Lucy and Abigail into their new lodgings. Lucy arranged a small pension for Nettie with money her father had sent. With his gift to Nettie he included a letter to Lucy, begging her to come to Yorkshire. However, heavily pregnant, she couldn't bear a week in a hot, bumpy carriage. She also refused to leave London without hearing back from Edward. She sent a parcel of clothes and food to him at the Tower, but she could not find out anything about his condition or his case. Finally, after several weeks had passed, Mr. Hosgood produced a reply from Edward:

Wife,

I am as well as can be expected under the circumstances. Mr. Hosgood told you about my plans. It is best to leave things as they are right now. You have my permission to sell the house to use as income.

"Sell the house?" Lucy wondered aloud. "I cannot. He must know that it has been taken along with the rest of his property." She looked up at Mr. Hosgood in anticipation, hoping to hear that their house in London would be returned to her, even if it was only to sell it. Edward had been in prison for two months and Lucy desperately needed money.

"I believe, Madam, that it is the house in Yorkshire to which he is referring."

"Chapel House? But that's my inheritance from my uncle! It is part of the estate. I cannot sell that house."

"Sell it to your father," he suggested.

"No," Lucy said, shaking her head. "No, Chapel House is my house. It is all I have. I will not sell it."

◆◆◆

It was September and her time was near. Keeping up with Abigail took every bit of energy Lucy had. When Teresa Maria visited Lucy's new accommodations, she looked with disdain on the two unkempt rooms, just a parlor and a bedchamber. Teresa Maria tried to give Lucy money, but she would not take it, insisting that she would go to Yorkshire as soon as the baby was born. Lucy also refused when Teresa Maria offered to send a girl over to help with the housekeeping, feeling that the older woman's charity was somehow an assertion of control over her and Abigail. Finally free of Edward's supervision, even if only temporarily, Lucy was not going to forfeit her autonomy to Teresa Maria, no matter how well-meaning she was.

In the end, it was Lucy's father who found a way to break through Lucy's defenses. She had put Abigail to bed and was looking forward to resting herself. The baby in her womb had been quiet today. It wouldn't be much longer now before her labor began. A knock at the door deflated Lucy's hopes of rest, but she waddled across the room to answer it just the same, hoping it would be Mr. Hosgood with news of Edward. But when she opened the door, she stood face-to-face with someone quite unexpected.

Dumbfounded, she simply stood in the doorway for a long moment, not even feeling the cold that he so wished to escape.

"May I come in?" Domingo asked, not sure how to interpret her reaction.

"Yes, of course, please," she said with distracted politeness.

After closing the door behind him, he pulled a letter out from inside his cloak. "Lucy, I received this from your father today. He cannot travel because Elizabeth's time is also near. He wishes me to escort you to his home in Yorkshire."

"Dominick, I cannot travel now," Lucy said, indicating to her womb as if he hadn't noticed she was pregnant. "Perhaps in a few weeks, after the baby is born."

He nodded, then looked about the cramped parlor to the other room beyond. "You are living alone here?"

She hated to admit this to him. "I've birthed a child before, Dominick. Your worries are ill placed."

"Lucy, please. What will you do when the baby comes? There is no one to send for a midwife, no one to care for the other child. You cannot do this alone. Let me at least take you to my home. My mother will care for you and call for our doctor when your time comes."

"No, I cannot."

"Why are you being so unreasonable? Think of your children if you won't consider your own well-being."

"I don't need your help. I'm staying here."

Domingo sighed in frustration. "Then I shall stay here with you, Lucita."

Lucy began to weep, but she did not know if it was in relief or anger. Why had it come to this? Why was it Dominick at her door and not her husband? Then she felt Dominick taking her into his arms, stroking her hair.

"Lucita, I've left you alone too long. Please come to my home and let me take care of you." She was crying so hard now that she could not speak. Years of sadness were pouring out of her. After she quieted, he led her to a chaise and gently eased her into it. "Stay here," he instructed. "I will get the child."

Despite what she'd told him, she was pleased that Dominick had come, but all she wanted now was sleep. Closing her eyes, Lucy drifted to a state beyond anxiety and exhaustion. But she soon felt the familiar pain in her back. Moments later, Domingo emerged from the back chamber with Abigail lying asleep against his shoulder, his hands protectively holding her in place. He offered Lucy an arm up. Just then, a second contraction seized her.

Domingo startled at the sharp intake of breath she took to ease the pain, but Lucy reassured him, "It is time. You can tell your mother to send for the doctor."

Early the next morning, Teresa Maria sent Domingo out of the house with Abigail for fear that Lucy's travail would scare the child. He accepted this charge gratefully, knowing that Lucy's labor was just as likely to scare him, although he felt a little anxiety about spending the next few hours alone with his daughter. Abigail was just two years old but Domingo could already see definition in her features. He felt like he was looking at a perfect blend of himself and Lucy: his hair, dimples, and high cheekbones; Lucy's eyes, mouth, and fair coloring. He had never seen Abigail up close. Though he knew that his mother visited Lucy and Abigail regularly, and on several occasions he had followed them just to get a glimpse of Lucy and the child. He had never done more than that, for fear of pushing either woman away from the other. It bothered him that Lucy had never tried to contact him during these last three years, but he accepted her silence as his penance for how he'd treated her years ago. Lucy seemed happy and his mother, consumed by her grandchild, had stopped pressing him to get married.

Nervous, he led the little girl out the door. "Avo?" she said, looking around anxiously for Teresa Maria as Domingo lifted her up and carried her across the gutter. Not seeing her grandmother, she squirmed in his arms and said, "Where's Avo?"

"Avo is tending to your mother."

"Mama?" The child's eyes grew wide with fear.

"Shh," he said, stroking her head, "she's going to be fine, and soon you will have a new brother or sister."

"Who are you?" she asked him.

He considered her question carefully. What was he to her? "I am your Avo's son, Amiel," he answered. He wasn't sure why he told her his Hebrew name, somehow it just seemed right.

He took her to the river to see the ships. Abigail's expressions of awe told him that his mother and Lucy had not ventured here with the child; it pleased him to be showing her something new. They ate a midday meal of sweet cakes and apples outside St. Catherine Cree Church, and then Abigail ran around the plaza chasing birds that came to feast on pieces of bread Domingo scattered on the ground. He was impressed with how fast and sure Abigail was on her little legs.

She scampered over to him laughing. "Ami, Ami! I chase birds!"

He caught her up in his arms and held her close. When she nestled her little face into his chest, he knew everything was going to be different from now on. His daughter needed him. He would not fail her. In late afternoon, he trudged home carrying the exhausted child. They were welcomed back by Avo with the news that Abigail had a sister.

That evening, he stood in the doorway of his chamber gazing at the three sleepers who had taken possession of his bed. Lucy lay on her side, her arms protectively sheltering the baby, with Abigail curled up against her back. He suddenly sensed his mother behind him, but it was a moment before she spoke. "This is not your family, Domingo."

He turned to her, stunned and hurt. She was so damn perceptive of his thoughts! "I know, Mãe." He turned away and went down to the kitchen.

She followed close behind. "Domingo, it is time for you to make your own family." He glowered at her, but she continued anyway, "I can arrange—"

"No!" He slammed his fist on the table in the center of the room. He drew a deep breath and continued more calmly, "Mãe, I am only twenty-six."

It was her turn to glower at him. "You make excuses, Domingo. As soon as she and the baby can travel, you will take them to her father. When you return, we will speak of your marriage. Senhor Caçeres has a daughter who's just come of age—"

"Mãe, stop," he said furiously. "You and Manuel got your way all those years ago. I abandoned Lucy and finished my apprenticeship. Now I am my own master and I will not submit to your schemes. I should have married Lucy, but since I cannot have her, I choose not to marry at all."

"Domingo!" she cried in shock. "You cannot! You are the last of our family."

"No, Mãe. Abigail is." He stormed out of the kitchen and shut himself up in one of the spare bedrooms.

♦♦♦

He went in to see Lucy the next morning. After he'd sat down on the edge of the bed, she handed the baby to him, grinning at his unease. "Remember when you held Thomas as an infant? That was ten years ago."

"It's hard to believe it's been that long. This one seems so much smaller. What will you name her?"

"She is Mary Teresa after my mother and yours."

He looked up surprised. "Lucy, what of your husband? He won't approve of such a Papist name, especially if he learns that one of her namesakes is Jewish."

Lucy's tone was hard when she said, "I've been without his support for three months. I've earned the right to name my baby what I like."

Her bitterness surprised him. He wished to talk with her about Edward's incarceration, but he didn't want to shame her. He knew that Lucy and her children had no income and had all but exhausted their resources. She had to start relying on the support of others now. He prayed that she would not be stubborn in this. The child began to root for her mother's breast so Domingo handed her back. "It is a lovely name, Lucy. My mother will be pleased."

♦♦♦

The following week they set out for Yorkshire in a private coach Domingo had rented. He was surprised at how easily Lucy complied

211

with her father's plan for her to move to Yorkshire. Living so far north would make it difficult for Lucy to see to her husband's case, which could still end in hanging, or worse, years spent in the Tower prison. Not many men, even in the best of health, survived long in prison without help from the outside. There was at least some small glory in hanging before a crowd, even a hostile one, as opposed to wasting away, forgotten, in the bowels of the Tower with only rats as spectators. As angry as Lucy had seemed to be with her husband, she could not wish such a fate for him.

The carriage ride would take six days, and as much as he hated this bumpy, noisy manner of travel, Domingo was glad to be away from his mother's attentive eyes. While Lucy had been in his house, he'd felt adulterous just breathing the same air as her. The baby slept most of the journey, and Domingo did his best to entertain Abigail so that Lucy could rest as well. He told Abigail stories, sang songs he remembered from his youth, and drew pictures with her. Sometimes he held Mary while Lucy slept. He marveled at how tiny and beautiful she was. Holding her little body against his engendered a confusing array of emotions in him. He wanted to protect her from every bump of the coach, and he became distraught whenever she cried.

They spent each night at an inn along the road. Still tired and sore, Lucy always retired early with the girls, leaving Domingo to find his own company in the inn's tavern. Generally, they would've all had to share a bed with one another or with other guests, but Domingo had paid the innkeepers handsomely so that Lucy and her girls would always have a private chamber. Domingo usually slept in a small room with one bed he had to share with two or more strangers. It was disconcerting after so many years of sleeping alone in his own bed. Domingo slept little those first few nights. But soon exhaustion won out and he welcomed the bed, no matter how crowded, at the end of each day.

When they finally arrived in Yorkshire, Domingo discovered why Lucy had been so easily convinced to move. She insisted on staying at her house, though, still stubbornly determined to live alone with her girls rather than with her father at his manor. So Domingo reluctantly unloaded his charges and their luggage at

Chapel House. It was a finely built, although small, house with three bedrooms upstairs and a kitchen, parlor, and dining room on the first floor. Chapel House was clearly a guesthouse for Thicket Hall, as it provided just one chamber for a servant in the attic and only a small stable. Nonetheless, it was cozy and comfortable, and Domingo could see why Lucy loved it. When Lucy and the girls were settled in, he hiked up the path to Thicket Hall to speak with her father.

"Domingo! Come in, come in. Where is Lucy?" John asked as he ushered Domingo into the parlor.

Domingo sighed. "She is at Chapel House. I could not convince her to stay here, even for the first night."

John just smiled. "She's got her mother's stubbornness, that's for sure. I should have known she'd do this when she asked me to remove the tenants. Well, perhaps it is for the best. God knows one screaming infant is enough in any man's home."

"How is Mrs. Dunnington, sir?" Domingo asked, remembering that Elizabeth was far along in her own pregnancy.

"Well enough. Any day now, the midwife tells us. Between you and me, I've no liking for infants. If children could arrive as seven-year-olds, with all that spitting up, drooling, and screaming behind them, so much the better. But of course, I suppose that would be hard on the women."

Domingo laughed politely and then, in a more sober tone, said, "I thought we might talk a bit about Lucy's situation."

"An ugly business, Domingo," John said, shaking his head. "Polestead left her with nothing. He even suggested that she sell Chapel House to pay his prison costs. I just don't understand. Edward and I fell out a few years back, but I never expected him to treat my daughter so irresponsibly. Naturally Lucy and the children must stay here, but it is not going to be easy for her to care for him at this distance."

"I've been thinking about that, and, if you allow me, sir, I think I can help."

"What do you have in mind?"

"If I might, and if Lucy would agree, every two months I can transport her and the children to London. My mother and I have a large house with separate apartments. Mãe has actually grown quite

213

fond of Lucy, and it would be good for her to feel like she was contributing to Lucy's comfort. I'm sure she'd care for the children while I escort Lucy to see Edward or the lawyer about his case. I've already met the man, a Mr. Jeremiah Hosgood. He seems to be competent."

"Domingo, do you realize how much time this plan of yours will consume? Why on earth would you want to do this?"

"For everything you did for us, Mr. Dunnington. You made a great sacrifice for my people. I feel that this is a way I can help you. I don't have a family of my own, so the time and money are of little consequence to me."

John sighed deeply. "This is an exceedingly generous offer, young man, and, as it is the only plan we have, I accept. I will pay for Edward's legal and prison fees if you would take care of the travel. And naturally, Elizabeth and I will ensure that Lucy and the children have everything they need here. You, of course, are most welcome to remain with us while you reside in Yorkshire."

"Thank you, Mr. Dunnington. I am most eager to retire. Will you be spending the night at Chapel House, then?" Though he'd been sitting all day in the carriage, Domingo was suddenly exhausted.

"Would it be too much trouble for you to stay there tonight? I hate to leave Elizabeth. Tomorrow I can arrange with Lucy to have a maid stay in the house."

"I won't be staying longer than the one night. I have to get back to London."

"Yes, of course. It is just for the one night."

"I'll need a lamp to manage the path back."

John sighed in relief, so Domingo did not voice his own concerns about the arrangement. His presence in Lucy's house did not suit propriety, but her father had never been one to worry about such things. He would stay at Chapel House tonight, but tomorrow he would return to London and John would have to figure out a new arrangement.

♦♦♦

It was on the return trip of their second excursion that it started. After settling the girls in bed at the inn, Lucy went downstairs, hoping to join Dominick for a meal. When she entered the dimly lit

214

and crowded main room, she noticed that there was some kind of celebration going on. After a few moments, she realized that it was the eve of the new year, the spring equinox. Tomorrow would also be Dominick's birthday. She'd been so consumed with her own life that she'd quite forgotten about the general passage of time. Two dozen villagers filled the small hall, all of them singing and drinking. A fiddler made merry with his instrument and was accompanied by a middle-aged woman who sang and played a whistle. After some rousing songs, she began a slower, mournful melody.

"*Black is the color of my true love's hair. His lips are like a rose so fair. He has the sweetest eyes and the gentlest hands. I love the ground whereon he stands.*

"*I love my love as well he knows. I love the ground whereon he goes. And how I wish the day would come, when he and I can be as one.*"

Her voice grew stronger as she reached the song's tragic climax. "*I went to the sea and there did weep. For satisfied I'll never be. I wrote him a letter, just a few short lines. And suffer death ten thousand times.*"

Lucy felt the words of the song merge with her memories. She looked over at Dominick where he stood by the hearth happily chatting with some of the village men. Did he even know she was in the same room now? He'd been her friend and her lover. What was he now? He acted toward her as a brother. Perhaps he had a lover among his own people. A surge of jealousy swept over her at the thought. It was too much to bear, even as she knew it was ridiculous for her to be jealous when she was married to another. She ran back upstairs, but to her surprise, he followed quickly behind her.

"Lucy. What's wrong? Are you ill?"

Ignoring him, she struggled with the key to her door. Her tears made it difficult to see the lock. She finally got the door open, but even then he followed her, shutting the door behind him.

"Lucy, please," he whispered, looking furtively at the sleeping children.

"I can't, Dominick. I've been such a horrid wife to my husband because I've spent almost every moment of my marriage wanting to be with you. I hate this life! I hate that you never answered my letters from Amsterdam! And I hate how much I still love you!"

"Lucita, I made such a mistake," he said and reached for her, but she moved away.

"Just leave, please, Dominick," she said with a finality that told him that further pleading was useless. He obeyed her request and retired to his own room. He despised himself for the despair he had caused her, but he could not help but be uplifted by her admission of loving him. There was hope.

◆◆◆

During the final two days of their trip, there was a strained civility between them. Domingo did not want to speak to Lucy in front of the children, and there was no privacy at the inns. When they arrived at Chapel House, Domingo quickly helped the driver unload Lucy's trunk and made arrangements with him for their trip in March. That task completed, Domingo entered the house and heard Lucy shutting the door to the girls' chamber upstairs. He took off his cloak, poured himself a glass of wine, and waited for her to come downstairs. But after a quarter hour, she still remained upstairs. Quietly, he ascended the steps and, seeing her chamber door shut, was disappointed to find that she'd already retired to her room. Frustrated, he went to bed. If she would not speak to him, then he would not force the issue. He determined to rise early to pay his respects to John, collect his horse, and then begin the journey back to London.

Late in the night there was a knock at his chamber door. Scrambling out of bed, he quickly donned his breeches and opened the door. Though she looked as if she'd just risen from her bed, the hard look on her face told him that she'd not been sleeping. Without a word of greeting, she strode past him into his chamber and tightened her shawl around her shoulders, as if arming herself for battle. Her anguish had finally fermented into anger and she was ready to confront him.

"Would you have married me, Dominick, had I not married Edward?"

The question took him by surprise. He was sure that she'd start by asking if he loved her. "We pledged ourselves when we first lay together," he answered.

"That does not satisfy my question, Dominick."

He tried again. "There has been no other, Lucy. I will always provide for you, even if we cannot be together. Under different circumstances I would have claimed you as my own. I have no right to call you wife, but this is how I will always consider you."

"I would have waited for you," she said through clenched teeth.

He tried to explain, "I thought I had to choose between you and who I am."

"I don't care that you are a Jew, Dominick!" she yelled, finally losing her composure.

"I know that. But my family cared that you were not one." He took a deep breath. "I cared."

Her expression fell at this revelation. "So you made love to me in secret while projecting the image of a good Jew? What kind of love is that? What kind of religion is that?" Her voice bordered on hysterical. It was an emotional purge to be able to scream at him. It wasn't so much that she needed the right answers from him; she simply needed to be able to expel the anger she'd felt since he'd left for Amsterdam eight years ago.

"I never denied loving you! Tell me what kind of life we could've had together, Lucy? What kind of life would Abigail have if people knew what she was?"

"Tell me what she is, Dominick! What is wrong with that beautiful child?"

"She is a Jew."

"Is she? Where is her Jewish father? Why has he not claimed her?"

"I was trying to protect you, Lucita. You never came back after that night. I thought that was how you wanted it."

She was holding back tears. "It was. You were right to stay away then. But how could you have left me after our pledge, Dominick? Why did you never even try to explain?"

"Because I knew you'd defy the world and marry me, and I loved that in you. But when all your friends turned on you and shopkeepers refused to serve you, what then? You would've grown to hate what I am."

"You don't know that! You never gave me that chance!"

"I couldn't take the risk." He placed his hands on her shoulders. The contact seemed to calm her. "Lucy, I nearly died the night I read your last letter, when you thought I might have been false to you. I learned to live with it because I knew it wasn't true. But I couldn't bear it if you hated me for being Jewish, because that is true."

"Please," she pleaded in a quiet voice. "Give me the chance now." She slid her arms around his neck and pressed her lips against his, her tears streaming down both their cheeks. The thin material of her nightgown offered little barrier against her nakedness. He needed no more convincing.

"I will never leave you again, Lucita," Domingo said. As they kissed, he tried to touch every curve of her body at once, as if he could make up for years of longing in a few moments. As he was leading her to his bed, she suddenly stopped and cocked an ear to the door. "What's the matter?"

"Shhh," she urged, putting her finger to his lips. "It's the baby. I have to see to her." Without looking back at him, she picked up her shawl from where it had fallen on the floor and slipped out the door. Domingo stood dumbfounded. Surely the baby needed Lucy more than he did at that moment, but her timing was terrible. Torn between joy over Lucy's desire for him and frustration at their interrupted tryst, he retired to his bed alone.

◆◆◆

He was falling again, this time off a high cliff above a turbulent ocean. A rush of cold air chilled his body and there was a tickling about his torso. When he looked down, he saw a striking blue butterfly fluttering about the hairs on his chest as if they were garden flowers. He didn't understand. Then he realized that he was no longer falling, but floating. And he was being carried out to sea by gentle, but determined, waves. The butterfly flew toward his face and alighted on his lips.

"Dominick." He felt her presence before he heard her whispering his name. She'd drawn back the quilt and was lying beside him, her fingers lightly caressing his chest. Still groggy from sleep, it took him a moment to realize where he was. As he came to full consciousness, Lucy snuggled up against him.

"Mmmm, Lucita." He reached down for the quilt and pulled it over them, hoping that Mary did not wake again for a long time.

◆◆◆

For three years, Lucy and the girls lived as nomads, living in Yorkshire two months and then traveling to London during the third. While in London, Dominick would escort Lucy to the Tower to visit with Edward as often as the guards would allow. Edward seemed to assume it was Lucy's father who brought her to him, and Lucy did not bother to correct him. There was no point in exposing Dominick to Edward. Occasionally Edward's advocate would join Lucy at these meetings, and at least once during each trip to London, Mr. Hosgood would invite Lucy to his office at Lincoln's Inn. Dominick always went with her to these meetings. He and Mr. Hosgood seemed to get on quite well.

There was little progress in Edward's case, but the conditions of his internment improved. After almost a year of incarceration, he was moved from a barred cell to a private room with a window, small fire grate, sleeping cot, and reading table. The new accommodations were still damp and cold, but there, Edward had privacy and some small comforts, such as books and writing supplies. His health was fair, although he had developed a racking cough in the months since she'd seen him last. Once, Edward had tried to bed her in the prison, but Lucy had stormed out, disgusted at both his selfish desire and her own unfaithfulness. Thus their conversation, which had been characterized for most of their marriage by the unease they felt at trying to avoid confrontation, became even more strained.

What bothered Lucy the most about visiting her husband was how infrequently he asked after the children. It was almost as if, now that they were living in Yorkshire, Edward had no reason to question their material circumstances. Certainly, her father and Elizabeth made sure that Lucy and her daughters had a well-stocked larder at Chapel House, and Dominick and Teresa Maria provided an allowance generous enough for Lucy to engage a local woman to help her during the day, but Edward could not have known this. Lucy, however, refused to complain to her husband for fear that he would bring up the sale of Chapel House again. Though the house had been willed to Lucy before her marriage, it legally belonged to Edward. If he wished it, he could instruct Jeremiah Hosgood to sell the house, and Lucy would have little recourse against the law. It was best to not bring up the matter with Edward.

If Teresa Maria suspected the nature of her son's relationship with Lucy, she kept it to herself. While in London, they lived as brother and sister. And as much as Lucy grew to dread the long trip between Yorkshire and London, the two-week trip was when she felt that she, Dominick, and her girls were really a family. If the weather allowed, they rode for eight to ten hours a day in the coach, covering forty miles sometimes. They filled the time by reading stories to the girls, singing songs, and teaching them their letters. By the time Abigail was five, she could read English and a little Latin. She could also converse with Dominick in Portuguese, and she knew how to write her name in Hebrew. Dominick was a natural teacher, and Lucy loved watching him with the girls. Mary had a great ear for stories, and as soon as she could talk, she would spend hours rambling on, to Dominick's amusement, about the strange food that Avo would serve them and about the antics of her Uncle Richard, who was three weeks younger than she.

During this time, Chapel House became their home. Dominick never stayed more than two nights, but he was the undisputed man of the house. The household revolved around his schedule and his preferences when he was there. Lucy would never have deferred to Edward or her father in this way, but perhaps because Dominick's presence was always so fleeting, she could afford to allow him this role. Though she was concerned with how her father would interpret her relationship with Dominick, Lucy was pleased to discover that her father's fondness for him remained intact, even insisting that Dominick dine at Thicket Hall whenever he was in Yorkshire.

Elizabeth was less enthusiastic about Dominick's company, but she never protested his visits. Lucy was not bothered by Elizabeth's suspicions because, despite the stress of Edward's incarceration, her financial worries, and her secret relationship with Dominick, Lucy found herself happier during these years than she had been since before her mother died. She was her own mistress, her children were safe and healthy, and Dominick loved her. Lucy knew that it could not go on like this forever and that soon she would have to make a choice. As satisfied as she was, she could see how the constant separation wore on Dominick and the girls. Deep down, she knew that this was not the family life he wanted or the one he deserved. But what to do? In the end, it was someone quite unexpected who pushed her to a decision.

◆◆◆

December always brought an increase in London's demand for wine and spices, making it a busy time of year for merchants like Antonio Robles. And after eleven years of being outlawed as pagan under Cromwell's Puritan rule, Christmas had been restored by King Charles II and had increased in significance and opulence each year. The feasts of the rich became more lavish, while the poor felt more and more their poverty. After justifying Senhor Robles's accounts for the week, Domingo's mind drifted back to Lisbon, to his childhood Christmas traditions. The Nativity Mass had been an elaborate affair of music, incense, and processions. At home, his mother would serve a special meal of *bacalhau* or dried codfish, egg-soaked fried bread topped with honey called *rabanadas*, spiced grapes, challah bread, and sweet wine. Before eating, he and his siblings would sprinkle grains on the hearth as an offering to the *alminhas a penar*, the souls of those who had died. He missed those times with his brothers and sister. He seemed to have so few memories of them now. It was Marcos and Gaspar who'd been the brothers of his formative years, and his childhood memories of them centered on the Sabbath. But now Marcos and Gaspar were gone too, living in Barbados and planning families of their own.

"Sir?" Domingo's reverie was broken by Sarah, a plain, but cheerful, young woman from Middleburg who had recently come to work in Senhor Robles's home. "A message was delivered for you."

"Thank you, Sarah," Domingo said and took the letter she held out to him. He waited for her to leave his office, then carefully opened it. Immediately scanning the bottom, he noted that it was from Jeremiah Hosgood.

December 18, 1663
Dear Mr. Lacerda,
    I've been able to arrange the matter of which we spoke last week. It is necessary for us to complete the business

before your trip north. Please come to my home at Star Yard
in Holburn near Lincoln's Inn this evening.
  Yours,
Jeremiah Hosgood, Atty.

The Hosgoods' servant led Domingo to the back of the house
where the lawyer made his study in the back parlor. A dining table
served as his desk, which was covered with strewn papers. "Lacerda,
thank you for coming on such short notice," Hosgood said, rising to
greet Domingo. "Please sit. Wine?" Without waiting for Domingo's
answer he poured a generous cup and handed it to him. "Just this
afternoon I received word that your petition was accepted."

Domingo sighed deeply. "Good. When will it be carried out?"

"Not so fast," Hosgood cautioned. "There is a condition. The
Crown requires a bond of five hundred pounds." Hosgood waited for
Domingo's response before continuing. Domingo said nothing, so
Hosgood completed his thought, unaided by his guest's commentary,
"You will have to ask her father for the money."

"I will pay the bond in full," Domingo stated firmly. "There is no
need to burden Mr. Dunnington with this matter."

Hosgood's jaw dropped in astonishment. "In full! Why would
you do this, Lacerda? What is he to you?"

"I don't know." Domingo looked away. "Redemption perhaps."

"Are you in need of so much redemption?"

"Which of us is not, Hosgood?" Domingo replied, locking eyes
with the older man. Hosgood simply shook his head. Domingo
rose to leave. "I will bring the note to your office at Lincoln's Inn
tomorrow morning before I depart. I would ask that my role in this
matter be handled with discretion."

"Yes, of course. Until tomorrow, then." Hosgood escorted
Domingo out, passing through the parlor where Mrs. Hosgood sat
with her two children, Clara and William. Domingo tipped his hat
to them, but the matron's angry eyes were on her husband and the
children stared blankly at their hands, folded neatly in their laps.

XVII. *REVELATION,* CHRISTMAS 1663

The day dawned bright and cold. An early-morning snowfall blanketed Yorkshire, providing a glistening cover to the muddy, gray landscape. By late afternoon, the snow had begun again, this time driven by a blustering wind off the North Sea. Despite the weather, Sebastian and Frances, who was proudly bearing their three-month-old son, had come to Chapel House to visit with Lucy and the girls.

"Lucy, what news of Edward? Is there any hope of his being released or shall you remain the wife of a traitor to the king?" Sebastian asked. Frances shot him a disapproving look, but she was just as eager for Lucy's answer.

Lucy ignored Sebastian's barb. In fact, she found it gratifying that her cousin expressed anger over her predicament rather than expecting her, like so many others, to feel nothing but pity for her husband. To be sure, Edward had been the victim of the king's vengeance; but after more than three years in prison, Edward was now simply the victim of the king's inattention. And Lucy had never forgiven him for trying to leave the country without her.

"His advocate does not believe that his case will come to trial," she answered. "It is now a matter of convincing the Privy Council that Edward is no threat. We are hoping that Edward's illness will persuade His Highness to mercy—" A knock at the door interrupted their discussion. Lucy sprang up to answer it. Frances cringed.

While Lucy was not unaware of her cousin's disapproval of her keeping her own house, she felt no desire to change her household management on Frances's account. The domestic arrangements suited both her needs and her purpose. It took little trouble to open a door. The real work was in explaining who passed through it. She paused at the foyer, smoothed her skirts, and took a deep breath to calm her excitement. She knew it would be him, even though she had not expected him until tomorrow. Pulling the door open, she was not disappointed to see his figure before her. "Dominick," she exclaimed then kissed his cheek. It was only then that she noticed how weary and pale he looked. As she drew him into the warmth of the foyer, he moaned and clutched his shoulder. "You're hurt!"

He leaned against the wall for support. "Just bruised."

Despite his dismissive comment, Lucy saw that he was in a great deal of pain. "Frances and Sebastian are here, but I'm going to prepare a hot bath for you." Too tired to speak, Domingo just nodded in reply.

She helped him to the kitchen and settled him in a rocker by the hearth, then she hurried back to the parlor. "Frances, Sebastian, I'm so sorry. Mr. Lacerda has arrived and he's not well. I need to tend to him."

"Ami is here?" five-year-old Abigail asked, jumping to her feet excitedly.

"Yes, darling, but please don't go to him just yet. He is in a terrible state and needs to rest." Abigail's face fell and Lucy found herself relenting. Abigail was his daughter after all. "All right, Gaily-girl. Why don't you get some wine for Ami. There's a jug and some pewter mugs in the kitchen cupboard."

Abigail's eyes brightened and she skipped away happily. Fortunately Mary, consumed with her doll, did not notice her sister's departure. It would have been near impossible to make her understand that she could not clamber all over Dominick right now.

Frances and Sebastian exchanged a look. Frances spoke for them, "Lucy, you tend to Mr. Lacerda. It's still snowing, so it's best we leave now anyway. We'll call on you tomorrow afternoon before heading up to the manor so Sebastian can finally meet your benefactor."

After seeing them out, Lucy rushed back to the kitchen and found Abigail trying to remove Dominick's boots, although with little success. Asleep now, Dominick did not notice the child's tugging. Lucy set a large kettle on the fire, dragged the wooden tub from the corner of the room closer to the hearth, and then shepherded the girls upstairs to their chamber, knowing she needed to keep an ear open to possible mischief. Abigail was fairly cautious and reliable, but three-year-old Mary was liable to burn the house down if she was not closely monitored. Downstairs, Lucy poured the hot water from the kettle into the tub and then added unheated water from the storehouse barrel. Refilling the kettle, she then set it back on the fire. Dominick was still asleep. She ran her hand softly along his cheek and whispered, "Dominick." He stirred, and she crouched down next to him and took his hand in hers. "Dominick, wake up."

His eyes fluttered and he turned toward her voice. "Hello," he said and kissed the hand that was still clasped in his.

Lucy smiled but replied in a no-nonsense tone, "I've made a hot bath for you. Let's get you in before the water cools." She helped Dominick undress. When he was in the tub, she gently bathed him. His right arm hung limp, the shoulder sporting a large bruise. She stroked it gently. "What happened, Dominick?"

"It was my own fault," he said, sighing. "I wasn't able to leave London until four days ago. I have important news for you, so I rode through the night yesterday instead of stopping. Earlier today I dozed in the saddle and fell off my horse."

He leaned forward as she poured a bucket of warm water on his head, causing his thick, dark waves to tighten into long curls. Then she wrapped his arm with a towel soaked in the steaming kettle water. "This is the shoulder you broke in Amsterdam?" He nodded. "Shall I send for the doctor, Dominick? It's not yet nightfall."

"No, I'll be fine," he told her. "I'll sling it for a few days. Thank you, Lucita."

When he was settled in his bed, she brought him some mulled wine and a bit of mutton pie. He was so tired he couldn't eat, but the wine eased the pain in his shoulder. Lucy sat on the edge of his bed and stroked his head. He was almost asleep when she remembered why he had come to Yorkshire early. "Dominick, you rushed here with news. What is it?"

His sleepy, satisfied expression became sober. Painfully, he sat up to face her. "Lucy, you know that Edward is very ill. If he remains in prison, he may not survive much longer, but there is a possibility that he may recover under your care if he is released. Mr. Hosgood is certain that, because of Edward's condition, he will be released by Easter."

Lucy said nothing at first. She looked down and began to fiddle with the loose threads of the shawl dangling across her waist.

Her silence worried him. "Lucy, say something. Tell me what you are thinking."

"That's three months before the baby is due."

"What?"

"The baby, Dominick. You are going to be a father again. I'm pregnant."

He didn't know how to react. He wanted to shout with joy, but at the same time, he was fearful about their circumstances. This would be the second time she'd bear his child while married to Edward, but this time was different. Edward was incarcerated, and it was well-known among their circle how much time he and Lucy spent together. There would be trouble over this. "What does this mean for us, Lucy?"

To his surprise she simply shrugged. "I will tend to Edward when he is released. Then I will have your baby. When Edward is well, I will leave him."

This scenario was scandalous, but it was typical of Lucy's tendency to oversimplify situations. "And then what, Lucita?"

She brushed her lips against his and answered mischievously, "I will find a handsome and kind Jewish man to take us in."

He smiled, despite his reservations with her plan. "Have you anyone in mind?"

She playfully pushed him, and his eyes screwed shut with pain as he groaned, fell back onto the pillows, and rolled onto his good side.

"Oh, Dominick!" Lucy's hands flew to her mouth in horror. "Please forgive me."

He reached out for her hand and squeezed it. "It's all right, Lucita," he reassured her. "And I am very happy about the baby."

She kissed him, then left him to sleep. They would speak more of this in the morning.

◆◆◆

Domingo slept through the next morning and well into the afternoon. When he finally rose, he felt much stronger. He was also ravenous. He managed his toilette alone, although it took him longer than usual. From some scraps of an old shirt in Lucy's mending basket, he devised a sling for his arm and headed downstairs. Unfamiliar voices coming from below alerted him that Lucy had guests, so he crept down the back staircase to the kitchen, hoping to find some means of satisfying his hunger without disturbing them. Despite his care, the girls heard his descent on the stairs and rushed to him.

"Ami! Ami!" they shouted together.

"Oh, my girls! Look at you! Prettier every day, just like your mother," he exclaimed, crouching down to receive them both with his good arm.

"Ami, come see the baby!" urged Abigail. He was confused by this until they entered the parlor and he saw Frances sitting on the settee holding a small bundle. Lucy had told him a few months ago that Frances and Sebastian had finally had a child after four years of marriage, but he had forgotten about it until now. Domingo had only met Frances a few times over the years and had no real opinion of her, except that she sometimes seemed haughty. He was certain that she must have a kind heart, however, as Lucy adored her. The girls scampered ahead of him into the parlor.

"Ami's up! He's here!"

"Good afternoon, Mr. Lacerda," Lucy greeted him, smiling broadly and striding toward him.

"Mrs. Polestead, I apologize for the lateness of the hour," he said in a rush, looking over at her guests. He hated meeting new people in settings like this when the focus was just on polite conversation and not some other diversion like business or entertainment of some sort. It made him feel like he was on display.

Lucy waved her hand as if to brush away his concern. "The hour does not signify. It is the company I value. You seem quite recovered today. Perhaps later you will let me refashion your sling so that it will give you more comfort." Her eyes twinkled with amusement at his sling of rags. "Come meet Mr. Bretton, my cousin and Frances's husband." She led him to Sebastian where he was standing by the hearth.

Domingo bowed to Lucy's cousin. "I am happy to finally meet you, sir. Congratulations on the birth of your son."

"Yes, at long last," replied Sebastian, his expression neutral, his bow slight.

Uncertain if Sebastian's weak greeting referred to the child or their meeting, Domingo decided not to pursue further conversation with him and turned to Frances instead. "You are looking well, Mrs. Bretton. What is your child's name?"

Frances pulled back the baby's woolen wrap so that Domingo could better see the child's face. "His name is James," she gushed, proud of her healthy son. "Three months old this very day, and already he's beginning to roll. Why just the other day I was telling Lucy that he'll be an early crawler and—"

"Ami, Ami! I want to see him!" pleaded Mary, interrupting Frances's maternal adulations.

"Mary, your Ami is hurt. He cannot lift you," chided Lucy.

"It's all right, Mrs. Polestead," Domingo said as he reached down for the child. He stifled a groan as he leaned in toward Frances and the baby with Mary in his arms. He was thankful Mary was young, but even so, it was a struggle to hold her for very long. She was sturdier than Abigail, who was often mistaken by strangers as Mary's twin rather than her older sister. Mary reached out her hands to James's face.

"Gentle, Mary," he instructed. "Don't touch the baby's head."

She stroked the baby's blanket and then squirmed down and scampered over to Lucy.

"Why do they call you 'Ami'?" Sebastian asked, showing interest finally. "Is it a play on the French term?"

Domingo cautiously accepted Sebastian's interest. "No. It is short for Amiel, the name I was given at birth."

Sebastian looked confused. "I've heard my cousin refer to you as Dominick."

"In Portuguese, my name is rendered as Domingo. It was Mrs. Polestead who dubbed me 'Dominick,' the English version of my name," he explained, wondering where this was leading.

"So from what language is 'Amiel' derived?" pressed Sebastian.

Domingo looked at Lucy. She bit her lip and looked at the floor. He realized that her cousins did not know. He met Sebastian's expectant stare. "It is Hebrew for 'God of my people.' I am a Jew."

Frances let out an audible gasp and said to Lucy, "You told me he was Catholic."

Before Lucy could respond, Sebastian spoke. "There's no need to be provincial, Frances. London is full of Jews because of the tyrant

Cromwell. They nearly financed his entire regime in exchange for being allowed to trade in London. He even tried to give them legal status a decade ago. What surprises me is that the king has allowed them to remain."

"Mr. Lacerda, tell us, what is the king's manner toward your congregation?" Lucy asked, trying to get Sebastian to recall that Dominick was her guest.

He answered with a curtness directed at no one in particular but seemed to imply all of them, "He has shielded the Jewish merchants from several expulsion petitions issued by the Lord Mayor of London on behalf of the Christian merchants. It is rumored that he may grant the Jews formal protection in writing to quell opposition against us."

Sebastian raised his eyebrows at this. "Is that so? I would not have expected that of the king, unless, of course, he is bound to them through debt."

Domingo had had enough. "Sir, I can assure you there is no blackmail involved. The king wants religious acceptance for all in his realm. By his word, Catholics and Jews are allowed to worship freely. Like it or not, our fates are tied as we are both minorities in this kingdom."

Before Sebastian could voice his retort about the obvious difference between Catholics and Jews in England, Lucy broke in, "Come, it is long past midday. Father and Elizabeth are expecting us."

Sebastian went to call for the driver to prepare his carriage, and Domingo made his way to the stables to bring round his horse. As the women dressed the children and donned their own cloaks, Frances excused herself and Sebastian from the family gathering at the manor. "Lucy, I am feeling tired, and there is still so much to prepare for Christmas. Please give our apologies to your father and Elizabeth. We'll not miss their festivities tomorrow night, and I promise to call on Elizabeth in January so she can see James."

"Yes, Frances," replied Lucy dejectedly. "Until tomorrow, then."

Frances, having her excuse met with little resistance, tried to make amends. "Your uncle is saying Mass tonight at Bretton manor. I'd thought you and Mr. Lacerda would come, but I suppose now he wouldn't have come."

Lucy's eyes briefly flashed with anger before she remembered herself. "We will be attending services in the village with Father, Elizabeth, and the children."

A moment passed in silence before Frances spoke again, "Why didn't you tell me, Lucy? This is no small thing."

"Neither is it a large thing, Frances," Lucy countered, not really believing her own argument.

"It's why he left, isn't it? You knew then?" asked Frances, suddenly understanding more fully what had transpired over a decade ago.

"Yes," conceded Lucy.

Frances gave a little shake of her head and said, "So you never would have been able to marry him, even if he'd come back for you. There was never any hope, Lucy."

There was so much Lucy wanted to say to Frances, but Sebastian reappeared and they left without even saying good-bye to Dominick.

After the Brettons left, Lucy loaded the girls into a sleigh she'd borrowed from Thicket Hall while Dominick hitched it to his horse. Normally they would walk the path to the manor house, but the recent snow was too deep for the girls to manage. As he finished buckling the harness, Lucy tried to speak with Dominick about her cousins. "I'm sorry for their behavior, Dominick. They speak from ignorance, not conviction."

Dominick replied briskly, "Don't concern yourself with it. Their response is normal."

She took his hand in hers. "I love you."

He responded by kissing her lightly on her forehead. It bothered him that Frances had not known he was a Jew. Was Lucy ashamed of his religion, or had she feared losing her cousin's friendship? Almost immediately he was angry with himself for entertaining such doubts. Surely it was the latter. Judging by Frances and Sebastian's reaction, Domingo was certain that they would cease their friendship with Lucy and he grieved for her. If Lucy was able to carry out her plan, Frances and Sebastian's friendship was only the first of many that she would lose.

Even without the Brettons, dinner at Thicket Hall was a noisy and lively affair. After a hearty meal of goose, mince pie, and posset, everyone gathered in the parlor. Elizabeth and Lucy chatted by the hearth while they kept an eye on Emma, now eleven, who was playing mother to her two nieces and her three-year-old brother Richard. Thomas, thirteen, planted himself by Domingo and hung on his every word. Thomas had a keen sense of adventure and idolized his sister's friend who had lived in three different countries, spoke five languages, and spent his days along London's wharves. Tonight, Domingo was telling them all about Manuel's latest letter from Barbados.

"You recall he no longer works for Senhor Robles? Anyway, he wrote that off the coast of Jamaica pirates intercepted a shipment belonging to one of his clients."

"Pirates!" exclaimed Thomas. "Did they take the ship?"

Domingo nodded and smiled at the boy's predictable enthusiasm. "When the pirates boarded, they demanded all the coin and all the rum. They were sorely disappointed that most of the cargo was sugar, because that meant that they would have to sell it to realize its profit. They then proceeded to dump the sugar out of spite. While they were engaged with this task, an East India Company frigate came along. After a short battle, the British overpowered the pirates and confiscated their ship."

"Were they hanged, Domingo?" asked Thomas eagerly.

"Manuel did not say, but I'm sure 'twas their fate."

John interrupted then, changing the subject before its crudeness drew a scolding look from Elizabeth, "Domingo, how is Manuel getting on? His family is well?"

"Yes, Manuel has several clients among the smaller plantation owners, mostly tobacco growers. His sons are also accountants. Marcos is about twenty-four now. He works exclusively for one plantation, a sugar operation owned by Lord Harleigh of Rutland. Manuel writes that Marcos is engaged to be wed next autumn after the harvest."

"And the younger son?"

"Gaspar completed his apprenticeship last year but has taken an interest in the law. Manuel is hoping to send him to London to further his studies. So much depends on the king's response to our petition for protection. There are lawyers in Barbados and Jamaica with whom Gaspar can study, but an apprenticeship in Doctors' Commons would serve him better. I have some contacts there who would accept Gaspar in their offices when we can be assured that he will be granted a license. Quite aside from that, Manuel is eager for me to come out to Barbados soon. I think he means to persuade me to stay."

Lucy, who'd only been half-paying attention to this conversation, having been engaged in arbitrating a dispute between Abigail and Mary over a doll's comb, was startled by Dominick's news and rose to join the men. "You mean to go to Barbados, Dominick?"

"I haven't seen Manuel or his family for over seven years, and I'm curious about the opportunities there. Perhaps I'll go in the next year . . ." He trailed off when he saw her stricken expression and soon the conversation shifted to a different topic.

When they returned to Chapel House later that evening it took awhile for the girls, silly with fatigue, to settle down. Tomorrow was Christmas and they eagerly awaited their grandfather's festivities. When he saw that they finally slept, Domingo sought out Lucy in her chamber. She was preparing for bed. "Are you tired, Lucita?"

"Yes." She put her arms around his neck and kissed him. "And no."

"There are matters we should discuss," he said.

Lucy sighed and sat down on the bed. "Which shall it be first? The baby, Edward, or Barbados?"

He sat next to her and placed his hand on her belly. "I want to raise this child. Abigail was two years old before she knew me."

Lucy had known from the moment she'd realized she was pregnant that things might be different this time, but now, after Dominick's plea, it became absolutely clear, this child had changed everything for them. A choice had to be made.

"And you are the only father that Mary has ever known," Lucy pointed out.

"But I am not with them even half the year," he argued. "Lucita, I want to be a true father to my children. I've been thinking about what you said last night, about leaving Edward. If you did this, we could never be together in London. We'd be shunned, or worse, arrested. If you come with me to Barbados, we could live as husband and wife. Things are different in the colonies. No one would have to know of our difficulties."

"I want us to marry, Dominick."

He took her hand in his. "I want this too, but there is just no way right now. We must be realistic, there may never be. I will go to Barbados after the baby is born and set up my business there. I'll return in the spring, and then we can all go together in the summer. That gives you a year to tend to Edward and settle matters with him. There is no need for you to argue over money or the house. Give him whatever he wants."

Lucy looked concerned. "What of Mary?"

"We'll find a way, Lucita. Remember, Edward is an enemy of the Crown. At worst, Mary will have to become your father's ward, and I don't think he'll object to your taking her."

"What if Edward wants to raise her? How can we take his daughter away from him?" Lucy argued.

"Perhaps we can convince Edward to come to Barbados," he answered, grinning.

"You are not serious! Dominick, am I to endure this conflicted life forever?"Domingo laughed and lay back on the pillows, pulling Lucy with him. "I think you were born for conflict, Lucita. You never would have fallen in love with me had you not been."

◆◆◆

According to Lucy, the Dunnington Christmas ball was always a splendid affair of music, food, drink, and dance. Despite her enthusiasm, Domingo halfheartedly dressed for it. A ball was not the kind of affair that he was comfortable with. He preferred more intimate gatherings of known friends and wished he could spend the evening in a corner speaking with Lucy. But to avoid suspicion, they'd agreed to behave as mere acquaintances. Domingo tried to mingle and make conversation with the dozens of guests, but he noted a distinctively dismissive response from Lucy's relatives and their friends.

Unsuccessful at socializing, Domingo made his way to the ballroom and took great pleasure in the music. He stood alone near the musician's corner watching the three fiddlers weave a spell of Christmas with their bows and strings. This music was not the solemn chant praising the Virgin Mary that he remembered from Masses as a boy. It was, instead, lively, with intricate harmonies that wove together crucifixion sorrow and nativity joy, farmers and shepherds with angels and demons, earthly flora with celestial bodies, and Christian theology with ancient tradition. Hearing such diverse images in the same song was unsettling yet irresistibly beautiful, and he felt that he wouldn't tire of it, even if he stood there all night. After an hour, Lucy made her way over to where he stood and dispelled his reverie with a strange and disturbing announcement. "I am going to give a speech."

"What? Whatever for, Lucy?" He often enjoyed her boldness, but the thought of her making a speech before her father's guests seemed unfitting.

"You'll understand when I begin. I have to do this for us." She said this with a conviction that told him she would not be persuaded to give up the idea.

"I'll be listening, Lucita," he replied, and she strode off with a swish of her skirts.

In time, the music stopped and John Dunnington called his guests to attention. Lucy approached the center of the room confident and beaming.

"Thank you all for coming tonight. Have not my father and Elizabeth provided a splendid celebration for our Lord's birth?" There was applause at this, and Lucy had to pause in her speech.

"One is not with us tonight who should be. My husband, Edward Polestead, has been these last three and a half years at the king's pleasure in the Tower of London. And to my joy, two days ago I learned that good King Charles has seen fit to release my husband and he shall join us by Easter. A true resurrection!"

Again, Lucy had to pause for the cheering that her news engendered. When it subsided, she continued, "I must honor tonight our dear friend, whose efforts on Edward's case have led to his imminent release. I give you Mr. Dominick de Lacerda."

Domingo was stunned at this acknowledgement, and before he had gathered his wits, John Dunnington had drawn him to the center of the room for all the guests to see. Tepid applause followed. After bowing to the crowd, Domingo drifted back to his corner. But Lucy had not finished with her revelations. "Finally, I want to announce to all of you, my friends and Edward's, as well as those who are dear to Father and Elizabeth, that Edward's prison term has not been without its tender moments. Soon after his release, Edward and I will welcome a third child to our home. This one is most certainly a boy." She drew her hands to her womb and smiled broadly. Then, in a brilliant move, Lucy raised her glass and commanded a toast, "To Edward's freedom and to our son!"

The room resounded with cheers and glasses clinking. In one short speech, Lucy had vindicated Domingo's presence and cut short any speculation about her pregnancy. Domingo was proud of Lucy's skill at self-preservation; at the same time, though, he felt unsettled. How could it be so easy for her to carry on their deception, and even earn applause, while he'd spent his life lying? There was a bitterness to this business. She seemed to give up nothing, while he felt as if he'd given up everything. She was publicly praised by her own, while he was suspect among the Jews on Cree Church Lane.

He had not been openly accused, but it was only a matter of time. He and Lucy were chaste in London, and she did not keep a live-in servant in Yorkshire who could be bribed to pass information about them. In the past year, however, he could feel the coldness from the other Jews. Matchmakers no longer begged Teresa Maria to convince her son to marry, and men no longer asked him to coffee or to study Torah in the evenings. Sometimes he felt that Lucy was the only one who loved him for who he was, yet she had managed to earn praise for what she was not.

◆◆◆

After slipping out of the party, Domingo wandered the grounds alone for hours. He went to bed in the early morning. Slipping under the sheets, he tried his best not to wake Lucy. But she had been restless, waiting for him. "Hello, my love." He did not reply, but he did peck her forehead before settling into his side of the bed. "Dominick, please talk to me," Lucy pleaded.

He rolled over to face her but said nothing.

"Dominick," she pressed her body against his and kissed him. She could feel his body respond, but he did not return her kiss. She pulled away from his rejection. "What?" she challenged.

"You've figured everything out without me. I'm just the lover in the shadows, cast aside when your husband returns, aren't I?" He said this without bitterness, but it cut Lucy deeply.

"How can you say that, Dominick? I am willing to risk everything to leave him. But I have a duty to see him through his release. I owe him that. My love is yours; my children are yours. Why do you doubt me now?"

This admission comforted him, but Domingo was still angry at her for some unknown reason. "'Tis a sharp contrast to your speech this evening. Where was your love for me then?"

"What! You would have me acknowledge you as my lover, the father of my children, before that crowd? You hypocrite! Would you stand up in your synagogue and do the same? Don't forget, Dominick, you did not stand for me when you had the chance. I am trying to do what is best for our children. If you cannot accept this, then leave us. But know that I have done everything I can to stand by you. I realize that there will come a time for fighting, but tonight was not the time. Tonight I tried to protect my parents, my siblings, you, and our children. I even protected Edward tonight, though he little deserves it."

"You carry my child, not his?"

Lucy sat up infuriated. "You rake! You fathered one of my children and have been father to another, yet you question the paternity of this one. What does it matter? This is my child and for that you should love him. Even Edward loved Abigail!"

"He thought her his!"

"So what of Mary? She is not yours, Dominick. Do you love her less?"

"No," he said, lowering his eyes. "Mary is as much my daughter as Abigail."

His confession lessened her anger, but Lucy still seethed at his accusation. "What of this child? Could you accept it as your own?"

"I hate that you were with him. But yes, this child I will claim."

Lucy's countenance softened. "Good, because I have not lain with Edward these four years. This child is most definitely yours, Dominick."

Domingo was relieved, yet annoyed by this revelation. Why did she play with him like that?

"It was never a question, Lucita."

She shook her head. "Yes, it was. I would not have you love this child less if he was not your sire. I promise to bear your children when I leave Edward. Until then you must accept my children no matter who fathered them."

He nodded, both relieved and exhausted. Lucy was true to him. He knew it was ridiculous of him to expect her fidelity, but as he had been faithful to her these last twelve years it meant something to him that she had not lain with Edward since he'd been imprisoned. "You seem convinced that this one is a boy. What will you name him?"

His acceptance of the child heartened her. "I would welcome a suggestion be it a boy or a girl."

"If it is a girl I would like Rachel, for Semuel's mother, who was like a mother to me when I lived with them."

"And if I bear a son?" Lucy asked.

"David," he responded without hesitation.

Lucy was curious. "Why David?"

"Because King David had the courage to marry the woman he loved, though he was advised not to."

"That is very romantic, but wasn't David punished for marrying her?"

"I have been punished, Lucita. I'm done with sacrificing. I want to live." He planted kisses on her neck and encircled her waist with his arms.

Lucy reveled in the knowledge that she carried his child. It made her feel more his than anything that had come before. She also knew that if this child was a boy, things would be much more different than they had been with Abigail or Mary.

XVIII. *RELEASE*, 1664

Lucy moved back to London on the first day of spring. It was Dominick's thirtieth birthday and marked the sixth month of her pregnancy. She knew Dominick was making plans to leave, and she hated the anticipation of it.

Four days later, she brought Edward home to a modest rented house near St. Paul's Cathedral. He was very weak and needed help with even the most basic functions. Although Lucy's pregnancy was apparent, Edward did not speak of it. When he was settled, she brought the girls to see him. Oddly it was Mary, who had never met her father, who approached him first with a smile and a curtsey so low that it landed her on her backside, earning a laugh and a hug from him. Five-year-old Abigail hung back, unsure of what to do and not wanting to admit that she did not know her father.

Edward gazed at her for a long while before he called her to him. "Come here, daughter. Do you not remember me?"

She hesitated until he held his arms open to her, and then she shyly placed herself within his embrace. "God bless you, Father," she said awkwardly, wishing Mary hadn't acted so familiar and foolish with him. It made her feel that her own greeting had been a disappointment to him.

At the end of May, Lucy sent the girls to stay with Avo until the baby was born. Domingo did not tell Lucy that his mother had not been well of late because he did not want to worry her, and he did not want her to send the girls to anyone else. So he hired a nursemaid to help his mother with the children during the day and cared for the girls himself when he was home.

Edward said nothing about the girls' departure but seemed finally ready to discuss her condition. "Lucy, we must speak of what has come to pass these last few years."

She sighed deeply. The baby was due any day now and she loathed a confrontation that would sap her energy. At the same time, she knew that she could not put this off indefinitely. "I will tell you what you need to know, but I will not suffer any abuse from you."

"Fair enough, wife. Tell me about the child in your womb."

"His father saved us all from your abandonment. If not for him, I wouldn't have been able to come to London and see to your case."

"So you became a whore for his money?"

"You would think that, wouldn't you? No, Edward. I love the father of this child. I loved him before I knew you," Lucy said passionately.

"You refused my affections these four years because you said you would not risk having another child while I was in prison. Now I see that that was just an excuse for your unfaithfulness. Who is he?" Edward asked.

"Does it matter?" she countered.

Edward took a deep, labored breath and reached for his pipe, lighting it and sucking deep of its embers. After a moment he replied, "The young Jew. He is your lover."

Lucy was unprepared for his comment. She had never spoken to Edward about Dominick. "Who do you mean?"

"The Jew! The guards told me that you always came with a Jew and that he waited outside for you. Even they suspected you a whore," he spat at her.

"Enough!" she yelled at him. "How dare you accuse me. You left us with nothing! You saved your fortune but you would've starved us while you were in prison!"

"I meant to leave London, yes, but I would have sent for you when I could. I assumed your father would care for you until then."

"To his own ruin, Edward? Is that what you wanted? To ruin my father while your fortune sat in an Amsterdam bank? When you knew you wouldn't be released, you could have authorized Mr. Hosgood to have the money transferred to me. Why didn't you?"

"Your father had plenty of money, more than enough to support you and his own family. No, Lucy. It was not for fear of your father's solvency that you chose not to live with him. It was your sin. You could have gotten a nice sum for Chapel House, yet you kept it so that you could carry on with him. I'd say you fared pretty well without me. It would seem you did not need my money with your generous lover to support you."

"You liar! He came to me three months after you were arrested. Three months after you knew we had no income. I was alone with a child, another soon to be born, and I could not even afford a midwife! We all could've died because of your selfishness!"

"And what of your father, Lucy? Where does he come into all of this? Are you not vexed with him for not coming to your aid?"

"My father? Why should I need my father when I had a husband?" She took a deep breath, trying to clear her head. "Yes, my father asked me to come to Yorkshire. I refused because of the baby and because I needed to be near you. I knew I couldn't help you from Yorkshire."

"Then why did you go finally?"

"Because he came for me. He offered to help me. He saved us." She ended in a whisper. He knew she spoke of the Jew and not her father.

"Let us speak no more of this, Lucy. I will not denounce you but neither will you cuckold me. If I catch you even looking at him from across the street, I'll have you both arrested."

◆◆◆

David was born June third. He was a healthy baby and, as with her other children, Lucy suffered no ill effects from his birth. Edward did not protest the diversion of his wife's attention, but he was completely uninterested in the child. Thus when Lucy slipped out with David two weeks after his birth, Edward paid little attention. He was growing stronger each day and was seeking to rebuild his business; consequently, he spent a great deal of his time writing to his former business associates.

Lucy took David to Stoney Lane to call on Avo and to retrieve the girls. When she arrived, she was disappointed to find Dominick away from home and Teresa Maria confined to her bed. However, the old woman's spirits rose at the sight of her grandson.

"What is his name, Lucita?"

"He will be called David."

Teresa Maria held the child close to her weak body and her eyes filled with tears. "A son. He is a Lacerda?"

"Yes, Avo. He is your grandson."

"What you have done to each other . . ." She shook her head sadly. "Domingo would die before giving up these children. Do you understand?"

"Yes, Avo. I gave him my pledge."

Teresa Maria handed David back to her. "Our people will never accept you. You know that, don't you?"

"I understand."

"This is, as the Christians say, your cross, but you must be loyal to him before all else. He has given up everything for you."

"I promise! Please believe me."

Teresa Maria's dark eyes narrowed as she stared unblinkingly at Lucy. "I do, Lucita," she said finally.

Lucy felt a lump form in her throat.

"And now, we must make arrangements," Teresa Maria said with her usual authority. "With boys it is different."

Thus over the next two days Teresa Maria arranged for David to be circumcised. The physician who would act as the mohel refused to perform the illegal procedure at first, but somehow Teresa Maria convinced him.

When David was four weeks old, Lucy took him back to Teresa Maria's one morning. "Avo, you are out of your bed! I am so happy to see you like this."

"I would be brought downstairs in a litter before I missed this. This will be the first infant circumcision in our family for over two hundred years." She smiled warmly at Lucy and grasped the younger woman's hand tightly. "Thank you for this. Now go to my son. He is waiting for you upstairs."

Lucy hurried up the stairs with her baby. She found Dominick pacing the second-floor sitting room. "Lucita, you are well? Let me see him." He held his arms out for the child and Lucy placed him in them. Dominick gazed at David lovingly. At one month old, David had a full head of thick dark hair and the same large, round eyes of his father and grandmother. "He is beautiful." He pulled her close and kissed her. "Are you sure about the circumcision?"

"Yes. We're committing our son; thus we're committing ourselves."

"No one must find out, Lucita. Our haham does not even know of this. You will be expected to baptize him."

"Yes, Dominick, it cannot be avoided. Our daughters were both baptized in the English Church."

"I was baptized a Catholic," he said.

"As was I," she replied. "Before I knew your true identity, I felt this was our strongest bond. Now it is not the church but our children who bind us."

Domingo frowned. "No, Lucita. The children are a result of our bond. Had there been no children, we would still be pledged. I will honor that pledge when I return." He shifted David to one arm and took her hand in his. "Please trust in this."

"I do, Dominick," Lucy said quietly. Letting go of his hand, she reached into the pocket of her skirt to pull out something lumpy wrapped in a blue cloth that she pressed into his palm.

Confused at this gesture but unable to examine the cloth he simply asked, "When will you come for him?"

"Tomorrow night. I cannot get away before then. He can take thin porridge, and you should give him a rag soaked in sweet wine for the pain after the doctor leaves. Avo will know how to prepare these things. She's the one who taught me with Abigail. I must warn you, though, he is not weaned, so he won't be satisfied until I come back. He will cry a great deal tonight."

He held the child close to his chest. "I will stay up with him until you come."

After Lucy left, Domingo set David down and opened the blue cloth. In it he found Filipe's carving of Mary. He'd given it to her just days before he'd left her for Amsterdam twelve years ago. It was the only gift he had ever given her.

♦♦♦

In early August, Domingo sailed for Barbados. It worried him to leave his mother but delaying the trip any longer was out of the question. In addition to the servants he'd hired to care for his mother, Lucy had assured him that she would visit her often. Leaving Lucy and the children, especially David, who was so young, tore at his heart. He expected to be gone ten months, staying with Manuel through the harvest season and the winter and then returning to England in the spring. Holding each child tightly, he was able to put off saying good-bye to Lucy. Their future together depended on his ability to settle them in the colonies, but he wished there was another way.

When he stood before her finally, Lucy's eyes were wet with tears. "Go with God, Dominick," she whispered, trying to hold back a sob.

"Lucita . . ." He couldn't think of what to say. "*Meu refúgio*." He kissed her for a long moment and then, before changing his mind, walked up the gangplank and onto the ship.

September 1664
Dearest Lucy,

I have been in the colony of Barbados for just a few weeks, but already I feel the strange power of this place. Here, sugar is king and the plantation owners are the barons who serve him. Most of the inhabitants of this island are African, but there are thousands of Irish slaves who have lived here since the time of Cromwell's campaigns in Ireland. My cousin Marcos tells me that Cromwell's policy was to slaughter the Irish men and boys and then ship the women and girls to the colonies where he forced them to breed with the Africans. Some of them work in the fields, but pureblood Irish women and children are preferred for work in plantation homes.

I've been staying with Manuel, though Senhor Robles has instructed me to purchase a house in Bridgetown to serve as his new base of operations. His current accountant here, João Mendes, suffers from the heat and wishes to return to Amsterdam. I will take on his duties when I return here next year.

After London's gray chill, Barbados is a wonder. It is sunny most days, and one can smell the ocean from any point on the island. If it were not for the slaves, I might think it was paradise.

Please give my love to the children.

אני אוהב אותך,
Dominick

A few weeks into Domingo's stay, Manuel called him to a formal meeting in his study. His cousin seemed worn with the passage of years, his cares seeming to have increased though he'd left London to escape them. And despite the warm welcome he'd given Domingo when he'd first arrived, Manuel's manner had been cool of late, almost uncivil. Domingo did not expect this meeting to go well. When he arrived, Manuel shut the door and strode over to his large bamboo desk and sat down, indicating that he expected Domingo to do the same.

"Domingo, I am trying to understand what the hell you have done with your life. I know about your plans, and I'll be blunt. There is no way you can settle here with her. It is simply unthinkable." He paused and shook his head in disappointment when Domingo made no reply. "When you were a boy, you had so much potential. Now look at you. You are thirty, unmarried, and having an affair with a married Gentile." Domingo raised his eyebrows in surprise, but Manuel wasn't finished. "Yes, Domingo, you think people in the London kehilla don't know about you? Do you realize that they are considering banishing you? Haham Mathias wrote begging me to talk some sense into you." Domingo remained silent, so Manuel pushed further. "You have no claim on your children. Even if she were free, no haham would ever allow you to marry her. Please, stay here and start over."

Domingo's anger exploded like a boil that had been festering for twelve years. "First it was Lucy, then Semuel. Now you would have me give up my children? Who else, Manuel? Who else should I give up to live according to the law?"

"I tried to stop you from having children with her!" Manuel banged his fist on the desk, causing the papers on it to scatter. "This is exactly what I wanted to avoid. You will be cast out, Domingo! Do you understand what that means? You cannot be a Jew and continue the life you've been leading."

"I will not abandon my children or Lucy for the sake of the law. You told me when I was a boy that being Jewish was what I am, not something I could choose to be. Is that still true, or was that just another one of the lies I've been told?"

"Lies? The only one telling lies is you, Domingo. You lie to yourself about your future with this woman and her children. You lie to everyone about your relationship with her. No one knows who you are anymore."

"No one knows who I ever was, not even God! In Lisbon I was raised Catholic, but it turns out I was Jewish. In Amsterdam I learned how to be a Jew who wouldn't offend the Dutch. Then, for ten years in London, I pretended to be a Spanish Catholic while secretly practicing a compromised version of Judaism. I was told to do this for the good of the community. Now I am supposed to shed every other mask and just be Jewish. My identity changes at the Ma'amad's will. As a child, I was lied to about who I was. When I was a boy, I was taught to lie about who I was. Somewhere along the way, cousin, I became that lie. I cannot live under the law after living so long under a semblance of it. I have been trained to blend in with Spanish, Dutch, and English Christians. Now you ask me to be just a Portuguese Jew. Do you have any idea what it means to be a Portuguese Jew? I'll tell you what it means! It means being Catholic! You have no understanding of this, Manuel, do you? You grew up in Amsterdam, safe from the Inquisition. You never had to watch your brother strangled to death because of a lie meant to protect him!"

When Domingo paused to take a breath, Manuel interrupted his tirade with a practiced tone of calm reason. "You have the chance to live freely here, Domingo. I see you are angry at the circumstances of your life. Perhaps I have not suffered as you have, but others have suffered as much and they don't excuse themselves from their obligations because of what they've been through. You had no right to continue a relationship with Lucy Polestead. And now you see the consequences of it. Your children are half-breeds. They belong to no nation and they will be rejected by both our kehilla and the English. This is what you created because of your stubbornness and your lust."

Domingo gave a bitter laugh. "You speak of obligations? I see, cousin. So what of Marcos's child by the Irish slave? How is that less of an offense than what I have done?"

Manuel seethed at Domingo's questions. "That is a different matter. The child is cared for and will be accepted among the mother's own. The Irish are used to half-breeds."

"So you are content to have your grandchild raised a slave in an English planter's household because the Irish are more accepting of half-breeds than the English or the Jews? Perhaps they are so accepting because they have little choice. At least I did not force myself on Lucy. My children may be rejected by others, but they shall not be rejected by me. I will not lie to my children, even if it means they think ill of me for it. I will not abandon them for the sake of the kehilla. Because you know what, Manuel? My duty is that of a father now, not some hypocritical 'good Jew' who changes who he is when the kehilla believes itself at risk."

"Get out of my house."

◆◆◆

Domingo moved to an inn by the wharf and wrote a letter of resignation to Senhor Robles. He could not stay in Barbados. That much was clear. Several days after his altercation with Manuel, Marcos came to see him at the inn's tavern. "Cousin, how are you keeping?"

Domingo nodded and responded cautiously, "Well enough."

"I heard you traded sugar prospects successfully this last week."

Was nothing he did unknown to the Delgados? But, of course, it was Marcos who'd encouraged him to bid on a percentage of his employer's crop weeks ago, so it was natural that Marcos would learn of his profits. "Yes, thanks to your excellent advice, I can now live as a man of leisure in Barbados," Domingo acknowledged, warming to the younger man.

"Of course you will be saving much of your profit to support your family," suggested Marcos.

"Yes, cousin. I have others to consider. However, it has been made plain that they will not be welcome here."

"My father is sick over this, Domingo. Please talk to him," Marcos pleaded. Domingo stared hard at his cousin. Marcos had his mother's blue eyes, which had always set him apart from most of the Sephardim in Amsterdam and London. They reminded Domingo of the blue eyes of Lucy and their daughters.

"No," Domingo said firmly. "There is nothing I could say now that would satisfy him. He was always kind to me and my mother as he did his duty by us. I love him for that. But he only sees me for what he would have me be, not what I am."

"Domingo, he grieves for you. You are like a son to him."

Domingo bristled at this comment. "No, Marcos, don't say that. I am a Lacerda, not a Delgado. I tried to be what he wanted, but I cannot escape who I am. Tell him that. I wish I could have done what he wanted. But there were choices I made . . . pledges I was bound to honor . . . pledges I want to honor." He suddenly grabbed his cousin's arms and said, "Marcos, don't abandon your child to slavery."

Marcos was startled at this change in Domingo's rambling. He was angry now. "I told you about her in confidence, cousin. My father was furious at your bringing that up."

"He called my children half-breeds and demanded I abandon them. How could any father do that? I love you well, cousin, but I cannot believe that you are the better man for allowing your child to be raised a slave. I may be cast out of the kehilla in London, and your father has made it plain that my family is not welcome here, but I swear, Marcos, I will find a home where my children will not be outcasts. I could never live as a gentleman while my children were slaves."

To Domingo's surprise, Marcos broke at his outburst. "Do you think that is what I want? My child was born of a slave belonging to my employer, not a free English woman. Fiona is far too valuable to Lord Harleigh for him to give her to me. And to be honest, cousin, I don't want her. She was a pleasant diversion at the time, but since she went and got herself pregnant she's been nothing but a nightmare, whining all the time about how she wants me to talk to Lord Harleigh about freeing her. Of course it is too bad about the child, but in all truth, our situations are not as similar as you would like them to seem. Your children could perhaps pass as either English or Jewish, but my child, even if I could save her from slavery, will always be Irish. They are a crude and ignorant people, white-skinned Africans."

Domingo let his cousin's characterization of the Irish pass, but Marcos's callous usage of the slave woman disappointed him. Domingo knew that a slave had little recourse to reject the advances of a free man, but he had hoped that his cousin had some feelings for her. Yet Marcos was right. It was not as easy to claim a child born of a slave as it was a child born of a free woman. "I am sorry, cousin. I made generalizations I should not have." He fell silent and the two men sat for a moment, each lost in his own thoughts.

Then Marcos spoke as if he'd just remembered something. "Listen, cousin, I've heard of a place where you would be able to go and live with your Gentile wife. Some in our kehilla are even considering going there because of the hostility of the English merchants and planters here." Domingo's surprise at this revelation urged Marcos on. "Don't let my father deceive you. Barbados is no paradise. The English here hate us as they do in London."

Domingo was intrigued and, frankly, desperate for some hope of living peacefully with Lucy and the children. "Where?"

"Newport, in the colony of Rhode Island. It was chartered by an Englishman named Roger Williams as a place where all men may follow their own consciences. Quakers, Baptists, Separatists, and Jews all live there in peace. It is said that Mr. Williams even makes friends with the Indians there."

"There are Jews in Newport?"

"Yes, Sephardim fleeing Recife settled there eight years ago."

Domingo was amazed. "Jews in the Americas," he mused.

"What?"

Domingo shook his head. "Nothing, it just reminded me of a conversation that I had long ago." He looked up at his cousin. "It would seem we have to live among savages to be free. It makes you wonder who the true savages are."

"But Domingo, Newport is not a colony of savages. Naturally, the colonists have their conflicts with the Indians, but Newport is a colony of merchants. It is not London, but neither is it a wilderness."

Domingo laughed. "Good. Because I don't know how to handle a firearm or a sword!" He rose to take his leave. "Thank you, cousin. I will consider Newport. Perhaps you and your child will follow us there one day."

In late October, he received a letter from Lucy.

Dearest Dominick,

It is with a heavy heart that I write to you. Your mother passed from this world this Wednesday last. She was peaceful at the end and asked that you say Kaddish for her. We buried her at the Mile End Cemetery.

She left in my care an inheritance for you with provisions for the children. It will please you to know that Mary received an equal share. Like you, Avo considered Mary a child of your heart if not your seed.

Yours,

Lucita

Her death was not unexpected, but it affected Domingo deeply. Theirs had never been an easy relationship, but he understood that his mother had transferred all her hopes to him and it grieved him that he'd disappointed her. The day he received Lucy's letter he found himself at a secret mass with the Spanish and Portuguese residents of Port Royal. Because the colony was controlled by the English, the Catholic Church operated covertly in Barbados. He had not attended mass since he was eighteen, yet the pattern of the liturgy was familiar, even comforting in an odd way. After the mass, he lit a candle for his mother and sat for a long time fingering Filipe's carving of Mary. He remembered Lucy telling him once that the Virgin reminded her of her own mother; he understood her now. It was somehow comforting to think of his mother still praying for him in the afterlife. Later in the day, he went to the Jewish cemetery and recited the Kaddish for his mother.

A week later, Domingo left for Newport. He planned to stay through the winter then return to England in the spring. But his plans were foiled when he received a letter from Marcos in late February begging him to meet the *Agnes*, scheduled to arrive in Newport in June. He loathed putting off his return to England, but Marcos was adamant in his letter that Domingo meet the ship. It was likely just a shipment of goods that any of Marcos's contacts in the colony could handle, and Domingo seethed at the delay. In the meantime, he met with the leaders of Newport and, finding the conditions of the colony satisfactory, petitioned them for a permit to settle and practice his trade.

With his sugar profits he was able to provide surety of his contribution to the colony and his permit was granted. By March, Domingo had three clients, all merchants who owned ships that traded in a triangle that brought sugar, tobacco, and rum from

Barbados; wood, candles, and hides from Newport; and flour, textiles, and home goods from London. The work was not unlike what he'd done in London, but trade in the colony involved far less haggling and speculation as there was such a great desire among the colonists for goods from England.

In May, with five clients now, he commissioned a two-level house to be built outside the village center. It was a large project for him, but Domingo happily anticipated many more children with Lucy. He also began to seek an associate who could oversee the business while he was away in London. This was not an easy task as there were so few Jews in Newport. Indeed, because of the small community, there was no synagogue, no haham, and no Ma'amad in Newport. The community barely supported a minyan for prayers. Including Domingo, there were just twelve men over the age of thirteen. Prayer services were informally conducted in the homes of those members of the community who could fit a dozen men into their parlors comfortably.

On June 9, the *Agnes* finally arrived. Domingo's house was still in the early stages of construction, and he now had six clients. However, he was eager to get back to London and prayed that this mysterious cargo from Marcos could be traded immediately or stored. He watched the unloading with a trained eye. There were few warehouses in Newport, so porters left the cargo on the docks for the agents to collect it. Often the goods were bought so quickly that there was no need to store them. In many cases, items such as glass windows, furniture, and books had been specially ordered and went directly to the owners after being unloaded.

While inspecting the various crates on the wharf, wondering which ones might be from Marcos, Domingo noticed a young girl disembark clutching a ragged sack. Her dress was of poor quality, and she was barefooted with reddish-brown hair hanging limp to her waist. Domingo shook his head at the despicable treatment of poor passengers. She was most likely an Irish indentured servant sent to the colonies to serve until she was twenty-one. Marcos had told Domingo the truth of the system, however. If an indentured servant was sold before his original contract was completed, the new owner had the right to add seven more years onto the servant's service.

Thus, a twenty-year-old indentured servant might be sold for seven years to a new owner, then at twenty-six, be sold yet again. This could go on indefinitely, and many of the Irish died before they ever saw freedom.

He looked around to see who would claim the girl but there seemed to be no one at the wharf other than sailors, porters, and merchants' agents. The girl approached one of the agents and began babbling in a language he did not understand. Domingo noticed she was limp and, on closer inspection, saw that she was missing toes on her right foot. The agent, busy with his cargo, waved her away like a fly, and she stomped her good foot in frustration. The agent raised his hand as if to strike the girl.

Domingo rushed over to them. "Peace, sir. Perhaps I can help. What language does she speak?"

"Blasted if I know! Look at her. She's as much a savage as the Indians."

Domingo turned to the girl. She did have a wild look to her despite her strikingly white skin. He tried Spanish. "Cómo te llamas?"

She replied by spitting with amazing accuracy at the ground in front of his feet and yelling in a garbled tongue Domingo had never heard before. He now sympathized with the agent's desire to strike her. Suddenly, in her diatribe he heard a word he thought he recognized, "coozhan."

"Cousin? Who? Who is your cousin? What is her name?"

Again the garbled speech but he clearly heard the word again. "Cousin? Who?"

"Mirchaz!" she screamed at him, pushing her sack toward him and peeling back one of its rags. Domingo couldn't imagine what she was up to until he saw the sack move on its own, then he realized that it was not a bundle of clothes but a child, perhaps a year and a half in age. Its face now exposed, Domingo saw that it had pale brown hair and blue eyes. "Mirchaz," yelled the older girl. Suddenly it dawned on Domingo. This was his shipment. The young one must be Marcos's daughter. Was the older girl her mother? No, she was too young. Marcos would never bed a child no matter how free he was with slave women. But who was she, and what was he supposed to do with her?

251

She seemed to understand English but did not speak it, or at least did not speak it well enough to make herself understood. But from a letter she produced from a pocket in her dress that Marcos had written, Domingo learned that this girl, Miread, was a half-sister to Marcos's daughter, Eimer. She'd been taken from Ireland when she was five and had lived as a slave in Barbados for the last eight years. Because he'd smuggled the girls out rather than freed them, Marcos instructed Domingo to say that Miread was an indenture hired to care for the child. There was nothing in the letter about when Marcos would come for them, and Domingo realized that this shipment might very well be his permanent responsibility.

Sighing, he indicated to Miread to follow him. He would have to take them to the Pratts, a middle-aged Quaker couple from whom he was renting a room until his house was ready.

Miread walked slowly. He could tell she was tired from carrying her sister, her limp becoming more pronounced with every step. But when Domingo reached out his arms to take Eimer, Miread screeched and clenched her teeth around his hand.

"Ow!" He quickly pulled his hand away, but her teeth had already made their mark. Fortunately she had not broken his skin. "Damned Irish savage," he muttered, cursing Marcos for sending this fiend to Newport. He glared at Miread and she glared back. Eimer laughed, but then looked confused when neither her sister nor Domingo laughed with her. After that they walked in silence, both of them ignoring the strange looks from passersby.

Fortunately Jonas Pratt overtook them with his cart on the road into town. "Mr. Lacerda, I went to find ye at the docks. Martha told me you had a cargo coming in, so I 'ave me cart." He cast a curious look to Domingo's ragged companions but waited for his boarder to explain.

"Praise God you've come, Jonas," exclaimed Domingo, hearing himself picking up the particular idioms of Newport's Quakers and Baptists. "This is Miread, and the infant is Eimer. They are my cousin's kin and they've had a bit of a rough journey." He hoped that this explanation would satisfy Jonas's unasked question about why the girls were so dirty. As if reading Domingo's thoughts, Jonas swung himself down without asking any questions. He was perhaps the tallest man Domingo had ever met, standing almost six feet, his broad shoulders preventing him from seeming like one of Newport's towering pine trees come to life. Were it not for his boyish face, Jonas would intimidate even the bravest of men. Eight years ago Jonas and his wife, Martha, had come to the colonies to escape the persecution of Quakers in England. Back then, Jonas and Martha had already been married ten years and childless. Now, after living in various New England port cities, the Pratts had settled down in Newport and supported themselves by renting out rooms and transporting cargo from the wharves. Domingo found the Pratts to be a pleasant couple who were intrigued, rather than offended, by his Jewishness.

Arching his neck to meet Jonas's gaze, Domingo cautioned him, "They don't speak English." Jonas nodded and without another word offered his arm to help Miread into the cart. To Domingo's surprise, Miread allowed Jonas to assist her up without so much as a sour look. Angered at her easy acceptance of Jonas, Domingo sullenly took his place next to the older man in the driver's seat and they set off for the Pratts' home in the village square.

Martha was delighted with Domingo's charges, much to his relief. "All we need here is a good bath, a hearty meal, and some new clothes. For meself, I'm charged by the good Lord with the first two tasks. You, Mr. Lacerda, must see to the third. You'll need to be getting a few yards of a light woolen cloth from Mr. Evans; then you'll need to be taking it to Mrs. Goodwin. She has a blessed gift with her sewing hands and can make you up a set of clothes for each child in a fortnight. Until then I'll send Jonas to borrow some dresses from Mrs. Brewer. You know her Molly died of the pox last winter. She was about Miread's size."

His head swam with her commands, but it was clear that Martha Pratt had taken it upon herself to see to the immediate physical needs of Miread and Eimer. Domingo allowed Bess Hale, wife of Newport's only shopkeeper, to lead him through the complicated matter of the female wardrobe, choosing fabrics that would hopefully suit Miread in her new life in Newport. Because Eimer was still so young, her wardrobe was far less complicated and Domingo was thankful for this.

When he returned after an evening meeting with his brethren, Domingo saw that Miread and Eimer had been transformed into respectable enough looking girls, although Miread maintained a brooding silence and tore at the food Martha served her.

When the girls were abed, Martha interrogated Domingo. "Mr. Lacerda, I am familiar enough with your people to know that Miread is not speaking Portuguese, and I am sure that there are no such curses as the ones that come out of that child's mouth in your sacred Hebrew tongue. You say she is kin, yet she has the look of the Irish about her."

Domingo hesitated before repeating the story Marcos had constructed for the girls. He knew he would have to include some truths for Martha to believe the lies. "The babe is my cousin's from a woman he loved but could not wed. The Irish girl is an indenture he contracted to care for the child. While my cousin settles his personal affairs, I will act as the children's guardian."

"And yet yourself's been preparing for weeks to settle your own affairs in London," she countered.

"My cousin did not know I was to leave so soon," he lied again, wondering what she was getting at.

"Do you have children of your own, Mr. Lacerda?" she asked.

He'd never been asked this before, and he rolled the question around in his head a second before answering with pride, "Yes. I have two daughters and a son. Abigail is seven, Mary will be five soon, and David had his first birthday earlier this month."

Martha's face broke out into a grin. "Such a large family, Mr. Lacerda. Your wife will be needing help with all those children."

It took him only a moment to realize her meaning. "Yes, Mrs. Pratt. Lucy would welcome your assistance I am sure."

"And you'll be traveling back to London for them now that your cousin's child has arrived?"

He nodded. "I hope to leave on the next ship." Last week he'd hired a young assistant, Benjamin Vieira, to maintain his business while he traveled back to England for Lucy and the children. Benjamin was only eighteen, but he was highly recommended by Moses Campanall, a Sephardic merchant with extensive business contacts in the colonies. Domingo liked Benjamin immediately, feeling an affinity with this young man who had escaped Recife as a child and had lived for some years in New Amsterdam. Domingo instructed Benjamin to oversee the completion of the house and was training him to maintain the accounts while he was away. He couldn't ask the boy to also care for Miread and Eimer. He would simply have to take the girls with him to London.

Martha discerned his inner conflict and boldly pressed her plan. "Well, you cannot be expecting your cousin's child and servant to travel to London just to turn around and come back here. Sea travel is far too risky, especially for the little one. If I might, Mr. Lacerda, I say you leave the girls with us while you collect your family in London. When you return, we'll have them safe and sound."

And so Martha Pratt offered herself and her husband as guardians to Miread and Eimer until Domingo returned. How this would all work out when Lucy and the children arrived remained a problem he was unwilling to contemplate just now. Suffice it to say that the immediate difficulty of caring for Marcos's daughter and her fiendish sister had an answer, and oddly, Martha Pratt seemed to feel she had gotten the better end of the deal.

XIX. *PLAGUE*, 1665

The girls sat waiting in the carriage. Their mother's urgency stilling their youthful irritation at having to embark on what they knew would be a long and dull trip. When Lucy finally appeared, she was carrying the baby, who she handed over to her eldest. "Gaily-girl, hold David for a moment. I'm going to find Mr. Polestead. I don't understand why he is taking so long."

When she found Edward, he was sitting before the fire in his study, casually puffing on his pipe and still wearing his morning gown. "Edward! What are you doing?" Lucy asked in a harried voice. "The children are already in the coach. We must leave while our certificates of health are still valid." Lucy held up a leather pouch containing the precious documents that would allow them passage out of London and into another town. Fear that the sickness gripping London would spread throughout the kingdom as Londoners fled north and west had resulted in a quarantine; only those who could prove they were free of infection were allowed to leave the city.

He looked at her coolly, removing the pipe from between his lips and balancing it on his thumb. It was a reckless gesture that defied Edward's cautious nature. It scared Lucy.

"I am not going."

"What?" she responded in disbelief. "Edward, hundreds are dying here each day! You cannot possibly stay."

"But I am staying, Lucy." He stood up from his chair and stood before her. "I was incarcerated for four years. I will not leave my city for a country prison."

"What do you mean? Yorkshire is not a prison. It is my home. It is untouched by this madness. Please, Edward, I beg you. If not for me, then come for the children."

"My children?" he scoffed. "Don't think I don't see. I won't go to that house where you lived with that Jewish whoreson."

She flinched at his attack but was not ready to give up on him. "Come with us and stay at my father's house then. Please, Edward. There is nothing but death in this city. Did you survive the Tower for four years only to perish like this?"

His tone softened at her genuine display of concern for him. "Perhaps I did, Lucy. I'll not go with you. Take your children to safety. I've sent ahead funds to your father for your upkeep."

"Edward, it doesn't have to be like this," she pleaded. Despite their troubles, they had shared ten years together.

To her surprise, he embraced her and kissed her forehead with a tenderness she had not felt from him for many years. "Lucy, this is my final decision. Go, please. Take the children to Yorkshire. I will write to you."

"Edward, I did try to love you."

"I know, Lucy."

A month later his first letter reached her in Yorkshire.

July 1665

Lucy,

Our neighborhood has thus far seen only ten deaths this week. I consider myself blessed, as I have heard that in St. Giles parish over a thousand have died over these last three days. All business is shut down now that the ports are closed. The Lord Mayor has ordered all animals slaughtered. It has been reported that during this last fortnight over ten thousand cats and dogs were thrown into the Thames. Down by St. Paul's, the dead are piled up by the dozens waiting for burial. Churchyards are so full now that the dead are being buried in whatever loose soil is available. Hardly any churchmen remain in London so burials are of the crude sort. No one bothers with mourning dress or coffins anymore. The dead are wrapped in bed sheets and dropped in mass graves.

I had a visit from Jeremiah Hosgood yesterday. The poor man buried his wife and daughter last Sunday. He does not look well to me and has asked me to check in on

him and the remaining child, a boy of eleven. If there were a doctor left in town, I would send him to Hosgood. But it would seem that our medical men fled with our ministers.
Edward

August 1665
Lucy,

Hosgood is dead and his boy, William, is staying with me. He says little and sleeps a great deal. I am trying to find a suitable situation for him, but many of my acquaintances who remain in the city will not take in a child whose family perished from the fever. I may want to send him to Yorkshire if you would agree to it and if I can get a certificate of health for him. Please send me your response quickly so that I may make arrangements.
Edward

September 1665
Dear Edward,

Please bring William to Yorkshire. We all worry after you and beg that you relent in your determination to remain in London. Father is most eager to have you stay at Thicket Hall, and Abigail and Mary ask after you. Please come, Edward.
Lucy

October 1665
Lucy,

I have put William on a coach bound for Northampton. The driver has assured me that he will deliver the boy and arrange for his passage to Leicester. I would ask that you come down to meet him. He is too distraught to make his own way to you.

Perhaps by the time this letter reaches you, I too will have perished. With this in my mind, I need to share some final thoughts with you.

First is the matter of Mary, who I am confident is my child as she looks so much like my mother. I will trust you to raise her in the knowledge of our savior, Jesus Christ. I would also ask that when you speak of me to her it is with kindness and not the bitterness of our last years together. I still find it difficult to forgive your treachery, but I do not want our daughter to be an alien among your brood.

As to your adultery, there is much I have to say. Perhaps we never should have married as your heart was bound to another. Yet I feel not all our years were unhappy. While I was in prison, the anticipation of seeing your face and hearing your voice carried me through many dark hours. But like you, I was sustained by the Jew.

Amiel Lacerda has been known to me these past five years, not as your lover, but as an advocate of my case. This, of course, bears explanation. The week following my arrest he visited me inquiring about my needs. It was he who provided my daily bread beyond the poor prison fare. He bribed the Tower guards to move me to a private room. He arranged for me to have adequate coal on cold nights and parchment and ink so that I could correspond with you and Mr. Hosgood.

I hated this Jew at first. He told me he had come on behalf of your father, and for this I did not reject him, even as the thought of being dependent on him filled me with self-loathing. But for lack of any other interesting company, I grew to anticipate his visits. He came each week on a Sunday when he was in town. Often he would bring books and newspapers for which I am sure he had to dearly bribe the guards. After the first year, he began to engage a doctor to accompany him once a month. Another damnable Jew. As much as I despised them both, I found myself impressed with their learning and charity. Lacerda spoke frequently with me of my case and, I confess, he was in many ways a stronger advocate than Jeremiah Hosgood. Indeed, Hosgood told me before he died that it was Lacerda who arranged my release with a large sum transferred to His Majesty's coffers. Dr. Abrunel testified to my imminent death due to a cancer in my bowels, and thus I was no longer considered a threat to the Crown.

While the Jewish doctor was incorrect about the time of my death, he was correct in his diagnosis of my ailment. I have known for some time that I should not be long with you. I had hoped that we might mend our divisions before I died, but I did not understand when I was released how completely you had betrayed me.

I am grieved at the Jew's deception because, through him, I had come to believe that there might be hope for his people. It was never apparent to me that he had any interest in you other than your being my wife. I must impress on you the vileness of your sin and your need for redemption before our God.

Perhaps he will still want you after I am dead. If this is so, you should make it your task to bring him to the true faith and therefore erase your sins.
Please remember me well.
Your loving husband,
Edward Polestead

As she reached the end of the letter, Lucy reeled with its revelations. Maybe there was more good in Edward Polestead than he'd ever let on. Or perhaps his goodness had always been apparent and she'd simply been blind to it. Clutching Edward's letter to her chest, she prayed God would someday forgive her for her sins against her husband.

The following week, Lucy found William Hosgood waiting for her at the Star Cross Inn on the Leicester road. He'd been alone at the inn for over a week, the other guests and the innkeeper not wanting to go near him but happy enough for the silver he paid for his keep. The poor child was sick with anxiety but fortunately not sick with the fever. Just to be sure, Lucy remained with him in Leicester for a week. During that time she did her best to draw him out of his grief, but recalling her own mother's death, she did not press him.

Lucy did not receive any more letters from Edward, and she fell into a state of anguish. Was her husband still alive? She wanted to go to him, but for the sake of her children, she dared not return to London until the fever abated.

At the end of November, Domingo returned to England and, after a week in London, he made the journey to Yorkshire. There he found Lucy and the children outside enjoying the first snowfall of winter.

"Ami!" Abigail saw him first trotting toward them on his mare, but Mary was at her sister's heels running to him. When he swung down from the horse, the girls fell into his embrace, laughing and crying at once.

"Oh, my girls. I've missed you so." He buried his face in their locks, breathing in their little girl scent. Kneeling before them he assessed how they'd changed in the last year and a half. Mary was looking more and more like a blonde version of Lucy with her pale blue eyes and tall build. Abigail's dark wavy hair and petite frame reminded him of his mother, although she also had Lucy's blue eyes. Despite the two-year age difference, they were so similar in size that they could have been twins. "Look how you've grown. Mary, you are as tall as your sister. And, Abigail, you have become a young lady."

"I am seven now, Ami," Abigail replied proudly.

"Ami, you were gone so long. David is no longer a baby," Mary informed him, pulling at his coat sleeve in an effort to make him turn around so he would see the truth of her report.

He looked over to where Lucy stood holding the hand of a wobbly toddler. David seemed torn. He held back from Domingo, uncertain of this stranger, yet his desire to be part of the attention his sisters were receiving propelled him forward. The child compromised by simultaneously pulling at Lucy's hand and hiding behind her skirts with the effect of blinding his path and causing him to stumble. He looked up at his mother and, satisfied that she'd seen him fall, began to cry. Lucy swept the child up into her arms and he quieted in her embrace.

Before even greeting Domingo, she held out the child to him. Bravely, David did not cry at being handed over to the stranger so suddenly, although he squirmed to be released from his grasp. But Domingo could not let go of the boy just yet. A lump formed in his throat as he took in his son. David had changed. He now had the look of Domingo's brothers with light brown hair that curled slightly at the ends and pale brown eyes that he'd inherited from Joseph Lacerda. It was like seeing them again in the face of his child.

"Mama!" David cried out finally, but Domingo set the child down rather than hand him over to Lucy. Then he embraced her, and, like her daughters, her tears flowed easily over her smiling lips.

Later, when they were alone, Domingo and Lucy spoke of London's plague. "The fever has slowed some with the cool weather, but many are still stricken with it. Lucita, it will not be safe for you to return for some months. The city is all but paralyzed for lack of able-bodied men. Mr. Robles estimates the dead at fifty thousand."

"Dominick, do you have news of Edward?" Lucy asked, unashamed of the emotion in her voice for her missing husband.

He took her hands in his. "I did not find him or hear any news of him." He paused here before telling her the worst part. "There was a red cross on his door." Lucy knew that this meant his house was marked as one in which one or more of the inhabitants had the fever. The cross was not a signal for help but a warning to the living to not cross the threshold. Unless he had received help from his friends in the city, Edward may have suffered and died alone.

She took a deep breath. "I must know for sure, Dominick. He was my husband despite everything. He . . ." Her voice caught on a sob. "He told me everything, Dominick. How you befriended him. I was always so angry with him. I never gave him the chance to be the husband he wanted to be."

"Lucita, don't judge your marriage by my actions. You were his wife. I was just a visitor to his cell. We knew Edward differently. He always spoke of you as constant and helpful. He was a good man, but not a man who loved you for who you are, who you want to be."

She wrung her hands while nodding her head in agreement. "I know. But that doesn't erase my sin."

"Don't do this," he said, worried now.

"Your mother always knew how much we would hurt each other and everyone else."

"Stop, Lucy," he pleaded. "People hurt each other, even with the best of intentions. Do you think you can make it up to Edward by telling me to go away now?"

"No, that's not what I meant."

"I love you, Lucita, sin or no sin."

She nodded, too overcome to speak, and they sat for several moments in silence before she took his hands in hers.

"There is another matter," she said. "Mr. Hosgood and his family perished, except for one. A boy named William. Edward entrusted him to me and he's been staying with us this last month. He does not know of any family who might take him. His mother had a sister who died in childbirth, and he said that his father seemed not to have any family relations. We need to find his people, Dominick."

There was something in the tone of her last words that seemed uncommitted to the task. "What if there are none who will take him? What then?" he asked.

Lucy nodded. "I've thought about that. I think he should remain with us until other arrangements can be found."

Domingo smiled to himself at her badly masked desire to keep the boy. He had not yet told her of the Irish girls in Newport. Suddenly their small brood of three had doubled. "May I see him?"

◆◆◆

William kept to the room he shared with David, even taking most meals there. Domingo drew a chair close to the bed where the boy lay and sat down. Trying to hide his interest in his new visitor, William glanced quickly at Domingo before returning his gaze to the ceiling.

Domingo began gently, "I knew your father, William. He was an honorable man."

This caught the boy's attention, and he sat up on the bed and faced Domingo. "I remember you. You came to our house. Mother said you were a damned Jew, but Father told her to hush."

"You have a good memory, William," Domingo said, genuinely impressed that the boy would recall him two years later after seeing him so briefly. "Your mother was right. I am a Jew."

Oddly the boy did not respond to Domingo's revelation. "Sir, what will become of me?" he asked.

Domingo smiled at the boy. In addressing Domingo as "sir" William seemed to be willing to accept him despite his mother's disdain for Jews. "William, can you read?"

"Yes, sir. I know some Latin and I can read and write."

"Good. Do you like figures?"

"I do not dislike them, sir."

This made Domingo chuckle. "William, I am in need of an apprentice, and you are in need of a situation. What say you to learning my trade?"

"Please, sir, what is your trade?"

"I keep account books for merchants. Most of the trade I manage is in imports of household goods for the colonies. I've just come from the city of Newport in the colony of Rhode Island where I have a home. Do you think you would like to go there, William?"

The boy's eyes widened. "On a ship across the sea?"

"Yes, across the sea to America."

"Thank you, sir. I would like that very much."

◆◆◆

In December, Domingo returned to London. He found a record of Edward's death at St. Bride's Church and visited the place where the parish sexton suggested Edward might be buried, a field north of London that had lain fallow for the last year. Many of the dead from the parish were buried there after its own graveyard became too full. Domingo rode out to the field even though he knew there would be no marker. According to the sexton, the dead were buried en mass during the late summer and autumn months. After dismounting, Domingo walked with his mare to the center of the field and gathered up a handful of loose soil. It was an awkward moment. The only prayers for the dead that Domingo knew were Catholic or Jewish, two religions Edward especially despised. Yet after their strange friendship, Domingo could not help but say an Ave Maria and the Kaddish for Edward. He knew he should despise the man for the anguish he had caused Lucy; instead, he felt a kinship with Edward. Both of them had failed her because they'd let themselves be ruled by fear. It was only Edward's abandonment of Lucy and the girls that had allowed Domingo to redeem himself in Lucy's eyes.

As he made plans to travel north again, Domingo received an unexpected letter from Amsterdam.

22 Sh'vat, 5426

Senhor Lacerda,

It has come to my attention that you have returned from the colonies and plan to settle once again in London. As haham of the London kehilla, it is my duty to inform you of the Ma'amad's complaint against you. Your adultery was known to me before I left London, having been told of it by more than one member of the kehilla. It has also come to my attention that, while living in Amsterdam, you consorted with Baruch Spinoza during times when he was under temporary ban. I'm sure you are aware of his permanent banishment in 1656.

I urge you to remove yourself from the company of the Gentile woman, only giving her what is your duty under the law. The Ma'amad has agreed that 50£ per annum is sufficient. Beyond this annuity, you are to cease contact with her. In addition, I require you to come to Amsterdam to atone for your sins before the congregation at Talmud Torah. Until such time as you complete these conditions, you have been placed under a temporary ban.

Haham Jacob Sasportas

♦♦♦

It was in a state of shock that he rode back to Yorkshire. Manuel had prepared him for this possibility, but Domingo had thought that while the haham remained in Amsterdam he would be safe from censure. Clearly one of his brethren in London had written to the haham urging him to carry out the ban. Even in London he was no longer welcome.

Lucy read the rabbi's letter twice just to be sure she understood. She couldn't believe that the rabbi and the other Jews in London would do this to Dominick when he was now trying to make things right. She had not seen him this upset since Semuel died.

"I am sorry, Dominick." Instinctively she moved to comfort him, but he pulled away. "Please, Dominick. Don't shut me out. I want to help you. I want to try to understand."

"You can't understand, Lucy," he said too loudly. Trying to calm his voice, he began again, "I'm sorry. I always knew it might come to this."

"What does it mean, Dominick? Are you still a Jew?" Lucy asked.

He sighed deeply. "One cannot stop being a Jew. Haham Sasportas has placed me under a temporary ban from the community. I have thirty days to repent. If I do not, the haham can invoke a *herem*, which is a permanent ban."

"Can you not appeal to your friend, Rabbi ben Israel? Surely he must wield some influence in the Amsterdam Jewish community."

He shook his head. "Lucy, he died two months after Semuel. He never even made it back to Amsterdam. Besides, bans cannot be appealed because the Ma'amad votes on them as a united body. This is not the decision of one haham but of all the council members."

"I don't understand. How can he invoke a ban on you in London while he is in Amsterdam?"

"He is the haham of the London community no matter where he resides. It is similar to the Christian system where bishops do not always live in their dioceses, though it is rare for a haham not to live among his people. The haham left because of the plague. He'll return soon, I'm sure of it. Besides, our kehilla in London still answers to Amsterdam because we are so small a community." Domingo sat down on the settee and put his head in his hands. "My family sacrificed so much. I'm the last one and I've done this."

"No," said Lucy. "You are not the last one. The children and I are your family now. And I know that Manuel, as angry as he is, will not forsake you. You are like a son to him, Dominick. He'll forgive you in time."

He became angry once again. "I don't want forgiveness! I want acceptance! I want to know why my parents were good Jews for allowing two of their children to be killed by the church, but I am cast out for not abandoning my children." He stood and kicked violently at the first thing he saw, a wooden candle stand that flew into the fireplace grate, smashing it into several pieces.

"Dominick, stop," Lucy cried. Without looking back at her, he strode from the room. Seconds later she heard the front door slam behind him. Running to one of the front windows she looked out and saw that he was already a good distance away from the house, headed toward the hilly meadow that her father used for riding. As much as she wanted to follow him, Lucy knew she had to let him be.

He walked about Thicket Hall's fields for hours thinking. The meadow stretched out before him, acre upon acre of grass with the occasional shade tree breaking up the landscape. In the sky a flock of ducks flew in formation, squawking at each other in their flight to southern climes. Was their noise chatter or warnings to stay together? Even fowl seemed to bully one another into submission. The sun began to set, a pale, weak glow amid the gray clouds. It was beautiful in a melancholy way. Why had he never noticed how beautiful Yorkshire was before? It reminded him of the uncultivated beauty of the marshes just outside of Newport. When darkness engulfed the day, Domingo began to walk back. But instead of going to Chapel House, he headed for Thicket Hall. He had unfinished business with John Dunnington that would not wait.

◆◆◆

"Domingo! Lucy said you'd gone out. I'm glad to see you're back," exclaimed John jovially, though his eyes were full of concern. Lucy had told him about the rabbi's ban and Domingo's reaction to it.

"Mr. Dunnington, may I speak with you alone?"

"Yes, yes! Come into my study. May I pour you a glass of brandy?"

"Thank you, sir. I'd like that." He accepted the spirit, hoping it would calm his nerves.

"What's on your mind, son?"

"Mr. Dunnington, we've suspected for weeks, and now I have confirmation, that Edward Polestead is dead."

"So it is true then. Why he would not come up with Lucy, I'll never figure out. I wrote to him that there would be no bad blood between us and that he was welcome here." John shook his head regretfully.

"Sir, Mr. Polestead may not have died of the plague," Domingo explained. "He was dying when he was released from prison, and he did not wish anyone to know. He was in great pain and took opium several times a day. When he was released the improvement in his care made him appear to be improving in health. However, his condition was grave. That he survived as long as he did was a surprise."

"From what did he suffer?"

"A cancer of the bowels according to Dr. Abrunel."

John seemed affected by this revelation but said nothing, shaking his head thoughtfully.

"Sir," Domingo began, "there is another matter. I'm not sure how this should be done, so forgive me if I am going about it all wrong. I'll come straight to the point. I wish to marry Lucy." He took a deep sip of his brandy and anxiously studied John Dunnington's face to determine his response.

To his surprise, the older man let out a hearty laugh. "It is early to speak of this so soon after Edward's death, yet I feel it's about time you came to me, for goodness sake! I've known your intentions for years, son."

Domingo began to relax. "So we would have your blessing, Mr. Dunnington?"

"I cannot think of a better man to marry Lucy." He rose and embraced Domingo. "You have my blessing and my warm welcome into our family."

Domingo took another deep sip of brandy. "What of my religion?"

"What of it? You both foolishly cling to the most despised faiths in England. You may as well marry each other. I am, however, curious how you two plan to marry. You are known to be a Jew, even here in Yorkshire. I'll wager even independent ministers will not perform a mixed marriage."

"Yes, it is a problem," Domingo answered glumly, then finished his brandy and placed the empty glass on John's desk. "It means a lot to me to have your approval, sir. I will find a way to marry her properly, and I promise to care for her."

"I'm not worried about that, Domingo. You've shown your quality over these last years. I know that Lucy and the children will be well looked after."

◆◆◆

When he returned to Chapel House, Domingo found Lucy and the children in the parlor. The girls played with their dolls as William, finally up to joining the family in the evenings, read to them, although Domingo noted with amusement that Mary's doll lay abandoned and she was attempting to comb William's hair with the doll's brush. Good-naturedly, William was allowing Mary to pull at his hair while he continued to read. David was working on knocking over Lucy's mending basket. All in all, it was a rare scene of calm at Chapel

House. Domingo strode in and planted a kiss on each girl's head, mussed William's already disheveled hair, and scooped up David just as he was about to put a knitting needle in his mouth.

"Lucy, can we talk?"

They went into the kitchen and sat next to each other at the table. Domingo held David in his lap. "I've spoken with your father about our marriage. He's given us his blessing."

She smiled and took his hand in hers. "I knew he would, Dominick."

David began to squirm. "Lucita," Domingo began, standing the child up in his lap, "your father asked me who would marry us. I was not sure how to answer him."

She did not answer right away and then it was almost a whisper when she did. "Shall I ask my uncle?"

"I don't want a Catholic wedding, Lucita."

She couldn't tell if he was angry or sad. In all likelihood he was both. She wanted to be sensitive to his disappointment, but the ban against him demanded action, not waffling.

"Dominick, you told me once that you could never return to Portugal because the church would always consider you Catholic. Your parents had a Catholic wedding and they remained true to the faith of your people. Let my uncle marry us, and I promise you we will raise our children as Jews."

He closed his eyes and sighed deeply. "I wanted to marry as a Jew. Had you been a Jew, the haham would have married us despite our adultery."

She caught her breath in shock. "Dominick, don't ask this of me. I will obey the law for you and for our children, but don't ask me to forsake my religion. There is another way. Marry me as a Catholic."

She was right, but he was not ready to give in. The irony was, of course, that had Lucy been a secret Jew, they would have easily married in the Catholic Church and then practiced their faith at home. Why was it so hard for him to agree to this arrangement then? Because she was Catholic. Lucy would marry within her tradition and allow his deception. It made him feel unclean. If she were sharing the deception, he would not feel this way. Yet he knew she was right. It was the only way. David began to pull Domingo's hair, drawing him out of his thoughts. He handed their son to Lucy. "Lucita, I have wanted to marry you since I was fifteen. If this is the only way, then I will marry you as a Catholic."

♦♦♦

A few days later Lucy paid a visit to Hugh Jowsey. "Uncle, I am ready to marry again. I would very much like to be married within the church this time. I'd be honored if you would perform the sacrament."

"How dare you," the priest said. "Your adultery with the Jew is even known to your cousins."

"Uncle, he was raised in the Catholic faith," she countered. "He is willing to be married under our law. He will not interfere with my religion."

"Lucy, he is a Judaizer, a heretic! How can you want to marry him? His very blood is tainted. How can you want to expose your children to this?"

Her expression hardened. "Uncle, he is the man I will wed, whether you perform the ceremony or not. If you will not, we will find another who will. But consider what you risk. I have been ever faithful to our religion. If you refuse me, you will lose me, my children, and any hope of bringing my husband back to the faith. Perform the marriage and you will have done your duty in trying to keep us in the fold. If you do this, I will remain Catholic. Do you want it on your conscience that you were the one to push your sister's only child out of the faith she loved, the faith you fought for, the faith your parents died for?"

"You have no right to play that card, niece," Hugh answered darkly. "You wear your religion like a seasonal cloak. Only when it suits you are you Catholic."

"Convince me to wear it evermore, Uncle."

"By marrying you to a Jew? Ridiculous!"

"Do this or lose me, Uncle. I would have my intended swear to my faithfulness. He loves me for it and has known since I was a girl what my true religion is. And he is the only one who has never tried to convince me to turn from my religion." Hugh scoffed at this, but Lucy persisted. "Does this surprise you? He knows what it means to have his faith taken from him by force. He knows, as we do, what it means to lose loved ones for the faith. He watched his brother die at the hands of the Inquisition."

"You said he was baptized in the true faith. He willfully rejected his religion."

"Uncle, please. If you still consider Dominick a Catholic, then you will be performing a Catholic marriage. If you do this, there is still hope."

"I must speak to him first."

"You will perform the marriage?"

"I will speak to him. Then I will decide."

"Thank you, Uncle."

◆◆◆

After Maundy Thursday, Domingo took William back to London to begin his apprenticeship and to help him prepare the house for Lucy and the children. Because of the ban, Domingo was not allowed to interact with other Jews, but he could still train William to keep accounts and to understand the intricacies of shipping and mercantilism. At the end of their first week in London, they went to William's abandoned house in Star Yard. Looters had already stripped the house of anything of worth, but Domingo hoped the boy would find something of sentimental value that had not been stolen. William combed the house while Domingo waited in the kitchen. All the furniture and linens, even the pots and pans, had been stolen. After a half hour, Domingo climbed the stairs to find William. He sat on the floor in what would have been a private bedchamber if any furnishings had been left.

"William, perhaps we should leave now," he said gently. "We'll go to Lincoln's Inn tomorrow to see what might be left in your father's office."

The boy glared at him with a vicious anger. "Go away, Jew! You don't know what it's like!"

Domingo paused before answering the boy. William's words were like daggers, yet Domingo knew that they were not aimed at him. He recognized the anger and respected the boy for having the spirit to express it. "No, William. I don't know what it is like to lose my entire family in just one month. But please listen to me. I do know how it feels to survive. I know how much guilt you feel when you find yourself laughing, or even enjoying a simple thing like eating or running through the streets. I know how many times you catch yourself just about to revel in being alive before you remember that those you love are dead. Within a year, I lost two brothers, my sister, and my father. I was the youngest, yet I lived. My mother and I clung to each other, but at the same time, I believe we hurt each other because we felt we did not deserve to be happy." He gently placed his hand on the boy's shoulder. "William, don't make the mistake of hating yourself or rejecting joy as absolution for surviving. God allowed you to live. Don't squander that in despair. You do no honor to your parents or your sister by living in sadness."

"But it hurts so much," William said, beginning to sob. Domingo struggled with how to respond. Manuel would have given him his space and let him cry alone. Lucy would have embraced him. Domingo decided to let the boy decide. He sat down next to William and soon the boy found comfort by leaning against him. Together they sat like this until the boy was spent. Then Domingo took him home.

XX. *FIRE AND WATER,* MARCH 1666 – SEPTEMBER 1666

Father Hugh Jowsey met with Domingo in the study at Thicket Hall. "You were baptized in the Catholic faith?" the priest began.

"Yes," answered Domingo. "At the Cathedral of Santa Maria in Lisbon, Portugal, in April 1634. I was three weeks old at the time."

"Have you partaken of any other sacraments?"

Domingo did not like the tone and direction of Hugh's questions but kept telling himself that it was the only way to marry Lucy. "I was confirmed at the age of seven. I made confession weekly and did penance; I also partook in communion. I did this until I was eight when we moved to Amsterdam."

"So when you were eight you became a Judaizer?" Hugh challenged.

"I returned to the religion of my people. The religion of which we were robbed generations ago," Domingo shot back.

"I understand that your parents were both Catholic and that your ancestors willingly converted to the faith."

"Under pain of death," Domingo added darkly.

"Yes, well, the particular circumstances of their conversions are not significant," said Hugh dismissively.

Domingo scoffed. "Did you not flee England when you were threatened with hanging for your allegiance to Rome?"

Hugh bristled at this accusation. "I left to attend seminary. I have been back these thirteen years."

"And yet during Cromwell's reign you hid your identity and did not live openly as a priest."

"I had an obligation to my parish. Without me they would have lost access to the sacraments. Without me there would have been no one to defend the faith to them. Truth would have been lost had priests not taken on the burden of secrecy during those years. I was honored to bear that cross for God."

"Is truth a defenseless child that needs your protection? Why is it necessary to defend God to those you consider heathen? Is not God powerful enough to defend himself against the Protestant and the Jew?"

"God anoints priests for the task of sanctifying humanity. God molds man to accomplish his will," Hugh retorted smugly.

But Domingo was not finished, "Yes, and often men mold God to achieve theirs." He stood to leave. "I will not let you use God to abuse my people. There is no need to try to win me for your church. I have agreed to marry under your law."

"Yes, but will you live under it?"

Domingo sighed. In many ways this was the one question that had been defining his entire life. Always he had been compelled by Catholic law or Jewish law and always he seemed to fail. "May God deal with me justly if I do not," he answered Hugh and then moved toward the door.

"Wait," the priest called him back.

Domingo turned to face Hugh, who continued with surprising sincerity, "You must know this marriage flies in the face of everything I've been taught, everything I believe. I cannot want this for her, but Lucy is all I have left of my sister, all I have left of our family."

Domingo chose his words carefully. "Her faith is important to me. It was the faith of my childhood. My mother was devoted to the Virgin her entire life. I want Lucy to remain Catholic."

Hugh nodded, satisfied at last, and leaned in toward Domingo in the intimate manner of close friends. "Perhaps she will help you find your way back to the church."

Domingo took this affront in stride. He actually felt sorry for Hugh and those Christians like him who needed the Jews to convert or to disappear altogether in order to bolster their faith in Christ. It was as if the very existence of Jews created a seed of doubt that people like Hugh could not bear. Domingo nodded vaguely, which seemed to please the priest.

◆◆◆

They were married quietly in the chapel at Thicket Hall shortly after Easter. While it was no longer illegal for Catholic marriages to be performed in England, Lucy had not observed the proper period of mourning for Edward and, for his own reasons, Hugh insisted the ceremony be private. John Dunnington led his daughter to the altar and, over her husband's protests, Frances stood for Lucy. Thomas witnessed for Domingo, and even though the boy was not Catholic, Hugh Jowsey let it go.

Their return to London in July was emotional. Thousands had died last year and the city was still in a state of mourning. The stillness of the poorer parts of the city testified to where the plague had hit the hardest. Entire neighborhoods stood lifeless, and the smell of decaying bodies buried in shallow pits drove away survivors who might have considered moving back. Cree Church Lane and Duke's Place had not suffered devastating losses, although, like every neighborhood in London, almost every family had suffered the loss of one of its own or someone dear.

Though still under the haham's ban, Domingo moved his family to his house on Stoney Lane. He knew it would have been easier to leave Lucy and the children in Yorkshire, but after being away so long, he couldn't bear to be apart from them, and there was much for him to arrange in London before their departure to Newport.

His Catholic marriage had rendered him dead to the community, although a permanent ban had not been pronounced against him yet. He was sure it was because he had let it be known that they would not be long in London. Even so, old women, many who had pressed Teresa Maria to marry her son to their daughters, now crossed the street when they saw him to avoid his contagion. Men he'd prayed with now looked right through him while their sons stared aggressively and their daughters cast their eyes downward.

Domingo tried as best he could to shield the children from the disdain of their neighbors, but Lucy saw it quite clearly and her heart broke for him every time he left the house, knowing how much time he spent steeling himself against the rejection of his brethren and then trying to recover from it. For Lucy it was easier, although, as Domingo had predicted, shopkeepers in the parish, both Christian and Jew, refused her service, even when she offered to pay with silver. Often she found herself at markets on the far side of the city in order to gain anonymity. London held little welcome for Catholics and Jews, but for now they had nowhere else to go.

Lucy and Domingo found comfort in settling into family life and in making plans for the future, for in just a few weeks they would set sail on the *Providence* for their new life in Newport.

By September, their preparations to quit England were complete. The house had been legally restored to its owner, an English agent who would then rent it within the Cree Church Lane community. Most of their belongings were packed, and they had bid good-bye to their Yorkshire kin. Lucy was also in the sixth month of another pregnancy. Traveling by sea for six weeks would not be easy, but they were scheduled to arrive in Newport in early November, well before the baby was due.

◆◆◆

It was Monday and Lucy woke first. The baby inside her squirmed as she sat up, and she giggled. Dominick lifted his head from his pillow, his eyes still closed in sleep. "Lucita?"

"Good morning," she answered cheerily. As the day of their leaving approached, Lucy felt her cares lifting. Emigrating was more than an adventure; it was going to be a new start for them. In Newport they would live free of fear, free of religious hatred. Running her hands over her belly, Lucy gave a satisfied sigh. Last night Dominick had likened Newport to Yorkshire and had surprised her by showing her plans of his house. While she found the exterior, which Dominick referred to as "saltbox," flat and dull, the inside proved to be a smaller imitation of Chapel House with a kitchen, two parlors, a dining room on the first floor, and three bedrooms on the upper floor. It was the perfect house for their family. Lucy leaned down to kiss Dominick and then set her mind to the tasks of the day. She was thinking they would visit Teresa Maria's grave one last time today.

It was when she lumbered up from the bed that she noted the sky remained dark, though it was well after dawn. "Dominick," she cried and ran to the window, opening it with a violent shove.

Alarmed at her behavior, Domingo shot up. "What's the matter?" But he did not need her answer when he smelled the air from outside wafting into their bedroom. "Mother of Christ!" He jumped from the bed and ran toward the window.

The air of the city was thick with smoke.

"Dominick, there's no fire. I don't see any fire," Lucy said in a rush, scanning the neighborhood.

He was already half dressed when she turned around. "Wake the children," he commanded. "I'm going out to see what's going on."

"No, Dominick," Lucy exclaimed, grabbing his arm.

"Lucy, we can't stay in the house if the fire burns nearby. The smoke alone will kill us. I have to see where it is."

But she was crying and wouldn't let go of his arm. "No! Not this! Not now! Don't leave, Dominick!"

"I promise I won't take any risks. I just have to see which direction it's coming from. We don't want to run toward it."

Half mad with fear, Lucy ran to wake and dress the children. When the older ones were ready and helping the younger ones, Lucy packed what food she could from the larder and gathered their traveling papers. It seemed like an eternity, but Dominick soon stumbled back into the house, sweaty and coughing.

"Everyone is headed toward Aldersgate. The fire is south of us, near the cathedral. I heard a man say that the king has ordered entire neighborhoods razed to stop the spread of the fire. We may never return here, Lucita."

Lucy looked around the parlor. Their trunks were packed neatly against a wall. Tomorrow they were to leave for Plymouth to meet the ship that would take them to Newport. "We don't have a cart, Dominick."

"Never mind about our clothes and household things. They can be replaced."

"I want my mother's rosary and Filipe's Virgin."

Domingo nodded. "You shall have those, Lucita."

She attended to David while Domingo searched through her trunk for the rosary and the statue. When they left, Domingo carried Mary, William held tight to Abigail's hand, and Lucy clutched David to her chest. The streets were thick with smoke and hundreds of living beings trying to make their way through it: horses bearing carts piled high with furniture, linens, and other household items; mothers and fathers bearing children and sacks filled to bursting with precious items they were loath to leave behind. People called out for loved ones lost in the melee or still in their houses, afraid to leave.

The Lacerdas joined the throng of evacuees moving north out of the city. They were not on the road long when Lucy suddenly remembered the packet of documents she'd left on the bed while changing David. "Dominick! Our passage papers, our marriage certificate, and your will. I left them!"

"Are you sure, Lucita? You told me you put them in your leather sack, and I see it hanging under your cloak," he replied, hoping against hope she was wrong.

"No! I meant to but I was distracted." She frantically handed David to Abigail and searched the sack hanging at her hip. "They're not here, Dominick. We have to go back!"

"No, I'll go alone. You take the children and meet me on the other side of the wall." Domingo set Mary down beside William and Abigail and turned to the boy. "William, Lucy must carry David. I am entrusting you with Mary and Abigail. Keep together and wait for me on the other side of Aldersgate."

William nodded wordlessly, feeling the enormity of his commission. Then Domingo kissed Lucy, turned around, and dove back through the crowds toward Stoney Lane.

Lucy stared after him until long after the smoke and the press of the crowds had obscured her view. "Mrs. Lacerda." It was William. "We should keep moving."

This broke her reverie. "Yes, of course."

They made their way at a much slower pace now, William dutifully following Lucy with the girls. As they neared the ancient fortification that surrounded London, the press of people grew greater, pushing, pulling, and inching their way toward the gates. Lucy felt sick from the heat and smoke, but she kept moving. With Dominick gone, she had to lead the children; she had to be the strong one. David began to cry and Lucy fumbled in her sack for a bit of bread to feed him. "There, love. No tears. Ami will be back soon."

She pressed her lips to his little forehead and hugged him tightly. When he quieted, she turned to reassure the older children that they would soon be on the other side where they would rest and eat. But when she did not immediately spot them, she felt panic rise in her breast. She scanned the crowd to see if they'd fallen behind, but William and the girls were now ahead of her, not having seen her pause to feed David.

Lucy made her way with David through the gate and saw that the crowd on the other side was just as dense as it was inside the city. But she was sure she'd seen Abigail wave to her just moments ago. Breathing more evenly now, Lucy began to look for her children.

◆◆◆

It was long past noon now, approaching the hottest time of the day. People still poured out of the city and it struck Domingo how many souls still lived here despite the devastation of the plague. He'd spent an hour outside Aldersgate searching for his family before he conceded that they must have continued north along with everyone else. Wearily he joined the throng of refugees, always scanning faces for those of his children and Lucy. He had not thought he would be separated from them for so long, but he took comfort knowing that they were together and that Lucy had thought to bring food. However, an ominous feeling began to settle on Domingo when he approached the refugees' destination and realized that London was taking shelter at Moorsfield, the graveyard for the plague dead.

To Domingo's relief, it took him less than two hours to find Lucy among the thousands gathered at Moorsfield. In fact, he heard her before he saw her. "Abigail! Mary!" Her hysterical cry rang out over the general hub. Domingo ran toward her voice and saw Lucy at last. She was making her way through the groups of refugees huddled together on the grass.

"Lucy!"

"Oh, Dominick," she cried, stumbling into his arms. She had David on her hip. Dominick lifted the child from her and took them both in his embrace.

"Where are the girls? Where is William?" he asked fearfully.

She shook her head. "I don't know. I've been looking for them for hours. We got separated. I know they're out of the city, Dominick. They were just ahead of me going through Aldersgate. I know they got out."

His instinct was to immediately begin searching, but he did not want to leave Lucy and David. "There is a small grove about a quarter mile back, just off the main road. Several families have set up camp there, so you should be safe from ruffians. I passed the king's men delivering food and ale on my way here. They will surely be at the grove before long. We'll settle you and David there while I look for the others."

"We should stay together, Dominick," Lucy argued as they began walking.

He stole a glance at her bulging middle and squeezed David to his chest. "No, Lucita, you must rest, and I can move much faster on my own. Stay close to the other families. I'll come back when I have the girls and William."

◆◆◆

He searched in every camp for them, and by dawn the following day, Domingo had begun to despair. He'd not slept or eaten since Sunday night, but he could not go back to the grove and face Lucy without Abigail, Mary, and William. As long as he searched, as long as he hoped, he could go on. The city was still burning fiercely and the thick smoke had begun to drift beyond the city walls so that at times he couldn't see more than three feet in front of him. There were dozens of men and women like him desperately searching for loved ones and, by Tuesday afternoon, a make-shift band of London marshals had organized to help the searchers. Domingo made for one of their tents and spoke to a Mr. Harlow, who seemed to be in charge. "Please, I need to find my children. They've been lost since Monday morning."

"All right, calmly now. Tell me their names and ages."

"My daughters, Abigail and Mary Lacerda, are eight and six. There is a boy as well, my apprentice, William Hosgood. He is twelve."

"Are you sure they are together?" the marshal asked. It had not occurred to Domingo that they would not be.

"No," he said, shaking his head. He related where he had already looked and gave a description of each child. The marshal told Domingo to return the next day.

Early the next morning, he returned to the marshal's tent, but there was no news of the children. The fire was still raging and Mr. Harlow told Domingo that it was concentrated by the river. Thus the neighborhoods by the north wall seemed to have been spared. In sheer desperation, Domingo found himself going back into the city. The smoke was blinding the farther in he went, and he found it increasingly difficult to breathe and to think straight. But the marshal was right; parishes to the north had been spared. With relief, he found his house still standing and it occurred to him that he could get supplies, food and blankets, for Lucy and David. However, once inside the house he feared for his sanity.

He thought he was hallucinating. They were all sitting at the kitchen table. William was pouring small ale and Abigail was cutting apple slices for Mary.

"Ami! You're back," Mary exclaimed. "Where are Mummy and David?"

Abigail stood and walked over to him. She took his hand in hers and looked up at him anxiously. "Ami, we couldn't find you, so William brought us back home to wait for you."

Domingo looked at the boy. Of course, it made so much sense now. He couldn't believe he'd spent three days looking for them. Like an empty sack he crumpled to the floor and, cupping his face in his hands, began to weep. Abigail looked stricken, fearful she'd done something wrong, but then Mary climbed into his lap and indicated for Abigail to do the same. After an awkward moment, William sat down with them, offering Domingo a cup of ale. No drink had ever tasted so good to Domingo.

They couldn't stay in the house for the danger of the smoke. After gathering supplies, the four of them set out for Moorsfield. By late afternoon they were reunited with David and Lucy, and they set up camp with them. Having delivered the children to Lucy safely, Domingo lay down on the ground and slept through to the next day.

By Thursday the fire was just smoldering in the rubble near the wharves. And on Friday they were allowed to go home. Lucy dashed off letters to her family to assure them of their survival, although she realized that she would have to post them from Plymouth. Surprisingly few had died in the fire that leveled eighty percent of London. Lucy and Domingo knew no one who had perished, and they only heard about a dozen or so deaths from the gossip in the field camps.

♦♦♦

The *Providence* was scheduled to leave from Plymouth on September 15, and the Lacerdas had already been delayed three days in getting there. Domingo hired a coach and, except for the change of horses, they did not stop until they reached the port. It was only when they were safely on the ship that, for the first time in a week, Domingo slept without nightmares.

Early on the third morning at sea, Domingo sent the children from the cabin so that he could speak with Lucy alone. "Lucita, I need to tell you about Newport and why I stayed so long there."

Her eyes grew wide and she steeled herself for a horrible confession of infidelity or insolvency.

"There are two girls living there," he began.

"Dominick, stop! I don't want to know. It was a long time to be away and I was still married to Edward. Please just tell me I am your legitimate wife." His laughter at her words angered her. "Don't mock me, Dominick!"

"Lucita, I have never been unfaithful to you." He took her hands in his and kissed them. "Please let me continue. My cousin Marcos has a daughter. He sent the child and her older sister to me last year because they cannot live in Barbados with him."

"Why not?"

"They were slaves. I don't know how he got them out of Barbados."

"Go on." So Domingo related the whole sordid affair between Marcos and the Irish slave. Then he told her about the capable Pratts who'd been caring for the girls in his absence. "In his last letter, Benjamin wrote that the girls are well. The older one, Miread, is quick to anger and given to running off, but she never gets far because of her lameness."

"That is lucky for us, I suppose," Lucy mused.

"No, Lucita," Domingo said, shaking his head sadly. "I suspect she was made lame. Her foot is too neatly damaged."

Lucy frowned. "What a despicable thing to do to a child."

"Unfortunately this kind of punishment is not uncommon for slaves."

"Did you speak to her about it?" Lucy asked. Despite her earlier misgivings, she felt herself drawn in by this mysterious Irish girl.

"When I left, her English was terrible. Her native language is forbidden in Barbados, but according to Marcos, the Irish slaves try to teach their children their tongue. I could not communicate easily with her. She tried to bite me once, and after that I left her care to Martha Pratt." He sighed and squeezed Lucy's hands. "I have no idea what to expect of her when we arrive. She is a broken child."

"Tell me of your cousin's daughter."

"Eimer will be about three years old when we arrive. She has the look of Marcos. What can I say about a child so young? She was confused, she missed her mother, yet she was quick to bond with Mrs. Pratt. Of course this angered Miread beyond telling."

"And what of Benjamin? What has he to say about them?" she asked, knowing that Dominick had a great deal of faith in his young assistant.

Domingo sighed. "Benjamin has no family. Miread has Eimer, he says, so why should she be so bitter? Yet he is kind to her and Miread responds in her own way. At least she has not tried to bite him."

Relieved that her husband's revelations did not meet her deepest fears, Lucy was willing to take on the challenge of his freed Irish slaves. But more than that, she saw Dominick in a new light. "It is an honor that Marcos would trust you with his daughter."

He smiled mischievously at her. "Wait, Lucita, I haven't told you about the horde of bastards I sired while in Newport." She laughed and heaved her heavy body up from the bunk and smiled at him.

"You sired two bastards in London and took on the children of two other men. Now you've committed to the bastard child of your cousin and her wild older sister." She caressed her belly. "This child is your only legitimate sire, Dominick. It would seem that bastards and orphans are your particular calling."

He laughed, realizing how happy he was. "I am more than willing to sire more legitimate children if my wife allows it." He circled her waist with his arms and planted kisses on her neck.

She giggled and pushed him away gently. "Your wife is willing but please let her birth this child before attempting a fifth, or would it be a sixth? Dominick, how many children do we have now?"

He added quickly in his head. "With the one in your womb, we will have seven. But there is also Benjamin. I've promised him houseroom."

"And will we all fit there now?"

"When I thought we had just three children, it seemed large. Now I suppose we'll have to add on some rooms."

Lucy leaned into her husband's chest and closed her eyes as he protectively wrapped his arms around her. "Will we be all right there, Dominick? Will they accept us?"

"*Tikvah*, Lucita. Never lose hope."

Author's note

I first discovered Domingo de Lacerda in the court records of the 1656 trial of Antonio Robles when I was writing my master's thesis on the readmission of the Jews to England. He was listed as a Portuguese accountant who worked for Robles in England, and his role in the trial was to verify Robles's nationality. While the entire case of Antonio Robles intrigued me, I couldn't stop thinking about who Domingo might have been because one of my grandfathers was a Portuguese accountant with the last name La Cerda. I wanted to know more about Domingo. There is no record of his death in the Jewish cemetery at Mile End in London, so I presume Domingo left the country.

The tragic life of another historical figure also fascinated me: Menasseh ben Israel of Amsterdam. The rabbi had two sons. Joseph mysteriously died in Poland on a business trip. The other son, Semuel, took over his father's press and later, he traveled to England to petition Oliver Cromwell to present his father's case for the readmission of the Jews to England. There is no record of Oliver Cromwell receiving Semuel, but we do know that Menasseh ben Israel traveled to England in 1655 to press the cause of the Jews to the Lord Protector. We also know that Semuel died in England in 1657 and that his father received four hundred pounds from Oliver Cromwell that he used to convey his son's body back to Amsterdam. Menasseh ben Israel died just two months after Semuel.

I knew I wanted to tell the story of the readmission of the Jews to England, but I wanted to do it in a way that put the history in the background, highlighting the relationships between the main characters. Domingo and Semuel might not have been friends, but, as they were both part of the small crypto-Jewish community in London in 1656, it is likely that they knew each other. Semuel surely knew Baruch Spinoza as the latter was a student of his father. I invented Lucy Dunnington as a way to connect Domingo's story

285

more closely to the events of the English Civil War and the crypto-Jewish community in London, though her father, John Dunnington, was a real person who also testified at Antonio Robles's trial. Indeed, John Dunnington is particularly interesting because he was Antonio Robles's front man in London and he went on record during Robles's trial as holding to no religion.

The following characters in *Hope of Israel* are based on historical figures:

Domingo de Lacerda:	A Portuguese accountant living in London in 1656 who worked for Antonio Robles.
Frade Francisco da Costa:	The grand Inquisitor of Portugal during the 1642 auto da fé in Lisbon.
Menasseh ben Israel:	Rabbi, printer, teacher, activist for Jewish sanctuary.
Rachel Abravanel ben Israel:	Wife to Menasseh ben Israel, mother of Joseph and Semuel.
Joseph ben Israel:	Elder son of Menasseh ben Israel.
Semuel ben Israel:	Younger son of Menasseh ben Israel.
Baruch Spinoza:	Philosopher, student of Menasseh ben Israel.
Franz Van den Ende:	Former Jesuit, scholar, friend of Baruch Spinoza.
Antonio Robles:	Portuguese Jewish merchant who lived in London, was tried for treason in 1656.

Antonio Carvajal: Portuguese Jewish merchant who may have been a spy for Oliver Cromwell.

John Dunnington: Agent for Antonio Robles, self proclaimed atheist.

Francis Knevett: Scrivener who denounced Antonio Robles.

Philip de la Hoyo: Portuguese converso who denounced Antonio Robles.

William Prynne: MP, lawyer, pamphleteer.

Henry Jessy: Dissenting minister, scholar .

Hugh Peters: Chaplain in the New Model Army.

John Sadler: MP, lawyer, scholar, private secretary to Oliver Cromwell.

Oliver Cromwell: Lord Protector of Britain 1649-1658.

Abraham Israel de Brito: Jewish merchant living in London, signed petition to Oliver Cromwell.

Isak Lopes Chillon: Jewish merchant living in London, signed petition to Oliver Cromwell.

David Dormido Abravanel: Jewish merchant living in London, signed petition to Oliver Cromwell.

Abraham Coen Gonzales: Jewish merchant living in London, signed petition to Oliver Cromwell.

Patricia O'Sullivan

Jahacob de Caçeres:	Jewish merchant living in London, signed petition to Oliver Cromwell.
Jacob Sasportas:	Rabbi of the London *kehilla* 1664-1665.

LaVergne, TN USA
13 January 2011
212317LV00003B/8/P

9 781605 945781